Praise for Wrightsville Beach

"Suzanne Goodwyn's debut novel Wrightsville Beach gives readers a poignant coming of age romance set in the current-day titular beach town in North Carolina. UNCW college freshman Jess is pursuing her passion for studying sea turtles, while troubled surfer Hank is floating adrift in grief, grasping for a break. When the two meet in the café where Jess works, an unexpected romance swells over breakfast, but Hanks's past seems to wipe him out at every turn. Years later, Wrightsville Beach calls them back together, but is it too late?

A timeless tale leaving you turning the pages way past your bedtime!"

—Mary Flinn, author of *LUMINA* and *The One*

"Suzanne Goodwyn's debut novel, *Wrightsville Beach*, is a compelling love story set against the backdrop of Wilmington, North Carolina. We watch love spark and develop between the two main characters, Hank and Jess, and then we see how misunderstandings and the interference of other people threaten their relationship.

Goodwyn has succeeded in creating a memorable first novel that will make people want to visit Wilmington to see all the places associated with Hank and Jess' romance. She perfectly captures the flavor of the area, from its beach and fishing pier to its elegant neighborhoods and antebellum homes, its university life and its upper-class social events. All the characters are thoroughly developed to the point where your heartstrings will be tugged on by many of them. Few novels reach such depths of character development, digging down into the gray areas of people's lives, while keeping us eagerly reading, wanting to find out what will happen next.

These are characters who will live with you long after you finish reading. They are characters who make you stop and think about life, your decisions, and why you might give people the benefit of the doubt when circumstances seem to be against them. Most of all, we are left with an understanding that while love is rarely easy, once found, it is worth holding onto."

— Tyler R. Tichelaar, PhD and award-winning author of
Narrow Lives and *The Best Place*

Wrightsville Beach

A NOVEL

[signature: Suzanne Goodwyn]

SUZANNE GOODWYN

Address all inquiries to:
Suzanne Goodwyn
Cartay Books
goodwynbooks@gmail.com
www.goodwynbooks.com

Print ISBN: 979-8-9858004-0-1
eBook ISBN: 979-8-9858004-0-1
Library of Congress Control Number: 2022903115

Editor & Proofreader: Tyler R. Tichelaar,
Superior Book Productions
Cover & Interior Layout: Fusion Creative Works, fusioncw.com

Printed in the United States of America
First Printing 2022

To order additional copies, visit: www.goodwynbooks.com

To Taylor,
My Favorite Youngest Child

You inspire me so.

Prologue

Hank didn't know where he was. As he came out of a black haze, his thoughts were blurry and disconnected. It was difficult to focus, but he forced himself to try. He could tell he was in a dark room. He could hear the sound of other people talking around him. Someone laughed too loud in the back. There was heavy metal music playing. He could smell stale beer and sweat and cheap perfume.

His eyes focused on the beer bottle in front of him. It was sitting on a stained wooden bar that he was leaning hard against. It was the only thing keeping him from falling off his stool. Slowly, it came back to him. He was in a bar, drinking. And as his recognition returned, so did the memory of the pain. He slowly reached for the beer, still unsure of his movements, and tried to drink from it, but it was empty. He slammed it down on the bar harder than he meant to, his arm heavier than he expected. The bartender, a burly guy named Rocky or Rocko, looked his way and scowled at him. Hank had heard that he'd been in prison, but he couldn't remember for what. He motioned for another beer, but the bartender ignored him and went to serve another customer at the other end of the bar.

Hank closed his eyes. He wanted to go to sleep, but sleep wasn't possible. Going to sleep meant going home, and right now he couldn't move. Right now he just wanted to dull the pain that was resurfacing before it made its way all the way up into his consciousness. He needed another drink, and he needed it now before he remembered why he was drinking. He had to push it back down. And the only thing that would do that was if he got another drink. He opened his eyes and looked for the bartender again, willing him to turn in his direction so he could get his attention.

"Well, look what the cat dragged in," a familiar voice purred. "I just don't seem to be able to go anywhere without you not far behind. Looks like someone has a little crush on me. Have you met Jimmy, sugar?"

Hank turned to see Roxy standing beside him, a tangle of wild white-blond hair and heavy makeup, wearing a tight leather skirt and a shirt that was too low cut. She was standing next to a guy who had his arm slung tight around her neck as if to show everyone she was with him, though he could also be leaning on her for support in his own drunken state. He was tall, like Hank, but lankier, with straight dark greasy hair that came down to his shoulders. He was wearing a leather vest with no shirt underneath, showing an array of tattoos down his arms and across his chest. Hank didn't know who he was and he didn't care. He thought he'd finally found a place where Roxy wouldn't find him, yet here she was again. *Not tonight*, he thought. *I can't handle this right now.*

Hank turned away from them and tried to catch the bartender's attention again, but he wouldn't look his way. Just one more beer, Hank thought, If I can get one more beer.... The bartender looked toward him, then away again before Hank could signal him. Hank was starting to feel desperate.

"Hey, the lady's talking to you," Jimmy said in a slurred voice. He moved closer, dragging Roxy along until he was standing over Hank in an attempt to be intimidating.

Hank turned to look at Jimmy and Roxy again, surprised they were still there and still talking to him. He could feel the anger start to surge inside him. He gave Jimmy a dirty look, shaking his head in a way that said, *No, no, no. Leave me alone* and threw his arm out to swat Jimmy away before turning his attention back to getting another drink. He drunkenly raised his hand to summon the bartender, but as he did so, he felt Jimmy grab his upper arm hard and jerk him off the stool, further igniting his anger and frustration. The movement caused his other arm to sweep across the bar where his hand came in contact with the beer bottle. Grabbing a firm hold of it, Hank took it with him as he felt himself fall toward Jimmy. The sound of breaking glass was the last thing he heard before descending back into the darkness he knew too well.

PART I

How They Met

Chapter 1

Henry Charles Atwater was angry. He'd been unloading boxes for hours, and his neck and shoulders were getting sore. It was hotter than usual for May under the North Carolina sun, and though he welcomed the idea of summer, the heat was starting to get to him. He stopped a minute, leaned against the truck, wiped his brow, and took a long sip from his water bottle. His brown eyes focused on the main cause of his distress: John DeGaulle. As in his employer, DeGaulle Delivery Service. John was busy sitting off to the side on a folding chair in the shade playing a video game on his phone, oblivious to the work at hand. This was the second summer Hank had been forced to work with John, who attended college the rest of the year. It had been bad enough last summer, when Hank did the majority of the work while John hung out and played on his phone, harassing him when bored. Hank was deeply disappointed when he saw they would be working together again.

"Hey," Hank said after waiting a moment for John to notice. "We could get out of here a lot faster if you helped with some of these boxes."

John finished what he was doing, put his phone in his back pocket, sat back, and looked up at Hank. Hank had the advantage of being taller at six-foot-four and was more fit than most twenty-year-olds, but one look from John could make him feel like none of that mattered. John had the handsome chiseled looks of a blond rich kid and an entitled manner that said he knew how to navigate the world, unlike Hank, who constantly felt like he was underwater. John was the boss's son, and he used it at every opportunity to avoid work.

"Watch it, there, Atwater, or I'll tell my father how you have been slacking off on the job. Then what would you tell your parole officer?" He held Hank's stare until Hank broke it off and grabbed another box. Hank knew there was no use arguing. He might as well get the job done so he could get out of there.

As Hank walked past, John was already on his phone playing another game.

Hank lived on a quiet street of bungalows in an area of town that the developers hadn't discovered yet, as they transformed the rest of Wilmington into a high-end beach haven. Each house on his block was no different from the others, a single-story rectangular unit with a long roof that overhung a front porch with white picket railings and square columns. When his mother had been alive, the garden area in front of the house had been well tended to, but that was a long time ago. Now the area in front of the faded blue house, which showed its age through peeling paint, only sported a few scraggly bushes and a small patch of dried grass worn down by the sun's relentless glare.

The front door opened into the living room, and the first thing Hank saw was his father sitting in his recliner watching a ball game. Or so he thought. He was dressed in an undershirt and some long brown pants, work clothes he had yet to change. From the heaviness of his breathing and the way his head lay tilted to one side, Hank saw he had fallen asleep.

"Hey, Pop," Hank said, not expecting much of a reply as he walked through the living room into the kitchen.

His father seemed to wake up, mumbled, "Hey," and then focused back on the television. Hank noticed how much older his father looked these last few years, partly due to him, Hank was sure. His once brown hair had gone gray and his physique had become soft. Bob Atwater had always been a quiet man, but the last few years, he had seemed defeated by life. And why wouldn't he be? Life had not been kind to the Atwater family. Hank went into the kitchen to see if his father had made any dinner, but there was nothing on the stove and very little to eat in the refrigerator.

Hank went back into the living room and started to ask his father if he planned to make something to eat, but he stopped in the doorway. There on the table next to the recliner was the photo album with pictures of Hank's older brother, Rob. That explained his father's solemnness. Hank decided not to bother his father in his grief.

"I'm going out to get something to eat," Hank mumbled as he grabbed his keys and headed back out the front door, slamming it behind him.

His father didn't even look up.

After stopping for food, Hank did what he always did when he needed to relax. He headed to the beach.

He drove a sturdy old black Jeep that used to belong to Rob. It was the perfect vehicle for a beach town—he could strap his surfboard on top and throw anything else he needed in back. It used to be a short drive from his house out to the Island, but over the last decade, Wilmington had grown exponentially, becoming both a well-known retirement community and a popular tourist destination as more people discovered it. At this time of day, the late afternoon traffic was pretty heavy, but Hank knew the back roads and made it across the Intracoastal in about fifteen minutes. He turned left on Lumina Avenue, which ran alongside the ocean, until he was far enough up island to avoid most of the crowds.

Surfing was only fun if you didn't have to watch out for some guy who would take waves he had no business taking because he didn't know the surfer code. Too many times, Hank had had to abort his ride because some college guy trying to impress his girlfriend or a vacationer who surfed only one week a year would get in his path. No, Hank preferred to steer clear of people in general. It was easier to avoid trouble that way. Trouble had already found him too often.

Hank parked on a side street and jumped out, grabbing his board. Just as most families were packing up to leave, Hank made his way down the beach, throwing his towel and keys in the sand before heading out into the water. Even though it was hot, there was always a good breeze at the beach cutting through the humidity. He dove into the water, clutching his board as he dove under the waves and started paddling his way out. The water felt cool on his skin.

The tide was coming in and the waves were well-spaced and starting to gain some height.

Hank went under a large wave that crashed in front of him and swam until he was behind the sand bar and could gauge the waves. He saw one on the horizon and started to paddle hard; then he jumped up on his board and rode the wave halfway in to shore. He swam back out and kept catching wave after wave until the day's stresses fell away from him and he felt himself start to relax. After a number of runs, the waves petered out for a time. Hank sat on his board, feeling himself moving in rhythm with the water, just looking at the beach houses lining the shore with their large windows to view the ocean and white picketed decks. He knew some of the townspeople who owned them, but he was always surprised at how often the homes looked empty. He couldn't even imagine what it would be like to live in such a house, where he could wake up and look right out at the ocean every day.

Then Hank noticed a group of guys coming up from the parking lot with boards. A bunch of college guys by the look of them, with newer and more expensive gear. Even the sacred places were no longer sacred. Hank caught the next wave in, and when he came out of the water, he pushed his hair back from his eyes and started walking up to his towel, giving a wide berth to avoid them.

A group of girls were lying on towels nearby, all wearing bikinis and looking around to see who was watching them. Hank was pretty sure that they all went to the University of North Carolina at Wilmington, the local college. One of them glanced up at Hank and smiled, obviously impressed with his physique. Being fit gave Hank some pride that he was worth looking at, and for a moment, he enjoyed being noticed. But then another one of the girls looked at him and turned to the others, whispering something that made them all laugh. Hank turned away. He knew college girls were not interested in a guy on probation working for hourly wages. And the local girls all knew about the trouble he had gotten into and stayed away. So Hank didn't think much about dating or the girls on the beach. Instead, he headed back to his Jeep and went home.

Chapter 2

On Sundays, Hank liked to head down to the beach for a run. He would leave early before the crowds started to arrive, park at the pier, take off his shirt, and start running. To the south end and back was about five miles, and if he were feeling particularly good, he would head up to the north end and back as well, another three miles. It was humid, but the breeze off the water kept him cool enough to keep going, and if he really started to sweat, he would do a quick dive into the waves to cool down.

The sand felt firm and cool under his feet. It felt good to get in a rhythm and feel his body respond to the movement. Rob had been in great shape even before he went into the Army, and he had passed that on to Hank, to keep fit as a way of keeping his head on straight. Hank focused on his breathing and the strength he felt in his legs, side-stepping the early risers looking for shells or doing their morning walk. When he made it to the end, he turned around and headed back, trying to go faster, thinking about John and all the other reasons his life was not working out. He knew his anger was the reason he had so many troubles, but here he could put it to good use, using it to push through the pain and sweat.

When Hank completed his run, he immediately started doing squats, followed by push-ups and sit-ups, doing a swim lap the length of the pier and back between each exercise. He was proud of his muscular build, which was defined and well-proportioned, and it was evident just by looking at him that he was quite strong—strong enough to take on John and pummel him into the ground if he wanted—but he also knew he did not build strength to use it that way. He had used his strength in anger once, and it had gone very badly, so he swore never to use physical force again. Any exit was better than using his strength to prove he was right.

When Hank was done, he went into the public shower at the pier, cleaned up, put on a fresh shirt and shorts, and ran his fingers through his brown hair to make it sit right. All that exercise had made him hungry, so he did the one other thing he always did on Sundays—he headed over to get breakfast at the Causeway Café.

The Café was another local favorite that had been overrun by tourists. Announced by white letters on a blue background, the Café welcomed all to come in and have a good Southern breakfast. Hank walked by the picnic tables scattered across the front lawn up to the front porch which was laden with rocking chairs, working his way through the groups of tourists waiting for a table. He walked in through the screen door to the bustle and clattering of the diner at full capacity, but before he could talk to the hostess, June waved him over to the counter where an empty seat at the far end sat open.

"Saved you a seat, hon," she said with a wink. June had been a friend of Hank's mother and had known him most of his life. This explained why she didn't avoid him the way most people did these days, seeing him as the young boy he used to be, rather than the man everyone else believed he'd become. She was heavy-set with lots of dyed white-blond hair that sat on her head like cotton candy, heavy blue eye shadow, and gum you didn't know she had behind those bright red lips until she cracked it if you said something she didn't like—her secret weapon against the more obnoxious customers, she would say. She'd been a waitress at the Café for as long as Hank had known her and he was thankful for her friendly presence since she always treated him well.

"Usual today?" she asked, pouring him some coffee.

"Sure," Hank said. "How's Bill?" he asked about June's husband.

"That man," June said, sighing as she put the coffeepot down, "you would think going to work was against God's plan…." Her voice trailed off in the din of voices as she headed into the kitchen to place his order.

Hank sat quietly watching the people in the restaurant, looking at the various families and trying to figure out where they were from. He could spot other Southerners easily enough by their mannerisms and the New Yorkers because they were louder than most. This used to be a weekend destination for North Carolina families, but the attraction of the place had started to have a farther reach. He had spotted license plates from Michigan and Maine and even Canada in the parking lot, a definite change from years past. When his food arrived, he found he was ravenous and ate quickly, enjoying the mixture of eggs and bacon and pancakes and stoneground grits. He finished in minutes and was about to wave June down for the check when he was startled by a loud voice behind him.

"What do you mean you have no grits?" Hank heard the man at the table behind him say angrily. "It says right here on the menu, grits. G-R-I-T-S. So that means you serve them. Now go get me some."

"Sir, I told you, the kitchen ran out. I will be glad to get you something else…" the waitress was saying calmly, trying to appease the customer.

"I don't come all the way down to North Carolina for hash browns. Get me some grits!" he said, practically yelling. The restaurant seemed to quiet for a moment and then started up again, most people not wanting to get involved in the matter, being either vacationers themselves or locals who were used to this kind of behavior from rude out-of-towners.

June appeared in front of Hank and filled up his coffee, redirecting his attention. "Everything all right?" she asked.

"Great," he said, wiping his mouth and putting his napkin on his plate. "Just the check."

"On the house," she said with another wink. It was their usual ritual. June would refuse to give him a check, paying for his food herself, and he would leave her twenty dollars under the plate to cover the food and a tip. Before he could respond, another waitress came up next to June with her back turned to him.

"What do I do?" she asked June in hushed tones. She was obviously younger, with a dark brown ponytail that swayed while she talked, emphasizing her words as she motioned to the table behind him.

"Honey, just get Sal. He'll deal with it," June said, comforting the girl with a pat on the shoulder and heading off with the coffeepot to her other tables.

"I thought you weren't supposed to annoy your waitress or she might spit in your food," Hank said. He had blurted out the words before he could stop himself, making him instantly freeze. Why had he said something? He should just stay out of it. No sense in getting involved.

The girl turned around and looked at Hank. She was about the same age as him, and now that she was facing him, he could see how pretty she was. He hadn't noticed her at all before, and now he wondered how he could have missed her. Even angry, she had brown eyes that were filled with emotion, and he could see her mind quickly assessing him. She wasn't the kind of girl you would notice right away, but once you did, there was something captivating about her.

"Well, there's one I haven't considered," she said, with a slight smile. "But now that you have given me the idea…."

"Hey, as long as I am not sitting at your station," he replied, smiling back at her without even thinking about it, feeling unusually at ease.

She gave a short laugh. "You better hope I don't ask June to switch, then," she said, giving a questioning smile and turning away to look for Sal.

Hank had not talked to a girl in ages, and he was surprised how relaxed he felt talking to this one. He watched as she headed over to the manager and explained what was going on. He got up and left June the money, then headed for the door, trying to act nonchalant but still buzzing from his encounter with the young waitress as if an electric shock had gone through his body. When he got to the door, he heard the voice as if it were right beside him.

You're going to marry her.

Hank stopped short for a second, uncertain about what he'd just heard. After all, they'd just met and he didn't even know her name. He quickly turned around and scanned the restaurant, hoping to catch another glimpse of her, to see if what he'd felt in those few short moments was real, but she was nowhere to be found.

Hank had only heard the voice two times before.

The first time was when he was seventeen and driving a couple of friends home from a party on a Saturday night. They had been blasting the music and were laughing about something as he drove down a dark back road when he first heard the voice shout as clear as if it had come from someone right next to him.

Turn.

In reaction, Hank had jerked the car to the right just in time to get out of the way of a drunk driver who had fallen asleep at the wheel and unknowingly veered into Hank's lane. Hank hadn't been able to see him because the other driver didn't have his lights on. As Hank passed him, he honked loudly, waking the other driver up, who immediately corrected his path. Hank pulled the car over and was a bit shook up, but no one was hurt, so they continued on, with Hank believing it was just his natural instincts that had made him react so quickly.

The second time he had heard the voice was the night he spent in jail. The officer had pushed him into a cell occupied with four other men, all tattooed and stronger looking than he was, with none of them looking friendly. As Hank heard the metal clanging of the jail door behind him mixed with the sound of the other prisoners yelling and making a racket, the voice came to him again.

You don't belong here.

He had been surprised to hear it and immediately remembered the incident with the car. He had gone to a bench on the side as far away as he could get from the other inmates and tried not to be noticed. He wasn't sure what to expect from them, but after giving him the once over and seeing what a drunken wreck he was, they ignored him, leaving him alone for the most part other than to give him the odd glance to make sure he wasn't going to cause them any trouble. He had nothing to do but think while he was in there; he knew between the noise and concern for his safety that he wasn't going to be able to sleep. So he spent his time thinking about the voice, remembering how it first came to him in the car that night and now here. He wondered where it came from, but he was unable to come up with an acceptable answer. Not that he was thinking all that clearly at the moment. He waited there, barely moving, until the cell doors clanged open again and his name was called for his arraignment; he had been relieved to get out of the cell for what he had hoped would be the last time.

And now the voice had come to him a third time. *Her?* he asked himself again, as he left the restaurant and headed back to his car.

But the voice didn't answer.

Chapter 3

Jesus, Mother Mary, and Joseph.

Jessica Taylor Wade wasn't one to curse, but good God, what could possible go wrong next? First, she had woken up to find beer cans left all over the front stoop, probably from the guys next door who were up late last night partying loudly. She liked staying at Anne's apartment at the beach, but between the party hours everyone kept there and the mess they left behind, it was starting to get on her nerves. Since parking was sparse on the Island, Jess parked her vintage light blue VW bug on UNCW's campus, preferring to walk or ride her bike as a quicker mode of transportation, particularly when traffic picked up in the summertime. But this morning when she went to retrieve her bicycle from the side alley, she found it had a flat. School had just ended for the summer, so she had started working Sundays at the Café, which was in addition to her waitress job at Oceanside, another restaurant on the Island where she worked several nights a week. Jess worked as many jobs as she could in the summer to make money to help her with expenses during the school year as well as had several volunteer activities she would do in her free time. Wanting to show she was a dependable worker, Jess left early, which was a good thing since now she needed to walk the mile to the Café. The distance wasn't a hardship, but even for mid-May, the day was already thick and humid with the Carolina heat, so when she arrived, she was sweatier than she, or Sal the manager, would have liked. She was able to clean up somewhat in the bathroom, but she still looked a mess. As if that was not enough, some kid at her first table dumped his orange juice on her, causing another trip to the bathroom to clean up. And it was only 8 a.m.

Then some vacationer got all bent out of shape because he couldn't get his grits. If she said they were out, what did he expect her to do? Lord knows they were more than happy to sell them if they had them. If he didn't like it, he could go somewhere else. But she had been working as a waitress since she was sixteen, so she knew the drill. Don't argue with the customer, just placate him, and then get him out of there as fast as you can. Still, it was a lousy drill. Being treated badly by people just because they were on vacation was not the kind of summer she hoped to have. But if she wanted to make the money she needed for college, it was best just to keep her mouth shut and pretend it didn't matter. After all, it wasn't like she hadn't dealt with difficult customers before.

But today she had already had her fair share of mishaps, so this was the last straw. Jess had been ready to explode when some guy at the counter said something about spitting in their food. She turned around and took him in, momentarily surprised that someone would even suggest such an act, but then realizing it was said in jest. Having him joke with her about it helped reduce her exasperation and made her take a minute to take him in. He was tan and in good shape, with brown hair pushed back from his forehead and close cut on the sides. More appealing was how he smiled at her with a warm look in his eyes, soothing really, playfully telling her to do exactly what she wished she could do as if they were planning it out together. He was average-looking, which was why she probably hadn't noticed him at first, but when she met his eyes, she felt a charge go through her. He was relaxed and self-assured, not over-confident like most of the guys at UNCW, and she was taken aback by the connection she immediately felt with him. She could hear the slight Southern drawl in his voice, identifying him as a local.

Then Jess remembered. Great. Here she was a complete mess, both figuratively and literally, and that's when the first interesting guy she has seen in a while decides to pay her some attention. Figures. Just add it to the list of today's misfortunes.

Jess had cracked something back and he had answered with something equally friendly and teasing. She had swallowed, said something else and walked off, hoping he didn't see how red her cheeks were getting. Why was she blushing? He was just a guy sitting at the counter. Someone who would soon be replaced with the next customer. She found Sal and explained her problem, trying to get her head back into her job. When he said he would take care of it, she headed back to the kitchen to check on her orders, determined not to let one customer get her down. After all, waitressing wasn't going to be her life forever. She just needed to get through today.

Still, she couldn't help herself. Had she imagined the connection she had just felt with that guy? It was like he could read her thoughts. She looked back at the counter, hoping to catch another glimpse of him, but another customer was already seated where he had been sitting, and a glance around the restaurant proved he was gone. He was the first person to say something to cheer her up, and she found she couldn't shake off their encounter. For the rest of the day, Jess had a smile on her face, remembering the sensation that vibrated through her when their eyes met. Even if she had only imagined it, it made the day better.

Jess had never lived in such a temperate climate before. She was used to the change of seasons common in her small hometown in Northern New Jersey. Living in a place where it felt like summer almost year-round made her feel like time had been suspended. It still impressed her even after attending two years of college here. When she first arrived, she marveled at how much more relaxed the people were, living at a slower pace than back home. It took a little getting used to, but once she acclimated to the new lifestyle, she enjoyed it as one of the perks of Southern living. Not that she had ever expected to find herself in the South. But she had wanted to find a good biology program, and UNCW had offered her more money than any of the other schools she had applied to. If she wanted to keep her student debt down, she needed to be practical, and with the money they offered and their reputation as a good school for science, it was an easy decision.

But there was another reason Jess had picked UNCW. She had always wanted to live by the water, and UNCW was just a bike ride away from Wrightsville Beach. Ever since her family's day trips to the Jersey shore when she was younger, she had developed a strong desire to be by the ocean. She had loved those family trips. She remembered how they would leave right after breakfast to beat the traffic and make the two-hour drive to get there early enough to find a parking spot. The beach itself would fill up quickly, with towels laid down by a neighboring family so close it would almost be touching theirs. Once they were settled, they would be there for the day, spending hours playing in the sand and swimming in the waves. Her mother would sit and read or sun herself, while her father would help her catch small fish in the water with a bucket or dig for crabs burying themselves in the sand. Sometimes, they would make sandcastles together with a chute to a moat, filling it with sea water, or she would bury her father's body in the sand and decorate him with seashells she found. Even their lunch of soggy tuna fish sandwiches out of a cooler had tasted so good because they were eating them at the ocean. She always hated it when it was time to leave, even when she was painfully sunburnt because her mother had forgotten to reapply her sunscreen. After her father passed away, they didn't take those trips anymore and she sorely missed them. She had always wanted to know what it was like to live so close to the ocean that you could visit it every day and at UNCW, she would get to do just that.

Jess loved living near the beach, and her need for it only seemed to grow with time. She would walk through the paths that cut through dunes covered with beach grass that led to the beach, and she would feel that need every time she arrived at the point where it opened up to the sprawling white sand and turquoise blue water. A sense of calm she didn't get anywhere else would come over her, instantly silencing any worries she had. She loved the feel of the sand between her toes and the sounds of the gulls cawing nearby, searching for food. She loved the heat of the sun on her skin and the smell of the salt water. She loved the coolness she felt diving into the waves and the exhilaration of riding them in on her boogie board. When she walked along the beach, she was still in awe of seeing pelicans swoop down to feed on the fish in the ocean, their incredibly long wings floating gracefully in the air as they would rise with their catch safely in their bill. Or at the sight of a pod of dolphins playfully jumping through the waves. She had never been in a place that made her feel so enchanted with the world around her. She felt like she could think when she was there, quieting the thoughts in her head that seemed to never slow down. Most of all, when she looked across the water that stretched endlessly into the horizon, she felt connected to something bigger than herself. Jess wasn't a religious person, but what she felt when she was here was nothing less than spiritual, and it filled her in ways nothing else did.

Once she settled into Wilmington, Jess was surprised by how at home she felt here. The warm climate allowed her to do what she loved most—swim in the ocean and bike everywhere she went. Jess equated riding with freedom. She liked exploring her surroundings, and riding a bike allowed her to cover ground while being at a slow enough pace to take it all in. She liked feeling the wind against her face and arms, and she enjoyed the weary but strong feeling she would get in her muscles after a particularly long ride. Any problem she was having could be solved by a bike ride because of the physical exertion and the time it gave her to think uninterrupted. In high school, when Jess couldn't afford a car, her bike gave her the ability to go anywhere she could ride, and it allowed her to discover parts of her town she would never have found otherwise.

At home up north, Jess could only ride in the warmer seasons; here, she could ride almost every day, and she often did. From the first day she arrived at college, she began exploring Wilmington. She already knew just how close the university was to the beach, but she discovered she could just as easily ride to other parts of the city. She spent time learning the different streets and exploring neighborhoods where people would wave to her from their porches even if they didn't know her, a definite Southern trait that she hadn't experienced before. They certainly didn't wave to you when she rode around in New Jersey, particularly since most of the homes didn't even have porches.

Jess found several parks she liked to ride through, some dense with greenery and many with tall pines that dropped red needles that covered the ground. But her favorite discoveries were the avenues lined with ancient oak trees covered in Spanish moss. She felt like she was in another time when she biked beneath them. Houses on these streets were often older, with large front porches framed in by fluted columns and white railings, and gardens that spilled over into the sidewalk. She was amazed how picturesque and peaceful it all seemed and how quiet it was save for the constant buzzing of the cicadas and the passing of an occasional car.

Jess was also taken with UNCW's campus. Filled with open green spaces amid colonial red brick buildings decorated with large white columns, the campus had a stateliness to it. You felt you were expected to do great things by being here. Though the buildings looked identical on the outside, giving a uniform feel to the grounds, each had its own interior personality, reflecting the area of study it served. Jess reveled in how many of the students rode bikes or skateboards to class even on rainy days and how the school made such equipment available for students to use if they didn't have their own. The campus was small enough for Jess to learn her way around quickly, but large enough that she could find a quiet bench or grassy area for some time alone. It suited her perfectly, and she was thankful that she had chosen it.

Her father had been the one who first gave her a love of how life formed and evolved. When he had explained how DNA worked to form an organism, it was so mesmerizing that she could have listened to him talk for hours. He'd been a high school biology teacher who had hopes of being a scientist, but he was never able to fulfill his dream. Her mother had gotten pregnant in college, causing her to drop out, and they had married. Her father had worked to support his new family during the day while he finished his college degree at night but pursuing another degree wasn't possible. So his way to enjoy the thing that inspired him most was to share that love with anyone who would listen. And Jess was his most rapt student. From a young age, she'd been drawn to the ocean and the creatures that lived in it, watching hour after hour of TV shows on underwater organisms from jellyfish to gigantic squid. Her father encouraged and built upon that desire for knowledge by explaining how life always found a way to survive even in the toughest of environments. She didn't realize it was a life lesson until much later, after he was gone.

He had been a wonderful father, always seeming to know when she needed to talk and when she didn't. When he passed away from a car crash when Jess was fourteen, it had been extremely hard on her, and it took her a long time to get over losing him. She continued her study of science as a way to remain close to him and his memory. He would have been so proud of her for getting into UNCW and doing so well in her studies.

Jess just wished he were here to tell her so.

Chapter 4

Mike James was Hank's best and only friend. Mike was currently a student at UNCW in the business school. He was getting ready to enter the family business, a local real estate company that managed summer rentals and sold beach houses. It was a job Mike knew he was expected to take and did not question. Mike's father made it clear he would not pay for college unless Mike kept up a 3.5 grade point average, so Mike took his grades very seriously. He was lucky to be smart enough to get his work done and still have time to engage in extracurricular activities. After all, it was much better to be in school enjoying the benefits of college life than working full-time, even if it meant he had to spend summers in his father's office learning the business.

Hank wondered if Mike would ever realize how lucky he was to have a job handed to him rather than having to worry about finding work in such a small town. Mike and Hank had been best friends since the third grade when they were put on the same baseball team. They had played a lot of sports together as they made their way through elementary and then high school, including basketball and some volleyball in the summer. They slept over at each other's houses, studied together, teased each other about girls, and told each other everything. Nobody except Rob knew Hank better.

Mike knew how close Hank had been with Rob, and he often expressed how he wished he had a big brother like him. Hank was secretly proud that he had something that Mike admired. He never said it out loud, but he often wished he had what Mike had, a mother at home who cared for the family and a father who, though often tied up in his work, seemed to really care about Mike and his future. Hank's dad had never gone to college and was a construction worker with a company that built homes until he had been laid off and started taking handyman jobs. Rob had gone into the Army right after high school, and Hank had just naturally assumed he would do the same. He had never thought about doing anything else and was happy to follow in Rob's footsteps if it meant staying close to his big brother.

When Hank's mother died, his father became barely functional. He found it hard to do much more than go to work, come home, and sit in front of the TV. When Hank asked him for help with homework or what was for dinner, he would tell him to ask his brother. He was a father in the sense that he put a roof over their heads and provided the essentials like food and clothing, but he wasn't able to give any more than that. Rob was the one who kept them going. He made sure Hank got to school on time and did his homework. He was the one who made sure they put up a Christmas tree and that birthdays were celebrated with cake and presents. It took some time, but his father slowly started to come back and be a part of their lives. Never to the extent he was before their mom died, but enough to show he still cared by showing up to school conferences or a couple of Hank's games each season. Meanwhile, Hank turned to Rob to help him with all the things his father couldn't.

Rob had been Hank's hero growing up. He was the best big brother anyone could ask for. When the bullies in fourth grade threatened to beat Hank up, it was his brother who taught him how to make them back down. When his grades started to slip in middle school and he started skipping classes, it was his brother who set him straight. And when he wanted to start dating a particular girl in high school, it was his brother who told him how to make a girl feel respected and special. Hank had worshiped his brother and wanted to be just like him.

Though they looked alike, Rob was definitely the better looking of the two. He was charismatic and could make friends wherever he went. He was taller than Hank or his father, with broader shoulders and one of the most well-defined physiques Hank had ever seen. He liked to lift weights and encouraged Hank to work out with him, even when Hank was still a scrawny young teenager who thought he could never be muscular. But Rob kept pushing him to do it, just like he pushed Hank in so many other ways. Sure enough, Hank started to catch up to Rob in the latter part of high school. Hank's nature was quieter and more subdued, like their father's, and he never developed the self-assurance his brother gave off so easily, but getting fit gave him confidence, as did Rob's belief in him.

Despite the number of vacationers that visited each year, the town itself was still small enough that names and reputations mattered. Hank wasn't the most popular guy at school, but he was liked by his peers for being an easygoing guy and respected by his teachers due to his work ethic and good manners. Being Rob's younger brother had something to do with it as well. For some guys, it would have been hard living in their brother's shadow, but Hank cherished Rob and the good feelings directed his way just because he was related to him. It was why Hank kept quiet when Mike would rave about Rob's latest accomplishment and how cool it must be to have him as his brother.

The real test of Hank's friendship with Mike came when Rob died and everything fell apart for Hank. When he stopped doing all the things he was supposed to do and, instead, started drinking and going out to the bars. Since he was tall, he looked older than his eighteen years and he quickly found the places in the less desirable neighborhoods that didn't care what age you were so long as you could pay for your drinks. Hank got to know them all. It was Mike who would often find him and drag him home. It was Mike who convinced his dad that Hank needed their help to bail him out that night when Hank was arrested for aggravated assault. And it was Mike who came to Hank's first appearance before the court and then drove him home once bail was set and paid. In the drive back to Hank's house, Mike had remained silent. Then, just before Hank got out of the car, he had quietly said one thing.

"Rob would never have wanted to see you this way."

Mike was right. Hank knew he wasn't the kind of guy who used his strength to hurt someone else. He had made it through school without ever having a fight; that he had been so drunk that he had hit another guy over the head with a beer bottle and sent him to the hospital was unthinkable to him. Hank had done the one thing he had worked all his life not to do, which was to let Rob down. As he watched the drunks and petty thieves shout at each other through the cell bars and heard the clanking of the cell doors as they shut him in, he knew he'd hit rock bottom. He had to come back from whatever hell he'd led himself into. It was either that or die. And he wasn't ready to die.

So as soon as Hank got home that day, even though it was painful due to his head aching and a hangover, he started working out again. He went to the beach and did some swimming, feeling the warmth of the summer sun for the first time in weeks, a feeling he realized he had sorely missed while sleeping days and being in bars at night. He made himself go for as long as he could until all he wanted to do was eat and go to sleep. Then the next day, he went back, this time going on a short run first. Every day he would return, doing it over and over until it started to feel natural. He quit drinking and picked up some history books at the library to fill his time since he enjoyed reading. When his hearing came up, he pleaded no contest and told the judge how sorry he was for the harm he had caused, how he was no longer drinking, and that he was looking for work. This impressed the judge enough to give him a suspended sentence and put him on non-active probation for two years. As long as Hank had a job and did not get in trouble with the law again, he was free to go.

Hank took very seriously this chance to turn his life around. But the locals were well aware of his drinking and the assault charge, so when he set out to get a job—any job—no one wanted to hire him. While Mike's dad helped with the bail money, he would not extend himself further by hiring him, no matter how hard Mike begged. He didn't even want Mike hanging out with Hank anymore because he saw Hank as a bad influence. Painful as it was to hear that, Hank understood. He knew he had to prove to Mr. James and everyone else that he was not the person he had been that night in the bar. That he was still the hardworking guy they'd always known.

So Hank kept looking for work, desperate to find anything. He tried to get every job he could think of with no luck until he heard they were looking for help at DeGaulle Delivery Service. He'd gone to school with John and disliked him for several reasons. John felt that because his family was one of the wealthiest in town, he could do whatever he wanted. When he got a new BMW convertible at sixteen, he would drive around town with his buddies, harassing girls on the street. He would randomly bully the less popular guys at school, and he was so untouchable that even the teachers looked the other way. It was evident his privilege knew no bounds when, even though there were better players, he made quarterback on the football team. Despite his insufferable ego, every girl seemed to want to date him due to his popularity, good looks, and money. However, if you weren't part of his posse, your best choice was to stay off his radar. John was known to be nasty to and demean people whom he didn't like.

Hank had somehow managed to steer clear of John during high school. He figured he wasn't important enough for John to bother like he did so many of the other students and, possibly, John may have cautiously kept his distance as Hank developed in strength. In senior year, some rumors started to float around about John taking advantage of a girl at a party. It didn't seem to hurt his reputation much, but some of the students became wary of him and his popularity started to wane as school ended. That was until he became a freshman at UNCW and it started all over again. Hank didn't understand why anyone liked John and wanted nothing to do with him.

But Hank was desperate to stay out of jail. He figured John would never work at such a low level at one of his father's many businesses, so Hank applied for the delivery job, thinking they would never cross paths. He was interviewed by Mr. DeGaulle himself, who looked at him sternly across the large oak desk of his expensively furnished office.

"Why should I hire you, Hank?" Mr. DeGaulle had asked, leaning back in his leather chair, assessing him. He looked like an older version of John, but more stately, in a starched button-down shirt and pressed pants that showed he was still in good shape. His age mostly showed by how his white hair had thinned, leaving a bald spot on top of his head, and how the skin on his face had started to sag. Still, it only added to his authoritative air, which he wore with reverence.

Hank clenched his hands together, trying not to appear nervous. His voice was earnest. "I know I've made a lot of mistakes recently, Mr. DeGaulle. I'm trying to make things right. I need this job. I promise, if you hire me, I won't let you down."

Mr. DeGaulle considered him a moment, appearing satisfied with his response. "How's your father?" he asked in a less severe tone. Though they certainly weren't in the same social circles, it wasn't surprising that in a town this size he knew Hank's family.

"Fine, sir," Hank replied. Rob had taught him always to call men sir. There was no sense in telling Mr. DeGaulle that his father was still devastated over Rob's passing.

"You know, I always admired your brother," Mr. DeGaulle said after a moment. "He worked for me for a while. He was always on time and worked hard. Is that something I can expect from you, too?"

Hank swallowed hard, trying not to let his emotions show. He knew Rob had spent several summers working at one of Mr. DeGaulle's restaurants. "Yes, sir."

Mr. DeGaulle hesitated a moment. "Good. Then you can start tomorrow," he said, dismissing Hank from his office.

And so Hank had found a job. It was fairly simple, making deliveries throughout the area. And it wasn't too bad. Most of the other workers were nice enough guys who'd dropped out of high school for one reason or another or who'd fallen on hard times. Hank kept to himself and got the job done, keeping a genial but distant relationship with the other employees. He knew he wasn't there to make friends. His only goal was to keep his promise to Mr. DeGaulle, and to not to let Rob down again.

That was until summer came. John was expected to work for his father, and apparently Mr. DeGaulle felt John should learn the business from the bottom up, assigning him to work with Hank. John was obviously unhappy with the arrangement, using it to bully Hank into doing his share of the work. If John's arrogance had been bad in high school, it was almost unbearable in college. Being wealthy and extremely good-looking made John very popular at UNCW, especially with the girls, and John had no problem using both to his advantage. Hank was more than glad to see John go back to school in the fall, relieved to be done with him.

But when summer rolled around again, John sought Hank out, knowing all he would have to do was show up while Hank did all the work. And Hank was stuck. He couldn't quit and let Mr. DeGaulle down after he'd taken a chance on him when no one else would. Hank knew if he fought back, John could get him fired, proving to everyone he was the screw-up they all believed him to be. And worst of all, if that happened, he would go to jail. The best he could do was remind himself that he only needed to keep this job until his probation ended and quitting would have no consequence. So he did what he could to ignore John when possible and just get the work done. As far as he could tell, he didn't have a choice.

He just had to make it until the end of summer.

Chapter 5

Mike served the volleyball as Hank got into place to block the spike coming from the other side. He jumped up to spike the return hit, sending the ball in such a sharp downward angle that it hit the opposing player's hands, causing the ball to deflect under the net to his side, giving Mike and him the winning point. He and Mike high-fived each other and then shook hands with the other players before going to the bench to get a drink. The game was part of a Memorial Day tournament held every year at the beach, and they were heading into finals, having won four games. Their opponents would be the guys from Carolina Beach who took first place last year, but who looked in bad shape today. They drank some water and sat on the bench waiting until the next round.

"Anne won't get off my case," Mike said, openly admiring some coeds who were walking by in thong bikinis. One of them smiled at him as she walked past, and he gladly smiled back. With his blue eyes, hair that had lightened with the summer sun, and perpetual tan, Mike had the look of a surfer. Because of his looks, Mike attracted a lot of attention, more than Hank, even though he didn't have Hank's physique. He was very good at attracting and flirting with girls, but he was currently dating Anne, another UNCW student, so all he could do was look. As far as he was concerned, there was nothing wrong with enjoying the scenery at these events, so long as Anne wasn't around.

"About what?" Hank asked, though he already knew. Ever since Anne had met Hank, she had been trying to set him up with her roommate.

"You know what—you meeting Jess," Mike said, wiping sweat from his brow. "C'mon. She's good-looking. Seems smart. Just meet her and then I can get Anne to drop it." He took another drink.

"I'm just not into dating right now," Hank replied, looking away and hoping that would end the subject.

"Right. Because you have so much going on," Mike said sarcastically, taking another drink of water and watching another set of girls pass. He put down the bottle and turned to face Hank. "Look, you're doing all the things you're supposed to do. The court didn't rule you weren't allowed to have fun while on probation, did it? Just do it for me."

Hank hesitated and finally said his biggest worry out loud. "Come on, Mike. I don't see a college girl going for me." Meaning a guy working a delivery job for an hourly wage. He watched more girls walk by. There was a never-ending parade at these games. He liked looking at them, but there was no sense in talking to any of them.

"You sell yourself short, man," Mike said, shaking his head and watching the girls. "The job isn't who you are. It's just temporary. A few more months and you're free. I'll make you a deal. If we lose the next game, you hang out with me and Anne tonight at Oceanside. Jess is working. You can meet her there. Decide if you're interested.

Or not. Quick and easy. And Anne gets off my case." At the sight of another group of bikini-clad girls, Mike leaned back and smiled approvingly. As he watched them pass, his eyes lingered.

Hank thought for a moment. They were playing with the guys from Carolina Beach next, and it looked highly likely they would win, so maybe he could use that to his advantage to get Mike off his back about the whole dating thing. "If we lose the tournament, I go. If we don't, you don't try to fix me up anymore. Deal?"

Mike laughed. "Deal, bro," he said, getting up to start the next match. "Let's show these guys which beach rules."

An hour later, the guys from Carolina Beach had crushed them. Whatever made them look like they were off their game earlier had been replaced with pure adrenaline as they made point after point. Hank and Mike played hard, but they couldn't get an edge, winning only one game. When it was over, Hank was tired and sweaty and wanted nothing but to go home.

"Well, that sucked," Mike said, looking as disheveled as Hank as he plunked down on the bench next to him, taking a long drink of water. "Where did that come from?"

"Yeah," Hank said. "Good save on that one spike, though." They talked for a few minutes more, recounting the game; then Hank put on a shirt and grabbed his stuff. "I'm beat," he said, throwing his bag over his shoulder. "I'm heading home to take a shower."

"Sounds good. See you at Oceanside around 9 p.m.?" Mike said, shooting him a sly look as he walked past him toward the parking lot.

Hank suddenly remembered the bet and stopped cold, a look of dread on his face. "Wait…."

Mike didn't stop but raised his hand in farewell, turning around to say one last thing. "And wear something nice, Atwater. It's an upscale place."

Chapter 6

Jess knew waitressing on Memorial Day weekend would be busy, particularly on a Friday night at Oceanside, one of the most popular restaurants on the Island, but she hoped the start of the summer would put people in a good mood so they tipped well. Things had started picking up at 5 p.m. when the families with small children arrived after spending the day at the beach, and now, at 8:30, work hadn't slowed down. But Jess didn't mind. She liked waitressing because she was constantly moving and it required her to think as she took orders, filled drinks, and served food. She also enjoyed interacting with the customers. She made more money waitressing than any other job she had worked, and she liked how the time would go quickly when the restaurant was busy. She knew she was good at it, and tonight it showed.

Jess placed some orders down on one table and took a drink order from another, then headed to the bar to get it filled. It was no surprise to see John there, drinking even though everyone knew he was underage. Being the owner's son, he was often there hanging out, and Jess, like the other waitresses, would just ignore him whenever possible. As Jess picked up her drink order, she passed Lynn, another waitress heading over to get her orders filled, and they both rolled their eyes at each other as a way of saying, *Guess who's at it again?*

Jess dropped off the drinks and had just gone back to the waitress booth to print out a check when she felt someone grab her butt hard. Surprised, she spun around to see John standing there, grinning stupidly. She'd heard about him groping the other waitresses, but under no circumstances was she going to put up with it. She glared at him and spoke in a low voice, trying to send a clear message. "If you do that again, I will tell your father how you harass the waitresses," she said, throwing out a threat.

John laughed at her. "Oh yeah? And who do you think he will believe…you? Or me?" He leaned in so close she could smell the liquor on his breath.

"How about me?" another voice said. Lynn was standing right behind Jess with her arms crossed, looking sternly at John. "I'll tell him that not only did I witness you grope her and several other waitresses, but you tried to pull me in your car one night after work with your drunken buddies. Sort of reminiscent of high school, don't you think?"

Lynn was a local who had attended high school with John, so she knew the rumors about his past.

John looked from Lynn to Jess and back to Lynn, contemplating his next move. He grinned and decided retreat was his best option. "Ladies…" he said, holding up his hands in mock surrender, slowly backing away. Then just before turning away, he gave them the finger with both hands and walked off.

Chapter 7

Hank sat at the end of the bar with Mike between him and Anne. He was drinking a Coke and planning his escape as he cursed Mike for bringing him here and making him do this. The last thing he needed was to be rejected by Anne's roommate. The faster he could get out of here, the better.

The large oak bar ran along the back wall, parallel to the tables that lined the windows overlooking the ocean. It was a Saturday night, so the place was quite noisy, busy with tourists and waiters going back and forth. The bar was less crowded since people tended to wait outside, but they were still lucky to grab three seats together.

Anne was going on about a movie she had seen the night before when suddenly John showed up on the other side of her.

"Hey," he said to the bartender, interrupting him while taking another customer's order, "give me another one of these." He put a glass down on the bar. "And this time fill it up, for God's sake." His voice was slurring slightly and it was obvious he was drunk. The staff knew John was underage, but since the DeGaulle family owned the restaurant, no one wanted him to cause them trouble. So the bartender did what he was told and gave John another drink, even though it was obvious he was not happy about it.

John surveyed the other customers at the bar and saw Hank, who had turned his back to him, trying to avoid him. John picked up his drink and sauntered over to him, standing so close to him that their arms were almost touching.

"Well, look who we have here. The local violent offender," he said with a chuckle, taking a long drink.

"Beat it, John," Mike said, knowing full well how John badgered Hank. "What, no underage girls to harass tonight?"

Hank ignored John, looking straight ahead, and taking another sip of his drink, but then John leaned over and got right in his face. "Perhaps we need to call the cops before you start swinging bottles? After all, a low life like you won't be able to contain his temper...."

Hank was already tired and on edge, and dealing with John tonight was too much. He jumped off his barstool and backed away, putting some distance between him and John while staring him down. He could feel the anger rising in him—and fast—but he held himself back.

"Go on, "John said, pointing to his chin and walking up to Hank until he was inches away from him again, though it was clear Hank had the height advantage. "Hit me. I can take it. I'm sure that's all it will take to put you back in jail...."

Hank leaned forward as if considering taking John up on the invitation, but he stopped when he heard someone speak.

"Anne, what's going on?"

While Anne and Mike had been watching the conflict play out, Jess had walked up to Anne. On seeing Hank there, she'd been so startled to see him again that she talked louder than she had meant to, causing all four of them to turn to look at her. Hank's eyes met hers, and he immediately recognized her as the waitress from the Café, simultaneously realizing that she must be Jess. His first thought was, *How long has she been standing there, witnessing John trying to humiliate me?* He had to get out of here and now.

Hank turned back to John, glaring at him with all the hate he felt for him putting him in this position, so ready to bring him down. But he knew the price he would pay if he gave in to his anger. Instead, he leaned into John's face and said through gritted teeth, "You're not worth it."

With that, Hank turned around and left, not once looking back at the three disconcerted faces at the bar behind him or at John's smirk at having succeeded once again in getting him riled.

Hank didn't sleep well that night, unable to shake off the events of the night before. When the memories wouldn't stop hounding him, he finally got out of bed, even though it was still dark, and decided to go to the beach to surf. He tried not to wake his father as he grabbed something to eat and then headed out in his Jeep.

When Hank arrived at the beach, it was early enough that the purple and pink colors of the sunrise were just beginning to peek over the horizon. This was his favorite time of day to be at the beach, when it was just him and a few beachcombers. But today, even the beach did not give him a sense of peace. The only way he knew he would feel better was to get his body moving and occupy his mind so he could forget about John, forget about seeing Jess at the bar, and most of all, forget about what a mess his life was.

Hank had remembered his conversation with Jess so many times this past week, half-believing something good might come of it, just enjoying the possibility that he might be able to talk to her again when he went back to the Café on Sunday. But now he knew that was over. Something always ruined whatever happiness he found, and now he just wanted to wear himself out physically so he didn't have to feel anything at all.

He was fortunate that the waves were coming in at just the right intervals and were high. He paddled hard and caught wave after wave, immediately heading back out to see how quickly he could catch the next one. The sun continued to rise until it was situated high in the sky, and still he went back and forth, thinking of nothing but his next ride. It took time, but he finally started to feel that sense of calm that came with pushing himself. He could feel his muscles start to ache, and even then he didn't stop, not wanting to think about anything but catching waves for as long as he could.

Hank finally got to the point where he had to take a break and headed back in to the beach. When he got back to his things, he took a long drink of the water he had brought with him, then lay down on his surfboard to catch his breath, closing his eyes and letting the sun dry him off. He felt worn out and empty, a feeling far too familiar these past two years. He just wanted to lie there and not think, feeling the warmth of the sun against his skin and listening to the far-off sounds of seagulls hawking in the distance and waves crashing against the shore.

But as he lay there, he sensed a shadow over him, blocking the sun.

"Hey," he heard a female voice say.

Hank opened his eyes and shaded them to see who was standing above him. It was Jess. He quickly sat up, placing his feet on either side of the board and resting his arms on his knees.

"Hey," he said, surprised to see her.

"You were pretty impressive out there," she said, nodding her head toward the waves. Hank sort of shrugged his shoulders in response. He was wondering what she was doing there. Jess hesitated, then sat down on the sand beside him facing the water. She had on a T-shirt, shorts, and sunglasses. Her dark hair was loose and the wind kept blowing it across her face, requiring her to reach up and gather it, then twirl it and put it to one side.

"Great day to catch some waves," she finally said after a minute of silence.

"You surf?" Hank asked, not sure what he should say, particularly after the events of last night.

"We used to boogie board when I went to the beach as a kid, but I never learned to surf. I never lived at the beach until I came here to go to college."

"And since then?"

She shrugged and smiled. "I don't know. I thought it was too hard to learn, not having grown up by the ocean. And no one ever offered to teach me."

They both fell silent and looked out toward the water again, the awkwardness growing. She took a breath and spoke.

"Look, Mike told me where to find you. About last night…."

Hank shook his head and looked away. He didn't want to talk about that.

"About last night…" she started again. "John can be a real jerk. He gives everyone a hard time. He was harassing me and another waitress right before he started in on you. He was obviously pretty drunk."

Hank winced at hearing her talk about the previous night's events. This meant she had seen more than he'd hoped.

"Anyway, Mike told me about…what had happened and why you couldn't do more to make John stop, although you probably wanted to."

Hank stared straight ahead and didn't look at her. She had been a good memory. He didn't want her knowing about his past or the person he had briefly been that no one seemed able to forget. "How much did Mike tell you?" he asked after a moment, fearing the worst.

"He told me about the arrest and how you work for John's dad and have to take whatever John dishes out."

"Anything else?"

She looked down at the sand and started drawing circles with her finger. "Yeah, he told me what happened to your brother," she said quietly.

Hank physically flinched at her mentioning Rob and turned away.

"Well, thanks for letting me know," he said, ready to end the conversation. He got up, picked up his board, and started walking back to the water, wanting to get away from her as fast as possible.

Jess quickly stood up.

"Wait, Hank…" she said, running up next to him. He stopped and turned to look at her, his body still facing forward toward the water, ready to keep going. "I wanted to say…" she hesitated and took a breath. "I wanted to say thanks for last week, you know, at the Café. I was having such a hard day and you were…you made it better. You made me smile when I needed it most. I guess I just wanted to see if I could do the same for you after last night…." Her voice trailed off and she waited for him to respond, but when he just stood there staring at her, expressionless and not seeming to care, she realized she had made a mistake.

"I'm sorry," she said, shaking her head. "I shouldn't have bothered you. This was a mistake. I…I'll leave you alone." She turned around and started walking back up the beach, leaving him standing there.

Hank was speechless. No one had been so genuinely kind to him in such a long time, and now he was acting like he didn't know how to respond to it. He couldn't believe she would come down all this way to tell him how much a few words he'd said had made a difference to her. That their quick exchange, which had kept him going all week, may have actually meant something to her too.

Hank looked up and realized she was leaving. He knew he couldn't let her go. Without thinking, he turned around and ran up the beach toward her.

"Hey, wait…" he said, catching up to her before she reached the dunes. He wasn't sure what he could say to make her stay, but he had to think of something and fast. She stopped and turned around; her eyes were hidden behind the dark sunglasses, but her facial expression was stern. He looked at the board in his hands, then back at her. "You said no one ever offered to teach you to surf…." he said, looking at the water and then back at her. He motioned with his head toward the ocean. "Do you want to learn now?"

She hesitated for a long moment, looking at the water and then back at him, and just when he was sure she was going to walk away again, she began to smile. "Yes," she said slowly, then more adamantly. "Yes. I would really like to learn to surf."

"Great," he said, relieved she had said yes, and he began smiling for the first time. She liked his smile. It had a way of lighting up his eyes and made his features more handsome. She felt herself starting to blush and didn't want him to see it.

"Beat you to the water," she said, thinking quickly and taking off before he could say anything else. When she reached his belongings on the beach, she briefly stopped and threw off her sunglasses, shirt, and shorts, revealing a well-fitting black bikini. Hank tried not to stare, but he couldn't help taking in her long shapely legs and how she had curves in all the right places. He never would have guessed she had such an athletic figure from seeing her in her waitress uniform. He caught up to her at the shoreline where she stopped and looked at him.

"Okay. You do know how to swim, right?" he said half-jokingly, not sure where to start. He had never offered to teach anyone to surf before. She laughed and ran into the water, diving under the incoming waves and coming up on the other side.

"Like that?" she asked, treading water, waiting for him to follow. He dove in after her.

Chapter 8

It was a perfect day.

Jess hadn't known she would end up surfing with Hank that day. She didn't really know what would happen, or if she would even find him at the beach. When she had come up to Anne last night and saw Hank standing there, she had gotten that same electric charge she had experienced at the Café, and she felt immobile at seeing him again. It only took her a few seconds to understand he was being hassled by John, and speaking loudly had been a reflex that seemed to shift everyone's focus long enough for Hank to walk out before she could say anything to him.

After Hank had left the restaurant, Jess had told Anne how Hank was the guy she had talked to at the Café a week earlier. Mike filled her in about how Hank had lost his brother and gone on a drinking spree that ended with a brawl in a bar, two years' probation, and working with John at his father's delivery service. When Jess voiced regret that she hadn't been able to talk to him, Mike told her where she could probably find him the next morning if she still wanted to. When she woke up the next day, something had told her not to wait. She got up early, threw on a shirt and some shorts over her swimsuit, and walked over to the pier, then started heading north up the beach to where Mike had told her Hank would be surfing.

It hadn't taken long to find him. When she first saw him out in the waves, she sat down on the beach and watched him from a distance. She watched how he swam ahead of a large wave, and when it caught up to him, he effortlessly transformed from lying down and paddling to an upright position, riding smoothly for a good distance before he jumped off and swam back out. He did this several times until, instead of heading back out, he walked a little ways inland where he had left a towel, took a long drink of water, and then laid down on his board.

Jess had gotten up and started walking over to him, uncertain what to say. He was wet and a little winded, lying on his back with his eyes closed, taking in the sun. His body was even more fit than she'd noticed earlier. When she spoke, he opened his eyes and sat up. She immediately felt her shyness hit her again when she looked into his eyes, so she sat down to the side of him, looking out toward the water instead of directly at him, but stealing glances when she was able, taking in his facial features and how his body glistened with salt water.

This was so unlike her. Guys normally had little effect on her. Even in high school, she rarely dated because no one seemed all that interesting. She thought it would be different in college, but here the guys were either trying to get her in bed or not interested in a girl working her way through school. With dating a distant prospect, it wasn't surprising that she easily relegated it to a lower status than school and friends. But then, no one had ever affected her like this just by looking at her. The feeling was both exhilarating and unfamiliar, and left her unguarded.

They swam out beyond the waves where Hank had helped her get up on the board. He instructed her to paddle until she felt the wave lifting her up, which was when she was supposed to pop up and ride it. He pointed out what to look for in picking a wave, telling her how to tell if it were going to maintain its speed and to make sure it wasn't too close to another wave that would weaken it. Jess was grateful to have something else to concentrate on other than Hank to keep her shyness at bay. When he saw a good wave coming, he pushed the board forward and told her to paddle as hard as she could. She tried a number of times, but she kept missing the wave, or would jump up too fast. Once, she jumped up too far forward and went toppling over. Hank swam over to help her, but she waved him off and got back on the board, determined to learn how to do it the right way.

After they had been at it a while, Hank started to wonder if they should call it a day since the waves were petering out when he saw one on the horizon coming in at the perfect height.

"Okay, this is it," Hank said, pushing her forward. "This is the one. Paddle!"

Even though her arms were tired, Jess paddled as hard as she could, and when she felt a slight lift behind her, she jumped up on the board. Squatting low to keep her balance, she steered herself down the front of the wave. The sudden dip was unexpected, but this time she stayed on, turning slightly to continue her ride as the wave crested along the shore, and she rode it a good distance up the beach. When she hit the shallows, she jumped off, turned around, and raised her arms in a victory cheer in Hank's direction. He waved back with a big smile on his face. He quickly swam in to where she was standing on the beach holding the board and feeling like a real surfer.

"Did you see me?" she asked, breathless and too excited to try to hide it. "That was amazing! And I made it all the way in!"

"Just like a pro!" he replied, holding up his hand for a high five, which she gladly gave him. "It must have been the teacher…" he teased, taking the board from her.

She laughed and started squeezing the water out of her hair. "Or maybe it was my excellent ability to pick it up so quickly…."

"So, are you coming?" he asked, walking backwards up the beach to his towel so he could still face her.

"Where?" she asked, following him.

"This calls for a celebratory lunch," he replied.

"Great, I'm famished," she said, and they walked up together to gather their things. "Where to?"

"We can walk down to Mercers Pier and can grab some burgers," he said, motioning down the beach.

"I didn't know there was a restaurant at the pier."

"Have you ever been out on it?"

Jess shrugged. "Not really. It's just a fishing pier, right?"

"Pretty much. But it has a lunch counter, too. Let's get something there."

They walked down the beach and up the long cement walk that led to the pier and inside to the cool interior of the building that separated the pier from the beach. They ordered some food at the counter and then they went out to the deck area, which had plastic tables overlooking the ocean.

"Wow. All the benefits of Oceanside without the insane prices," Jess said, jokingly.

"It's a pretty well-kept secret," Hank said, biting into a burger. "Don't go telling all your college friends or you'll ruin it for us locals."

"Ha," she said. "No worry about that. I barely have time for friends as it is."

"How come?" he asked, taking her in now that she was seated across from him and they were no longer fighting waves. He liked how her long, dark, wet hair hung down her back and over her shoulders. She was tan, which seemed to set off her brown eyes; they had such an intensity to them that he sometimes had to look away because of the way they pierced through him. They were animated with whatever she was feeling at the moment, and when she started talking about school and what she was studying, she came alive. He liked that she was very straightforward, making it easy for him to talk to her. It had been a long time since he'd talked with such a good-looking girl; he tried not to think about it so he wouldn't get too self-conscious. *Keep it together, Atwater*, he told himself. *Just hang out.*

Jess told him how she was from New Jersey and was a biology student at UNCW. Most of her friends had gone farther north to New York state schools, but when they had complained about the long winter, she knew she'd made the right decision to go south. However, maintaining the scholarship required she maintain a high grade-point average. It was difficult to work much during the school year, so she worked hard over the summer to cover as many of her living costs as she could that weren't covered by her scholarship.

During her freshman year, Jess had taken the introductory biology classes, which included a lab class the second semester. She discovered the labs were what she enjoyed most. They involved going out on a boat or wading into the marsh to collect and study specimens. During one of these trips, they encountered an injured sea turtle they had pulled into the boat and brought back with them, handing it off to the Karen Beasley Sea Turtle Rescue and

Rehabilitation Center. Jess had gone to the Turtle Rescue the following weekend to check up on the turtle; she discovered he had been named "Waffle" and his two front flippers had been deeply cut by some discarded fishing line, limiting his ability to swim and seek food. She started to research sea turtles and would visit the Turtle Rescue to check on Waffle and talk to the staff about the other turtles that came in. She had ended up volunteering there last summer and loved it. She would help feed and care for the injured turtles and give presentations to visitors wanting to learn more about them. When she returned for the fall semester, Jess continued volunteering on weekends and did a study for one of her classes on how light pollution disrupts sea turtles' nesting behavior and leads the hatchlings and nesting mothers away from the sea. After talking to her advisor, Jess realized she really enjoyed studying sea turtles, so she switched her major to marine biology to make them a focus of her studies.

This summer, Jess had volunteered to help monitor the nests with another local group, the Wrightsville Beach Sea Turtle Project. Sea turtles would start coming ashore to the Island in May to bury their eggs. Volunteers from the group walked the beaches each morning, and when they spotted turtle tracks and found a nest, a makeshift enclosure would be posted around it to protect the nest from being disturbed by people.

"It doesn't help much with the raccoons or the crabs that try to dig up the eggs to eat them, but it does give them some protection from beachgoers who aren't familiar with the nests," Jess said between bites.

"Did you ever see a nest hatch?" Hank asked. He had seen the protective enclosures on the beach consisting of wooden poles arranged in a square around the nest. They were wrapped in black plastic and stood three feet high, with a long chute dug out on the ocean side leading down to the water. He knew what they were, but had never thought much about them. He had thought they were to protect the turtles from people who wouldn't think twice of setting up their beach gear on top of a nest.

"No, but I have looked it up online to see what it's like," she said, enthusiastically. "The nest actually looks like it is bubbling because of how the turtles climb over each other to get out. It's amazing to me how they instinctively know to wait until the sun has gone down and the sand has cooled before emerging from the nest to avoid predators, like crabs or seagulls that try to swoop down and take them as they head to the ocean. The theory is that as few as one in ten thousand of the hatchlings may make it to adulthood, though that is still being studied. I really hope to get to see a nest hatch this year…." Her voice trailed off as she momentarily got lost in thought.

Jess stopped and looked at Hank, who was sitting back and smiling at her. "Sorry," she said, realizing how she'd been going on. "I'm sure you never intended to learn about the life and habits of sea turtles as part of your lunch." She took his silence for polite interest and hoped she hadn't bored him.

"Actually, you make it sound fascinating," he replied, shaking his head, impressed with her passion. "I never thought much about them, even though I've seen sea turtles swimming in the channel."

"I've actually made conservation of them the focus in my studies," she said, enthusiastically. "When I see these incredible creatures come to the Turtle Rescue so hurt and hear it is due to being hit by a motorboat or being caught in fishing line, it breaks my heart. It's amazing what some of them live through."

When they were done eating, Hank told her he wanted to show her something. He took her out to the pier, making the long walk to the very end, which was quite a ways out, where a dozen fishing poles were set up.

"Look down," he said, and she looked over the edge down to the deep blue water. "What am I looking for?" she asked, and then she saw them. Sharks were circling around the poles, obviously attracted to the fish being lured by the bait.

She looked back at Hank, stunned. "I swam in the water that close to sharks?" she asked, suddenly not so excited about her surfing success.

"Well, not that close," he said. "I think the feeding is better down here. Don't marine biologists like sharks?" he asked, trying to joke to ease her concern.

"Some of them do, but I prefer to see them from a distance and in tanks. Have you ever encountered a shark while surfing?" she asked, not sure she wanted to know.

"Once," he said. "I was on my board waiting for a wave when I looked down and saw about a five-foot shark swim underneath me."

Jess was amazed. "What did you do?" She knew full well that would have been enough for her to give up the sport.

Hank laughed. "I rode the next wave in and called it quits for the day. It was my own fault. It was dusk, when they go hunting for food. I knew better. You just have to pick your times right. I've been surfing for years and no shark bites." He turned and smiled at her. "Yet."

"Yeah, *yet…*" she said.

They talked some more as they slowly walked back the length of the pier and then returned to the beach. Neither one wanted to leave, but Jess looked at her phone and realized she had to be at her Oceanside job in less than an hour and she needed to shower and change.

"I have to get ready to go to work," she said reluctantly. "This was so much fun. It was really...incredible."

She looked at him with such earnestness as she spoke that he was taken aback. He was enjoying their interaction so much, and it had all been so relaxed, but he wasn't sure what to do next. "So let me know if you need any more surf lessons..." he started lamely, trying to figure out what he should say. She smiled, but when she realized he wasn't going to follow up with anything else, she knew it was time to leave.

"All right. Thanks again, Hank. Bye," she said and turned and started walking away.

Hank mentally banged the side of his head. *Get a grip, Atwater,* he told himself. *Don't blow this.* He ran in front of her, blocking her exit.

"So when's your next day off?" he asked, making sure he set up a date before she left.

Chapter 9

Jess's next day off turned out to be Tuesday night since she was working extra shifts for the holiday weekend. Hank said he would pick her up around 7 p.m. for dinner with the promise there would be no sharks involved.

All day at work, Hank couldn't stop smiling. He kept telling himself to chill and just do the job. He didn't want to give John any ammunition, but it was hard. He was able to ignore John's taunts and one-sided recap of Friday night because that event had led to Jess coming to find him on the beach. When John realized he wasn't getting a rise out of Hank, he busied himself with his phone and left Hank to do all the work; plus, he was probably nursing a hangover. Hank was unusually quick and compliant, finishing up his shift fifteen minutes early. He left as soon as possible to shower and change before heading over to pick up Jess.

The wait was worth it. Jess was staying at Anne's apartment, the bottom half of a house on the Island and a half block from the beach. The houses came right up to the street, so Hank was able to pull right up to the house where her apartment was. When she opened the door, she walked out in a stunning pink spaghetti-strapped sundress with red flowers and white sandals with her dark brown hair lightly waving around her face and over her shoulders. She had on just a touch of makeup and silver earrings. She seemed to sparkle. He couldn't believe how pretty she was and how lucky he was to go out with her. She stood there waiting for him to say something back to her hello.

"Everything okay?" she finally asked when he just stared at her.

He came to and quickly turned to open the car door for her. "Everything's great," he said with a big grin on his face as he helped her into the Jeep.

Hank got in on the driver's side and started the engine. "I have to warn you, my ride gets a little windy...."

"No kidding." She laughed since it was an open vehicle. "I came prepared." She pulled out a hair tie and tied her hair back. "So where are you taking me?"

"Somewhere we hopefully won't run into any college students," he said, smiling at her before driving off.

The restaurant was on the Cape Fear River in an area Jess had not ventured to yet that catered to locals. It had a big deck overlooking the river with red umbrellas shading the tables during the day and rows of string lights overhead to provide ambience at night. They sat outside feeling a cool breeze off the water, and Jess could hear the river flowing. When the waitress came, Hank ordered a sweet tea with his meal. When she left, Jess couldn't resist teasing him.

"So, drinking sweet tea," she said. "Does that make you a Southern boy?"

"No, being from the South makes me a Southern boy," he replied, smiling back at her. "Why, what do you think of when you think of a Southerner?"

Jess shrugged. "Oh, you know, pick-up trucks, dogs, good ole boy mannerisms...."

Hank sat back in his chair and looked at her, trying not to laugh. "Well, I wish I had the dog; you've seen my vehicle, which isn't exactly a pick-up truck, and I thought you Northern girls would appreciate good manners since you so rarely see them."

Jess pretended to be shocked, but she was extremely impressed with his sharp comeback. It wasn't often she ran into someone who could relate to her sense of humor and respond in kind.

Hank asked her where she grew up and she told him about living with her mother, who was a receptionist for a local law firm. When he asked about her father, she said he had been a high school science teacher, but had died in a car crash when she was fourteen. They'd been very close, and he had been the reason she'd developed a love of biology; he had loved talking about how what sort of effect the environment had on life and how life continued to evolve in spite of it.

"He loved amphibians and reptiles, but was especially into frogs and how important they were to the ecosystem," said Jess. "He would often catch tadpoles at one of the local parks and bring them home to raise to understand them better. Of course, my mother was not fond of his hobby since the tank water smelled so bad. She would make him keep them in the garage, and he would spend time each day feeding them and watching them grow."

"What did he do once they were grown?" Hank asked.

"Well, he wasn't always successful, which was probably a good thing," she replied, laughing. "One year, he released a bunch of frogs in our yard, and I remember every night when we would go out to see the fireflies, they would start croaking loudly. Too loudly. Those little tree frogs were small, about the size of a silver dollar, but you could barely hear yourself talk once they got started. They would croak to each other, which my father found infinitely fascinating, but it annoyed my mother, who couldn't enjoy time on her patio without hearing them or finding them on the furniture or in the grill. After that, I think she required that he release them in the park."

"What about you? Do you like frogs?" Hank asked, thinking he had never known a girl who did.

Jess shrugged. "They were more my father's thing. I liked learning about anything that lived in the ocean. Once a year, my father would take me into New York to visit the aquarium, and that was just amazing." Jess talked about how she loved the darkness of the jellyfish room where she would watch them float silently in a purple-lit tank. Or she would stand in awe in front of the coral reef that had been recreated with all of its colorful fish, manta rays, and sea turtles.

"And yes, even sharks," she joked. "Like I said, as long as they are in a tank, I'm good."

As Jess got older, she had started learning more about sea life through books and videos, everything from the tales about gigantic squid to marine life so far beneath the ocean that they lived in total darkness. She hadn't thought about studying such creatures in college until she had taken the marine science course.

"But it's different from reading about them in a book or watching them through a video," she said. "Here I get to study them in their natural habitat in the marsh and the ocean. It's even more amazing in real life."

"Didn't you ever go to the beach back home?" he asked.

"Well, beaches in New Jersey are not the same as Wrightsville," she replied. "You had to drive over an hour for a day visit on a beach so completely covered with people that you had to weave your way around the towels to get to the water, which was also crowded. I have never seen beaches as open and sparsely populated as the beaches here. And forget about surfing. I always thought that was more a West Coast sport, so I was surprised to see how many people did it when I first came down here."

"Welcome to Wilmington, pioneer of East Coast surfing. It's actually a fairly popular surfing site. I've met guys from the West Coast who like to come here to surf."

"I just figured that everyone I see out there grew up surfing and I was too old to learn how. I'm glad that's not the case."

"Me, too," he said, smiling. "You'll pick it up eventually."

Jess mock hit him for that comment, feigning being insulted. "You mean I do it so well with such little practice, thank you very much."

"You're right. I didn't do anything but hold the board. It was all you," he said, making her laugh. Hank took a sip of his drink and changed the subject. "How did you manage to get such a great place living by the beach?" he asked. He knew rentals at the beach were expensive, so it was not the place he would have expected her to live if she was having a hard time making ends meet.

She told him how she had met Anne when they were in an English class together freshman year and they had just really hit it off. Anne's parents had rented the apartment for her at the beach last summer, paying all of the lease fees so she wouldn't have to have roommates, which they worried would distract her from study-ing. Without telling them, Anne had invited Jess to take the extra

bedroom so they could hang out together when Jess wasn't working. It worked out so well that Anne invited Jess to stay when their
sophomore year started, and Jess had been there since. It was Anne's
way of helping Jess, whom she knew was struggling to make ends
meet while making the grades she needed to keep her scholarship.
Plus, she enjoyed having the company. Anne was a business major
who took her studies seriously, but not having to worry about bills
meant she had more free time. She could afford to take an unpaid
internship downtown at a marketing firm a few days a week and to
have an avid social life. Living together made it easier to hang out
whenever they were both around.

When the check came, Jess realized she'd spent the whole dinner
talking about herself again and hadn't asked Hank anything about
himself. He seemed genuinely interested when she spoke, asking
questions and paying attention to everything she said, but she still
felt self-conscious about revealing so much so quickly. It had been a
long time since she felt like telling her story to anyone, and though
she felt comfortable doing it at the time, she wanted to know more
about him. *Next time I ask him questions*, she thought.

But Hank had been a riveted listener. He was more than glad
to sit back while she told him how she had come to Wilmington,
asking questions when he could to keep her going. He had no interest in talking about his own life since telling his story would put him
at more of a disadvantage. He wanted to hear everything about her.

As Hank listened, he kept thinking about how much he wanted
to kiss her. Rob had taught him that the first kiss set the stage for everything else, so you had to make sure you chose your moment. He
knew he wanted it to be right. But the restaurant was too crowded
and the parking lot too unromantic. So he hoped for an old-fash-
ioned kiss good night at the door.

But that didn't quite work out.

When Hank pulled up to Jess's door, he could hear music blaring from next door. He parked and jumped out to open her door, noticing some guys at the neighboring house on the second-floor deck, shirtless and drinking beer, hanging out and watching them. As she was getting out of the car, one of them sat on the edge and called over to her.

"Hey, Jess! Looking good! Been on a date?" he asked, somewhat drunkenly while toasting her with his beer can. He wore a backward baseball cap and looked the very picture of the frat boy.

"Yes, Grant," she said as if talking to a child. "Been drinking with the boys on the deck again?"

"Hey, it's summer!" he said with a huge grin, throwing his arms up, which caused him to spill his beer on himself. He made a feeble attempt to wipe it away, then smiled and shrugged. "When are you going to come join us?"

Jess laughed. "When I don't have a life anymore? Have you thought about heading out to some of the bars on the strip? Maybe expand your horizons a little?"

"Why do that when I have all I need here?" Without thinking, he threw up his arms up again to emphasize his point, only to fall backward onto the deck.

Jess turned back to Hank. "Sorry. One of the hazards of living at the beach. There's always a party going on."

Hank nodded, not sure what to make of it. It had been such a great night, but he felt a little threatened by having these college guys so close by and friendly with Jess. He wasn't sure how to handle it, and now he was disappointed since he couldn't kiss her with a drunken audience nearby. "No problem. I really enjoyed tonight."

He awkwardly reached out and gave her arm a quick squeeze and then started to back away toward the car. "I'll text you," he said and then got in and started the engine.

Jess walked up and held on to the passenger window before he took off. "I really enjoyed it, too," she said, recognizing his discomfort and giving him an assuring smile. Then she backed away, heading safely inside before he drove off.

Even with the awkward ending at Jess's door, Hank had had a great time. He drove home singing with the radio, and when he pulled into his driveway, he practically leaped out of the car and through his door.

When he walked in, he saw his father sitting in his chair, watching television.

"How's it going, son?" he asked, looking up and turning down the volume. He noticed Hank was dressed up more than usual. He looked surprised. "You're looking good tonight. What have you been up to?"

Hank sat down on the couch, eager to share his good news with someone. "I went on a date," he said, smiling widely.

His father's eyebrows went up in mock surprise. "A date. Well that's great. How did it go?"

"All right, I guess," Hank said, shrugging, but it was easy for his father to see he was smitten.

"Says the man with a crocodile smile…" his father said with a gentle laugh. Hank hadn't heard one of his father's sayings in a while. See you later, alligator. In a while, crocodile. He always liked them. They were a part of his good memories of him. "Well, I'm glad it went well. Is she pretty?"

"Yep. Very."

"I figured. Is she good enough for you? No need to bother with the ones who aren't…."

Hank thought about this for a moment, his smile diminishing a little. Wasn't it more a concern whether he was good enough for her?

As if reading his mind, his father said. "Don't sell yourself short, son. You're a good man. You've just had some setbacks. But you and Rob were always good men…."

At the mention of his brother, the conversation faltered. They sat in silence for a moment, which Hank decided to use as his exit.

"Well, good night, Pop," he said, getting off the couch and heading toward the stairs, not wanting to think about Rob after such a great night.

"Good night, son," his dad replied, turning back to the TV.

Hank didn't want to appear too over-anxious and had planned to text Jess the next day, but he ended up doing it before going to bed.

> Thanks for coming out tonight. Really liked the dress.

He didn't expect a reply so late but got one anyway:

> Thx. My hoop skirt was at the cleaners, so I had to make do.

Hank laughed.

> Sorry if I used too many manners. I am sure you Northern girls aren't used to that. I'll try to hold back next time.

She replied:

> Good idea. Maybe you could start hanging out shirtless
> on a deck somewhere with a beer in your hand. So
> much more appealing....

With that comment, Hank realized he had nothing to worry about from a couple of college boys next door. They texted back and forth for a little longer before Hank headed to bed. The next day they both had off was Saturday, so they made plans to go surfing again. Hank liked the idea of hanging out with her at the beach, plus there was the added advantage of seeing her again in her bikini. But Saturday seemed like a lifetime away. How could he possibly wait until Saturday?

Chapter 10

"You squeezed her arm?" Mike said in a teasing voice. "Dude, what were you thinking?"

It was early Wednesday morning, and Hank and Mike were sitting on their boards surfing before heading into work. They were waiting for the next set of waves while letting the water gently bob them up and down. Apparently, the guys next door had not been Hank and Jess's only audience; Anne had looked out the window to see what all the talking was about and had seen their goodbye exchange. Jess had texted him that Anne was teasing her about it and had probably told Mike.

"Hey, man, there were like ten guys watching us. It wasn't the place," Hank said, enjoying the light-heartedness of the conversation.

Mike laughed. "Ten? Now there were ten guys? I thought there were, like, three."

"You weren't there. It was a tense situation."

"Well, you must have done something right. Anne says Jess has been in too good a mood since your date. It's driving her crazy."

Hank smiled even bigger at knowing she was feeling as good as he was. "So?" he said, trying to play it off

"So, the Jess I know is a pretty serious girl. I'm not sure I've ever even seen her smile before."

"Who the hell would with you hanging around?"

"Oh yeah?" Mike said, splashing Hank, who playfully splashed him back, both trying to outdo the other. When they stopped, Mike looked at Hank for a moment, and then his expression turned thoughtful.

"It's good to see you back to your old self, man," he said, looking at the horizon, then back at Hank. "I've missed that guy."

"Yeah," said Hank, nodding in agreement, giving a small smile. "Me, too."

Chapter 11

While Jess may have divulged a lot of her life story to Hank, she had purposely left out some parts. Everything she had said about how she had become interested in sea turtles was true, and she was really taken with Wilmington, feeling like it was a second home, but there were details she was not ready to disclose, especially this early in their getting-to-know-each-other stage. She had left behind a lot that she did not want to be a part of her life in North Carolina, such as how hard it had been for her and her mother after her father had died.

When Jess's father was alive, they were a happy family, but after he died, money became very tight. He had not had life insurance, leaving her and her mother to struggle to find ways to support themselves. For a while, Jess was not sure they would be able to stay in their home. She could see the bills piling up on the counter, and she started to worry what would happen to them when she heard her mother cry in her room at night when she thought Jess was asleep. It was a huge relief when her mother finally landed a job as a receptionist. Though it was barely enough to cover their basic living expenses, they were both grateful she had found it. Knowing the

financial bind her mother was in, Jess did everything she could to
help out. She would spend hours in thrift stores finding clothes that
her classmates had donated rather than shop at the more expensive
stores in the mall. She would do any job for the neighbors she could
to make money from washing cars to taking care of their pets and
babysitting. And when she was old enough, she found there was
good money in waitressing in restaurants.

Jess knew early on it would be up to her to figure out how to
pay for college. UNCW had not been her first choice. She had been
accepted to better-known schools, but UNCW offered to cover
more of her costs than any of the other schools, and it was the best
choice for graduating without incurring substantial debt. It had a
well-respected biology department, and once she started attending,
she found the classes informative and her professors accessible. Plus,
it had the added benefit of being in a beach town. It didn't take Jess
long to realize she had made the right choice as she quickly became
enamored with the school and Wilmington.

The only person Jess had even talked to about how hard it had
been growing up in New Jersey was Anne, and that was after a year
of getting to know each other and a night of too many drinks. She
was glad to talk to someone about it, but she was otherwise guarded
when it came to talking about her past. She didn't want to be known
as the girl who had lost her father and scraped by, but rather to
be seen as the hard-working and determined college student she'd
become.

Jess also didn't tell Hank that when she decided to pursue the
study of sea turtles, she'd applied to transfer to the University of
Central Florida last January. When she had transferred her major
to marine biology in her sophomore year, she was assigned to a new
advisor, Professor Williams. When she explained her work with the

Turtle Rescue and the research project she had done on light pollution, Professor Williams could tell Jess had found her calling. But she also explained that Jess could only do so much hands-on learning at UNCW, which didn't have a program or a lab that specialized in the study of sea turtles. UCF not only had such an in-depth program, but it would give her the opportunity to conduct field research at a wildlife refuge that was considered one of the most important green turtle nesting sites in North America. Jess could continue to work with the Turtle Rescue and have access to sea turtle nests in North Carolina, but the exposure she would receive at UCF would be much more focused and immersive. If Jess was serious about becoming a sea turtle biologist, she would have to get her master's or PhD, and to get into the better graduate programs, she needed a resumé that showed the type of experience a school like UCF would give her.

When Jess went home to research UCF, she knew instantly it was exactly where she wanted to be. The problem was the application deadline to transfer was coming up quickly, so she had to act fast. She spent most of her winter break at home putting together her application, which required an in-depth essay and recommendations from two of her professors and the Turtle Rescue. She even returned to UNCW early so Professor Williams could review it and help her refine her essay before sending it off.

But there was one major concern. Though UCF's tuition cost was not much more expensive than UNCW's, UNCW had only been affordable due to the scholarship money they had given Jess to attend. In addition, more expenses would be involved. Right now, Jess didn't have to pay housing, which would certainly be expensive living in a tourist destination like Orlando. Jess knew how lucky she had been to live rent-free with Anne, a gift she reciprocated by being the one to clean the apartment and buying whatever groceries they needed. But if UCF did not offer her the same scholarship money, there was no way she could afford it. Once she finished her undergraduate degree, she still had to pay for her master's, and there was only so much debt she would be able to take on with the salary she would have when she completed her degrees. Professor Williams said her 4.0 GPA and her work at the Turtle Rescue should encourage UCF to offer her financial aid. But first, she had to get in. All she could do was keep her fingers crossed and stay focused on her studies while waiting for UCF's decision.

When the acceptance finally came in March, Jess was elated. UCF was pleased to invite her to attend their program starting next fall. They would accept almost all of her UNCW credits and were excited to welcome her to a learning experience unlike any other. Jess had never been so excited about her future. She could barely focus on her schoolwork and was so ecstatic that she chattered constantly to Anne about the program and what she would learn. Anne was happy for her at first, but after a while, she just couldn't take Jess's nonstop enthusiasm and decided to go home for a few days to visit her folks. Jess sensed Anne was also bummed to be losing her as a roommate, but she couldn't focus on that right now. All she could think about was going to Florida and what it would be like to work at a wildlife refuge so populated by turtle nests. Jess had read about the thousands of nests they saw each year and that more nests were laid there in one night than she might see in an entire season in North Carolina. She would not only have the opportunity to see the nests hatch but also to see the turtles actually lay their eggs. It was all she wanted to do, and she couldn't wait for it to begin.

That was, until she got the second letter. It came on Friday, the day Anne had left for her parents for the weekend. This one came from the financial aid office at UCF telling her what her tuition costs would be. They were sorry to inform her that all available financial aid money for that year had already been disbursed, so they were unable to offer her any type of scholarship, but she was encouraged to apply again next year. Jess stared at the numbers on the letter and knew right then it was over. If she were to take out loans for that amount, she would never feel comfortable taking on more debt to attend a master's program, and just having an undergraduate degree would not be enough. She made a call to the Office of Financial Assistance to see if there was any way they could help her, but while they sympathized with her, there was nothing they could do. Jess hung up the phone and just stared at it, not knowing what else to do. Transferring at the start of her junior year was her last shot since they didn't allow seniors to transfer into the program. If she didn't go now, it was over.

Jess sat for a long time staring at the phone, her mind desperately trying to find a solution. There had to be a way, she told herself. She decided to take her bike out and go for a ride. She rode without caring which direction she was headed, her mind going over and over what to do, trying to find a way to make it work. Could she work more during the summer to make up the difference? Not if she wanted to keep volunteering at the Turtle Rescue, which would be necessary since it was part of her eligibility for getting accepted to UCF. She had no extended family to ask—Jess's parents had been disinherited when they had gotten married so young, and besides, Jess hated the idea of asking anyone for money; the idea was even more insufferable than borrowing it. Every solution she came up with all came down to the same answer. Unless she was willing to take out loans, she would not be able to go.

Jess rode until her legs felt stiff and tired, finally heading back to the apartment where she locked up her bike. She couldn't stomach going inside just yet, so she walked down to the beach, sitting herself down on the sand in an exhausted heap, watching the waves roll in as the sun set behind her. She sat watching families pack up to head home for dinner and the surfers catch a few remaining waves before heading in to shore. She wanted to feel the sense of calm that being at the beach had always provided in the past, but this time it wouldn't come. UCF was so close and within reach, and now it was falling through her fingers. She was so disappointed that she had gotten this far and then could not go. She could always apply to their master's program, she told herself, but she knew without the experience she would gain in their undergraduate program what a long shot that would be. *There's just no way to do it,* she told herself. *You just have to make the best of it here.*

Jess remained there, silent and unmoving, until night had descended around her. Even the twinkle of the stars above offered no comfort. Not until she felt herself getting chilled did she rise with great reluctance and head back.

When Anne returned on Sunday afternoon, she instantly sensed the change in atmosphere in the apartment. Jess was no longer the enthusiastic roommate who had gotten on Anne's nerves. Now she sat on the couch in front of the TV, barely saying hello, just keeping to herself. There were some dishes on the kitchen counter and trash that hadn't been put away, all very unlike Jess, and it looked like she had slept in the clothes she was wearing. It didn't take Anne long to find the letter from the Office of Financial Assistance, which Jess had left out on the kitchen table. Anne took one look and knew how disappointed her friend must be. She'd pilfered a couple of bottles of wine from her parents' house, so she figured some cheering up was in order. She took one out and filled two wine glasses, handing one to Jess as she sat next to her on the couch.

"Drink this; you'll feel better," she said. Jess had only tried drinking a few times before and wasn't a fan, but the wine was sweet and tasted good, and after a few sips, it started to ease her pain.

"The way I see it, you are looking at this all wrong," Anne said. "With the humidity in Florida, you were just going to sweat all day, causing sweat stains on those T-shirts you pick up from that thrift shop, which you would miss, not to mention how frizzy your hair would be. Big hair was never your look, even if you did come from New Jersey. Plus, do you even know what Orlando is like? Everywhere you go, it's Disney this or Disney that, trying to convert you into a freakin' Mouseketeer or something. Trust me, you are much better off here where you have an excellent living arrangement, if I do say so myself, and the beach is half a block away where you can find your fair share of turtles or nests or whatever without having to head to the land of humidity and tacky tourists. And let's face it," she said, pausing dramatically to give her crowning reason, "you'd miss me too much."

Jess smiled and even laughed at her friend's efforts to cheer her up. She sipped her wine, and after a couple of glasses, she agreed she probably would not like the heat or the bugs, for which Florida was well-known. They finished off the first bottle and started on the second. By that point, Jess was feeling a little tipsy and the wine was making her reflective. When Anne started asking her questions about her father, Jess decided to open up and told her what had happened. She hadn't talked to anyone about it since coming to college, but right now really wanted to.

Jess explained that her father had gone out one night to pick up some supplies he wanted for his science class the next day. After he left, a huge thunderstorm moved in and it started raining really hard. When he'd been gone a while, Jess's mom started to get anxious, thinking maybe he had pulled over to wait until the rain had passed. She tried calling him on his cell phone, but the call kept going to voice mail. When the rain stopped and he still didn't come home or answer her calls and texts, her mom really started to worry. They only had the one car, so all she could do was wait for him to pull up in the driveway, telling herself it would be any minute; she just had to wait a little longer. But it kept getting later and later, and still, he hadn't come home.

When the police car parked in front of their house, her mother knew it could only be bad news. She answered the door when the officers knocked and politely let them in to sit in the living room. She listened quietly while they told her that her husband had been making a left hand turn into the shopping center when another driver who had been driving at high speed had come over the hill from the opposite direction and been unable to stop in time due to the wet streets. Just like that, her husband was gone. Jess listened from the doorway, trying to comprehend what she was hearing. A loud buzzing noise filled her head, making their words unintelligible. She watched wordlessly as her mother thanked the officers and walked them to the door. Jess didn't understand it at the time, but her mother was in shock, and she would continue to be so through the following days and even the day of the funeral itself, staring numbly at the casket that held her husband's body, unable to offer any comfort to Jess as she was swallowed up by her own pain.

Her mother's sadness at losing her father was very hard on Jess. After the funeral, her mother barely ate, and after a while, she rarely got out of bed. For months, Jess did what she could to take care of her, getting the groceries and taking care of the house, all while trying to keep on top of her schoolwork, but it weighed on her. Finally, with encouragement from her mother's friends, her mother started to come around a little bit. She started getting out of bed, fixing dinner for Jess, and doing the shopping. She started going to church and looking for a job. When she finally got one, life became more normal, settling into a routine. Once more, Jess was able to hang out with her friends and go to sleepovers without worrying about her mother all the time.

"Wow," said Anne when Jess had finished, not only at the story but at how much Jess had actually told her for the first time. "That must have been really rough."

"Yes, it was," said Jess.

"What was your dad like?" Anne asked.

Jess thought for a moment. "He was…curious. He loved thinking about how life evolved. Why the frogs would croak only at night, why some tadpoles lived and others didn't; things like that fascinated him. We would take walks in the woods and find insects that we would later research online to see what they were. He had really wanted to be a scientist, but was never able to get his master's degree."

"How come?" asked Anne. "Let me guess. White lab coat wasn't his color?"

"No," said Jess, throwing a pillow at her and laughing before getting a bit more solemn. "No, my mom got pregnant with me in college and had to drop out, and that is why they ended up getting married so young. My dad managed to finish his college degree, but then he had to support us. Becoming a teacher was the closest he ever got to his dream."

"Geez, can you imagine one of us with a kid at this age?" asked Anne, shaking her head.

"No and I don't want to," said Jess, laughing. The idea of having a baby now when she barely felt able to take care of herself was unthinkable. The thought of it made her think about her mother and how she must have felt when she came along. She knew her parents had loved each other, but they also had repeatedly warned her against getting married so early in life. It was romantic as a story to meet the love of your life so early, but the day-to-day reality was much harder.

"First, you need to go after your dream," her father had said to her more than once during one of their long hikes. "Do the things you really want to do. That time when you are just starting out as an adult and can explore the world at your leisure, you never get those years back. Once you take on responsibilities, everything changes. As for love, it will find its way to you when the time is right. It always does. Don't let it worry you, Jessie girl," he would say with his broad smile.

"I won't, Dad," she told him, storing his words in her memory as she took his hand and followed him through the woods.

Chapter 12

Jess and Hank started texting each other during the day. When something didn't go as planned with a restaurant customer or when a visitor at the Turtle Rescue where she gave tours was difficult, she would send him a message asking for advice. He would always come back with some absurd scenario that made her laugh and melted the problem away. It helped her cope with a bad day and gave her something more cheerful to think about. She liked that their easy conversation translated into an ongoing texting dialogue. It gave her a chance to get to know him better, even if she wasn't able to see him as often as she would like.

Thursday night, she got off from her job at Oceanside at 10 p.m. She was grateful for the night to end since the customers had been unusually difficult. She'd walked to work but now regretted not having ridden her bike because it was dark and she was tired. Anne hadn't come by tonight, and she had forgotten that Lynn had the night off, so walking home was her only option.

"Need a lift?" she suddenly heard a voice say in the darkness. Startled, she turned to see Hank leaning against his Jeep, smiling at her. She broke into a relieved grin and tried to hide her shock at seeing him there.

"You have no idea how good your timing is," she said, letting him open the door for her and getting in the Jeep.

"Sure I do," he said. "All Southern boys have good timing. It's in our breeding." He didn't know where this bravado came from when he was around her. He felt he could let down his guard and just be himself.

He got in the vehicle. "Where to?" he asked, starting the engine.

"Home," she said. "I need a shower and to get out of these clothes. I probably don't look as good as the last time you saw me...."

"You're right," he said, turning to look at her before backing up. "You look even better." Then he smiled at her and started backing out of the spot.

Jess laughed. "Oh my. I think either swimming in the ocean has diminished your eyesight or you're taking this Southern charm a bit too far."

It was a short drive to her house, where she asked him to wait outside while she went in and changed out of her work clothes. He parked the car in the street and got out. *No parties on the deck tonight*, he thought, looking up at the dark apartment next door.

When Jess came out, they walked up to the beach, leaving their shoes at the path entrance so they could feel the sand on their bare feet. They could hear the waves crashing against the shore, but there was very little light. They carefully made their way down to the water's edge and then started walking along the shoreline. The night was extremely dark, with no moon or stars, indicating it was going to rain shortly. He had never thought about why there were no lights down at the beach, but Jess told him how an ordinance had been passed by the town to diminish the lights of the houses lining the beach to avoid disorienting the sea turtles that would come in to lay their eggs.

"This is one of the few protected areas left where they come to nest," she said.

"When do you start nest-sitting?" he asked, knowing that was the work at the Turtle Rescue she was looking forward to most.

"This is when the season starts, so we should start finding nests soon. Once we do, the waiting begins. It takes about sixty days for the hatchlings to be ready to emerge from their nests, which won't begin until late July at the earliest. Every morning, I walk up and down Wrightsville Beach to search for them, but I haven't found one yet."

"That's dedication for you," he said, impressed with her enthusiasm.

Jess laughed. "Sorry. I don't mean to go on. I never thought I would enjoy learning about turtles so much. Sometimes I think about all the events that led up to my being here. It's not the path I thought I would be on, but here I am," she said, starting to think about UCF, but then putting it out of her mind.

After a moment of silence, Jess spoke again. "I don't know; do you ever feel like…do you ever think some things are just meant to be?"

Hank thought for a moment, remembering the voice that had come to him the first day he had met her. "I want to believe that's true," he finally answered.

"Yeah, sometimes it just feels that way."

They walked together closely, occasionally bumping against each other. Hank used one of these opportunities to reach down and take her hand, entwining his fingers in hers. She felt that charge again at his touch, and they both fell into a comfortable silence, broken only by the sound of the waves in the distance.

Even in the darkness, Jess could sense him grinning. She was grateful how the darkness allowed her some cover from showing too much of her own feelings, the excitement rising within her when she was with him. She wasn't ready yet to show him just how much she liked him. She knew that she needed to take this slow. What did she really know about him other than a few dates and Anne's complimentary picture of him? Jess recognized that Anne had her own motives, wanting to double-date so she could hang out with her boyfriend and her best friend together. That was why Jess hadn't put much credence at first into Anne's pushing for her to meet Hank. In all honesty, if she hadn't run into him at the Café first, the meeting at Oceanside would have been the end of it. She knew she needed to get to know him because so far everything she had seen was too good to be true.

It was getting late, so they turned around and started heading back. As they neared the beach path back to the street, it started to drizzle.

"Well, that's one way to shower," Jess said, laughing. She looked up at the sky and held up her free hand to catch some drops as they misted over her face and body.

Hank looked over at her catching raindrops. He dropped her hand and took her by the waist, lightly but firmly pulling her to him. His other hand came up and tenderly held her face. She stiffened for a quick instant, making him hesitate, but when she looked up into his eyes, he felt her body relax and accept his embrace, tilting her face up toward him. Slowly, he leaned in to kiss her—one soft, warm kiss that vibrated through her, lingering even after it was done. He placed his forehead on hers for a moment, letting them both take in the moment, but then the rain started coming down hard and fast. He grabbed her hand and they ran back to her house, where she ran inside while he waved goodbye and ran for the safety of his Jeep.

Lying in bed that night, Jess recounted everything from the moment Hank picked her up to when he had kissed her. That was the part her mind kept going over the most. All she could think about was how incredible it had been. That it was even better than she had imagined it would be, and that she wished it hadn't all happened so quickly.

Even though it was late, she had to share her excitement with someone. Anne was out so she instinctively dialed her mother, knowing she was probably waking her up, but needing to share her euphoria.

"Hello?" her mother's groggy voice answered. "Jess, are you okay?"

"Hi, Mom. I'm fine," Jess said, trying to sound calm, but the excitement resounded clearly in her voice. "Sorry to wake you, but I had to tell you something. I met someone."

Chapter 13

Hank was there the next night to pick Jess up again from work even though her Friday night shift ended later. He waited over an hour in the parking lot until he saw her familiar figure exit the restaurant, then drove her home where they talked a short while in his car before he leaned over and kissed her again, using the same tender touch as he held her face. This time the kiss lasted longer and became more intense. He pulled back after a few minutes, getting out and opening her car door to let her out. He kissed her a few minutes more, then told her he would pick her up at 7 a.m. sharp to do some surfing.

It was all Hank could do to pull himself back from her. The scent of her intoxicated him, and she was so soft and warm to the touch. He had decided during work on Thursday that he could ab-
sol   nother day to see her, and he made a plan to show
                 r shift to offer her a ride. It was the right choice.
                 g the beach, it had felt so good to be with her.
                 ght about taking her hand; it had just hap-
                 e he did, he liked how it felt in his and how
                 every moment speaking; they could just walk

together side by side along the water. It had all been so easy. As they approached the beach exit, he knew he could not let this moment pass, and so, he had taken a deep breath and made his move. One kiss, that was all he wanted. And he got it.

That day at work, Hank's mind was a million miles away thinking about being with Jess the night before. Twice, he delivered the wrong boxes, and even though John chastised him about it, he couldn't care less. There was no question he was going to show up again at the end of her shift. He planned to take it slow and only kiss her once more, but seeing her sit next to him in the car, he suddenly found himself leaning over, anxious to be close to her, and one kiss just led into another. When he could feel himself getting lost in her, he stopped, slowing things down. The sensations were overwhelming. He got out of the car and then took her hand to help her out, pulling her to him and kissing her again. He could feel himself slip away again, and it was all he could do to step back and say goodnight.

Saturday they would keep it simple, he told himself. They would do some surfing and at some point grab something to eat. But his mind was racing with so many things he wanted to show her and do with her that he didn't know where to start. He decided to let things play out and see where they went. He went to bed smiling to himself, excited about seeing her again the next day, thinking tomorrow could not come soon enough.

Saturday morning, Hank showed up early, but Jess was already waiting for him outside. She jumped into the Jeep before he could get out to open the door for her and gave him a quick kiss.

"Quick," she said. "Let's get out of here before Anne wakes up and decides to join us with Mike. Today I want you all to myself."

He was all for that idea. He quickly put it into gear and headed down the beach to an area at the south end of the Island that was less crowded and where Mike wouldn't think to look for them. He had brought Rob's board this time, which was easier to use, being slightly bigger.

They got in the water, and Hank put her on the board and told her how to swim past the incoming waves. Jess was a quick learner, and he followed, swimming right behind her. Once they reached a good place to pick waves, he had her stay on the board while he remained in the water holding onto the board while they waited for a good wave to come. When he looked at her, he kept thinking how pretty she was, so he tried to avert his eyes by looking toward the horizon watching the water. He would push the board forward to help her catch the incoming waves, and when she caught one, he would tread water, watching her ride into shore. She loved the feel of being on the board, and when she swam back out to him, she would pop back on the board, ready to ride again.

After a few runs, Hank asked if he could try something with her—for them both to ride at the same time. Rob used to do it with their dog, and though Hank had never tried it, he thought he could make it work. He put her squatting in front and then got behind her, paddling hard when the wave came and then jumping up as it crested. The first time they went toppling over, but they decided to try again, and by the third time, they were able to ride a whole wave with both of them upright on the board.

"That was amazing!" Jess cried out as they jumped off the board. She threw herself into his arms. He dropped the board and started kissing her, her wet body against his, holding her tightly, almost inhaling her, until a large wave knocked them off balance. Laughing, she ran back into the surf, splashing water at him, encouraging him to follow. He threw the board on the beach and quickly swam out to her.

They played a while longer in the water and then decided to eat. Hank drove them to the Trolly Stop, where they picked up some hotdogs and drinks. They ate outside at one of the round cement tables with large blue umbrellas that protected them from the hot June sun.

"So, tell me what it's like to grow up here," Jess said.

"I don't know. What do you want to know?"

"What's your family like?" she asked.

Hank felt himself tense a bit. It was still hard to talk about Rob.

"Well, I live with my father, who is a handyman."

"And what about your mother?" Jess asked, sensing there were some delicate issues and hoping she wasn't prying too much.

Hank shrugged. "She died. When I was eight. She got sick with cancer. She was only sick a few months before she passed." Hank could still picture his mother in the hospital bed looking sickly, his father not leaving her side for weeks. He shook off the memory.

"I'm so sorry, Hank. What was she like?"

He liked that she asked about his mother rather than to go on about how sad it all was. It had been so long ago and he'd been so young. Still, he remembered that he had felt loved by her, even if the memories he had left were distant.

He thought for a moment. "I remember her being happy, singing around the house. She liked to garden and used to fill the area in front of the house with all sorts of flowers, making it pretty. I remember how she used to read to me every night until I would fall asleep. But I especially remember," he said, smiling, "how she would take me to the beach and we would run up to just where the waves were coming in and run back just before they touched us."

He suddenly remembered doing this very vividly, the way his mother would laugh and he would chase her, as they darted to and from the waterline. He could see her shoulder-length sandy-colored hair moving with her as she ran. He remembered how she would let him catch her and then run away again. He could picture her infectious smile and her nails that were always painted red. She'd loved songs from the Big Band era, singing along with them as she made dinner. If he or Rob entered the room, she would take them in her arms and start dancing with them, swinging them around. He hadn't thought of any of those moments in a long time. He came back from his reverie. "She was great," he said, reaching for his hotdog.

"She sounds like it," said Jess.

"What about you?" Hank asked, hoping to get the attention off of him. "You told me about your father. What is your mother like?"

But before Jess could answer, she heard a familiar voice behind her.

"There you are," Anne said, sitting down next to Jess with Mike sitting down next to her. They'd also gotten some hotdogs for lunch. "I thought we were going to do something together today?"

"We are," said Mike, shooting a smile in Hank's direction. "We're eating."

"Oh, ha-ha. No really. Where have you been?" Anne asked Jess.

Jess explained that Hank had picked her up early and that she didn't want to wake her. Then she told them how they had surfed together on the same board. After eating, the four of them decided to head back to the beach and hang out. The girls laid out on their towels talking while Hank and Mike went for a short run.

"So, how's it going?" Mike asked, although it was obvious it was going quite well.

"Okay. She's great. What do you want to hear?" Hank replied, trying not to give away too much but obviously bursting with how good he felt.

"Just checking in. Anne will ask me later. I've done my duty. How's life with John?"

Hank scoffed. "It's going. How's it going working at your dad's office?"

"Not too bad. I actually got to tag along while he showed a house this week. Real big stuff."

"Sounds promising."

"If you're into that kind of thing. Did you know there are guys my age who have their realtor's licenses already?"

"So, once again, you're a slow learner…."

Mike used that as an excuse to wrestle Hank into the water where they tussled for a moment, trying to throw each other in, before diving into the waves.

Anne and Jess watched from their towels.

"Boys…" Anne said with a sigh.

Jess laughed. "I know. Aren't they great?"

Jess was walking on air that night. She was accommodating and had endless patience with all her tables. Her good mood was infectious, and everything seemed to be going smoothly for once. She couldn't stop smiling, despite herself, thinking that maybe it was a good thing that she was staying in Wilmington after all.

Lynn finally pulled her aside to interrogate her. "Okay, so who is he?" she asked. "This is not the Jess I have come to know and love."

Jess laughed and told her about Hank, including how they'd been hanging out having a good time and she was learning to surf. As Lynn listened, she seemed to get quiet and her expression went from smiling to thoughtful. She seemed like she wanted to say something, then decided against it.

"That sounds great, Jess," she finally said, turning to print out a check. "I mean, I hope it goes well." Lynn's sudden lack of enthusiasm was obvious.

Jess was taken aback at this response. "What do you mean?" she asked, seeing the change in Lynn's expression.

"Hey, I've known Hank a long time. He was always a nice guy to me, so who cares what anyone else says? He definitely has a great body. Just enjoy him. It's just a summer thing, right?"

Before Jess could ask what she meant, Lynn rushed back onto the floor to serve her customers. Jess pondered Lynn's words for a minute. Lynn must be referring to the bar fight Anne and Mike had told her about since everyone who knew Hank knew he had been put on probation. Jess of all people would never be with someone who was violent. Her own father had been kind and attentive to her, and that was the expectation she had from anyone she dated. She didn't understand women who stayed with men who hurt them. Besides, she felt she really knew Hank. She couldn't see him being the kind of guy who went to bars to pick fights. The Hank she knew was very different from that. From what Anne and Mike had told her, it had been a one-time event brought on by his grief over the loss of his brother. She shook off Lynn's words and went back to work, trying to resurrect the good feelings from earlier that day, avoiding any more discussions with Lynn that night.

Chapter 14

Jess and Hank started seeing each other every day. On the nights she worked at the restaurant, he would park at the far end of the parking lot waiting to pick her up to avoid John seeing them together. Having John find out about their relationship would not benefit either of them and so they were both cautious to avoid him finding out. Hank would take Jess back to her place, where they would talk in his car or go for a walk on the beach, or sometimes he would come inside with her and they would hang out. On Sundays, Hank would still go to the beach for his run and then head to the Café to eat breakfast, but now he would linger longer, watching her work. He couldn't take up a seat at the counter all day, so when he was done, he would wait outside on the porch for her until she had finished her shift so they could spend what little time she had together before she headed to Oceanside for the Sunday night dinner shift.

Hank liked sitting on the porch and watching the customers, particularly how the different families interacted. He had memories of eating here with his own family, running around the wooden picnic tables outside while waiting for their table and once inside, being served by June. Most of the vacationing families seemed happy to be together, though sometimes the long wait for a table would end up with someone's child having a meltdown. He liked the mothers who talked to their children and weren't occupied with their phones or a magazine, remembering that's how his own mother had been. Sometimes he would hear a woman laugh much like his mother used to, and he'd wonder what life would have been like if she hadn't died when he was so young.

Hank's mother had been the center of household—a cheerful, energetic force of motherly love that had made everything bright. It was easy to see where Rob got his charms. Somehow, she made them all feel special. "My men," she would call them, as in "I am going to make my men a good dinner." Hank remembered how his father would beam at her, taking her in and letting her happy attitude fuel him. He had spent his free time with his sons playing ball or showing them how to fix things around the house. Hank remembered how his parents would hold hands while walking along the beach, and even though he was very young when his mother died, Hank knew they had loved each other.

The Café was right next to the drawbridge that spanned the Intracoastal waterway, and when Hank got too deep in thought, he would be grateful to hear the sirens from the bridge go off, indicating it was going to open up and let the boats too tall to make their way underneath pass through. It brought him back to where he was now, sitting on a porch on a bright summer day waiting for Jess.

It didn't take long for June to figure out they were an item the way they kept eyeing each other. One day when she picked up Hank's plate, she gave him a big smile and a wink. "I approve a hundred percent. You got yourself a real sweetie pie in that one. You make sure you treat her right," she drawled, pointing a finger in his direction.

Hank felt like he had received the equivalent of his mother's approval when she said that, and he thought how his mother would have really liked Jess and Rob would have definitely approved. He felt proud that he could get a girl like Jess to notice him, much less be his girlfriend. It felt strange to call her his girlfriend, but when she would come up behind him and give him a quick hug in passing, he knew that was exactly what she was.

They spent a lot of time with Mike and Anne as well, sometimes watching a movie at Anne's place or grabbing something to eat. Saturdays, the four of them would spend the day together at the beach until Jess had to leave for work.

One day after they had all been swimming in the ocean, they came back to their towels to catch their breath and dry off. Jess put in her headphones to listen to something on her phone and lay back with her eyes closed. Hank wanted to know what she was listening to, so he took out one of the headphones and put it in his ear. It was like being back in his mother's kitchen. She was listening to a song by Tony Bennett he had heard many times years ago. When he asked to see her playlist, he discovered it was a collection of all the same songs he used to hear in his own house, some from similar singers of that era and some by newer artists with a more updated twist to them. But still, he knew this music and found he had missed hearing it and the happy memories that came with it.

"I just like to listen to these songs once in a while," Jess said, a little embarrassed.

Hank smiled at her. "My mother used to play these songs. I liked listening to her sing to them while making dinner."

Jess relaxed. "They're just so….romantic. There's not much romance anymore," she said with sigh, and she closed her eyes again
as she lay back down.

And that was what gave him the idea.

When they were walking back from the beach, Hank pulled
Mike aside and asked him where he could find a place to set up a
nice outdoor dinner for Jess. Somewhere private where they could
be alone. Mike said he could get him in one of the rentals on the
Channel with a deck for a night. They could watch the sunset while
eating. That suited Hank perfectly. The sunsets overlooking the
Channel were particularly striking and would set the perfect mood.
Hank himself had pulled over in his Jeep a few times to watch the
sun sink behind the homes along the water and to see the colorful
display that lingered afterward. They set it up for Monday when Jess
would be off of work.

Hank smiled secretively to himself, excited about his plan.

Chapter 15

"Going out again tonight?" Anne asked Jess, who was putting on a sundress instead of her usual work uniform. "It's like I don't see you anymore." She flopped herself down on Jess's bed.

"You see me every day," Jess said, laughing as she brushed out her hair and put in some hoop earrings.

"Yeah, but when are we going to have some girl time?" she asked, leaning on her side and watching Jess apply makeup.

Jess laughed. "You have been on my case for the last year about lightening up and going out with someone, and now that I am, you're complaining about girl time?"

"True. You do seem much more fun these days...."

Jess picked up a small stuffed animal and threw it at her.

"I was always fun. That's why we're best friends."

"That and you work a lot, so I get the place to myself when I want."

"Another added benefit."

Anne sat up. "You know, if you ever need the place some night for you and Hank, just let me know. I can always go hang out at Mike's house."

Jess looked at her with surprise. "Mike's parents are okay with you staying over there?"

Anne gave a cunning smile. "Well, Mike has access to a lot of beach houses through his dad's office, so there's always a place we can go...."

Jess laughed and shook her head. "Well, I'll keep it in mind if it comes up."

"You mean Hank hasn't made any moves on you yet?" Anne asked, obviously trying to get the inside scoop. Jess stayed silent, not giving away anything. "He hasn't, has he? Wow, that's a surprise. I thought the boy had a little more to him than that, especially with that bod. What's the hold up?"

Jess looked down at her dresser. She wasn't sure why Hank hadn't tried to do more than kiss her with all the time they had spent together over the last month. In fact, he was the one who always pulled away when things got too intense. She was beginning to wonder herself why he kept holding back, but at the same time, she was in no rush to move things along either. "What's the rush?" she replied. Then, before Anne could respond, she turned and faced her. "How do I look?" she asked.

"Gorgeous. He doesn't deserve you," Anne replied.

Funny, Jess thought to herself. *I was thinking I don't deserve him.*

Hank picked her up at 7 p.m. sharp.

"Where are we going?" she asked as he opened her door and helped her into the Jeep.

He wore a huge grin. "It's a surprise."

Hank drove a short way down the Island, then turned onto one of the side streets, pulling into the driveway of a large house sitting on the Channel.

"Who lives here?" Jess asked as he stopped the car and got out. He went over to her door and opened it.

"For tonight, us," he said mysteriously. Jess felt a little nervous; the talk with Anne was still fresh in her mind.

Hank opened the front door and she slowly stepped into the large family room. The house was beautifully decorated in hues of blue and green with art meant to remind you of being at the beach. Someone had spent a lot of money making it look just so. Jess was impressed with how nice it all was, but she was still unsure why they were there. Hank told her to close her eyes and wait there for a minute. She did as she was told, hearing some noises before he returned and offered his hand.

"This way," he said, grinning at her. The other end of the room was a kitchen area, which opened up out onto a deck looking over the waterway. He had set the deck table for two for dinner. A candle was flickering in a hurricane lamp on the table, and the deck railing was lined with a row of votive candles in large clam shells. The sun had just begun to set, turning the sky from a pale blue to paler shades of orange and yellow over the horizon as the sun hung low, just hovering over the houses across the Channel. She had seen sunsets over the Channel, but never from this viewpoint, and she noticed how the water was a silvery blue, with streaks of yellow from the descending sun. She could hear the far-off rumble of motorboats lazily going through the water and cars crossing the bridge. Boat lines were clanging against their masts on their docks below as the boats bobbed lightly with the moving water. A breeze brought her the salty smell of the brinish water. She just stood there taking in how beautiful it all was.

Hank led her to the table and pulled out her chair, waiting for her to sit down. She moved very slowly like she was in a daze, sitting down while still looking out at the scenery in front of her.

"Can I borrow your phone?" Hank asked once she was seated, pleased at her expression. "I just need to do one thing...."

Jess reached in her purse and handed it to him. He hooked it up to a small speaker on the table, then found her playlist and started to play the music she had been listening to on the beach. She had never had something so romantic done for her, and she was speechless, taking it all in.

Hank went into the kitchen and brought out a carafe, sitting down next to her. "I hope you don't mind sweet tea. It's the house special...." She laughed as he poured some tea into their wineglasses. He raised his glass and looked at her.

"To the most beautiful girl I have ever seen," he said, with a sincerity that was reflected in his eyes.

Jess felt her cheeks grow warm at the compliment. They clinked glasses, and then she leaned over and gave him a kiss. "It's wonderful," she said, starting to relax. "And so beautiful..." she said wistfully, looking out over the water just as the sun was reaching its lowest point before disappearing behind the houses on the other side. With its disappearance came more color, vibrant shades of red and purple through a scattering of clouds.

"Wait, there's more," Hank said. He went into the kitchen and came back with two salads that he put down on the table.

Jess took a bite and looked impressed. "This is delicious. Did you make it yourself?" she asked, wondering if his talents extended into the kitchen.

"No, I picked up the food at one of the restaurants on the Intracoastal. I hope you like shrimp and grits."

Jess laughed. "Are grits part of the memory of our first meeting?" she asked, reminding him of the rude customer at the Café.

Hank laughed. "I hadn't actually thought about that, but I guess it is appropriate now that you mention it. I have a lot to thank him for." They sat eating and watched the sky grow dark as the colors faded into a deep purple.

At one point, Hank switched out their plates with dinner. When Jess asked to help, he told her no, that tonight she was the one being waited on. By the time they were done, night had fallen and they could see the lights of the houses reflect on the water through the flickering candlelight. Jess couldn't get over how picturesque it all was.

Hank started talking about how there used to be a dance hall on the Island called Lumina, built when electricity was new and named for how it lit up the night so people could see it for miles. Jess imagined what it must have been like to go to a dance hall on the beach and dance like they did in the old days. An Etta James song came on, and Hank suddenly felt just like he had when he was in the kitchen with his mother singing along, her long shapely arms reaching for Hank so she could hug him and they could dance along with the music. Heartened by this memory, Hank got off his chair and offered Jess his hand. Jess took it and got up, uncertain what he meant to do.

"I warn you, I don't normally do this," he said, pulling her close to him and starting to slow dance with her.

Jess knew she should just enjoy it, but after a moment, she suddenly felt herself grow tense. Was he trying to seduce her? She pulled away and stepped back.

"Look, before this goes any further, I have to let you know, I'm just not ready to sleep with you. I just want to be clear up front."

Hank was startled by her declaration. He had not brought her here to seduce her; he was surprised that was what she thought he was trying to do.

"I didn't bring you here for that," he said, uncertain what he should say. He could tell she was upset. "I just wanted to…do something special for you. You made that comment about romance at the beach the other day. And I've always loved these sunsets. I just wanted to share that with you."

Jess hesitated, still looking worried. "Why haven't you tried to do more than kiss me?" she asked bluntly. "I mean, most guys would have tried to sleep with me by now." She didn't mean to ask so frankly, but she didn't seem able to stop herself.

Hank felt flustered and was visibly uncomfortable. Did she want him to do more? "Um, it's not like I haven't thought about it. I just…don't feel we need to rush things. Just being with you and kissing you is so….intense," he said, trying to find the right words, but then once he started, the words just started spilling out in quick succession. "Look, I think about you all the time. No one has ever made me feel like this before. I was barely existing when I met you, Jess. I would go to work, hang out with Mike, and work out. That was my life for almost two years. I didn't feel anything for anyone, and I was beginning to wonder if I ever would. That day at the Café, talking to you was like getting hit with a lightning bolt. I instantly felt connected to you, and you were so easy to talk to. And when you showed up that day at the beach, I couldn't believe you came to find me. You brought me to life again, Jess. You helped me feel again. You made everything be…right again."

He hadn't meant to tell her all this, but there it was. And now he waited, barely daring to breathe, his heart racing as he waited for her reaction. Had he said too much? What if she didn't feel the same way? Had he blown what had been the best thing to happen to him since Rob had died?

Jess was still a moment, taking his words in. She hadn't expected him to feel so strongly about her this early on, but hearing him say his feelings out loud only put into words her own feelings for him. She didn't doubt that they felt connected to each other in a way most people never do. The two of them felt so right together.

She quietly stepped back into his arms and held him tighter than she ever had, putting her head on his chest. "You make everything right for me, too," she whispered, as they started swaying again to the music.

He gave a silent sigh of relief and held her tight, wanting the night to last forever, knowing that he never wanted to let her go.

Chapter 16

Jess had never dated anyone as tall as Hank. Even though she was tall for a woman at five-foot-nine, his six-foot-four frame required she stand on her toes to reach up and kiss him, often resorting to the use of a stair or other type of leverage to put her on equal footing. He seemed to enjoy his height advantage, amused at her attempts to get to him when he was standing at his full height. Yet for a man so tall and muscular, he was exceedingly gentle. If she had seen him on the beach before knowing him, she would have taken a nice long look at his athletic build and then moved on, thinking he looked good but that was not enough to hold her interest. His looks weren't what had drawn her to him. Rather, it was how he treated her and the way he thought about things. She still hadn't forgotten how familiar it felt to talk to him the first time she saw him at the Café. It was like they had picked up on a conversation that had been started a long time ago between old friends.

Jess was embarrassed by how she had accused him of wanting to sleep with her that night on the deck, and she had apologized later, explaining it had come from the conversation she had had earlier with Anne just before he had picked her up. Though secretly, she knew she couldn't completely blame it on that. She herself had thought many times about what it would be like to be intimate with him, even though she had never slept with anyone. He had been very reserved with her, always pulling back before the kissing progressed to something more, but that didn't stop her from thinking what it would be like to have him fully naked and pressed up against her, passionately wanting her. There were times when they were kissing that she could feel him tremble and she knew he wanted her as well. It was so easy to get lost in each other. She had a feeling that making love with him would be very passionate and beyond anything she could imagine, and she would get aroused just thinking about him.

But the thought also worried her. She was deeply infatuated with him, more so than any other guy she had ever dated. She could see herself falling in love with him, though she told herself that wasn't possible in such a short time. Her parents had told her over and over, it takes time to really get to know someone. Her rational mind said there was a lot she didn't know about Hank, and she needed to take it slow or she might get hurt. But her heart told her she had never met anyone like him before, and she wanted to be as close to him as she could possibly get. It was an ongoing conflict inside her, and she was not sure which side would be the ultimate winner.

Jess had thought about saving herself for marriage, but that could be a long time away. Her parents were adamant that she wait until her late twenties to choose someone to settle down with—something to do with knowing yourself better and the statistics of marital success. Jess knew their real worry was that she might get pregnant in college like her mother had, and Jess sometimes wondered if that was why she also hesitated about having sex. If she didn't have sex, she couldn't get pregnant, and since she hadn't found any of the guys in college she had dated to be interesting enough to question that logic, it really wasn't a sacrifice. But the feelings she was having for Hank were much deeper than anything she had experienced before, making her consider it for the first time. She was just glad he wasn't pushing her while she worked out her feelings on the matter.

From what Jess saw at college, sex was expected as part of a dating relationship, so she had wondered when the subject would come up. Jess knew her ideas about sex were much more conservative than those of other girls her age. She saw how Anne would change boyfriends like clothes, and knew she'd had her share of one-night stands. Jess didn't know how anyone could be so casual about giving someone such access to her body. To Jess, sex was not something to be done lightly. She wanted it to be special, not an extracurricular activity she did on a Saturday night half-drunk. If anything, she respected and admired Hank even more for not being the type of guy who felt the need to bed her as quickly as possible. That they were spending time getting to know each other first made the idea of making love in the future even more exciting.

Jess knew Anne had different ideas. Anne liked sex and had no issues discussing it or doing it. That she had lasted this long with Mike was quite a feat for her since she often got bored quickly. And considering she was quite attractive, with her long black hair and piercing eyes, she had no problem finding men who were interested in her. Jess had felt a little envious at first of how open Anne was, and she had even reconsidered living with her since she knew Anne's way of life, but she felt more comfortable once she knew Anne never brought them home. Anne felt her home was her sanctuary, and if someone wanted to hook up with her, they better find a comfortable spot where it could happen. Even Mike had never slept over, though Jess wouldn't have been surprised if they had enjoyed time in the apartment together when she wasn't around. She was just appreciative that she didn't have to worry about running into Anne's latest conquest coming out of the bathroom the next morning. She couldn't care less what they did when she wasn't around.

Hank was so many things Jess hadn't expected. She didn't expect him to be so smart, for one. Or as much fun as he was. Or as attentive and sweet. When Anne had first wanted to get them together, she had just said he was Mike's best friend, as if that were explanation enough. She didn't mention that he was making deliveries for a living, which would have earned a resounding "no" from Jess. Really, what would be the point? Having a short exchange with him before she knew these facts about him had made a huge difference. Feeling that connection had her completely hooked. What's more, she could tell he felt it, too. It was like the decision had already been made for them and they were just following along.

Which was why she was hesitant to get involved sexually. She knew it was better to wait to get to know more about Hank and for him to get to know her. That would take some time, she realized, but they had a whole summer. And maybe more. He had already proven he was patient. He had already told her she meant a great deal to him. At some point when the time was right, she believed she could let him in in a way she never had before.

She felt she could trust him with anything.

Chapter 17

A few nights later, Hank picked up Jess after work, and after she changed, they brought a blanket down to the beach to look at the stars. Lying down, they fell right into kissing and did so for a long time until it started getting too passionate and Hank pulled back. Then he lay on his back, with Jess's head on his shoulder, holding her close while looking at the night sky and catching his breath. The smell of the ocean was so familiar to him, and yet he had never experienced it like this, lying quietly with a night breeze keeping him cool and a girl he was in love with in his arms. He had fallen for her the first day they had spent together, though he didn't dare admit it to himself, not wanting to think about how hard it would be should it all fall apart.

"Hank, when does your probation end?" Jess asked out of the blue.

He was caught off guard for a moment, then answered, "August 14th. Why?"

"And what happens then?" she asked.

"What do you mean?"

"I mean, what do you plan to do once you it's over."

Hank was quiet a moment. "I'll quit my job for one," he said. That was the number-one thing he knew he would do. He had put up with John's abuse only because he couldn't disappoint Mr. DeGaulle, who had given him a chance when no one else would. But once his probation was done, so was that obligation. "I guess I really haven't thought about it," he finally said, realizing he had no idea what he would do next. Knowing his history, would anyone else be willing to take a chance on him even though he had not gotten into any further trouble the past two years?

"Never?" she asked, sitting up on her arm so she could look at him. He had the most moving brown eyes, and when he smiled, which he always did at her, they just had such love and life in them. The better she had gotten to know him, the more handsome he had become in her eyes, and looking at him now, even in the dim light of the moon, filled her with longing for him. "You never thought about what you would do with your life once it was over?" she asked, lying back down so she could look up at the stars with him.

For the past two years, the goal had always been to reach the day he was done with this stage of his life, but Hank hadn't given any real thought to what would happen after it was over. It had been hard enough just making it through each day so he could make it to the end.

"In high school, I always knew what I was going to do with my life. To follow Rob into the Army. That was the plan. And when Rob died...." He hesitated a second, realizing he had not said this out loud in a long time, then forced himself to resume his thought. "When Rob died, I knew I was only doing it to be with him." He was getting more used to talking about Rob to her. She never pushed him, and lately, he found himself wanting to talk about Rob more often, to think about and remember him now that the grief was less pronounced and more distant. It was still there, particularly at home with his father mourning the loss of him, but it was not as all-consuming as it had once been, and even less so since Jess had come into his life.

"How did he die?" she asked quietly, not sure if he would want to talk about it. It was a subject he always seemed to be skirting, so she had been waiting for the right moment to ask him about it. Hank took a deep breath and hesitated, wondering if he really wanted to talk about Rob right now, but when he started to speak, the memories came flooding back so quickly that he couldn't stop them.

Hank had hated it when Rob had enlisted in the Army. His brother leaving before his junior year in high school was one of the toughest things Hank had ever had to endure, almost as bad as when his mother had died. On their last night together, Rob had looked at him and told him to remember everything he had taught him. He had put his hand on Hank's shoulder and said he knew Hank knew the right thing to do when he thought about it. If he would listen to what was in his heart, he would be fine. Then the next day, Rob was gone.

The house had a certain emptiness without Rob there, a definite absence of his energy and spirit. With him gone, things were different, quieter and more solemn. But Hank wanted to make his brother proud, and he didn't want to dwell on his absence, so while Rob was off to boot camp in Georgia, Hank would inform him through FaceTime or email what he was up to and how well he was doing in school. Even when the contact got more sporadic, depending on where his brother was stationed, Hank looked forward to telling Rob how he had aced the physics test, or made the Varsity baseball team, or started dating a girl for the first time in his senior year. Rob had been able to come home for a couple of quick weekend visits, but they always went too fast, making his absence more pronounced. When Rob got stationed overseas, Hank knew he wouldn't be seeing him for a while.

Hank always knew he was going to follow in his brother's footsteps by enlisting in the Army after graduating from high school. He was strongly motivated and even excited about enlisting, thinking that even if they were not stationed together, joining the Army would allow him to remain close with Rob in shared experiences. He had a goal he was working toward, so he worked hard, both in school and in getting into the enviable kind of shape that would fare well at boot camp. Hank had heard of Rob's experiences, so he knew it wouldn't be easy. He kept up the weights, and he would go for runs on top of whatever sport he was playing at the time, preparing himself mentally and physically.

Until the day they got the visit.

Two men in uniforms looking grave had stood at the door. His father had let them in without asking who they were, closed the door, then silently walked into the living room and sat in his chair. Hank had been in the kitchen, but when he saw who came in, he, too, had stood in the doorway leading into the living room, wanting to hear what was being said. The men introduced themselves and stood uneasily for a moment, then sat down when it became clear they were not going to be asked and delivered the bad news. Rob had been in a convoy that had headed off-base on a mission. The convoy had met with a surprise attack. While Rob had fought admirably and was a hero for saving a group of men by shooting a terrorist about to throw a grenade into their truck, he did not survive the attack.

And just like that, Rob was gone. Just one week before the end of high school and just eight days shy of Hank's walking into the Army's headquarters on Oleander Avenue and enlisting, having turned eighteen a month earlier.

The days after that were a blur. Hank remembered standing with his father at the airport hangar where the Army officers ceremoniously removed the casket draped with the American flag from the plane and put it in the hearse. He remembered a well-attended funeral where a large number of Rob's high school friends, teachers, and even the parents of his friends who had always thought well of him had come to say how sorry they were that this had happened to such a fine young man. He remembered standing by his brother's gravesite while the Army chaplain said some words and staying there until everyone else had gone, not wanting to leave his brother. He remembered thinking that Rob deserved so much more than this for all the things he had been to everyone, especially Hank. He couldn't believe his brother was in that box and he would never see him again.

Afterward, Hank spent days lying on his bed, barely leaving his room. The school knew of Hank's loss and decided that even without taking his finals, the work he had done throughout the semester was more than adequate for him to graduate. But he didn't attend graduation or the parties that followed. He didn't call Mike to go to the beach to surf or hang out. He didn't do much of anything until one day he decided he couldn't take it anymore and started to drink away his pain.

Whereas Hank's father Bob became withdrawn after the death of his wife, the death of his son seemed to permanently sink him.

Rob had always been the bright spot in the house, keeping Hank and his father from falling too deeply into their own serious natures. Rob had been Bob's namesake, passing down the name his father had given him to his oldest son, but now that line had ended. When Rob joined the Army, the empty space he left was apparent but manageable. After all, they knew he would be coming back to visit. But the funeral made it clear he was never coming back. He would never be there to shake Hank's hand when he made officer or to be the best man at his wedding. There were so many things Hank had thought he would do with Rob, and as new ones came to mind, it was just more reminders that his brother was truly gone.

Hank stopped talking after he described the funeral. He just stayed quiet after that, lying with his eyes closed, the image of the coffin at the gravesite achingly clear in his mind, not wanting to venture into the sorrow and drunkenness that came after. Even now, there were so many questions he wanted to ask Rob. Questions about things happening to him now and ones he knew he hadn't even thought of yet but wanted Rob there to help answer when they came.

Jess hugged Hank tightly when she recognized he wasn't going to go on. Then she got up on one arm and stroked his face and hair, leaning down to kiss him softly on the lips. "Thank you for telling me," she finally whispered. He pulled her close to him and held her tight until the fresh feeling of grief passed.

Chapter 18

Jess thought about her first meeting with Hank. She had been drawn to him from the beginning, never seeing him as the local guy who worked making deliveries as that description didn't fit even from the start. She thought about how he consistently surprised her. Teaching her to surf. Planning the sunset dinner on the deck. All the little things he did for her, like picking her up at work. She was particularly impressed with how smart he was and how they never ran out of things to talk about. He liked hearing all about what she was studying or what she was learning at the Turtle Rescue, and he seemed to absorb the information as if he were there every day learning it with her. He naturally picked up information from whatever source he listened to and he was always reading, analyzing the knowledge he picked up from books in ways she had not considered. He may not be in college, but Jess saw no difference between Hank and any of the guys she had met at UNCW in terms of intelligence. If anything, he seemed more mature than the college guys she knew, and she had no doubt he would do better than most of them if he ever were to attend.

Wilmington was Hank's hometown and she loved seeing it through his eyes. He took her to local places to eat that she hadn't been to before and never would have found on her own. As they walked on the beach, he sometimes talked about the houses along the shoreline because he knew the families they belonged to and he told her how two hurricanes a while back had wiped out the fishing pier as well as a good part of Oceanside. He talked about the Island as if it were a living thing, explaining how it was constantly changing in shape and size, due to the shifting of sand from storms and tides. He knew the area and its history better than anyone she had ever known.

Not that everything they did together turned out well. Hank had tried to take her running on the beach one Sunday, but after two miles, she couldn't go any farther, a stitch in her side causing her to stop. They had to walk the rest of the way back. She felt bad she had cut short his run, which he took well, but inside, she had gained new respect for him after seeing how hard it was to run on the beach and that he had barely broken a sweat. She actually hoped he didn't think any less of her for being unable to keep up.

The next Saturday, she decided it was time to level out the playing field a little and see how he would do biking with her. She asked if he had a bike and told him to bring it since she was taking him riding.

Hank found his old bike in the garage, and once he pumped up the tires, discovered it was still in good shape. In high school, he had ridden it around town, like Jess, because he didn't have a car. He only stopped when Rob passed on his Jeep to him right before he left for boot camp.

They started off early from the beach with Jess in front. If she didn't have good running legs, she definitely had good riding legs, and Hank found that, not having ridden in a while, he had to work to keep up with her. Jess, seeing it was more difficult for him, slowed down to a leisurely pace.

Jess seemed to know the route well, and before long, they were on a less populated street, able to ride side by side, and talking as they rode. Jess talked about one of the turtle tours she had given the day before at the Turtle Rescue and how funny some of the kids were. Hank liked that she was so good with them and enjoyed hearing some of the questions they asked her. He had had little experience with young kids, but she seemed to know instinctively how to talk to them, and he could hear how she enjoyed it.

Jess had asked before they left if Hank had ever been on UNCW's campus. When he admitted he hadn't, she told him she was taking him there. He felt a little uncomfortable at first, thinking he would feel out of place, but as they rode around and she pointed out the various buildings, he started to feel more at ease. Other students were also riding their bikes or walking about, and some were lying out on the grass, reading or talking. Jess waved hello to a few of them as they rode. They got off their bikes at the student center, which she took Hank inside to show him around, and then she walked with him around campus, showing him the library where she spent too many late nights studying and the dorm she had lived in her first year on campus. After walking around for a while, they got back on their bicycles.

"Where are we headed now?" Hank asked.

"That's a surprise," she said and started riding away. He followed her off of campus and down several back roads he was not familiar with until they reached the end of a dirt road that backed up to a waterway.

"We're here," she said, getting off her bike and leaning it against a large oak tree next to the water with long branches that reached out parallel to the ground before bending upwards. It was a secluded area with no homes nearby. She had a backpack she had carried with her that she now took off and opened up. Hank also put his bike up against the tree, and when she took out a blanket and started to lay it down, he helped her.

"Please. Sit," she said, motioning to it. He sat down, not knowing what to expect, watching as she laid out some sandwiches, grapes, and bottles of water. She put the backpack down and sat down next to him, leaning against him, a closeness he liked even in the summer heat. She opened a water bottle and handed it to him. "I thought it would be nice to have a picnic in my secret place," she said, opening another bottle for herself.

"Ah. So what makes this your secret place?" he asked, taking a sip and looking around.

"This is where I go when I need to get away from everyone and think," she said. "It's quiet and seems to be one of the few undiscovered places where I can escape from the world when I need to. The one place I haven't shared with anyone until now."

She looked at him with a smile, and he leaned over and kissed her gently as a way of thanking her. "I can see why you like it," he said, enjoying the peacefulness of the lake and trees. After a few minutes of taking in the scenery, Hank looked down at the food. "So, were you going to feed me the grapes or make me forage for them on my own?"

Jess laughed. "Oh, I'll feed them to you, but you better open wide because it will be a one-shot deal."

"I hope you don't treat your customers like that. And here I thought you were a professional," he said giving her a nudge.

"You'd rather I feed them grapes one by one?" she asked, testing him.

He thought about this. "Good point. Pass the grapes, please. And a sandwich. I'm starved."

They sat under the tree, quietly eating, as they watched a heron in the marsh nearby standing still in the water, looking for fish and undisturbed by their company.

"That's a great blue heron," Hank told Jess. "It may not look it, but watch it when it flies off. Its wingspan is over six feet."

Jess shook her head and laughed. "You know so much about this place while I barely know anything about my hometown. Where do you get all this information?"

Hank shrugged. "I like knowing where I come from, I guess. The city has a lot of history you wouldn't expect from a coastal town. I've always enjoyed learning about it because I like knowing why things have become what they are, what made them. I didn't really have extended family or a heritage that I belonged to growing up, so I learned about the town as a way to feel like I had some sort of history."

Jess sat back and looked at him. "You amaze me," she said.

"Why?" he asked, taken aback but obviously thrilled by the compliment.

"You're so smart, and you don't even seem to realize it. You know so much about so many different things...." She sounded a bit exasperated, like he should know this already.

"Like what?" he asked, uncertain what she meant. Hank was a capable student in high school, but he attributed that to the discipline and hours of studying he put in. Being told he was smart, particularly after the events of the last two years, was not the first word he expected anyone to attribute to him.

"Everything. All the information you tell me about your town, the beach, those houses...."

"Those are just facts I know from living here," he said, trying to downplay it.

"No, Hank," Jess said insistently, facing him so he could understand what she was saying. "It's a mark of someone who pays attention and absorbs knowledge. It's an indication of someone who thinks about the world around him. Something not a lot of people our age do."

"Well, I think about you a lot. Does that make me smart?" he asked in a teasing voice, trying to deflect her comments.

Jess laughed and lightly smacked him. "Yes, but only in the sense of how to make me adore you. You know what I mean. You are smart enough to do almost anything. You are smart enough to go to college if you want."

Hank was surprised to hear her say this. He had never considered college. His father had never gone, and his brother hadn't even considered it, knowing they could never afford it. It wasn't an option in his family. Even if it was, he didn't feel comfortable there, almost like the buildings and other students were too good for him. Riding through campus with Jess was fine, but the idea of going to school there seemed too far off an idea. That was for guys like Mike.

"You should think about it," Jess said, her voice sincere as she leaned back against him and put her head on his shoulder, looking out at the scenery before them. "You need to think about who you are going to be, Hank Atwater. Because you have outgrown whoever you thought you were before."

You have outgrown whoever you thought you were before.

Jess's words had reverberated in Hank's mind the entire ride back and all the way home. He went to sleep thinking about them, and when he woke up, they were still there, hanging in the air like an unanswered question.

So who was he now?

He had never had to think about it before. It had always been a given that he would follow Rob into the Army. No one in his family had gone to college, so it was never even a consideration. And after his circumstances had changed, well, he had stopped thinking about the future. It had become a battle just to get through each day. To Hank, two years had been a life sentence. And with so many options closed off to him, he hadn't seen himself doing much of anything.

But his probation was quickly coming to an end. Soon he would be able to walk away from his delivery job and John, his debt to Mr. DeGaulle paid. He had stayed until it was over. But now he needed to figure out his next step. As far as he could see, his options were still limited. Just because his probation ended didn't mean that his past mistakes would be easily forgotten, particularly in a town this small.

Could he go to college? After hanging out with Jess and knowing Mike and seeing what college was like, maybe it was something he could do. He had always liked school and had done well, though mostly because he was doing it for Rob. But even if he were capable, he had no idea how to get in. Not to mention, how would he even pay for college? He had saved most of the money he had made from working the delivery job, having lived at home and having few expenses, but he was sure his savings were far from enough. He just didn't see how he could ever do it.

So what was he going to do with his life?

Hank didn't know what it was, but he knew he needed to figure it out and soon. He didn't want to be the guy who messed up anymore and was trying to pay for his mistakes. He wanted to be the guy who knew where he was going and deserved a girl like Jess.

Chapter 19

A few days later, Hank gathered his board and headed to the beach to do some early surfing with Mike. The sun was just rising as he drove the back roads to his favorite surfing spot, parked, and headed to the shore. He made his way out into the water and managed to catch some waves before Mike joined him, looking worn-out.

"Late night?" Hank asked, assuming he had been out with Anne.

"Yeah, but well worth it," Mike said, grinning.

"I bet," Hank said with a laugh. They managed to ride in a few times before there was a lull in the waves, and then they sat bobbing on their boards. Hank took the opportunity to tell Mike what Jess had said about his going to college. He thought if he brought it up, Mike would laugh it off as a dumb idea and he could finally put it to rest, but the exact opposite happened.

"I think she's right. You should think about it," Mike said with a serious look. "You're smarter than most of the guys I know. You just never gave yourself the credit."

This was the second time Hank had been stunned by how highly his friends regarded him.

"I wouldn't even know where to start, man…" Hank said, thinking again that the cost alone made it impossible.

"You start by talking to someone in the admissions office. They will walk you through the application process. And I bet you would qualify for all sorts of financial aid. Even if you don't, whatever they don't give you, you can get student loans to pay. Hey, you could easily do it, Hank," he said in earnest, looking at his friend. "The real question is, what do you want to do?"

I want Jess, Hank thought. The desire to be with her now and in the future resounded through him. *I want to build a life with Jess.* Of that he had no doubt. But how to attain that goal? There was no question that Jess would want to be with someone who was educated. But could he go to college? He enjoyed learning. He had liked the challenge of getting good grades in high school. He realized he had sorely missed being mentally stimulated the last two years, trying to fill that gap with reading and discussions with Mike. But what would he study? Whatever it was, the thought of being with Jess in college and beyond was what he wanted.

Now he had to make it happen, as Rob would have said.

Chapter 20

By July, life was going at full speed for Jess. She worked Wednesday through Sunday nights at Oceanside, and Sundays she worked the day shift at the Café. This was on top of giving tours several days a week at the Turtle Rescue, which was getting busier as they got into the heart of summer. Tourist season really took off in July, so she was making good money, but she found herself getting worn down. She finally decided to give up the Café job to be able to spend weekend days with Hank and give herself a much-needed break. She realized the summer wouldn't last forever, and besides, the other girls her age at the Café had been cliquish and unfriendly, making a difficult job even harder. Only a few of the older waitresses, like June, were ever nice to her. Hank's smile when she told him showed he had no objection whatsoever. "As long as it's what you want," he had said, squeezing her hand, obviously happy to have more time together.

The other reason she decided to give it up was she wanted to volunteer to monitor nests with the Wrightsville Beach group in hopes of seeing one hatch. She had already been helping out by walking the beach in the morning looking for nests and now signed up to spend Monday and Tuesday nights at a nest that was located close to Mercers Pier.

On her first night out, Jess was very excited, and Hank, always happy to spend more time with her, had offered to go with her. He had gone home after work to quickly change and grab something to eat, then swung by to pick her up in his Jeep, driving them down to where the nest was located. He brought a couple of folding chairs and set them up next to the other volunteers, who were friendly and told Jess what she needed to do. Basically, her job was to explain to onlookers why they should turn off their cell phone lights that they were using at night to view the nest and why they shouldn't disturb any nests if they saw one. Occasionally, she would be asked questions about sea turtles in general. Over and over again, she would explain that the nest would take about sixty days to hatch and that this one had just been discovered, so it would be toward the end of August before any hatchlings would appear.

Jess loved being out there, talking about something she really enjoyed, breathing the scent of the ocean and sitting under the night sky. She found most people to be respectful of the rules once she explained them, and she was happy to answer as many questions as some of them would ask. She felt she was actively doing something to help the turtles by relaying information to passersby who hadn't regarded the turtle nests before and maybe now would help protect them. Hank was content chatting with the other volunteers when Jess was busy, and when she would glance over at him to see how he was doing, she could see him watching her, smiling in her direction. Having him there seemed to make everything just perfect because his presence put her in a good mood and she enjoyed that she could share this experience with him. *If this is what watching turtle nests is like*, she thought, *let me do it every night.*

Jess loved having Hank as her boyfriend. She was constantly amazed by how hard he tried to please her. She had never imagined having a boyfriend who paid such close attention to her and who really listened when she spoke.

The one boyfriend she had had in high school was much different. One of her friends had taken her to a school baseball game where Ben was pitching. After the game, they had met and he had seemed a fun guy, joking around and popular with everybody. He was good-looking with dark curly hair and a look like he just knew something you didn't. He liked the look of Jess and tried to get her number, which she had refused, but he got it from her friend and started texting her. At first, she wasn't interested, but then he finally got her to agree to meet for coffee. Once he was away from everyone else, his demeanor changed and she was able to get to know him better. They dated a few months and even went to the prom together, but things fell apart soon after. He started saying he wanted them to have a sexual relationship, then seemed to demand it. Jess had seen glimpses of this side of him early on with some of his friends, but had ignored it, thinking he would never treat her that way. Realizing her mistake, she had quickly broken it off and never looked back. Instead, she had set her sights on starting college and what life would be like at UNCW.

But Hank was different. The way he looked at her sometimes with such warmth in his eyes would give her butterflies in her stomach. She told herself it was just the infatuation stage and that it would pass, but then the way he would kiss her for long periods sometimes left her breathless. He never pushed her to do more. It was as if even asking would disrespect her somehow. With him, she felt special, and even though he hadn't said the words, she felt loved. She was not the type to have a summer fling, and she didn't see Hank being that way either. She sensed this was something much deeper. They were taking the time to really get to know each other, and the more she learned about him, the more she wanted him in her life.

Jess looked in her dresser mirror at her reflection. What did Hank get from being with her? She was not as pretty as Anne or so many of the other college girls who were constantly around. Yet to him, she knew she was always the most beautiful girl in the room. At least that was how he made her feel. She noticed how other guys would openly watch girls on the beach who were wearing thongs or tight-fitting bikinis. She had seen Mike do it plenty of times, with Anne waving it off as a guy thing. But Hank focused on her as if no one else were around. Not in the sense that he smothered her, but by being aware of her and doing small things that showed he cared.

Just like her father had used to make her feel, Jess realized, sighing. She didn't need lots of boys to notice her, she thought. Just this one was enough.

"Hi, Mom," Jess said into the phone. It had been a few weeks since she had last called her mother with all the running around she was doing, so she wanted to catch up.

"Jess? Is that my long-lost daughter?" her mother asked, her familiar laugh making Jess smile.

Jess caught her mother up on her jobs and working at the Turtle Rescue and with the Wrightsville Beach group. Then she brought up Hank.

"I was wondering if I was going to hear more about him," her mother said. "So, how is this young man treating my daughter?"

"Very well," said Jess. "More than very well." Jess told her mother about the sunset dinner on the balcony, leaving out the more sensitive parts, as well as the walks on the beach and how Hank picked her up at work.

"It sounds like you like this one," her mother replied, hearing the excitement in Jess's voice.

"I do," she said, unable to hold back her excitement. "I'm having a great summer, much better than I thought it was going to be. But I have something to ask you. You were my age when you dropped out of college because you were pregnant with me. Did you ever regret having to leave college?" She had never asked the question before and waited while her mother carefully phrased her answer.

"I never regretted having you," her mother said. "I felt bad for your father because I knew he wanted to go on to graduate school after college and having a baby changed that. But once he knew you were on the way, he proposed to me, telling me that even though we hadn't planned this, he would not change any of it. Are you two getting serious?" she asked tentatively, not sure where this conversation was headed.

"No! No, nothing like that. I just realized that by the time you were as old as I am now, you were already getting married and having a child, something I cannot fathom doing. I just didn't know how you felt about it."

Her mother thought for a moment. "Well, I was in love, but I was also scared. We married young, Jess, and because we did, there were many hard years of adjustment and sacrifice for both of us. It was because we committed ourselves to each other and you that we made it through. Most people who marry at that age end up divorced. What I want for you is to explore all those things you want to do in life and to really learn who you are so when you do get married, you choose the man and the life that is right for you. For the rest of your life is a big commitment, bigger than you can imagine at your age. Right now, you are doing something your father would have loved to see you do, following that dream you both had to be scientists."

"But you had a great marriage," Jess said.

"Yes, we did," her mother said, thinking fondly of Jess's father. "But it took years to get to that point, of learning what marriage was about and how to live with another person. Love takes time to grow, and there are always challenges. You know that, right?"

"Yeah, absolutely," Jess said, listening to words she had heard before from her mother to some extent. But inside, her mind was racing, thinking how much Hank already meant to her and how much she had already begun to rely on him. *If this isn't love,* she thought, *I can't imagine what is.*

Chapter 21

As he sat off to the side of the turtle nest, Hank watched as Jess interacted with passersby. She was always patient with them, even those who turned on their phone flashlights and shined them on the nest; she kindly let them know why that was not good for the turtles. He loved how she would describe the turtles hatching and escaping from the nest, making it sound like an event not to be missed, and getting others excited about seeing it. He liked how she so easily engaged with everyone and how she never tired of talking about the turtles, making the whole process a fascinating experience, even though she would give the same information over and over. He never could have done it, but then, it was easy to see this was something she was passionate about, and the reason she was able to do so was because of how much she enjoyed it.

Watching Jess, Hank wished he had something he was that passionate about. Ever since their talk about college, he couldn't get the idea out of his mind, especially after Mike had seconded the motion. He had been avoiding it for the past week, telling himself all the reasons it would never work, but he knew he was just making excuses because he was scared he wouldn't be good enough. If Rob were there, he wouldn't have let him get away without at least trying. And if Jess and Mike had such faith in his ability to do it, he knew he couldn't let them down. But if he was going to apply, he needed to find out what he needed to do and now.

The next day at lunch, Hank looked up the phone number and called the admissions office, setting up a meeting for later that week. After he hung up, he felt relieved and even excited for the rest of the day. No matter what happened, he knew he was heading in a new direction. And for the first time in a long time, it felt like it was the right one.

Hank took off work on Thursday and went down to the school to meet with the admissions officer without telling Jess. He was visibly nervous as he sat in the waiting area, not sure what to expect. Finally, a Mrs. Woodson introduced herself and took him back to her office, where she asked numerous questions about Hank's high school experience and what he had been doing the last two years. He told her everything about his brother, the arrest charge, and his delivery job, and how he was now looking toward his future, which he hoped would include college.

She listened quietly, and when he finished, she said she would very much like to help him. She explained the application process to him and gave him several forms to fill out. She didn't make any promises, but she said she thought he had a very good chance of being accepted for admittance mid-year if he could get them his high school transcripts and a completed application. Then she walked him down to the financial aid office and introduced him to another woman, who walked him through the process of what applications he would need to fill out to qualify for financial aid. He was overwhelmed by the amount of paperwork they wanted him to do, but when he finally walked out a few hours later, he felt inspired. He was starting to believe college was a real possibility if he really wanted to go. He went home and immediately started working on the forms he had been given, trying to figure out how to obtain all the information they requested.

Hank wanted to tell Jess everything that night, but when he picked her up, it was obvious she had had a bad night at work, so he decided to hold off. He started to tell her the next night while they were hanging out at her apartment, but Mike and Anne came in just as he was about to, and he wasn't sure he wanted to make it common knowledge yet, so he held off again. Even though it was Jess's idea, he wanted to be sure she would be happy that he had applied. They had never talked about what would happen when summer ended and if she saw their relationship continuing, and he wanted to be sure she would be comfortable with having him on campus with her before he let their friends know what he was doing.

By Saturday, he couldn't keep it to himself any longer. They were at the beach with Mike and Anne, so to get her alone, he asked her to go for a swim with him. As they walked down to the water, he tried to be casual, mentioning that he had talked to someone in the admissions office that week and he was thinking of applying.

Jess stopped dead in her tracks and turned to face him, holding his arm. "You mean you're going to do it?" she asked. He started to get nervous because he couldn't read whether her expression was good or bad, but he had already started to tell her, so he continued.

"Yeah, I'm taking your advice. I'm going to apply and see what happens. I don't know if I will get in...."

Hank wasn't able to finish his thought because Jess excitedly screamed out "Yes!" and jumped into his arms, wrapping her arms around his neck and her legs around his waist and kissing him all over his face.

"Well, if I knew this would be your reaction, I would have applied sooner," he said, holding her up, surprised and pleased by her response. She jumped down, but still held him around his neck. "What made you decide to do it?"

"You," Hank said, getting quiet and looking at her intently. "You made me believe I could do it, Jess."

She pulled him down to kiss her again, then looked at him adoringly. "I think it would be great if you came to college. I didn't want to think about losing you when summer ended." It was the first time she had said anything about their relationship lasting past the end of summer, and if he was pleased by her response to his applying to college, her statement of their relationship continuing was even better news.

He kissed her softly and touched her face. "I don't plan on letting you lose me at all," he said with a look that showed he meant every word.

Chapter 22

If their relationship had been going well before, it was now more solidified than ever. Jess knew they were still in the infatuation stage, but when she thought about what she wanted, it now included Hank. He was the kind of man she had always wanted to be with. Even Anne noticed just how close they were and pretended to be jealous.

"Does he pick you up every night?" she asked one day after Hank had dropped Jess off. They were sitting on the couch together, hanging out.

"Yep."

"Wow. Such dedication. I don't think Mike would do that for me."

"I don't think that's Mike's way of showing his devotion."

"You're right," Anne said, with a devilish look in her eyes. "He does have other ways, though...."

Jess threw a pillow at her. "Is sex all you can think about?" she asked, jokingly.

"I'm a twenty-year-old college girl. What else is there to think about?" Anne asked, causing both of them to laugh before her tone became serious. "Mike is great. He's just not 'the one.' And to be honest, I hope I don't meet the one until I have had my fill of fun and adventure, which I plan to use most of my twenties to achieve."

"How do you even know if someone is the one?" Jess asked. "When I think of how differently I thought about life even two years ago, I know I'm nowhere near ready to make such decisions. But how do you know when someone is the right person for you?"

Anne got thoughtful for a moment. "My grandmother once told me that marriage is very simple if you understand what it is all about. That the right man would go to the ends of the earth for you if you treat him right. She would say if you can see yourself waking up each morning and saying to yourself 'What can I do today to make this person glad he chose me?', then you have found the right one, for in return, he will treat you like a queen." They both sat there for a moment thinking about what she had said before Anne resumed her usual bravado. "Which, in my experience, is not what your average twenty-year-old guy is capable of."

They laughed at her last comment, but Jess couldn't help pondering over Anne's words. She felt she knew Hank and she felt very strongly that she wanted to be with him. Even though she recognized their relationship was still new, she couldn't imagine what he could ever do to change her opinion of him. She just knew no one had ever made her feel this way and that she had never wanted to do so much for someone else. And when he looked at her the way he did, she couldn't imagine ever being without him.

Chapter 23

Hank picked up Jess to take her to the turtle nest to do her volunteer work. He was smiling when she got in the car and gave her a big kiss hello, his excitement obviously showing as she gave him a look and asked suspiciously what he was so happy about.

"Being with you," he said, not revealing his surprise. That day, Hank had gotten up early to go surfing with Mike. All the late nights had taken a toll on him, so he had quit early. He knew it was going to be a long day at work, so he stopped at the Del Mar coffee shop on the beach to get some caffeine to kick him into gear. As he was walking back to his car, he passed a local art shop. He had never been inside, but this time, he noticed they had some jewelry for sale. He walked in and started looking through the cases, suddenly spotting a sterling silver turtle on a silver chain. The shell was detailed with swirling designs and the legs and head were similarly crafted with intricate designs. He could barely contain his excitement as he bought it, knowing it was the perfect gift for Jess.

The necklace was now in his pocket, and Hank wanted to give it to her, but he also wanted it to be a moment when she wasn't preoccupied. So he went with Jess to the nest and sat patiently on the sidelines as she interacted with onlookers until the hour got late and the number of people walking along the beach dwindled. The other volunteers started breaking down at eleven and headed off one by one. Hank was slow in folding up the chairs, waiting for them all to leave so he could be alone with Jess.

"Ready?" she asked after the last person had left and the two of them were alone on the beach.

"Not just yet," he said, reaching in his pocket and pulling out the necklace. "I have something for you."

He held up the turtle necklace. She took it from him, looking amazed to receive such a thoughtful gift.

"It's beautiful," she said, stunned and looking at the turtle in her hand sparkling even in the dim moonlight.

"Just like you," he said, pleased she was so taken with the gift.

She looked up at him, looking like she was ready to cry. "It's just...."

He grew concerned. "What Jess? Is something wrong?" He put his arms around her, hoping he hadn't upset her somehow.

She swallowed, trying to hold back the tears suddenly welling up, and shook her head, trying to explain. "No one has ever treated me like you do. You make me feel so special. You just do everything so right." A tear came down her cheek. "I can't imagine being without you. And I wonder how you can become so important to me in such a short time, but you are. I love you, Hank." She looked at him with earnestness and open devotion, hoping she hadn't said the wrong thing.

He immediately began kissing her, wanting to hold her closer than was possible. "Jess," he whispered between kisses, "oh, Jess, I love you, too. I love you so much."

He was so happy he could finally say the words he had longed to tell her, never wanting to let her go.

When Hank woke up the next day, he knew everything had changed. He no longer felt the emptiness that had been a part of him for so long. Now he felt whole and more directed than he had ever been. He had a girl who loved him, and he knew what he wanted to do. Life had purpose, and he was ready to fulfill it. He just had to hold on for a couple of more weeks until he ended his probation and his new life could fully begin.

The promise of a new life couldn't have come at a better time. At work, John was showing up hungover more often and occasionally even drunk at times, making him more cantankerous than ever. Even through the haze of his alcoholic stupor, John began noticing something was different about Hank. He sensed Hank's happiness, which made him work even harder to rile Hank whenever he was sober enough to put more than a few words together. But Hank no longer cared. Two more weeks and he wouldn't have to deal with John ever again. As far as he was concerned, it would soon be over and a whole new chapter of his life would begin.

Jess had told Mike and Anne about Hank applying to college. Mike helped Hank with his application, giving him pointers on what would impress the admission office, and getting his father to write a recommendation letter. Mr. James had seen how well Hank had done over the past two years and had slowly welcomed him back into his good graces. For the first time, Hank felt like his life was coming together. He saw college as a fresh start. Even though he knew he would likely run into some of the locals who knew about his past, he was more likely to be just another face in the crowd in a college of more than 10,000 students. He was trying not to get too excited as he handed his application in to Mrs. Woodson, telling himself he hadn't been accepted yet, but she felt his chances were good, which left him feeling like it would all work out.

Now he just had to wait for their response.

Chapter 24

A big storm on Saturday night made Sunday a much cooler respite from the usual August Carolina heat. Hank and Jess decided to ride their bikes downtown as a break from the beach.

Jess knew the route well, and before long, they were on a street where they were able to ride side by side and talk as they rode. They went by creeks surrounded by sea grass, local neighborhoods lined with trees that shaded the streets, and some wooded trails before heading into the downtown area and its historic homes.

Here Jess rode even slower, more interested in looking at the large antebellum houses. She would stop at houses she particularly liked, some so old they had accommodations in back originally built to be slave quarters. "Not something you would find in New Jersey," she told Hank. Hank started to tell her about some of the homes, how many of them were built only to be abandoned a few years later during the Civil War when a ship of sailors with yellow fever came into the port and spread the disease throughout the city. He understood certain aspects of the architecture, pointing out how the columns from one house differed from another or why another one had Spanish railings instead of white posts.

"How do you know all of this?" she asked, impressed.

"I had a teacher in high school who tied learning about the Civil War to the town to make it more relatable. I remember learning about how Wilmington was the last port able to receive supplies for the Confederate Army from ships that were able to get past the Union blockades. They were called blockade runners, and when the Union Army captured Fort Fisher, it was a big blow to the South because it cut off their supplies. I enjoyed hearing about it enough to come down and see some of the places he talked about. I found it interesting to see how these older homes were constructed and what set them apart."

Neither Hank nor Jess were very fond of the red-brick-style homes, preferring instead the white homes with large front porches and tall columns, many of which had well-tended gardens. There was something welcoming and homey about them with their colored shutters around the windows and decorative moldings along the rooflines. They went up and down the various streets until they were at the end of one particular street and saw a white house set back much farther than the others, with an actual yard out front and a large overgrown garden that spilled out onto the sidewalk. At closer look, it seemed to incorporate all the favorite traits that they had picked out in other houses. It had a staircase that started at the top of the porch and opened up as it reached the ground, where a circular driveway wrapped around a flowing white cement fountain. The porch was wide and wrapped itself around the house. In front were large white columns that spanned past the second floor, where another wraparound porch extended from the rooms above. The windows were long and reached from floor to ceiling, the paint on their white trim looking fresh, as it did on the house itself. The garden was full of wildflowers and large flowering bushes, giving the well-manicured gardens a more natural feel. Hank thought about his mother's garden and how it had made his house feel like a home when she was alive.

"This one is my favorite," said Jess, standing on her bike while looking at the house. "This is the kind of house where the kids would be running around the front yard while Mom and Dad sit on the veranda watching, drinking sweet tea…" she said, with a quick smile at Hank. The kind of house she'd never had, she thought as she looked at its tall columns and stately manner. The kind of home she could only dream she would have one day.

"It's certainly in good condition," Hank said, looking at the house's structure. "And the bones are good."

"Bones?" Jess asked.

"Meaning the structure itself looks sound. The porch is in good condition and not uneven; the columns are straight; nothing looks like its sinking or leaning. And it's obviously well cared for."

"And where did you learn about bones?" Jess asked, amazed once more at the extent of his knowledge. Hank thought back to where he had heard these terms before. He had a vague memory of his father talking about houses as they walked down the street in his neighborhood, telling Hank and Rob why some of them were in good shape while others were ready to be bulldozed. He had forgotten that his father had done construction work before working as a handyman. "My father," Hank replied. "He used to do construction work when I was younger."

"Did you ever do any construction work?"

"No, but I helped my father fix things around the house. It made my mother happy," he said, reflectively, remembering how proud she was when he told her he had fixed something, even if all he did was hand his father the tools.

"I would love to live in a house like this," Jess said, absentmindedly.

"With how many kids?"

"What?" she asked, surprised at the question.

"How many kids? In the yard."

She laughed. "Um, two I guess. A boy and a girl."

"And a husband who adores you."

"Of course. That goes without saying."

"All right then," he said, getting back on his back and turning around.

"All right what?" she asked, getting on her bike and following him.

"All right, I'm ready to head downtown to get something to eat," he said, riding ahead so she couldn't ask him any more questions.

But he was thinking how much he would like those things one day with her.

Chapter 25

A few days later, Jess had a free morning and decided to go on one of her long bike rides. It had been a while since she had had some time to herself, and she had missed the opportunity to just slow down and think about her life.

So this is what it is like to be in love, Jess thought, her fingers absentmindedly clutching the turtle that hung around her neck as if trying to memorize its every detail. The turtle was a constant reminder of Hank telling her he loved her. She didn't realize until she had said it out loud that she didn't even know if he would feel the same way, and the fact he had, well, it was everything to her. The world was a glorious place in a way it had never been. She had someone she cared about and who cared about what happened to her. It was a strange and exhilarating feeling she had never expected to experience, and now that she had it, she never wanted to lose it.

Jess was starting to see Wilmington as a place where she felt she could stay and live after college, maybe even continue on here to do her master's degree. She thought of her work at the Turtle Rescue and how she had found real direction in her career working there, as well as through her work with the Wrightsville Beach group monitoring nests. She thought of her teachers who had taken a real interest in her future and were helping her along. And she thought about the pelicans on the beach and the oaks she could ride beneath on sunny days like this. Being here this summer had given her a sense of belonging she had never felt before. She thought about how she liked living with Anne, and yes, how she liked that she was part of a group with Hank, Anne, and Mike, even if she knew that was unlikely to last since Anne would eventually move on to her next boyfriend. But she believed it wasn't just a fluke that she had ended up here because it was the school that had given her the largest scholarship. Things happened for a reason. Here, she had found herself in so many ways, from how she wanted to make her mark on the world to what type of relationship she wanted. It wasn't hard to see why she felt so attached to this place.

With all that had happened these last few months, she told herself it had actually been beneficial that UCF had fallen through. If it hadn't, she would have been spending the summer thinking about how hard it was going to be to leave Hank behind just as they had started this relationship. She knew the chances of them lasting were still very small, but she also knew there was something different about this relationship. She knew she wasn't ready to get married at such a young age as her parents had, but how do you ignore something that is so right, even if it shows up at the wrong time? Hank was everything she had ever wanted in a man. But they needed more time. A lot more time. And staying in Wilmington would give her that time to continue to get to know him and see where this went.

Jess had thought about telling Hank how she had almost gone to UCF, but what was the point? She couldn't go, and now that they were together, it felt right to be here in Wilmington with him. Why bother telling him about something that was never going to happen?

Jess rode home excited about how great she felt about her future. On the way, she kept touching her turtle necklace and thinking about how good her life was. Everything was working out in ways she never could have imagined.

It had been a good decision to stay.

Chapter 26

Thursday night, Hank picked up Jess from work as usual. She invited him in to hang out while she quickly showered and changed. When she came out, she smelled so fresh and clean that he couldn't help but start kissing her. He could feel himself getting completely lost in her, and he knew he had to slow down before he reached a point where he wouldn't want to. But as he pulled back, Jess held on to him.

"No," she said adamantly. She had thought about him so many times. She knew she loved him and felt he loved her. "I...I don't want to stop."

Hank felt conflicted. He had held back for so long, even though he had wanted her. Was now the right time?

"I love you, Hank. I love you so much. You have become everything to me, and I want to share everything with you," she said, kissing him around his face as she spoke. "I want to be as close to you as I can get," she whispered as she continued to kiss him.

Overcome with emotion, he grabbed her and kissed her passionately. "I want that, too," he said between kisses, getting lost in her, but then he suddenly pulled back again.

"I, uh…I don't have anything. You know, protection," he said, feeling embarrassed. Jess thought for a second.

"Wait here," she said. She went into the bathroom and opened Anne's toiletry drawer. When she came out, she held up a line of condoms. "Jackpot!" she laughed. "I knew Anne would be supplied."

Hank laughed too. Were they really going to do this? Jess had already told him she had never been with anyone else. And Hank had only had that one drunken encounter he couldn't even remember, so technically it was the first time for both of them.

Jess sat down next to him on the couch and held his face with her hands, kissing him gently. "I want to be with you," she said, looking deeply into his eyes.

Hank didn't need any more convincing. He stood up, scooping her up in his arms. She threw her arms around his neck and kissed him again as he carried her into her bedroom, closing the door behind them with his foot.

The next morning, Hank woke up and felt like he was in a dream. He was curled up next to Jess, both of them naked, and he immediately remembered the night before. The first time had been passionate and quick, the waiting and the withstanding having taken its toll. He had placed her on the bed, and they had rushed to remove each other's clothes; then, feeling each other fully naked for the first time, it had all happened so quickly, though he did his best to be gentle with her. After, they didn't move, staying as close as possible, whispering to each other as if the sound of their voices would break the spell. Eventually, their hands started to explore each other again, and this time it was very sensual and slow, even more intense than the first time. When they were done, they lay entangled in each other and fell asleep that way.

Upon realizing where he was when he woke, Hank immediately began kissing and stroking her, waking her gently. She immediately responded to his touch, and they made love again. When they were done, she lay her head on his chest, feeling more connected to him than she had ever been. Even though Hank knew he had to leave for work, he could not pull himself away.

"Good morning," he said, smiling down at her.

"Is that what that was?" she joked, "your good morning greeting?"

"Only for those I truly appreciate." He laughed. He suddenly looked at the clock. It was late. "Uh, I really don't want to go but…."

"I know. You have to get to work. I understand. Text me later. Tell me how memorable I was."

Hank laughed. "I don't think there are enough words to describe that."

She curled up to him and kissed him one last time before pushing him out of bed. "Go," she said.

"Are you kicking me out of bed?" he asked, pretending to be incredulous as he got up and started putting on his clothes.

"If I don't, I may not get up for weeks," she said, smiling seductively.

He kissed her again and looked at her devotedly. "I love you, Jess. I'll call you later."

"I love you, too," she said.

She heard the front door close behind him as she got out of bed and put on some clothes. She went into the kitchen and poured herself a glass of juice just as Anne entered the apartment. Anne closed the door behind her, then leaned back against it in mock surprise.

"Was that *Hank* I just saw leaving this apartment?" she asked.

Jess smiled from ear to ear but said nothing, sipping her juice.

"It was!" Anne said, throwing her keys on the table by the door. She sat at the kitchen table across from Jess, sitting on the edge of her chair, chin in her hands, showing full attention. "Oh, do tell."

Jess played it cool. "Nothing happened," she said, nonchalantly. "Are you just getting back from Mike's?"

"Oh, you're good," Anne said, leaning back. "But I know you, my friend. How was it? Can you at least tell me that? Was he good?"

Jess laughed, bursting with happiness, but still saying nothing.

Anne just nodded her head up and down with a cunning look. "Don't worry; it may take a few drinks, but I'll get it out of you."

Chapter 27

Hank's feet didn't touch the ground once that day. At least that's how it felt. His face with its broad smile said it all. Nothing and no one would be able to reach him today. He was tired yet felt full of energy. He couldn't believe he and Jess had made love last night. He hadn't expected that to happen, at least not yet, but when she had proposed it, he had just felt the time was right. He knew he loved her. He knew he would do anything for her. With her going back to school, there would be some changes, but he saw this relationship going into fall and then winter. He saw it going as far as she would let it. Because he knew from the beginning their relationship was special and not something to let go of, and he planned to hold onto her as long as she would let him.

The real question was how Hank would be able to show her he was worthy of her. He really hoped he would get accepted into college. He still had trouble picturing himself there, but he would do what he needed to if it got him Jess. The admissions officer had been positive about his chances of getting in, so maybe college was where he belonged. The Army had always been Rob's path, but now Hank realized it wasn't where he wanted to be. It had never occurred to him that there were other choices or that life would lead him in this direction. Knowing he was working on a plan gave Hank a new sense of confidence and inner peace, and it was noticeable to everyone who came in contact with him.

Including John. Because Hank spent a lot of time at work thinking about Jess and college, he was able to tune John out as if he weren't even there, ignoring his comments and just working his shift. This did not suit John at all. Hank had obviously been in much better spirits these last few months, but today, it was worse than ever. It was starting to get on John's nerves, particularly since pushing Hank to the edge was one of his favorite hobbies. It was his way of paying back what Rob had done to him. Not that Hank had any idea that was what John was doing. John had learned that the less your adversary knew about your motives, the better. So he needed to find out why Atwater was so damn happy-go-lucky lately. If he could figure that out, then he would know which button he could really push to get Hank worked up again.

John's father had been all over him this summer, more than ever before, and it was really getting old. His father seemed to think Hank was someone worth paying attention to as the idea of the ultimate working man. Who needed that crap? John was never going to be a blue-collar worker like the friggin' Atwaters. He thought of them as scum, particularly holier than thou Rob, who had snitched to John's father about some of John's extracurricular activities. John was just lucky his father hadn't believed Rob or his lifestyle would have been seriously curtailed. And that, John thought, was not a scenario he wished to entertain.

It turned out John didn't have to wait long to learn what had Hank so revved up. The next night, he was eyeing the waitresses again as he drank at the Oceanside's bar, and in his half-drunk state, he decided he liked the look of Jess. He waited until her shift ended and then he stumbled out to his car, thinking when she came out, he would pretend they just happened to be leaving at the same time and he could give her a ride. No girl ever turned down a ride in his convertible. But as John got to his car, he saw Jess was already at the far end of the parking lot, and before he could call out to her, he saw someone with her. It took a moment to figure out who it was, but even in the dark, John knew that Jeep all too well.

"Well, well, well…" he said to himself, watching as Jess got in the Jeep and it headed off. "Looks like we are up for some real fun now."

Chapter 28

Hank picked Jess up on Friday night as usual, and they went for a walk on the beach, stopping to kiss every so often. Saturday, they spent the day at the beach with their friends, and when Hank picked her up on Saturday night, Jess invited him to spend the night again since Anne was staying out with Mike. Sunday, it was raining outside, so they spent a quiet day sitting around the apartment, reading and just being together, curling up on the couch until Jess had to go to work. So many times she would look up to see him just smiling at her, and when she asked what he was thinking about, he would just say "You."

Monday night, the four of them decided to go to a local restaurant downtown on a side street, a new place that Mike had heard about. When they walked in, the place was very artsy. A variety of paint colors were splattered on the floor and walls, with multicolored chairs and tables of different designs. Painted fish made out of wood and other recycled materials were hung up as artwork. They sat down, ordered some po' boys, and talked about how summer was almost over with school starting soon. Jess was really on tonight, too, with some really good one-liners that had them all cracking up.

This is what it should be like, she thought at one point, looking at her friends and feeling she really belonged. She had found her tribe.

When they were done eating and the guys had asked for the check, Anne and Jess went into the ladies room to freshen up. Anne finished first and went back to the table. As she exited the bathroom, one of the waitresses entered. Jess was toweling off her hands when the woman sat on the counter next to her and crossed her arms, looking right at her.

"So, you with Hank?" she asked in a friendly Southern accent. Jess turned to look at her. She had tattoos on both arms and piercings in her nose and eyebrows. Her makeup was heavy, her lips bright red, and her hair, dyed a stark white blond, was short and spiky.

Jess smiled politely. "You know Hank?" she asked.

"Oh, Hank and I know each other real well…" she said, turning toward the mirror and checking her teeth for lipstick. She stole a glance in Jess's direction. "We used to date. I'm Roxy. You mean he never mentioned me?"

Jess was surprised. Roxy did not seem like Hank's type. "Really, when?" she asked, reaching in her purse for her lipstick, trying to find an excuse to stay and find out more.

Roxy knew she had Jess hooked by her tone. "A couple of years ago," she said, turning around again and leaning back against the counter. "So, I guess we both go for the bad boys," she said with a conspiratorial smile.

"Hank's not exactly a bad boy," Jess said, feeling the need to defend him, but uncertain what this woman was saying. "He just got into that one fight…."

Roxy threw her head back and laughed. "Is that what he told you? Oh, honey, that man picked fights wherever he went. If he wasn't fighting, he just wasn't right, you know what I mean? And I was there the night he got arrested."

Jess froze. "You were?" she said, stunned.

"I sure was. Some guy just looked at him funny and he let loose on him. Grabbed a beer bottle and started beating on him until the man was bloody unconscious. He always was a loose cannon. That's the problem with the shy ones," she said, leaning in a little too close, "Just when you think you know them, they go and explode."

Jess put away her lipstick and looked at Roxy, who seem a little too happy to give her this information.

"I have to go," she said, turning to leave, not wanting to hear anymore.

"Sure, sugar," Roxy said, giving her a sly smile as Jess walked by her to get to the door. "Say hello to Hank for me."

When Jess got back to the table, she was completely flustered. She didn't even sit down, just told everyone she needed some air and went to wait outside. Confused at her sudden change of attitude, they all looked at each other questioningly. Hank turned to Anne, who shrugged her shoulders in a way that said she had no idea what was going on. Mike and Anne followed her while Hank pulled out some cash for a tip and threw it on the table. As he turned to leave, his eyes went to the back of the restaurant where, in the kitchen doorway, he saw Roxy, leaning against the frame, arms crossed, looking right at him with a menacing grin. His stomach dropped at the sight of her, surprised to see her there. He turned away and headed out the door, not giving her another look, but he had a very bad feeling she was somehow the reason Jess was acting so strangely.

Jess was quiet all the way home. When Hank pulled up to the apartment, she jumped out with Anne and Mike and said she was going in for the night. When he asked her again what was wrong, she told him nothing; she was just tired and wanted some time alone. But Hank could tell there was something else as he pulled away and headed home. Something had happened. He went through the evening in his mind, how they were all having fun and then how the girls had gone to the bathroom, and how Jess had changed when she came back. Something had happened in the bathroom, and Hank was pretty sure it had to do with Roxy. Had she talked to Jess? If she had, he knew whatever she had told Jess was a lie. He had to find out what she had said to her.

Hank turned the Jeep around and headed back to Jess's apartment.

Anne opened the door and let him in, quietly telling him that Jess was in her room crying. Anne and Mike left to give him a chance to talk to Jess in private.

Hank knocked gently on Jess's door. "Jess," he said quietly, "can I come in?"

He waited for an answer but only heard muffled sounds.

"Jess?" he asked again.

Hank opened the door a crack and called her name again. He waited, and when she didn't answer, he slowly pushed it open and looked into her room. Jess was sitting on the bed wiping her tears away with a tissue. She had obviously been crying hard. Hank had never seen her so upset and wanted to put his arms around her and comfort her, but the look on her face told him he had better keep his distance, so he stayed in the doorway.

"Jess, what's wrong?"

"Tell me about Roxy," she said bluntly, throwing the tissue to the floor.

"There's nothing to tell."

"Really, Hank? She sure had a lot to say about you."

Hank didn't know what to say. He had hoped to spare Jess the details of that dark period of his life, yet here it was again in full-blown color, invading the one place where life had been so good.

"Like what?" he asked, wanting to know what Roxy had told her.

"Like how you used to date."

Hank scoffed. "We didn't date, Jess. I can assure you of that."

"Then why did she say that?" she asked, looking at him accusingly. Hank looked down, not wanting to look at Jess.

"She said it because she wanted to date me, but I didn't want to date her. I guess she's still upset about it."

"Really? So you never went out with her?"

Hank shifted his weight from one foot to another. He really didn't want to talk about Roxy. It was a humiliating reminder of whom he had been during those few months—a person he never wanted to be again. "No," he finally said, clenching his teeth. "We did not go out. She liked me and sought me out. And one night when I was drunk, we...hooked up."

The look on Jess's face was total devastation. It was obvious what she was thinking. *How could he sleep with a girl like her? What kind of person was he to do that?*

Hank came into her room a little farther, stopping when she backed away as he entered. "Jess, it was...a really bad time for me. I did a lot of things I deeply regret...."

"Like start fights? And hit other guys with beer bottles?" she retorted. The anger she felt was so strong that it felt it like a physical punch. He could feel the hatred she had for him at that moment, and he felt like he was losing her. He was starting to feel desperate. Roxy could not destroy this as well....

"Jess, please, you have to listen to me..." he said in anguish, reaching out his arms to her.

"No," Jess said, backing away crying and yelling back at him. "You lied to me. You are not the person I thought you were. I want you to leave."

Hank could feel the panic rising in him. All he could think was he couldn't lose her. Not like this. He had to make her understand that he was not that guy in the bar.

"Jess, that's not true. You know I would never do anything...." Hank said desperately, throwing his arms out in emphasis as he said this, not realizing how close he was to her dresser. His arm smashed into the lamp on top, which went into the dresser mirror, breaking both instantly. Hank jumped back when he heard the startling loud crash.

There was a second of silence while they each stood there stunned, and then Jess spoke.

"Get out," she said, barely a whisper, a look of sheer terror on her face.

"Jess, I..." Hank started to apologize.

"Get out!" Jess screamed, throwing a book from her night table at the wall next to him and then throwing herself down on the bed, crying.

Hank shielded himself from the book and then quickly turned around and left. He went out the front door, got in his car, and started driving, not allowing himself to think as he drove off the Island. It had been an accident, he told himself. A stupid accident. He didn't mean to break the lamp and the mirror. He didn't mean to scare her. But like all his other mistakes, it was going to cost him. And the cost this time would be Jess.

He had to make her understand he would never hurt her. He just needed a chance to explain. Certainly, she would let him do that once she calmed down. She knew him better than anyone. She had to know he was not the person his past tried to make him out to be.

Chapter 29

Jess didn't know what to think. Had she been looking at Hank through her own delusions of what she wanted him to be? The guy who finally came into her life and made things better? After Hank left, Mike had come back in to hang out with Anne. Jess didn't want to talk them, so she stayed in her bedroom. When she woke up the next morning, her stomach was immediately in knots remembering Roxy's words.

I guess we both go for the bad boys.

That man's a loose cannon.

Just when you think you know him, he goes and explodes.

Jess wasn't ready to talk to Anne, who was still asleep, so she quickly got dressed, got on her bicycle, and started to ride. She could think better on her bike, and as she made her way down the familiar streets, she kept going over what she knew about Hank.

She thought back to Lynn's reaction when she had first started dating Hank and how she had seemed to be holding something back.

She thought of Anne's telling her that Hank had a past, but that he really wasn't that type of guy. But then what type of guy was he?

He worked an hourly job and had had no future plans until she came along. And Anne's motives were also suspect since she liked hanging out with Jess, and what better way than to double-date with Mike's best friend?

Her mind kept berating her for putting herself in this position. What was she thinking? They were only twenty for God's sake. And she barely knew him. How could she have let things go so far so quickly? She had given him everything, and now she wished she had waited. She should have taken the time to find out more about him and not just see him as the person she wanted him to be. The ride only seemed to get her more riled up rather than soothe her the way it had in the past.

When Jess got back, Anne was eating at the kitchen table and looked up. "Been riding?" she asked.

"Yeah," Jess said, going to the refrigerator for a bottle of water. It had been humid and she was sweaty.

"I need to know something," Jess said in a serious tone, sitting across from Anne at the table. "How well do you really know Hank?"

Anne looked at her suspiciously. "Did you and Hank have a fight?" she asked, trying to figure out where this was coming from.

"Answer my question. How well did you know him before setting me up with him?"

Anne sat back defensively. "What is up with you, Jess? I know Hank through Mike. Mike said he was a good guy."

"Did you know he used to get into bar fights? That there wasn't just the one fight where he got arrested? That he attacked another man with a beer bottle? What kind of guy does that, Anne? When you left the bathroom at the restaurant, one of the waitresses who had dated him came in, and she made it very clear that he is known for being exactly that kind of guy."

Anne looked perplexed. "I knew about the beer bottle, but I didn't know about there being more fights..." she started, trying to recall what Mike had told her, but Jess was too upset and cut her off.

"Really, Anne? You knew about the bottle and you didn't say anything? What kind of friend are you?" Jess shouted, suddenly feeling betrayed by everyone.

"Jess, c'mon, you're overreacting. You know Hank. How could you think he would be like that?"

Jess looked at her friend in astonishment. Her voice got very low and she emphasized her words with her finger, her anger being palatable. "Last night when he came into my room, he broke my lamp and mirror. Did you know that? Don't tell me I'm overreacting."

Anne fell silent, unable to respond. Before she could think of anything to say, Jess was already heading back out the door.

Chapter 30

Hank tried texting Jess a number of times that day, and he even called and left messages, but he got no response. This was not good. She had never ignored him before, and he was getting really worried. This was the first time they had fought, and he didn't know what to do. There had to be a way just to talk to her and work it out.

As soon as he got off work, Hank went over to the apartment. Anne answered the door and told him how Jess had left earlier that day and she hadn't seen her.

"Do you know where she went?" he asked, hoping to find her.

"No. We had a fight and I saw her take off on her bike. I figure she needed to go off and cool down."

"A fight about what?" Hank asked, now knowing something was really wrong. As long as he had known her, Jess had never had a fight with Anne.

Anne leaned into the doorframe, seeing how upset he was getting. "She was angry at me for not giving her all the details of your arrest. I never gave her any information other than it was a bar fight, but some waitress at the restaurant last night told her you had hit that guy with a beer bottle and said a bunch of other things that upset her."

"Do you have any idea where she would go?" he asked, feeling desperate. "I really need to talk to her."

"Your guess is as good as mine at this point. Once she's on her bike, it could be hours before she comes back."

Hank thanked her and told her to let him know if she returned. He got back into his Jeep and stared out the window. He needed to talk to her, to explain what Roxy had said was not true.

But first he had to find out what Roxy had said.

Hank drove back downtown to the restaurant. He walked in and saw Roxy by the bar, talking to another waitress. He walked over to her before she saw him.

"What did you say to my girlfriend last night?" Hank asked, grabbing her by the arm and turning her around to face him. It was all he could do to contain his anger at this girl who kept screwing up his life.

"Well, hey, sugar," Roxy said, leaning seductively on the bar and giving him a big smile. "It's been some time, hasn't it?"

"Tell me what you said to Jess last night," Hank said, not up for Roxy's games.

"Jess? Is that her name? Oh, she and I had some real nice girl talk in the bathroom last night. Turns out she didn't know much about that night in the bar at all. I also mentioned it was probably not your first fight. But then I always get confused as to who is fighting all the time. And what kind of relationship is that if you aren't truthful with each other, Hank?" she asked, smiling deviously.

"Why did you tell her that, Roxy? It's been two years. Haven't you done enough?"

"After the way you used me and just threw me away? I'd say you deserved that and more. Though I have to admit seeing your face when they had you believing you were the one to hit Jimmy with that beer bottle...."

"What?" Hank asked, confused by what she'd just said.

Roxy looked at him and smirked, putting one hand on her hip. "Oh, come on, sugar; certainly, you know by now...." She considered his puzzled reaction, and suddenly, a look of realization crossed her face, causing her to shake her head in disbelief.

"You must be the dumbest son-of-a-bitch alive," she said, as she demurely leaned into his face with a big smile, happy to be the bearer of bad news. "You didn't hit Jimmy with that beer bottle, hon. That was Rocko, the bartender. You see, unlike you, Jimmy does have a reputation for starting fights and for breaking apart bars when he gets a little, shall we say, agitated? So when Rocko saw he was going to get into it with you, he decided to take some preventive measures, you could say. But the trouble was that Rocko already had two strikes against him for some other things he'd done and couldn't get arrested again. So I told him we could just say you did it. And no one had a problem going along with that."

Hank felt like he had been hit in the stomach. He couldn't move, much less breathe. "You mean I didn't do it?" he finally said, his voice almost in a whisper.

Roxy threw her head back and laughed. "Of course not! Not a little lamb like you. But the cops didn't know that, and all I had to do was sign some statement saying I saw you do it. That was all it took for them to take you away. And you, you didn't even fight it! It was almost too easy. Made me think twice about why I ever slept with you in the first place."

Hank tried to swallow. He needed air. He felt frozen in place, but he knew he had to get out of there. He took one last look at Roxy's smug face, seeing how delighted she was to tell him the truth, and turned and stumbled out of the restaurant as fast as he could. He made it about halfway down the block before he had to stop and hold onto the wall, bending over with pain, afraid he was going to throw up.

Two years. Two years of everyone believing he had cracked open the skull of another man with a bottle and having to work a shit job taking John's crap. Two years of his life wasted because of some lowlife who wanted to sleep with him. And to find out now, just days before he had finished his sentence, that he didn't do it. He took several moments to steady his breath and collect himself, finally making himself stand up and walk to his Jeep despite the pain he felt. Once he got in, he sat thinking for a long time, the shock of it all still reverberating through him.

He had to tell Jess. He had to let her know everything Roxy had told her was a lie and that he had never done it. He had to let her know he was never the person he thought he had been in that dark period, capable of such violence. It all made so much more sense now. Of course he hadn't taken a bottle to beat another man. He would never do that, even stone drunk. He had been in the wrong place at the wrong time with the wrong people. And he had paid for it dearly.

He texted that he had to talk to her and that it was urgent—that he had to see her in person and explain. She still wasn't answering his texts, so he decided to go look for her. It was Tuesday night, so first he drove to the turtle nest to see if she had gone there. The volunteers said she hadn't shown up that night, so he went back to his Jeep. It was getting late, so he went back to her apartment to see if she had returned or if Anne had heard from her, which she hadn't. Anne allowed him to sit and wait, but at midnight when Jess still had not shown up, she said he should go home and try again tomorrow.

"Just be patient," she said. "She'll come around. She just needs to cool off."

Despite his better judgment, Hank left and went home. As he lay in bed that night, he did something he had never done. He prayed, first that Jess was safe and just cooling down as Anne said. That was the most important thing. But if he could have one more wish, he prayed she would give him a chance to explain his side of the story because he knew if did, he could make everything right again.

Chapter 31

Having fought with Anne, Jess didn't feel right about returning to the apartment, so she called Lynn and asked if she could come over. When she got there, Lynn offered her a beer and they sat on the couch talking. Lynn asked what was wrong, and Jess told her about the fight with Hank and how he had broken her lamp and mirror. She said she had heard about Hank getting into other fights and asked Lynn if it was true.

Lynn sighed and tried to remember. "Well, everyone knew about the incident with the beer bottle. But I don't remember hearing about more fights. That doesn't mean that they didn't happen; I just wasn't really paying much attention to the whole story, if you know what I mean." She took a long sip of her beer. "I had really hoped this would work out for you, Jess. You were so happy there for a while. Like I've never seen you before. I was pulling for you guys," she said with true remorse. "Do you really think he broke those things on purpose? I mean, could it have been an accident? That's just not the Hank I grew up with. But then, I would never picture him hitting someone with a beer bottle. But he must have done it because he got convicted, right?"

Jess didn't know what she believed at this point. And when she looked at her phone, she saw dozens of texts and calls from Hank, all saying how sorry he was, how he loved her and just needed a chance to explain. But she just couldn't face him tonight. She really needed a moment away from him to think and get her head straight.

She and Lynn ended up talking until 2 a.m., and then Lynn told her she could spend the night on the couch since it was so late. Jess was grateful not to have to go back to Anne's apartment and gladly accepted, though she spent most of the night lying in the dark unable to sleep as thoughts about Hank ran through her mind.

The next morning, Jess left Lynn's, but when she rode back to the Island, she found she was not ready to return to her apartment just yet. Instead, she headed to Kohl's to grab breakfast, then made her way to the beach where she took a long walk along the water. Watching the surfers made her think of Hank, and she started to miss him, thinking of all the good things he had done for her and how he had made her feel. Maybe she was overreacting. Maybe Lynn was right that the lamp and mirror had merely been an accident and she had been too upset to see it that way at the time.

She took out her phone again and reread his messages. *How could I not give him a chance to at least explain?* she asked herself. After all they had been through the past few months, she owed him at least that. She hesitated, then texted him back.

Pick me up tonight after work. We can talk then.

She closed her phone and put it in her pocket, but it immediately buzzed. She looked at it again, seeing his response.

I'll be there waiting for you.

She smiled to herself at the quick reply. Maybe everything would work out after all.

At work that night, Jess felt stressed and was grateful for the distraction her job provided. The one good thing about waitressing was that it kept her busy. Between taking orders, getting drinks, bringing the food, and just being aware in general when the customers at one of her five tables were ready for their bill, there was no time to think about anything other than her work.

Until she noticed John slouching over the bar, drinking as usual. Maybe it was because she was already agitated. Or maybe it was seeing him grab the butt of another waitress as she passed by him while carrying a full tray of food that he almost made her drop. Whatever the reason, she had one thought: This has to stop.

She turned and headed to the back of the restaurant where the manager had an office, knocking on the door before opening it. When she entered, she was surprised to see Mr. DeGaulle there. She knew he sometimes dropped in to handle business matters, but she hadn't known he was there tonight. She hesitated a moment while both men looked at her, uncertain if she should file a complaint against John's behavior with his father right there, then decided she needed to set things straight. She stepped inside, closing the door behind her, ready to let them know what John had been doing.

Chapter 32

Hank counted the minutes until he could pick up Jess tonight. He was going to do whatever it took to get her to listen to him, to explain he had never done any of the things Roxy said he had. He had to make her understand because he had no intention of losing her.

Hank hated thinking about those days. During that time, he had become the darkest side of himself, a person he did not recognize. It started with him going out at night and drinking until he would almost black out. The late nights turned into late mornings, and soon he was sleeping in until midday and would start drinking as soon as he woke up, hitting the bars by 3 p.m. He didn't remember a lot of that time. He knew he would sit at the end of the bar at one of the local establishments on the edge of town and drink whiskey, trying to drown the anger he felt over losing Rob. But the pain was always there just under the surface, and the slightest thing could set it off. If someone bumped into him by accident or said something he didn't like, Hank was up and yelling in some guy's face. But as far as he knew, he was always too drunk to do anything more and just ended getting thrown out of a lot of places for being belligerent. As far as he knew, he had never hit anyone.

And then one night, Roxy had appeared. Hank usually managed to deter any women who tried to talk to him, but Roxy was relentless. She would show up wherever he was and try talking to him for a while, wearing tight little outfits that left little to the imagination and rubbing up against him when saying hello. When he tried to deflect her, she only came back for more. He finally gave in and bought her a drink one night when his despair got the better of him, thinking maybe having someone else to talk to would help drown out the pain. It was a night when Mike didn't show up to get him and he was too drunk to drive home, so Roxy took him back to her place. He was trying everything he could to get rid of the pain of losing Rob, and the alcohol wasn't working, so when she came on to him, he didn't stop her. In the distance of his foggy mind, he thought maybe sex would make him feel better—feel anything. He was too drunk to do anything, so he just lay there, letting her do all the work until at some point he just passed out.

When Hank woke up and saw where he was, he was disgusted with himself. He left without waking Roxy and went to a different bar the next night, hoping to avoid her, but somehow she found him. She came up to him and started kissing him and calling him baby, and it made him sick. He threw her off of him and told her to stay the hell away. Roxy got insulted and called him white trash and a whole bunch of other things he couldn't remember, but he didn't care; he just wanted her to go away.

A few nights later, she showed up at the bar he was at with some greasy guy in a sleeveless leather vest showing off his tattoos that involved skulls and knives. Roxy was hanging all over the guy, hoping to make Hank jealous, and when he ignored her, she got mad. The greasy-looking dude decided to be a big man and take Hank on, daring him to fight. Hank remembered being pulled off the bar-stool, but he was so drunk, he didn't remember anything after that until he felt himself being handcuffed and lifted off the cold cement floor. It wasn't until he was at the station that the police told him he had taken his beer bottle and slammed it so hard over the guy's head that he had knocked him out and caused him to bleed all over the floor.

He found out it was Roxy who had called the police and had him arrested, making the guy press charges.

And once again, it was Roxy still trying to get back at him by turning Jess against him.

Hank had decided that morning that he would tell Jess every-thing and make her understand what had really happened. That he had never been the type of person who could do something like that.

When he got to work, he was obviously distracted, thinking how he would get her to listen to him. But that was not all he was going to have to worry about that day.

"So, how's your girlfriend, Atwater?" John started in on him shortly after he arrived. Hank pretended not to hear him, but inside he was thinking, *Not today, John, not today.* He didn't know how John had found out about Jess, but he couldn't focus on that right now.

But John had no intention of letting up. Seeing Jess and Hank together explained a lot about how mysteriously elated Hank had been the past couple of months, and now that John knew the source, he had every intention of sticking a knife in it.

"Dating a college girl, huh? Isn't that a little above your pay grade?" he started, sitting in his chair like he always did. "What makes you think you're good enough for a girl like her?"

All day long, John made comments about how a guy like Hank could never live up to what a college girl like Jess would want. That she was just using him for a summer fling. Hank tried to shake it off, but John had found his most vulnerable spot, his concern about what would happen to them when Jess started college again next week. It had been in the back of Hank's mind for several weeks, and John pointing it out now when their relationship was already tenuous only confirmed his worst fears.

Hank held it together until quitting time came, relieved when the day finally ended. He raced to his car to get away from John and go talk to Jess, hoping to get her to break from work for a minute. But when Hank got to his car, he realized he would not be going anywhere quickly. One look at his Jeep and it was obvious his rear left wheel was completely flat. Not just low but flat. Upon inspection, he could see it had been slashed. He looked over to John, who was leaning against his car, watching Hank with a satisfied look. It was all Hank could do not to go over and flatten him, but he knew it was more important he get to Jess. He pulled out the spare and started changing the tire, ignoring John's jeers about watching where he parked his Jeep so he wouldn't get flats. He managed to put on the spare, but he could tell it was old and not going to hold up well. The only tire place he could find open at that hour was a place in Carolina Beach, about a thirty-minute drive away, but he had no choice. He set out to get it fixed, hoping he would make it back in time to pick up Jess from work and settle this mess once and for all.

Hank drove as fast as he could, but reached Oceanside fifteen minutes later than he wanted. Worse, his phone had died as he raced around to fix his flat, so he couldn't text Jess to let her know he would be late. He sat there, uncertain if she had left yet and wondering what to do, when he saw Lynn come out, having finished her shift. When he asked if she had seen Jess, she told him Jess had left about ten minutes ago. Hank thanked her and got back in his vehicle, then headed to Jess's apartment, driving slowly down the street, hoping to catch her walking home.

He had only gone about two blocks before he heard the screams. Hank gunned it down the street, seeing a car stopped not far ahead by the side of the road. He could hear some guys laughing, and one of them was trying to pull someone into the car with them.

"C'mon," he heard a familiar drunken voice say. "We just want to take you for a little ride."

John had Jess by the arm and was trying to drag her into the car. Jess was fighting as hard as she could to get away, screaming at John to get away from her.

Hank sped up right behind them and jumped out of his Jeep as fast as he could, leaving the vehicle door open. John had his back to Hank, so he didn't see him come flying out of the dark. Without even thinking, Hank grabbed John's arm and spun him around, forcing John to release his grip on Jess. Then Hank hit him three times in the face in quick succession, sending John reeling back against the car. Slowly, John sank to the ground, the car being the only thing holding him upright. Hank quickly looked around for Jess and saw her running down the street away from the scene. He stepped back to take a breath as John's two friends jumped out of the car, coming to their friend's rescue.

They both started to go for Hank, but before they could do anything, John held up his hand and shouted, "Stop! Don't touch him!" He touched his mouth where Hank had hit him and looked at the blood on it. Then he started to laugh, too drunk to feel any pain just yet. "Call the cops. This asshole's going to jail." He looked at Hank, half-leaning against the car and half-lying on the ground. "I finally got you to break, Atwater. Less than one week to go and you were done. I knew you wouldn't make it."

John rolled down to the ground, laughing as he lay there bleeding, but Hank didn't hear him. He looked at his hands and the blood on John's face and started backing up slowly. John's words suddenly hit him and he realized what he had just done. He quickly turned and ran back to his Jeep, driving away as fast as he could.

"Go ahead," John happily called after him as Hank disappeared into the darkness. "Run. We know where to find you."

Chapter 33

Hank drove around for a long time trying to figure out what to do. He tried to call Jess, but she wouldn't answer. He texted her and pleaded for her just to tell him if she was all right, but she wouldn't respond. He finally texted Mike to contact Anne to see if Jess had gotten home safely. Once he knew she had, he turned off his phone, not responding to Mike's questions about what had happened and where he was. He knew he had really blown it and he was going to jail. It didn't matter that he had never done the assault that put him on probation in the first place since it was his word against Roxy's and any other witness they had. The only difference was this time he didn't want to drag his friends down with him. Mike had done enough for him. They were all better off without him.

After driving around the city for what seemed like hours, Hank finally ended up at the beach's north end. He parked on the side street he often used when surfing. If he were going to be incarcerated, he wanted to feel the sand and sun one last time. He got out of the car and slowly walked to the beach, hearing the sound of the waves colliding along the shore. He made it halfway to the water, then sat in the dark, waiting for the first strands of sunlight to appear, knowing it would mean the end of this terrible night and the start of the day when he would lose everything he had ever wanted.

Hank sat watching the sunrise, thinking of nothing but the colors that lit up the sky, watching the initial yellows and oranges fade into a pale blue, the water shimmering as the waves came closer and closer into shore. As the scene's peacefulness overtook him, his mind started to find clarity. He had learned so many things about himself this summer. About the person he thought he was and how his friends saw him. But more importantly, about the man he believed he could become. He thought of Rob and what he would have done. Not that Rob ever would have been in this position in the first place. But Rob would have told him to do what he knew to be right. Face the music. Own your consequences. That is what a man would do. And so, as the sun made its full appearance, Hank knew what he had to do.

He sat a bit longer taking in the beauty of it all, thinking how lucky he had been to enjoy it like he had. Then he stood, brushed off the sand from his pants, and headed slowly back to his car to what he knew was waiting for him.

It didn't take long before Hank was driving up the oak-lined driveway to the stately white mansion at the end. The DeGaulle residence. Probably the largest home in Wilmington and one of the oldest. A massive structure, its large Corinthian columns reached past the second floor and surrounded the house on all sides with a full colonnade, holding up an immense roof that covered the house and wraparound porch alike. The bottom windows spanned from floor to ceiling, while the upper windows were rounded at the top and had their own balconies. The house's stark whiteness was contrasted by the black shutters adorning the windows and the flowers blooming in the surrounding gardens. It was the most magnificent antebellum home Hank had ever seen. He just wished he was here for any reason other than what he had come for.

Even though it was not yet 8 a.m., Hank rang the doorbell, hoping for the chance to explain to Mr. DeGaulle what had had happened last night before he had him escorted to the police station for hitting John. Hank felt he owed John's father an explanation after all he had done for him, even if Hank knew it was unlikely Mr. DeGaulle would believe his version of the events. Still, all his thinking told him this was the right thing to do, so here he stood, anxiously waiting for someone to come to the door so he could get the conversation over with.

Hank was somewhat surprised when Mr. DeGaulle himself opened the door. He looked as if he had not slept the previous night either. He wore a polo shirt and some chinos, very unlike the well-kept man he usually appeared to be. He didn't seem surprised to see Hank standing there, and without a word, he held the door open for him to come in as if he were expecting him.

When Hank stepped into the large entryway, he was immediately taken aback. If the outside of the house was impressive, the inside was spectacular. A circular staircase cascaded down either side of the massive room laden with a black and white marble floor. Hank stared in awe at the detailed craftsmanship in the banisters' woodwork and the large crystal chandelier suspended over the room's center. He knew the DeGaulles were wealthy, but Hank had never seen a home like this, making him feel immediately out of place.

"This way," was all Mr. DeGaulle said as he started walking down the hall to the left. Hank followed him into a study where a large oak desk sat covered with papers, flanked by finely crafted bookshelves that reached the ceiling. An expensive oriental rug covered most of the hardwood floor. Mr. DeGaulle went behind the desk, then motioned for Hank to sit on one of the two chairs opposite him. The chairs had lion heads carved into the ends of the armrests and were a deep rich wood with brown leather upholstery. Hank sat upright in his chair, trying to touch it as little as he could, intimidated by the grandeur of it.

Mr. DeGaulle leaned back in his office chair, which was identical in design but much larger, and folded his hands, looking at Hank and waiting for him to speak.

Hank cleared his throat. "Sir, I know what I did was wrong. And I plan to turn myself in. But first, I wanted to apologize to you. You gave me a chance when no one else would, and I feel I owe you an explanation for why I hit John last night."

Mr. DeGaulle sighed and shook his head, then turned to look out the window as he spoke. "No need, son. I saw what happened. I've suspected what John was doing for a long time. I just didn't want to admit it to myself. But I can't turn away from it anymore. I spent a good part of last night thinking about John, and I have come to one conclusion: I don't want to be the type of father who raises such an irresponsible and callous son."

Mr. DeGaulle turned back to Hank and leaned forward on his desk, clasping his hands as if to impart to Hank how important his words were. "I didn't come from money. My father was a tailor, and my mother cleaned houses where I grew up in South Carolina. We lived in a two-bedroom house I shared with three brothers. I had to scramble for food, and my only clothes were whatever they handed down to me. One day, I visited Charleston with my mother, a rare retreat, and I remember walking down those streets looking at all those beautiful houses, each dripping with more gingerbread than the last. I'd had no idea that houses like that existed. And the people who lived in them wore such fine clothes and seemed so happy. That day, I made a promise to myself. I promised that one day I would live in a house like that—that I wanted to raise my family in a house that would make them feel the happiness I saw in those people.

"From that day on, I put everything I had into making more of myself. I was the first of my family to go to college, paying for it myself by working nights in a meat-packing plant. I opened my first business, and it was so successful that I opened another one. Making money came easy to me." He waved his arms to emphasize his point, then leaned back in his chair again. He thought for a moment. "I came to Wilmington to expand my business plans and liked the town, everything from its size to the people that were in it. Here, everyone assumed I had always been rich. I liked them thinking that. It made me feel elevated, like I had finally become the person I was striving to be. So, this is where I decided to settle down. I got married, bought a house, had a son...."

His voice trailed off for a moment as he sat in thought. Hank sat quietly listening, uncertain where Mr. DeGaulle was going with this.

"I bought this house because I wanted everyone to know I was rich. I wanted to give my family everything I'd never had. There would be no hand-me-downs for John, and there would be plenty of food and other opportunities. I got involved with the town and became a prominent member of some of its more distinguished organizations. I thought if I did all that, I would be like one of those happy people in Charleston. I would finally feel what I thought I had seen on their faces that day. But last night, I realized I've been working toward the wrong goal all along. Money hasn't brought me the happiness I was looking for. In fact, money is what destroyed the things I truly wanted—happiness for my family, a son I could be proud of...." Again Mr. DeGaulle hesitated, choking up for a moment. He stood up and went to the window, standing there with his hands behind his back as if to conceal this moment of emotion from Hank. Hank didn't know what to say, averting his eyes while the older man collected himself.

Mr. DeGaulle cleared his throat and continued, strong in tone again. "I blame myself for how John turned out. By not teaching him the value of hard work, I have created a spoiled child instead of a man. Not someone like your brother. Or you."

Hank was startled to hear Mr. DeGaulle say this.

"You know Rob worked for me for a few summers?" he asked, sitting down again, facing Hank.

"Yes," Hank said.

"Did you know he was the first one to come to me and tell me the things John was doing? He felt I should know. All my other employees were too scared to say anything, but Rob, he always tried to do the right thing. I didn't believe him at first and waved it off. But it made me watch John more closely and realize that what he needed was more discipline. That's when I started making him work the harder jobs. And he knew Rob had been the one to spoil his fun, at least for a short while. He would have found a way to seek revenge if it had been anyone else, but Rob was older and much stronger, and I am sure John was too scared to confront him. However, once Rob was out of the picture and you showed up, well, I guess he thought he could exact his revenge on you. Oh, he wouldn't have touched you when Rob was alive, but with Rob gone...." He let the words trail off, shaking his head at the thought.

"There has only been one other person who has been brave enough to tell me the things that John is still doing. That waitress, Jess. When I came in to check on a few things last night at the restaurant, she came into the manager's office. She told me how John had been treating the staff at the restaurant. I didn't realize there had been issues, but she was very candid about what he had put one of her friends through. Just like that mess back in high school. I had to know if what she said was true. So, last night, I followed him."

Hank sat silent, suddenly realizing what Mr. DeGaulle was saying.

"Yes, I was there, parked just down the street from John's car. I saw John get out of his car and start to pull Jess in with him and his friends. I got out of my car and was just about to call out to him when you appeared out of nowhere. You brought him down right away. Three hits I believe it was. And then you stopped. After all the things he did to you, you could have easily knocked him unconscious. Or worse. And no one would have blamed you for it, least of all me. But you didn't. You did just enough to stop him and then you backed off. Quite a feat of restraint if you ask me. If I had your strength and that moment had come up, I don't think I would have been as...reserved shall we say."

Mr. DeGaulle looked at Hank, who was sitting there stunned. Hank had hit his son and he was saying how restrained he was?

"I saw Jess run away as soon as you removed John's grip from her arm. She was crying hysterically. I called her over to my car and told her to get in and wait. You were gone before I got to John. I told his friends to drive him home right away. He was upset, yelling about calling the police for what you had done, but I made it clear I was going to handle it. It just wasn't in the way he expected."

Mr. DeGaulle leaned back again, resigned.

"I now see how depraved my son has become. I had hoped that by having him work with you, he would learn a few things—like what it means to put in a good day's work and how hard it is for some folks who don't have everything given to them. But he is just too entitled. He is never going to be the man I hope he will become unless he has to do it for himself. Like I did. Giving him everything only ruined him."

Mr. DeGaulle leaned forward on his desk again, his stern posture indicating how resolute he was. "I was up all night thinking about what I need to do to fix John, and I finally concluded there is only one thing that might save him. So this morning, I told him I wanted him out of my house. I told him I would no longer pay for his college or his cell phone and I was taking back his car. I said I was disgraced to have him bear my family name and until he straightened himself out, I wanted nothing more to do with him. I gave him ten minutes to pack a bag and get the hell out of here or I would call the police on him."

Mr. DeGaulle sat silently for a moment and then spoke again in a much quieter voice. "It was the hardest thing I have ever had to do. And his mother may never forgive me for it." Hank, surprised by his openness, could see the sadness in his eyes.

"I couldn't make a good man out of him, Hank. I couldn't make him into someone like you or your brother. At that I have failed. Like how you came here knowing I could very easily turn you in and send you back to jail, but you came anyway because you wanted to do the right thing. I was never able to teach that to John."

"It was Rob who taught me," Hank said, finally speaking. "He was the one always making sure I was doing the right thing." He could hear the pain in Mr. DeGaulle's voice and didn't know what he could say to ease it.

"Your brother was a good man," Mr. DeGaulle replied. "He was always going to get by. But you, you have something your brother never had. Where Rob had street smarts, you always had the brains to be more. Sure, the Army was a good place for him, but you, Hank, you could make something more of yourself with a good education and the right attitude. You remind me of myself when I was your age. Determined and capable, someone who has what it takes to succeed."

Hank shifted in his chair, wondering how much he should say, then decided with all that Mr. DeGaulle had told him, he had nothing to lose.

"Actually, I applied to UNCW this month. The admissions officer said I might be able to get in by the spring semester. I don't know how I'll pay for it or even if I can do it, but…I know I have to try."

Mr. DeGaulle shook his head and smiled. "You never cease to amaze me," he said. "You apply yourself and you'll do fine. But wait until spring semester? I see no reason for that. I'm on the university board. Let me talk to them. And when you get your degree, there's always a job for you here. If you want it. But I suspect you are the kind of man who wants to make his own way."

"So I am not going to jail?" Hank asked, more to convince himself that what he had been fearing wasn't going to happen.

Mr. DeGaulle waved away the thought. "No one's going to jail. John deserved everything you gave him and more. I saw how he treated you. I would never have held out as long as you did, Hank, after what he did. I believe you should never use force unless absolutely necessary. And you obviously had a good reason to use it in this case."

"Mr. DeGaulle, there's something else you should know," Hank said. Mr. DeGaulle listened as Hank told him about his shameful descent into drinking and his interactions with Roxy, ending with how Roxy had told him he hadn't actually done the assault for which he had been sentenced to probation. When he was done, Mr. DeGaulle sat quietly for a moment and looked very concerned.

"I don't like seeing good people facing such a grave injustice," he finally said after thinking for a moment. "I am a good friend of the DA. Let me have a talk with him about what can be done to fix that situation."

Chapter 34

As Hank left the DeGaulle residence, he was in complete shock at how things had turned out. When he had entered John's house, he was sure he would be led out in handcuffs. Instead, Mr. DeGaulle was going to help him get into college. He still couldn't believe it. He had to tell Jess what had happened. He was feeling elated at the turn of events and felt invincible. He couldn't believe she wouldn't hear him out. And if she refused to see him, he would just wait outside until she finally relented, showing her just how determined he was. She was too important to him. He would show her just how much.

Hank parked in front of Jess's apartment and knocked hard on the door. Anne opened up the door, not at all surprised to see him there.

"I need to talk to Jess," he said, running past her and through the apartment until he was in Jess's room.

But the room was empty. All of Jess's things were gone, from the items on her desk and dresser to the closet of clothes. Hank stood there, staring in shock, trying to wrap his mind around what he was seeing.

Anne came up behind him, looking into the room. "She left early this morning. She was pretty upset and wouldn't tell me why."

"John and some of his friends tried to attack her last night as she was leaving the restaurant. I showed up just in time to get him off of her before pummeling him," Hank explained.

"Well, that explains a lot. I'm sorry I missed that. John certainly has been asking for it. I hope you really gave it to him," she said, smiling.

Hank faced Anne, the desperation showing on his face. "You have to tell me where she went. I have to talk to her."

Anne shrugged and walked back into the living room with Hank following her. She sat down on the couch, then said, "Well, we haven't exactly been the best of buds lately, so maybe I'm not the one to ask. She didn't tell me anything, just left me a note saying she wouldn't be back. But my guess is she was going to see if they would still accept her at that Florida college, so she had to leave right away."

"What college?" Hank asked, confused as he sat down in a chair across from her. "What are you talking about?"

"She didn't tell you, did she?" Anne sighed. This was not the quiet morning she had planned. "Jess applied to a program in Florida last January that was big on sea turtles. She was dying to go, and they accepted her as a transfer, but when the tuition bill came, she couldn't afford it. She was pretty bummed about sticking around here until you showed up. Suddenly, Wilmington wasn't so bad. But then she heard stories about you from that waitress and grilled me about why I hadn't told her more."

"Which is why you had that fight," Hank said.

"Oh, yeah. I couldn't fill in the blanks she needed, so she went off on me before storming out. When she came back last night after her little get-together with John, she was so shook up that she wouldn't even talk to me. Just locked herself in her room and started packing. I heard her talking to someone on the phone, but I thought it was you."

Hank sat in disbelief. "She wasn't talking to me. She won't answer any of my calls or texts. She really left? But why so quickly, Anne? Why wouldn't she at least talk to me...?"

"I don't know," Anne said. "Jess heard what you did when you drank, and then you broke her lamp and mirror—"

"That was an accident!" Hank said, defensively. "I would never hurt Jess! And it turns out I never hurt that guy in the bar either. When I saw how upset Jess was, I went and talked to Roxy. She told me she had set me up, and I had been too drunk to know what had really happened. Why do you think I stopped drinking altogether? Because I thought it had made me hurt someone when I was drunk, and I never wanted to do that again."

"But you just told me you hit John right in front of her."

Hank shook his head, unable to comprehend how Jess could view that as anything but protecting her. He tried to keep his voice level. "John was drunk and pulling Jess into the car with his two friends. You know as well as I do that if I had not shown up, they would have raped her. Yes, I hit him, but just enough to bring him down and set her free. I couldn't bear the thought of his touching her...." He felt the anger surge through him again at the thought of John grabbing her. "I have to speak to her and set things straight."

"She loaded up her car this morning and left," Anne said, tired of the conversation and picking up a magazine to indicate she was done talking to him. "I think we both know she is on her way to Florida."

Hank tried all that day and the next to text and call Jess, with no response. Anne said Jess wasn't answering her texts either. Anne knew the school was in Orlando, so it didn't take long for Hank to figure out Jess had applied to UCF. He thought of driving down there to talk to her, but the day after talking to Mr. DeGaulle, he got a call from the university. Mr. DeGaulle had gotten Hank into UNCW for the fall semester and the university had given him a full scholarship based on financial need. The problem was he was expected to show up for freshman orientation at the beginning of the following week. That didn't leave enough time to drive down to Florida and back. And he couldn't just leave after everything Mr. DeGaulle had done to get him in so fast. So he kept trying to reach Jess by phone, hoping she would finally break down and talk to him.

He missed her so much that he kept going to all the places they shared together, blindly hoping that she would just suddenly appear. The turtle nest where they had sat together was getting ready to hatch, and Hank knew how important that was to Jess. Every night, he would sit there, believing she would come back to see it. She had spent so much time taking care of it and wanted so badly to see the hatchlings emerge and scramble their way to the water. And if he was here, then maybe he could talk to her, put some sense into her head, remind her of what they had and tell her how everything about his arrest had been a lie. Every night, Hank sat by the nest, often until midnight, just waiting under the stars for his life to return to what it had been.

For the first couple of nights, Mike came to hang out with him. Hank was pretty sure Mike was checking up on him to make sure he wasn't drinking again, but Hank had no interest in drinking. What he wanted was Jess, and if by some chance she did come back, the last thing he wanted was for her to see him drunk. He had also learned that getting drunk only put him in a position to be taken advantage of by people like Roxy, making it totally unappealing as a way to soothe his pain.

It didn't take long for Mike to realize that Hank wasn't going down that path, so Mike stopped coming, claiming he had to prepare for his classes. Hank didn't mind. He actually wanted solitude right now. He used the time to relive each moment with Jess and think about how she had made him feel. Then he would wonder what he could have done differently, how he could have kept her from going away. He kept coming up with the same response. He loved her as much as he could, and anything he had done was to protect her, not hurt her. He just wanted one last chance to explain it all to her, to show her they belonged together. To prove that everything he had said and done was the truth about who he really was. That her believing in him made him see a future he had never known existed, and that he so greatly wanted that future to be with her.

The night before Hank was to check in to UNCW, the sand started to bubble just like Jess had told him it would, and he stood and watched in amazement as dozens of little brown hatchlings started crawling over each other to make their way out of their sandy nest. As volunteers watched nearby, the turtles started their trek to the ocean, making their way down the chute that had been built for them and into the water, carried off by the outgoing tide. It was a slow process because they were so tiny and it was such a long journey to the water's edge, but one-by-one they made their way.

Hank watched until the very last one had reached the water and was swimming anxiously away. He kept looking even after he could no longer see them and the other onlookers had departed, knowing that they were somewhere out there.

It was over and she hadn't come.

PART II

Hank

Chapter 35

Hank showed up on campus as required on Monday to start classes on Wednesday. UNCW required he live on campus as a first-year student, so he packed up some clothes and drove over to move in. All the freshmen dorms had already been full, but Hank lucked out because one of Mike's suitemates was not going to return. Mike went with Hank to the housing office and arranged for him to move in with him and two other guys in the upper classmen dorm, getting permission due to Hank's age.

They dropped off his clothes at the dorm and Mike introduced him to his suitemates as a friend from home who had finally gotten his act together and made it to college. Rick, from Greensboro, was studying engineering, and Matt, from Richmond, was an English major preparing for law school. Hank wasn't sure if Mike had told them anything about his past, but both guys were friendly and welcomed him to UNCW, saying if he needed anything to let them know; then they went back to their own conversation, treating him as they would have any other new student. Mike gave Hank a look like, *That's your story now*, knowing how important it was to Hank to have a fresh start. Hank nodded gratefully.

Hank quickly realized that even though he had visited the campus with Jess, he didn't know his way around. So as soon as he signed up for his classes and picked up his class materials, he changed and went for a run to get his bearings. He remembered a few places, like the Student Center, but it took some exploring before he found the academic buildings where his classes would be held and figured out how to get to them from his dorm.

Hank felt sure he would stand out as someone who didn't belong on campus, but when he sat down on one of the benches to catch his breath and just watch people pass, it became apparent no one was paying any attention to him. Except for an occasional smile from a girl who would pass by, the other students were busy greeting friends they hadn't seen all summer and getting settled. As far as anyone else was concerned, he was just another student. He started to relax and instead thought about how he had done it—he was finally starting a new life. Here was the opportunity to become the person Jess had seen in him. He couldn't help but think what it would have been like if they had been here together, but he quickly pushed those thoughts away. It hurt so much to think of her, and though he kept reaching out, he still hadn't heard anything back. To avoid thinking about her, he quickly got up to do another few laps around the campus to push down his thoughts and all the pain that followed, trying to get back to occupying his mind so he wouldn't think about the fact she was no longer there.

A lot of activities were being held to welcome back the upper classmen and as orientation for the freshmen; they were activities Hank could have attended, but most weren't of much interest to him. He didn't trust his ability to relate to the other students, not wanting to share his story of how he got there, and he wasn't in the mood to meet new people. Mike had tried talking him into going to Beach Blast with him and the guys, an annual UNCW tradition where the school welcomed the students back with a day at the beach that included music, food, and free T-shirts, hoping it would make Hank feel more a part of things. But when Hank saw the event was held at Crystal Pier where Oceanside was located, the memories were just too raw for him to handle, so he begged off, saying he needed to prepare for his classes. It was easier to keep to himself without complicating his new life with social activities.

Some days, Hank felt so torn up inside that he was sure everyone could see his world had been shattered and how hard he was working to keep it together. Those were the days he had to fight to concentrate on his studies. When that proved unsuccessful, he would work out, sometimes going for two runs in one day. It took a while for him to realize his pain was not as evident to others as he thought and that when he talked to other students, they were more focused on their own lives.

About a month in, Hank ran into Anne while walking around campus. She had broken up with Mike just before school started. His ego had been a little bruised, but it didn't take Mike long to bounce back and find new girls he was interested in. However, his disconnecting with Anne was a downside for Hank, who had hoped she would provide him with information about Jess if she heard from her. When he ran into her, he used the opportunity to ask if Jess had contacted her.

"Honestly, Hank, I haven't heard from her either. It's like she disappeared off the face of the earth. I mean, I know she was mad at me, but whatever. Sorry I can't be more helpful. How do you like college?"

So he wasn't going to be able to reach Jess that way.

Hank began his studies with some general required courses while trying to figure out what he wanted to major in. He was slightly self-conscious that he would be older than the other students in the first-year courses, but he found that along with the many eighteen-year-olds who enrolled just after high school, there were also adults of all ages, people who had left the military after they had finished their tours or were unable to get a degree when they were younger for various reasons. He quickly realized his age didn't matter, and he instead worked on applying himself, trying to keep his mind clear of the heartbreak that would suddenly appear at odd moments and require him to fight to push it back down.

It was so hard at first. Every time Hank walked through campus, he kept thinking he was going to turn a corner and run into Jess. He would find himself looking at everyone who passed to see if he could catch sight of her. A lot of people were on skateboards and bikes, so he half-hoped he would see her ride by, even though the rational part of him knew that wasn't going to happen. *She's gone*, he kept reminding himself. There was nothing he could do about it. He knew he needed to stop thinking about her, hard as it was. After weeks of texting and calling her, he finally told himself to stop trying to contact her. She knew he wanted to talk to her, and he would just have to wait until she was ready to do so, if that day ever came. He made himself numb after that, trying not to think about her or feel anything, knowing that if he did, he would fall so completely apart that he wasn't sure he could recover.

Hank put all his energy into his studies, spending hours in the library between classes and in the evenings, mostly keeping to himself. When he wasn't studying, he was working out, pushing himself harder than ever, using exercise to manage his pain when it tried to rear itself. When other students tried to talk to him in class or would join him at lunch, he would be friendly but somewhat reserved. Mike's story that he had started late because he'd taken time off before going to college worked well for Hank. When questions followed about what he did during that time, he said he had worked to earn money for college, and when some students pushed for more information, he learned to deflect their questions by asking them about themselves. This proved successful since most of them were more interested in talking about themselves anyway; Hank found that a relief since he would just have to sit there and nod in response.

In his off time, Hank enjoyed hanging out at the Student Recreation Center. He was impressed with the amount of athletic equipment the university made available to students and would go whenever possible. It was so much better than the dumbbells he had used in his garage with Rob, allowing him new ways to strengthen himself. He even befriended some ex-military guys in the weight room. Occasionally, Mike would invite him to join some other guys for pick-up basketball games. He still did his Sunday run at the beach and would go surfing with Mike a couple of times a week when the weather was good, but otherwise, his life revolved around the campus.

Going to college had effects Hank hadn't counted on. When he moved into the dorm and started getting on with his life, it also seemed to spark something in his father, who started acting more like his old self. Rather than go to the Café after his run, now Hank would go home on Sundays to help out around the house. His father would make dinner for the two of them, using that time to ask about Hank's classes. He was obviously impressed to have a son in college. He kept telling Hank how he knew it would work out for him, and though he didn't say it out loud, Hank knew his father was proud of him.

They were also finding it easier to talk about Rob, less with sadness and more about the good memories they had of him. For the first time, their home life wasn't centered around the loss of Hank's older brother. Now it focused on Hank and his achievements. While Hank still missed Rob, he also could see that Rob's absence was allowing him to grow in ways he never would have if he had followed in Rob's footsteps. It was a bittersweet feeling to be his own man and still miss being able to share his accomplishments with his brother.

Hank was also relieved that his father didn't bring up Jess. He had met her briefly a couple of times when Hank had dropped by with her to pick up his surfboard or to change so they could go out, and he had been very friendly to her. Hank was obviously devastated by her sudden departure, and his father must have picked up on the fact that things had changed, but he had the good sense not to press Hank for details about what had happened. He steered the conversation to Hank's studies and life on campus, avoiding the subject of girls and dating altogether. Hank felt like that was one of the most fatherly actions he had done for him in a while. Though he worried that the subject would eventually come up, Hank soon came to realize his father was not going to mention it, and he was grateful not to have to talk about it.

Chapter 36

Mr. DeGaulle had kept his promise to Hank to look into his assault charges. About a month after Hank started at UNCW, he got a call from the district attorney's office, asking him to come down and answer some questions about his arrest. Hank was nervous at first, wondering if the charge had not been dropped after all, but it turned out they were looking into Roxy for filing a false report when she named him as the perpetrator on the night of the bar fight. Hank told the young district attorney what he remembered and explained his relationship with Roxy, making it clear she had repeatedly sought him out. The attorney asked Hank to write out his version of the story and sign it, which Hank did, handing it to him. The attorney thanked Hank for his time and said they would be in touch. Hank walked out, relieved to have the meeting over with and wanting to forget all about it, particularly with his life going in a new direction.

After the interview, Hank didn't hear anything for a couple of months, so he put it out of his mind. Then, just before Thanksgiving break, he got another call from the DA's office. They had been interviewing other witnesses at the bar that night and had received new information. One witness, in particular, had had it in for Rocko after he cheated him out of some money. He ratted Rocko out for the beer bottle assault, telling them Roxy had it all wrong blaming it on that kid and Rocko was the one who actually did it. The DA managed to back up his story with testimony from a waitress who had worked at the bar at that time. She also admitted it was Rocko who had hit Jimmy; she had felt bad that Hank was blamed but had not wanted to lose her job at the time. When they confronted Roxy with this information, she finally admitted she had made it up and was now being charged with filing a false police report, plus other charges.

For Hank, this meant his record would be expunged. He hung up the phone, feeling elated and yet still angry for all the grief Roxy had caused him. She had cost him two years of his life and made people believe he was someone he'd never been, a reputation he was still trying to get past. She had even made him—not to mention Jess—believe he was capable of such violence. The anguish he felt over that time was still raw, recognizing how much time he had lost and the pain he had endured because of Roxy's lie. He was relieved when Mike came back from class so he could tell him what had happened.

"Unbelievable," Mike said, when he heard the whole story. "What a bunch of dirt bags. Man, I'm glad you got away from that."

Hank thought about how Mike had been the one to help him during that time and all he had done to get him back on track. "You know, Mike, I never thanked you for all you did for me back then. I wouldn't have made it without you, man. And all the ways you helped me out since. You are like a brother to me, as much as Rob ever was."

"Yeah, me too, man," Mike said thoughtfully, warmed by the compliment and the comparison. "You're the brother I never had, too."

They decided Hank's news had to be celebrated, so Mike recommended they head down to Dockside for dinner, a restaurant on the Intracoastal with a large deck overlooking the waterway with live music. Saying they just needed a break from studying, they asked Rick and Matt to join them, and the four of them headed down in Hank's Jeep. When they arrived, they found the place was already crowded, being an unusually warm evening right before the Thanksgiving holiday.

"Looks like we're not the only ones who need to blow off some steam," said Rick as he surveyed the deck and saw a number of fellow students.

They managed to find a table, and while the other guys enjoyed a few pitchers of beer, Hank was content to sit back with his seltzer water and just enjoy the camaraderie between them, feeling a part of their group for the first time. He recognized it was mainly due to his isolating himself so much, but his feelings of missing Jess were still with him on a daily basis, and it helped him just to stay focused on getting his work done. Somewhere in the back of his mind he told himself if she ever did come back, he wanted to show her he had done well at college and that everything she had believed about him before had been right. He still hoped that day would come.

After a few hours of music and drinking, it was time to head back. Hank was drunkenly thanked by the other guys all the way home for being the designated driver, a position he welcomed since it not only kept him from having to explain why he didn't drink but also seemed to solidify his place in the group. For the first time, he felt like a college student, and it was a good feeling.

The next day, everyone including Hank headed home for the Thanksgiving holiday. As soon as he got home, Hank told his father about the charges being reversed and his record expunged. To his surprise, his father gave him a hug when he heard the good news, something Hank couldn't remember him doing in a long time.

"I never believed you were capable of doing it, son," was all he said as he held Hank tightly. When he let go, Hank was sure he saw a tear in his eye. His father quickly wiped it away as he turned away from him. To know his father had believed in him all this time was uplifting, and it put his father's perspective of the situation in a whole new light.

After a quiet Thanksgiving dinner together, Hank spent most of the day preparing for his finals. Then they watched a football game and later sat out on the porch while Hank talked about what it was like going to college and how he was starting to feel more like he belonged there. Then he turned in, eager to get an early start on his studying the next day.

Hank knew there was something else he needed to do this weekend, so on Friday morning, he drove up to the DeGaulle residence. He wasn't sure if the family would have company for the holiday, but the house and grounds were oddly quiet when he arrived. He walked up to the large black front door and knocked, waiting for a response.

This time, a maid dressed in uniform opened the door and let him in. Asking his name, she told him to wait in the foyer while she told Mr. DeGaulle he was there. Hank used the time to admire the dark mahogany staircase he had seen last time, noting how it was floating and not supported underneath with beams, as well as the intricate scroll work under the banister. He was so caught up in looking at it that he didn't notice when Mr. DeGaulle walked in.

"Beautiful, isn't it?" he said, noticing where Hank's attention was pointed and interrupting his thoughts. He offered his hand.

"Yes, sir. Very much so," Hank said, shaking it. "I hope this is a convenient time…."

"Of course, let's just go back to my office," he said, leading Hank down the familiar hall and into his study. Hank remembered how he had felt the last time he had been there, and he was relieved this visit had a much different purpose.

When settled, Hank took a moment to thank Mr. DeGaulle for all he had done, both in getting him into college and in talking to the district attorney's office, telling him how they had investigated his case and reversed his charges.

"You have no idea how much it means to me to have my name cleared," Hank said. "And I know I wouldn't be in UNCW without your help. I don't know how to thank you for all you have done for me."

Mr. DeGaulle waved off Hank's words. "All I did was make a few phone calls. If I was able to help, then I was glad to do it. You were a good employee and someone who reminded me of myself at your age. The rest was up to you. How is college going for you?"

"Very well, sir. I am working hard, and I feel I am well prepared for my finals."

"Good news. I didn't doubt you would put everything you had into it. Keep up the good work. And if there is anything else I can help you with, don't hesitate to call. Nobody makes it on their own, Hank. Everyone who has gotten somewhere has done it with the help of others. Understand?"

"I understand, sir," Hank said, realizing he would not be where he was now without the help of Mike and Mr. DeGaulle.

Hank thanked Mr. DeGaulle and got up to leave, but as he reached the doorway, he felt he had to find out what had happened to John. He turned around and asked Mr. DeGaulle if he had heard from him.

Mr. DeGaulle's expression instantly changed, taking on a defeated look. "Mrs. DeGaulle has seen to it that he be put in a rehabilitation facility," he said, grimacing. "We'll see how that goes."

Hank nodded, sorry to have brought up such a sore subject. He thanked him again and left, thinking how strangely things work out.

When Hank returned home, another surprise awaited him. His father said he had received a call from a reporter at the *Star News*, Wilmington's newspaper. Uncertain what it was about, Hank dialed the number his father had written down and the call was answered right away. The male reporter said the newspaper was doing a piece on the reversal of Hank's charges and asked him if he wanted to comment. Hank was taken aback and didn't know what to say. He managed to say he was thankful to the district attorney's office for all their work and was pleased that the truth was finally being told, which seemed to be all the reporter wanted. He said the article would run in the Sunday paper and hung up.

Hank stood there stunned for a minute. He told his father what the call had been about, and then he called Mike to tell him the good news. Mike was equally excited for him. At first, Hank was concerned that other students at UNCW would read the article and find out about his past, but he then realized it no longer mattered.

He had been declared innocent. He no longer had to be ashamed for something he had never done. It was truly over.

Sunday morning, Hank was so excited that he got up earlier than usual. Nothing would be open yet where he could get a copy of the newspaper, so he headed to the beach to do his usual workout of a long run and some calisthenics. The adrenaline he felt from the events of the weekend made him push harder than usual, but not so hard that he didn't enjoy watching the sunrise as he did his run and thought about how it truly was a new day.

When he was done, Hank wasted no time going down the street to the Del Mar coffee shop where he purchased breakfast and a copy of the paper. He eagerly sat down at one of the tables and put aside eating while he anxiously opened the paper to look for the article. He found it quickly on the bottom of the cover of the second section covering local news.

Wrongfully Charged Local Man Has Name Cleared.

It described how he had been convicted of an assault charge due to a false report and that the district attorney's office, after reopening the case, had his conviction overturned when other witnesses came forward declaring his innocence. A mug shot of Roxy accompanied the article, stating how she was being charged for falsifying information. Hank read it twice before he started to eat, absorbing every detail. Seeing the article made him feel vindicated since it announced to the community that he had been innocent all this time. He didn't have the words to describe how relieved he felt that it was finally over, and he sat for a long time letting it sink in.

While walking on campus the next day, Hank passed another student he had known in high school but whom he hadn't talked to at UNCW. As they passed, the other student looked at him and gave him a smile and a thumbs-up. Hank smiled and gave a nod in return, knowing it was about the article. He remembered that gesture all day long, feeling like his life had finally taken a turn for the better.

And yet the one person he needed most to see it probably never would.

Chapter 37

When the first semester grades came out and Hank saw he had made the dean's list, he started to believe he could make it. Here he was, pulling top grades and gaining the respect from his teachers that he remembered seeing Rob receive. He wished his brother could see him now, though he wondered what Rob would have thought about him being at UNCW. Mr. DeGaulle's words about the differences between him and Rob were stuck in Hank's mind, and he wondered if Rob had ever wanted to go to college. It was one of the many questions he would never get to ask him. Rob was becoming part of his past in a way Hank had never thought he would.

When the second semester came around, Hank took a heavier course load, trying to make up for lost time. Even Mike said he was insane taking so many courses, but since Hank didn't drink and didn't have any interest in the party scene, staying in nights to study wasn't a hardship. He had saved enough from working his delivery job the last two years to cover any textbook or other expenses not covered in his scholarship, allowing him just to focus on his schoolwork. He found he really enjoyed learning in general, though it bothered him that he couldn't decide what he wanted to major in.

He wasn't that interested in science, even if he was fairly good in math. He didn't have an interest in computer programming, the arts, or education. As a matter of elimination, he finally decided he would work toward earning a business degree, which he felt would be the most practical for finding a job after college.

One of the history classes he took that semester was on the Civil War. The teacher had an interest in how the Civil War had specifically affected Wilmington and offered extra credit to anyone who could write a paper providing greater insight into the subject. Hank already knew a lot about Wilmington's history. He decided to drive downtown to the historic district to see some of the houses built during that period to think about a topic for his paper. He had walked down a couple of streets when he came across the house he and Jess had loved, the white-columned home set back with the large front lawn. He remembered how after she had talked about living in such a house, he had thought of what it would be like for them to be married and live there with their own kids. He remembered how much he had wanted to make that a reality, imagining the two of them fixing it up, and at the end of the day, sitting on the porch together, watching the kids play in the lawn as neighbors walked by.

Hank froze. Suddenly, he knew exactly what he wanted to do with his life.

He went home and started researching firms in the area that built and restored houses, focusing on the ones whose specialty were older and historic homes. It didn't take long to find out which one was the most reputable in the area. MacMillan Home Builders kept coming up as winning a number of major awards for its innovative designs and the superior quality of its craftsmanship. Hank wasted no time. He called Mr. DeGaulle, told him he wanted a job at the company, and asked if he knew anyone he could talk to. It turned out that Mr. DeGaulle played golf with Wayland MacMillan, so with one phone call, Hank had a job on Saturdays on one of the restoration crews.

Hank knew little about house construction other than what he had learned from his father, but he did like using his hands, and the thought of being able to build a home appealed to him. At first, the other workers dismissed him as another college student making some extra bucks on the side. He was given the grunt work of hauling items around, handing over tools, and cleaning up. But soon it was obvious Hank was interested in the work they were doing from all the questions he asked. When he wasn't studying, he found books at the library on carpentry and learned what he could from watching online videos. He was always on time for work, and he took care with even the smallest tasks. Before long, he had earned the respect of his supervisor and the other workers as someone dedicated, reliable, and deserving of more responsibility.

Mike had breathed a sigh of relief when Hank first told him about wanting to renovate houses. He saw how Jess's leaving had devastated Hank, and he was still concerned about him. He had asked a few times early on if Hank had heard from Jess, but he had stopped asking when he saw how much it hurt Hank to talk about it. Though Hank was functioning on the outside, Mike knew him well enough to see he was still in pain, and he wasn't sure how to help him other than to offer to meet up with him at mealtimes or invite him out with him and the other guys, which Hank turned down more often than he accepted. There was a moment of celebration when the charges were reversed and the newspaper article came out, but shortly after, Mike had noticed Hank withdrawing again into his studies. He was glad to see his friend find a new interest after all these months of being so stoic, and he thought such a career was a good fit for him. He knew it wasn't good for Hank to keep his feelings inside like he did, but what could he do? Hank wasn't drinking or doing anything harmful to himself. Mike knew he just had to wait until Hank worked through it.

Once Hank added working to his schoolwork, Mike rarely saw him. Mostly, they would get together to surf a couple of times a week in the mornings, or Mike would join Hank in a workout session to keep tabs on him.

"Man, I wish I had your motivation," Mike said after hearing some of Hank's plans for the summer to work on houses. He had joined Hank on one of his Sunday runs at the beach, and though he hated to admit it, he was having a little trouble keeping up because his friend had gotten into such good shape. "And the freedom to choose what you want to do."

"Don't you want to go into your father's business?" Hank asked. He had always envied how Mike's life was already planned out, but he had never asked him if that was really what he wanted to do.

Mike thought for a moment. "Yeah, I'm starting to think I do. I mean, it may not be what I would have chosen on my own, but I can see how I can make really good money. And I see my dad helping people find their homes, which I like. I think I would be good at it."

"Yeah, I could see that," Hank said. "You're good with talking to people and helping them out."

They ran together in silence for a bit until they came back to where they had dropped their things on the beach.

"Water," was all Mike said, heading up to his things to pull a water bottle out of his backpack and take a long sip. He was breathless but didn't want to admit to Hank that the run had been harder than he had thought it would be, so he sat down in the sand to show he was done.

Hank, who had barely broken a sweat, followed, taking a sip of his own water and then sitting on the sand next to him. They looked out over the ocean, which was a steely gray this time of year. It was March and a little warmer than usual for the season with temperatures in the seventies, but in the sun, it could feel much hotter.

"So with spring break coming up, do you have any plans?" Mike asked.

"Just work," Hank said, not thinking much of it. "You?"

"I may go down to Florida with some of the guys. They're talking about driving down to Orlando." He waited to see Hank's reaction since Hank had told him that was where Jess had gone.

Hank was silent, then took a sip of water. "Sounds like fun," he said, but did not offer anything more.

"I was wondering if you wanted to come. Maybe drop in on an old friend?"

Hank knew what Mike was offering. A chance to go down and find Jess if he wanted. He had thought about driving down so many times, about texting her to tell her about the article, or just to wish her a Merry Christmas, but each time he came to the same conclusion: She didn't want to talk to him. There was no choice but to respect her wishes. If she was this resolute to avoid him, he couldn't see how showing up at her doorstep would make things any better. In fact, doing so would likely make it worse because if she were to reject him then, he would know it was over. At least while he was in limbo, there was a chance she might change her mind and contact him again.

"Thanks, man, but I already signed up to work. You know how it is. Thanks for thinking of me, though," Hank said. He knew Mike just wanted to help him out, but this was his pain to get over. He looked at his friend and smiled. "You're a good friend, Mike," he said, trying to convey in those simple words how much he appreciated what he was trying to do for him.

"You, too, man," Mike said with a smile back, but still feeling the run. He lay down on the sand. "Jesus, you do this every Sunday? How the hell do you do it?"

Chapter 38

Hank finished off his second semester on the dean's list again, and he enrolled for a couple of summer courses that he could take while working at his construction job. He had been taken on as an apprentice by a master carpenter, a man named Tim Brenner who had worked with the company for more than twenty years, which meant he would spend the days assisting Tim while learning different building skills. Tim was a tall, thin, older man with white hair and a quiet manner who would tell Hank about how he had started his apprenticeship at age fifteen and shared some of his own learning mistakes. For instance, he had once fallen three stories off of a scaffolding and been in a coma for five days. He was very explicit that construction could be a very dangerous job and safety was paramount, having almost died three times on the job himself. Tim reminded Hank of his father, as he could see his father being just like Tim if he'd continued working in home construction. Between Hank's eagerness to learn and Tim's methodical and patient approach, they got along well, and Hank began picking up new techniques.

For the summer, Hank moved back home, which gave him more time to talk to his father about the jobs he was working on. His father was more than happy to share his own work stories, something he had never done before. Hank was impressed with how much his father knew about the work he was doing, forgetting that this was his trade before he became a handyman. It became their conversation topic at dinner, where Hank would tell his father what he and Tim had worked on that day; then he would listen to his father's own thoughts about how he would approach certain jobs.

When summer classes ended, Hank continued working, but now he had time to turn his focus to another project he had been thinking about before the fall semester began. Their home had been neglected for a number of years, and he started to get ideas about how he could fix it up. One night, he walked through some ideas with his father, who was equally enthusiastic about fixing the front porch and doing some other repairs around the house. Together, they planned out which project they wanted to start on first, and then the next Saturday, Hank picked up the supplies they needed.

They did the majority of the work on the weekends, completing it all in record time. When they were done, Hank was proud of what they had accomplished. While the changes were minor, they gave the house a fresher look just by putting in a new white railing, repairing a number of rotted boards on the porch, replacing some of the shutters, and adding a new coat of paint to the outside of the house. Inside, they laid a wooden floor in the living room, which was easier than Hank thought it would be, and they gave that room a fresh coat of paint as well. When they were done, it felt like a different house. Hank was already eyeing what other changes he could make, but with school starting again soon, those projects would have to wait.

Still, there was one final touch Hank knew he had to make. He told his father to stay inside while he worked on it, wanting to surprise him. The last Saturday before school began, he picked out some plants at a nearby nursery and then planted a garden out front. It took almost the entire weekend to remove the old, dried-out bushes and prepare the dirt properly to plant new ones, then put in a border of pavers marking off the garden area, but when Hank was done, the difference was astounding. What had been a sad little house that needed work now looked bright and cheery.

When Hank's father came out and saw what his son had done, tears formed in his eyes. "Just like your mother's garden," he said, remembering.

Hank nodded, feeling the same way. For the first time in a long time, it felt like home.

Hank returned to UNCW ready for his second year of college. For their senior year, Mike and the guys had rented a small place near campus and they asked Hank to come live with them again. Hank was glad to be included, and he could pay for rent with his construction earnings, so he agreed to join them. He had never gotten very close to Rick and Matt while they lived on campus due to the amount of studying he did and his work schedule, but they were good guys and being off campus meant interacting a bit more since they had to coordinate such items as shopping for food and paying bills. As Hank began to feel more comfortable with what he was doing, he started to warm up a little to them, occasionally watching a game or eating dinner with the group. Rick and Matt were big gamers, so many Friday nights were spent watching them duel it out on the latest video game. Even though he didn't enjoy playing such games himself, these evenings allowed Hank some down time and helped him feel a part of the group.

Through their encouragement, Hank also started thinking about dating again, though he was in no hurry to start. It had been over a year since Jess had left with no word, and though he still thought of her almost every day, he was starting to believe that she might never be back. Though he still bore a faint hope she still might someday return, he knew the possibility of that happening at this point was small and he had to move on.

The problem was he wasn't interested enough in any other girl to ask her out. A number of female students had made it clear they saw Hank as an attractive prospect since he did well in school and worked out, but most of those girls held no interest for him. He didn't like the idea of dating someone in his classes in case things didn't work out. And he could tell for a few of them, he was just a challenge they wanted to conquer but they had no real interest in him. He was particularly turned off by the forwardness of some of these girls who made it clear they just wanted to have sex with no attachment—an offer he had no interest in as it seemed so impersonal. When he turned down one girl in particular, she actually got angry and told him how full of himself he was. That only made him retreat further from the idea of dating, uncertain how to navigate a world where he had suddenly become so sought-after.

It took a while, but eventually he started to find a few girls he was attracted to and thought he might like to get to know better. A sophomore named Catherine had been in his English class last year and loaned him her notes once when he had missed a class. She was pretty, had dark hair like Jess, and was also athletic, playing on the school tennis team, but that's where the similarities ended. Hank took her out a few times, but then stopped calling her, finding her immature since she was more concerned about her social life than what she was studying in college. He tried dating another girl he met in the gym, a tall girl named Annie who played basketball and was a nursing major. She had curly red hair and a bit of an attitude to go with it, a reminder of Jess's no-nonsense manner, but he found her too brusque after an evening out. A couple of more girls followed, but none he saw more than a handful of times, getting bored quickly and being more concerned about taking time away from his studies.

Hank knew what the problem was. He shouldn't compare them to Jess, but in the end, he always did. None of them ever came close to her. He didn't have the interest or energy to plan the type of outings he had done for her, so the dates were rather ordinary and unimaginative. He never discussed his past, saying only that he had lost his brother shortly after high school ended and worked some odd jobs before deciding to go to college, which seemed to be enough to explain his late start but not enough for the girls that really wanted to know him. One of them had asked him to teach her surfing when she found out he went regularly, but Hank no longer wanted to share that part of his life. That was his time, spent only with Mike. He didn't say no, just put it off, and eventually the relationship ended, making it a moot point.

After a while, he just had to admit to himself that dating was more trouble than it was worth. He preferred the orderliness of keeping his life focused on work and school. Trying to date only got in the way of what he saw as important. He wasn't as happy as he had been with Jess, but he felt content, having a direction and a few friends to hang out with when he had the free time.

For now, that was all he really needed.

Chapter 39

When Mike and the guys graduated in May, Mike and Hank found a new apartment together, staying close to the university so Hank could walk to classes. That summer while Mike went to work full-time at his father's business, Hank spent his time much as he had the previous year, taking additional classes and working with Tim at construction sites. Tim had been slowly allowing Hank to take over some of the easier tasks, impressed with his ability to learn quickly. At the start of the summer, he gave him his first job to build out a wall, which consisted of laying out the pieces on the floor before nailing them up and then standing the wall in place. Hank did such a good job his first time that even Tim was impressed, stating that he was well suited for this job, a compliment that had Hank smiling for the rest of the week since Tim didn't hand them out often.

After that, Tim started showing Hank how to do more complicated tasks and began trusting him with doing some of the work on his own. Hank worked hard, making sure his work was well done, even if it meant he had to do it more than once, staying late if necessary, without taking overtime. Weekends he often spent at home with his father so they could work on house projects together and he could have a quiet place to study, leaving the apartment to Mike to conduct his own social activities.

When Hank returned to UNCW in the fall, he again loaded up on his classes. He had gotten far enough ahead that he could finish up his degree that year if he continued to push ahead, and so he did, enjoying his classes even more because they were specifically related to what he was planning to do when he graduated. He knew he needed a lot more experience to become a master carpenter, but once he felt he had sufficient knowledge, he wanted to open up his own construction business. He had learned from Mr. DeGaulle that owning your own business could be very profitable, and he also liked the idea of being in control of a job, both in terms of delivering quality workmanship and in deciding who he had to work with. Some of the supervisors at MacMillan had been poor at managing people, which only made what was already technical work more difficult. Hank felt he could do a better job if he were in charge. He decided to get his Bachelor of Science in Business Development to learn about marketing and management so when he was able to open his own shop, he would be ready.

The schedule he had set up made it a hard year, but it went by quickly. He was constantly busy, getting through by remembering how far he had come and motivated by the challenge to get it done. And at the end of that year, he had something he never dreamed he would have, a college degree with honors. His father and Tim came to his graduation ceremony, and he could hear them, together with Mike and a few other friends, cheer loudly as he walked across the stage to get his diploma. Afterward, there was picture taking and congratulations from a number of his fellow students, more so than Hank would have thought, and then a special dinner at Oceanside to celebrate. While they were there, Mr. DeGaulle dropped by to congratulate him personally, telling him what a fine thing he had accomplished. That day, Hank looked around him and felt grateful for all the people who had gotten him there, thanking the ones he could for the support they had provided, knowing that without them all, he never would have made it.

It was only after dinner was done and he had stepped out of the restaurant into the parking lot that he thought of the one other person who should have been there.

If only Jess could see he had done it.

After graduation, Hank wasted no time going to work full time with Tim. For the next three years, they worked side by side on several projects with Hank advancing to more difficult tasks as his skills improved. He found he had a knack for figuring out the best way to stick build a home, and he even did the majority of the work on a free-floating staircase he and Tim had to rebuild after termites had destroyed the original. He could see that a window ledge or ceiling beam was out of alignment just by looking at it, even if it was only off by 1/8 of an inch. At one point, Hank asked Tim why he didn't start his own business. Tim replied that he had thought of it, but he didn't care for all the administrative work required. He loved doing the work itself, but he didn't want the hassle of running a business. Hank nodded in agreement, understanding his concerns, but after dealing with poor supervisors, he thought he could do a better job of it.

Hank continued to live with Mike after graduating, and the arrangement worked well. They would surf together or hang out when they could coordinate their schedules, only holding off when either of them had to work or when Mike was involved with a new girlfriend. Mike always managed to find a fair share of pretty girls to date, but his relationships never lasted more than a few months. Often, the girls would stay over, which Hank didn't mind since he would spend weekends at his father's house.

However, after two years of a revolving door of girlfriends, Hank noticed a difference when Mike started dating Lila, the daughter of one of his clients. Mike would go out with her and then come home and hang out with Hank if he was still up, which was unusual since Mike was known to bring his girlfriends home. After a couple of months of dating, Mike invited Hank to join them for dinner one night so he could meet her. Hank was struck by how different she was from Mike's other girlfriends. She was a slight woman with blond hair that came down to her shoulders in a straight bob with bangs, and she had delicate features that made her look very feminine. While her manners were precise, she was also warm and engaging, drawing you in with her subtle Southern accent. She quickly engaged Hank in talk about the historic homes around Wilmington, fascinated with his knowledge about such matters and wanting to hear everything he had to say about them. It was quite a pleasant evening, and Hank could see why Mike would be charmed by her. When Hank would glance over at Mike, he could see him watching her admiringly, making it clear he was quite infatuated.

As Mike continued to date Lila, Hank noticed some other changes in his friend. For instance, Mike started drinking less with his college friends and working out more with Hank, getting into a more regimented schedule. He was doing well at work and making good money, which he started to invest in the stock market, spending his spare time researching companies and discussing his purchases with Hank. Most noticeably, one day Hank realized that Lila had never come over to spend the night, and Mike had never had a night when he didn't come home since dating her. When he asked Mike what was up, he just smiled knowingly and said, "Hey, I really like this girl." Hank realized Mike was in love at that point, and he wasn't surprised when, within a year, Mike was ready to propose. Mike showed Hank the ring he had picked out and told him of his plans to ask Lila on a walk along the Riverwalk downtown after dinner at Elijah's, a romantic restaurant that overlooked the Cape Fear River. Hank couldn't be happier for his friend, congratulating him on finding such a wonderful woman to marry.

Still, it was a bittersweet moment for Hank since he still had not dated anyone seriously since Jess, and the idea of Mike getting married only reminded him of how much he missed her. When he did think about dating, the issue was how to meet women. He rarely met them at work, and he had yet to start participating in any community organizations that were likely to offer such opportunities. He knew of some friends who had tried online dating, but the whole idea was too unappealing to him. He remembered the charge he had felt the first time he met Jess and knew how important it was he meet someone face-to-face to determine if he was attracted to her. But now with Mike moving on, he needed to find ways to develop his social life, and yes, hopefully find someone to share his life with like Mike had.

It had been five years since Jess had left. Five years of the distant thought in the back of his mind if she would ever come back. But he couldn't wait any longer. It was time to let her go or he would never be able to let someone else in. He already resolved himself to believing he would never love someone again like he'd loved her, but that didn't mean he couldn't find someone with whom he could build a life. He just didn't know who that could be.

Chapter 40

After three years of working for the MacMillan company, Hank decided he was ready to go out on his own. He mentioned his plan to Mr. DeGaulle during one of their talks. He had told Hank to come talk to him when Hank was ready because he might have an interest in working with him. Hank researched what he needed to do get started. He first took an exam to get licensed. While waiting for the test results and board approval, he set out to figure out all the other various conditions he needed to meet, such as setting up liability insurance, registering his business, getting a tax ID, and familiarizing himself with the regulations involved with the hiring of employees. He also knew he needed to learn a number of computer programs that would allow him to manage inventory, suppliers, and contractors, and to do his accounting. It was a dizzying amount of work, but he tackled each item one by one, marking them off his list as he completed them.

When Hank was done, he still had two key elements to figure out: how to finance the company, since the Board of Regulations was stringent on meeting certain financial qualifications, and how to start getting jobs. When his license approval came through, he set up a meeting with Mr. DeGaulle at his house, hoping he could offer some assistance in tackling these next two steps.

Hank was initially hesitant to approach Mr. DeGaulle. About six months ago, he had read in the paper that John had hit a tree while driving and died. After being sent to rehab, John had moved to Raleigh to attend college, though Hank had heard he was still drinking. There may have been more visits to rehab, but Hank didn't like to listen to gossip and knew better than to ask Mr. DeGaulle after the first time he had done so.

When Hank told Mike about John's passing, he expressed out loud exactly what Hank was thinking. "Well, I guess the drinking finally did him in." As Mike scanned the article, he added, "It happened late on a Saturday night. What does that tell you? At least he didn't take anyone down with him."

Though Hank did not care for John, he did empathize with the loss Mr. DeGaulle must feel at losing his only son. He remembered how Mr. DeGaulle had taken responsibility for John's misconduct and wanted to help his son be a better man. Now that could never happen. Mr. DeGaulle had done so much for Hank, he felt he owed it to Mr. DeGaulle to go to the funeral and offer his condolences. His father came with him, as a parent who knew the depth of such a loss. When they arrived, Hank was glad they attended since the only other people in attendance were a handful of curious former high school classmates and some business colleagues of Mr. DeGaulle. It was quite in contrast to the attendance at Rob's funeral, where the pews had been filled with people who would truly miss him.

Hank had not seen Mr. DeGaulle since the funeral, so he was uncertain whether this was a good time to approach him. However, when he called, Mr. DeGaulle said he would be pleased to meet with him and talk about his business plans.

As it turned out, Mr. DeGaulle was very interested in financing Hank. Mr. DeGaulle had made his money finding good investment opportunities and he believed Hank would work hard to run a successful business. They agreed to set up a partnership whereby Hank would be the majority owner and Mr. DeGaulle would be given part-ownership in exchange for providing financial backing. When they talked about how to start getting business, Mr. DeGaulle offered some ideas on how Hank could market his services, and he promised to spread the word around to see if he could generate any interest among some of his friends.

When the meeting was over, Hank stood up to shake Mr. DeGaulle's hand.

"Thanks, Mr. DeGaulle. You have been so helpful to me in so many ways. I really believe I can make this work."

"I wouldn't be backing you if I didn't believe in you, Henry. Is it all right if I call you Henry? I think it's better suited to a business owner. Though now that we are going into business together, I believe it's also time you start calling me Richard."

"Certainly...Richard," Hank said, feeling a bit awkward in saying it but also realizing he had passed another milestone. As Hank walked out through the large black door and felt the warm sun on his face, he was excited for what the future held.

It didn't matter that he had no idea how to start a business. He just knew he would do everything he could to make it work.

Getting his first client was easier than Hank thought it would be.

Hank gave his two-weeks' notice to MacMillan the day after his talk with Mr. DeGaulle. When he told Tim of his plans, Tim said he would miss him, but wished him the best. Then he mentioned that he might know of a few smaller jobs Hank might be able to do, jobs too small for a company like MacMillan but which would be just right for someone starting out. Tim provided him the contact information for two families who needed work on their homes and said he would be a personal reference for him. One was a job building a deck, and the other was building some bookshelves, both of which Hank was already familiar. Hank contacted and met with each family to provide an estimate for the work. Based on Tim's recommendation and Hank's pricing, both families hired him. Hank was officially in business, and even though he was still working for MacMillan for another week, Hank wasted no time in getting started that weekend.

As Mike was getting married, the timing was right for Hank to move back home to save money while starting his new business. He planned to find someone to work with him on these and other jobs when his father offered to help out. Hank wasn't sure how he felt about his father working for him, but they ended up making a good team. His father had no qualms about Hank being in charge of the work, and his experience and knowledge proved more than helpful. When these two jobs were completed, both families were very satisfied with the work and said they would recommend Hank to their friends. Within a week, Hank was called two more times to give estimates, one of which again hired him. The work came in like that in pieces, with some weeks being busy and others spent more on how to grow the business. Hank worked nights and weekends with little rest, and had several moments of uncertainty when he had to figure out what to do next, but he had come too far not to keep pushing forward.

And he had done it. He had started his own business, and with his attention to detail and quality of work, jobs were slowly coming in. Now when he went for a run on the beach, his thoughts were no longer about the anger or hurt he had felt in his past or uncertainty about his present, but how excited he was for his future and what he hoped would happen next.

Anything was possible.

Chapter 41

Richard DeGaulle encouraged Hank to get involved in community events as a way of networking and growing their business. He invited Hank to an annual event held each spring, a members-only formal gala at Thalian Hall, Wilmington's performing arts center. Hank knew such an invitation was a favor and he should go, but he had a lot of concerns about attending. He had never attended a black-tie event before, so he thought through what he needed to do to prepare, such as renting a tuxedo and getting a haircut. He even made sure his nails were clean, knowing all the work he did with his hands, and wanting to look as presentable as possible.

Preparing his appearance was easy enough, but his real apprehension was how to act. He was fairly certain he would not know anyone there other than his benefactor, and he didn't want to disappoint Richard by not fitting in. Richard made it clear this event was an opportunity for Hank to start selling himself to acquire more work for their business, but selling himself was not one of Hank's strong suits. His strengths were in his knowledge and the quality of his work. When he met with a potential customer, he relied on past references to state why he was the one they should hire. He didn't know how to convey his skills in this type of setting without sounding like he was boasting. He tried to think of things to say about the work he had done that he felt showed confidence and would hopefully entice someone to contact him later, but he couldn't quite figure out what that should be.

Having lived in Wilmington, Hank had known about Thalian Hall all his life, yet he had never been inside the historic building. He did some quick research online before heading out to the event, discovering it was one of the oldest operating theaters in the country, a fact he had been unaware of until now. But even more interesting was that the building retained much of its original design, despite having survived the Civil War, multiple hurricanes, and a number of other events that had befallen the city since the hall was built in the 1850s. Hank admired how the stucco building was able to mix a combination of restrained Classical Revival elements with features of Late Victorian design, and he thought it would be interesting to see some of those design elements up close. By concentrating on seeing the historic aspects of the building, he hoped to make himself more relaxed and enthusiastic about attending the gala.

That focus didn't alleviate his nervousness the night of the event, however. When Hank arrived at the large white building with its looming bay windows and imposing Corinthian columns lining the front, he hesitated. Watching the other event-goers enter the building, he felt out of place and started having second thoughts about going in, reconsidering whether this was such a good idea after all. The last thing he wanted to do was make a fool of himself, and this was the right place for that to happen. He could feel himself backing away from the building when he heard it again.

Go inside.

It had been some time since the voice had come to him, and that it came at this moment when his decision could affect his business was not lost on him. Without thinking any further, he followed its directive and quickly made his way up the stairs and into the building, determined not to let Richard down.

Even with all his planning, Hank was unprepared for the grandeur inside. While the lobby was what he would expect, ushers instantly guided him up the large staircase to the second-floor ballroom where the event was being held. The ballroom was spectacular, with a large open space, a ceiling two stories high, and tall arched windows on three sides, giving various views of the river and city. White decorative patterns were molded across the walls, interspersed with elaborate antique chandeliers that hung gracefully from the ceiling. Hank was in awe of the craftsmanship it took to create such a space, focusing on the architecture to ground himself before he turned his attention to the event itself.

The festivities themselves were well underway. A swing band was set up at the end of the room, and people were elaborately dressed, holding drinks, and in high spirits. Hank made his way to the bar where he ordered a seltzer water with lime to give himself something to hold. Then he stood to the side, taking in the scene before him of a group of women dressed in ball gowns adorned with expensive jewelry and men who very much looked like they ran the town, standing tall in what he was sure were not rented tuxedos. Hank had no idea how to start a conversation in such a setting, and he was about to put his drink down and make his exit when Richard came up to him followed by a very attractive young woman whom Hank had never seen before.

"Glad you could make it, Henry," Richard said, shaking his hand and patting his back.

"Thank you, sir. I appreciate the invitation," Hank said, uncertain how else to respond.

"This is Alanna Moore," Richard said, introducing the young woman at his side. "She worked with the board to put this event together." Hank reached out his hand to Alanna and looked into her green eyes, noticing they had flecks of gold. Hank normally didn't notice someone's eye color, but she had such warm and beautiful eyes they were hard to miss. She had a very pretty face, set off by the blond hair she wore in a loose bun at the nape of her neck. She looked elegant in a fitting rose gold dress with beading that clung to her slim figure and then flowed out toward the bottom, a look both understated and perfectly suited for such an event. She was striking in a classical way, and Hank was instantly attracted to her, though he had no doubt she was well out of his league.

"Very nice to meet you, Alanna," Hank said, gently shaking her hand.

"You as well," she said with a demure voice that had a hint of drawl. "I hear from Mr. DeGaulle that we are to expect great things from you."

"Well, hopefully you will find that to be true," Hank replied, unsure how to handle the compliment.

"Of course it is," Richard said. "I've asked Alanna to introduce you to a few folks tonight since she's familiar with most of the people here. I think they will take more kindly to having you be introduced by a beautiful young woman than an old man like me," he said with a smile at Alanna.

"Oh, Mr. DeGaulle, you know that's not true," Alanna said with a laugh, "but I am more than happy to help out a family friend by introducing Henry around. Don't you worry about him while I'm here." She linked her arm into Hank's and started to lead him over to a group located on the other side of the bar.

"Let's go introduce you to the esteemed citizens of Wilmington," Alanna said conspiratorially in a hushed tone, seeming to sense Hank's anxiousness and trying to ease it with her smile, "and let them know you are the answer to their restoration prayers."

Hank wasn't sure if she was kidding, but he followed along as Alanna introduced him to several businessmen and their wives as one of the innovative new builders in town whom Mr. DeGaulle had invited to the event. This seemed a sufficient introduction for everyone to greet Hank in a friendly manner and ask about his work. After doing it a couple of times, Hank started to pick up on what to say and to feel more comfortable about conversing with some of the more receptive attendees, even handing out a few business cards to people who showed more than a casual interest or talked about what work their houses needed. Alanna stayed by his side the entire night, holding onto his arm as she led him from one group to another, which Hank found he did not mind the least bit. She had an engaging manner that seemed to draw people in and made the mood lighter.

As the evening started to wind down, Hank realized the event had not been nearly as awkward as he had expected and he had actually enjoyed himself. When it was time to head out, he turned to Alanna, grateful for all she had done.

"I don't know how to thank you for making this such a pleasant evening for me," he said sincerely, looking into those green-gold eyes that sparkled, noticing once again how pretty she was, but feeling fairly certain that now that her duties were done, he wouldn't see her again.

"I do," she said with a mischievous smile. "You're taking me to dinner tomorrow night." She handed him a card with her number and address on it. "You can pick me up at 7 p.m. Good night, Henry Atwater. It was quite a pleasure meeting you." Then she turned and faded into the crowd that was making its way out the door before he could reply.

When Hank returned home that night, his dad asked him how the event had gone, knowing Hank's nervousness about attending.

"Not at all what I expected," was all Hank said, smiling but not mentioning Alanna or the date he had planned for the next night.

Chapter 42

Getting ready to go out the next night was even harder than preparing for the gala. Not knowing where they were going and knowing Alanna came from money, Hank wanted to dress appropriately, but he wasn't sure if anything he owned would be suitable. His wardrobe was woefully outdated. The last time he had bought a new pair of dress khakis and a button-down shirt was for his graduation. He was lucky they'd been barely used since then and still fit. He added a jacket, but ditched the idea of a tie as too formal. He made a mental note that he needed to go shopping as he looked himself over in the mirror, hoping he had made the right choice.

The next issue was what car to drive. He had bought a truck that he only used for work purposes, which he knew he couldn't show up in, and though he had managed to keep his Jeep in good repair all these years, that wouldn't work either. He decided to call Mike to ask if he could borrow his car for the evening. Mike had bought a BMW sedan that he used to take clients to see houses. When Hank explained he needed it to take Alanna out to dinner, Mike was floored.

"Alanna *Moore?*" he asked. "As in Councilman Moore's daughter? How on earth did you score that?"

"Thanks, Mike; now I'll never be able to go through with it," Hank said, only half-kidding. He still wasn't quite sure how he had landed it either. And now that he knew her father was a councilman, it only increased his nervousness. He explained how the previous evening Alanna had shown him around at the gala and then asked him to take her out.

"Well, she seems to have good taste. I'm liking her already," said Mike, happy to hear his friend was going out on a date. "Come by on your way over and I'll give you the keys."

Hank left early to pick up Mike's car, then headed downtown to pick up Alanna. He had looked up her address earlier in the day to make sure he knew where to go. It was on Front Street in the historic district, a part of the downtown area he knew well, having spent hours admiring the homes there. When he got there, he immediately recognized the house, its size and beauty being very impressive. A white neoclassic revival style house, it had a Queen Anne porch sporting Doric columns with giant ferns hanging between them. The property was surrounded by an elaborately scrolled black, wrought-iron fence with a gate he walked through that led to the front walk. On either side of the house were spectacular magnolia trees, and gardens of tropical fauna were placed strategically around the yard to give it a homey Southern feel. Once again, Hank felt out of place, but he pushed down the feeling, reminding himself he was here by her invitation.

Hank rang the doorbell at exactly 7 p.m., not wanting to be early in case Alanna wasn't ready and most certainly not late. She opened the door right away as if she were standing there waiting for him.

"Well, hello there, Henry. So good to see you again," she said, her voice warm and inviting and those green eyes smiling right at him. She was wearing a white sundress printed with pink and red roses and ruffled trim; it was very feminine while outlining her figure, and tonight her straight blond hair lay loose around her shoulders. Again, Hank was struck by how pretty she was, looking so elegant and yet casual. But looking at her, Hank wondered if he had overdressed.

"I'll just grab my purse and we can go," she said, turning behind her to take her purse off the table in the foyer. Hank stood in the doorway, getting a quick glimpse of a curved oak staircase that elegantly ran up one side of the round foyer entrance. An antique walnut table sat in the middle of the entrance area that looked to be of French design. Hank could tell at a glance that the banister was handmade and the large white long-stemmed flowers in a vase on the center of the table were fresh.

Alanna stepped out onto the porch and closed the door behind her. "My, but you do look handsome," she said, touching his collar. "Still, it's a little warm for a jacket tonight, and I was hoping we could eat outside. Would you be all right with removing it for dinner?"

Hank didn't have to be asked twice, and he appreciated the way she had asked so as not to embarrass him. Now he was glad he hadn't worn the tie. "Of course," he said, offering his arm and walking her to the car. "You look quite nice yourself." He was trying to return her compliment, but between seeing how she was dressed and getting a glimpse of her house's grandeur, he was a bit overwhelmed. *Better to just keep quiet unless you know what to say*, he told himself. He opened her car door and helped her in, taking notice of the dress's crisscross strap over her bare back. Once she was settled, he wasted no time taking off the warm jacket, folding it over, and laying it in the backseat before getting into the driver's seat.

"Any idea where you might like to go?" he asked, starting the engine and then turning to her.

"I was hoping we could go out by the beach to the Bluewater Grill. They have such a nice view of the sunset over the Intracoastal, and on Sunday nights, they have a jazz band. How does that sound to you?" she asked with a dazzling smile.

"That sounds great," he said, smiling back, glad they were going somewhere familiar. The Bluewater Grill was a large two-story restaurant situated right on the water with a large area for open-air seating downstairs stretching the length of the building. He had gone a number of times with Mike and Lila to enjoy the view of the boats docked outside of the blue-roofed building, as many locals liked to do.

Hank headed out to the restaurant as Alanna started talking about the evening before. They had been so busy socializing that this was the first time he had actually gotten to converse with her. On the way over, she told him how well she felt he had done in meeting so many new people, and she told him some background on a couple of people they had met, such as one couple who was getting a divorce, and how the DeGaulles had been friends with her family since she could remember. Hank briefly thought about how that meant she knew John, but then he thought better about asking her about him.

When they got to the restaurant, they were placed at a waterside table with a clear view of the evening sky, the water below serene and gently lapping the dock. Hank listened as Alanna told him how she had graduated from Duke University a year ago and gone to work at Thalian Hall part-time helping to train the docents and manage the volunteers, as well as help with events like the gala. She also volunteered with the Wilmington Historical Foundation, doing research on historic properties or helping out with the events they put on to raise funds. She encouraged Hank to look into getting involved with the historical organization since they recommended contractors they had worked with on their website. If he volunteered on some of their restoration projects and they recognized the quality of his work, they might add him to the list. This lined up with the advice Hank kept getting from Richard to get involved in the community, and he liked that he now had a concrete suggestion he could look into.

It didn't take Hank long to realize he liked listening to Alanna talk. Their mutual love of Wilmington was an instant connection between them, and he listened intently to her thoughts on how Wilmington could better itself, amazed at her in-depth knowledge of the area's history and how passionate she was about maintaining its character and traditions. She had earned her degree in history, and through her own efforts, she was well-versed in Wilmington's past, just like Hank. She came across as more mature than her twenty-three years would suggest. With a full view of the sun setting across the waterway and the sound of soft jazz playing in the background, they talked for hours about the town and its development over the years, plus where they thought it would go in the future if the rate of development that had started in the last decade continued and certain safeguards were not put in place. With Alanna's easygoing manner and soft drawl, Hank lost all sense of nervousness before they had even reached the restaurant, settling in to their conversation and feeling very much a kinship with her. He hadn't enjoyed talking like this with another woman since Jess, but he quickly put her out of his mind, not wanting to taint the connection he was having with Alanna.

They closed the restaurant, talking the night away, and Hank felt completely at ease with her until they pulled up to her house so he could drop her off. Suddenly, he wasn't sure what to do. Would it be too forward to kiss her? He had thought about it several times tonight, but pushed away the thought every time it came up. He didn't know the rules of dating a woman like Alanna, and he didn't want to blow it the first night out.

Hank jumped out of the car as soon as he parked and went around to open her car door and help her out.

"Now that is what I call a magnificent evening. Much better than having to make conversation with friends of my parents at a society event," she said in a teasing tone, squeezing Hank's arm as he walked her to her front door. When they reached the top step of the porch, she turned to face him. "Do you want to see me again?" she asked bluntly, her eyes sparkling at him invitingly. Hank felt her stare right through him as if she could see everything he was thinking.

"Yes. Absolutely," he said, not hesitating, wondering if she wanted him to kiss her goodnight as much as he wanted to.

"Good," she said, obviously pleased before she turned around, opened her front door and then turned back to look at him once more. "I'll be waiting to hear from you, Henry Atwater," she said softly with a tender look as she quietly closed the door.

Hank smiled all the way home, thinking it really had been a magnificent evening.

Chapter 43

On Monday morning, problems started arising at work before Hank had even drank his coffee. He got a call from his father, who was on site at a project reconstructing a porch in the downtown area, saying the three workers he had hired had not shown up. It turned out they had been offered more money to work on another job and bailed on him. Hank told his father to hire some new workers, paying the additional salary if needed because he wanted that project completed on time, and he would be down to help him out shortly. It was the only project he had gotten in the last two weeks, and he was starting to worry when the next job might come in.

His concern was soon allayed by a call from a Mr. Anderson, whom he had met at the Thalian Hall event. Mr. Anderson owned one of the historic wood-clad cottages on Wrightsville Beach. Though many of the cottages had been torn down to make way for larger and more modern housing, a couple of dozen still remained. Mr. Anderson asked Hank to come look over some work that needed to be done at his property. He had two quotes already by other contractors, one of which said the foundation had problems. Mr. Anderson wanted Hank's opinion on whether he agreed there was a problem, stating that if Richard DeGaulle trusted him, he could, too. Hank set up a time to go see the site, and when he hung up, he was again pleased he had attended the gala since the event might provide him some potential business.

Using the new business as an excuse, Hank called Alanna to tell her about the call he had received, thanking her again for her help, and then asking when he could see her again. Alanna recommended a walk through her neighborhood after dinner, to which Hank readily agreed.

After work, Hank showered, dressed, and headed downtown to meet her. He figured since they weren't driving anywhere, he could use his Jeep and just park it a few blocks away so she wouldn't see it. He knocked on her door, and again, she opened it almost immediately as if she were waiting by the door. They started walking down Front Street, where she gave him a tour of the homes in her neighborhood. While Hank already knew some of their history, Alanna knew their more recent background, such as which ones had been renovated and who lived in them, giving rather humorous depictions of some of the residents. This tour gave Hank some valuable information on what people in her area liked or wanted when it came to working on their homes, and he filed it away for future reference. He liked that he could talk to her about his work and that she had an avid interest in how such buildings related to the city and made up the character of Wilmington. He found he really enjoyed just walking with her, holding her hand and talking about their city.

Eventually, they came to the street where his Jeep was parked. Hank stopped as they came upon it, deciding right there it was time to talk to her about the two things that he worried might cool her affections. He needed to tell her before he asked her out again, which he was already planning on doing. The first was his false conviction.

He took a deep breath and started on a brief summary of what had happened, but it turned out she already knew the story from what had been in the paper and waved it off, saying how horrible it must have been for him to go through all that.

"There's one other thing I need to tell you if we're going to go out again," he said, not knowing if this would be a deal breaker.

"What's that?" she asked questioningly.

Hank pointed at the Jeep. "That's my real car. The one I took you out in yesterday was my friend Mike's car."

Alanna looked at the weathered Jeep, beaten up after years of use and looking very much like something a college boy would drive. Hank waited for her reaction, which seemed to take an inordinate amount of time as she stared at the car with a blank look on her face.

"Well, we can just take my car the next time we go out," she finally said decidedly, smiling at him as she linked her arm in his and continued on with their walk.

Hank liked Alanna. He liked her smile and her laugh, not to mention she was a beautiful woman he could talk to for hours about the city's history and the beauty of its buildings. She was interested in his business and gave him ideas to keep it growing. She was sweet and thoughtful, yet had a sharp mind for how things worked, whether it be the politics she encountered at some of the organizations she volunteered at or the social circles she moved in so freely. And she had chosen to be with him. When she looked at him with those eyes, he felt something in him stir, and it was a good feeling.

Hank was clearly interested in her, but his feelings of attraction were usually paired with a feeling of apprehension about how different their backgrounds were. She was rich and used to nice dinners, expensive clothes, and galas. While he had certainly risen up from his roots by getting his college degree and starting his own business, he had not been exposed to all the refinements she had grown up with, and he worried that would make him look less appealing to her once she understood just how little he knew of her world. Once they started talking, those doubts would temporarily disappear, only to rear themselves up again when he was alone. While he certainly liked the security of having money, he was not someone who needed a lot of expensive things. He found satisfaction in what he built, not what he owned. The question was whether she could admire that in him or if she would eventually find him too unsophisticated for her taste.

They had spent their first two dates with him guiding the conversation to her interests, mostly due to his uncertainty about how she would react once she knew his background. It made him hold back, creating a small but distinct distance between them. He felt he had to prove he could take her to the places she was used to and he could treat her well before he revealed too much about himself. With that thought in mind, he decided to make their next date at one of the more expensive riverside restaurants downtown, a place called The George that had a romantic setting and a view of the Cape Fear River. He had lived modestly the last couple of years, saving up for when he started his business, so he had some means by which he could take her out. But that money would only go so far. The question was: How far would she expect it to go?

When Hank picked Alanna up on Friday, the familiar nervous feeling was there, but he was also looking forward to taking her out. He had picked up some new clothes earlier that week, which she immediately noticed, commenting on how elegant he looked. It was a pleasant and cool evening, so they decided to walk downtown to the restaurant.

The George turned out to be one of Alanna's favorite restaurants, so she was delighted he had chosen it. At dinner, he again tried to ask her questions to get to know her better, but this time she stopped him, saying she felt she knew so little about him and wanted to know everything. He had hoped to put off this moment, but with her urging, he started to tell her a few things about his mother and what he was like growing up in his part of Wilmington, which led to talking a little bit about Rob and then getting into UNCW and finding his interest in building. He glossed over the part about his actions after Rob died and his arrest, instead focusing on how he had worked hard through college and learned to be a carpenter, talking about his passion to build as his way of improving his community and other people's lives. He explained that by starting his own business, his goal was to preserve those very buildings that gave his hometown such character and told its history.

When they were done with dinner, Hank felt like he had run a marathon, and he suddenly worried he had said too much. As if she realized this unspoken thought, Alanna reached over and stroked his cheek. "Thank you for sharing all of that with me," she said, looking at him adoringly. "You are a fascinating man, Henry." With that one gesture, he knew it was all right that he had opened himself up, and he liked how he felt when she touched him.

When he had paid the bill and was about to get up to leave, though, Alanna stopped him. "There's something I want you to know," she said, putting her hand on his arm to make him wait, her demeanor suddenly serious. "I love that you brought me here. I have many wonderful memories of this place, and now I have a new one, having shared it with you. This was very special to me. But

I need you to know I don't need you to go to great expense when taking me out. I admire that you are starting your own business and know that must be difficult in many ways. I am here because of all the interests we have in common and I enjoy our time together. I never met anyone who loved talking about this city as much as I do and who lets me go on and on about its idiosyncrasies and charms. I love sharing that with you, and I want to continue doing so if you will let me."

Hank sat quietly as she spoke. They were the exact words he needed to hear, and in listening to her, all of his uncertainty suddenly fell away and he knew what he had to do right then as a strong and undeniable emotion rose within him. He stood up, reached out his hand to take hers, and said, "Come with me."

Alanna could sense his urgency and took his hand. He led her out of the restaurant onto the boardwalk. They walked a short ways until they reached a spot where they had a perfect view of the moon reflecting off of the water, giving it a silvery glow, and they were alone, with no passersby for the moment. Hank stopped and turned to face her, putting his hands on her waist as he looked into her eyes, trying to convey all the emotions he was feeling for her.

"Here," he said definitively.

"What's here?" Alanna asked, as he gently pulled her closer to him, breathing in her perfumed scent that reminded him of lilies of the valley.

"The place where I first got to kiss you," he said, and then he leaned in, his lips touching hers, sharing a quiet and soulful kiss that lasted for a long moment, neither of them wanting it to end. When Hank started to back off, Alanna put her arms around his neck and pulled him back in, and they continued for several more moments until Alanna broke away, her hand touching his face.

"I have been waiting for you to do that," she said, breathless and exhilarated, and they both smiled.

"I have wanted to do that since I met you," said Hank, looking deeply into her eyes. He pulled her to him and held her, feeling the space that had been empty for so long finally start to fill.

Chapter 44

After that dinner, they embarked on a slow and steady courtship, spending as much time together as their busy schedules would allow. They wanted to show each other the places each had discovered that were unique to Wilmington. Alanna took Hank on a tour of Thalian Hall, where she showed him the Thunder Roll, a sound-effect machine from the 1800s that used cannonballs to imitate the sound of thunder, and she told him about the history of the hall's original hand-painted theater curtain, which had been lost over one hundred years, then found randomly stored at a board member's home. From her job at the Historic Wilmington Foundation, she got a map of all of the historical wood-clad cottages on Wrightsville Beach like Mr. Anderson's and they rode around looking at them, with Hank explaining why each was unique. During their walks around her neighborhood, he would tell her stories about the Civil War and how yellow fever had caused the owners to abandon their homes and flee the city. They took long walks through Airlie Gardens, admiring the outdoor sculptures while talking about its roots as a garden estate. It became a game, each trying to show the other some new part of Wilmington the other had yet to discover or share some new and interesting facts about the places they both already knew.

When it became evident that Hank was becoming a recurring visitor, Alanna's parents told her to bring her new beau to dinner so they could meet him. "They just want to know who this handsome stranger is that keeps appearing on their doorstep and taking up so much of their enchanting daughter's time," she teased, though Hank knew there was more to it. Alanna's father was not only a council-man but one of the more prominent attorneys in town, and her mother was well-entrenched in Wilmington society, being a former President of the Cape Fear Garden Club and, like Alanna, involved in several other local organizations. Hank had no doubt they did not see their only daughter settling down with a local contractor.

He was right to have reservations. Meeting them, Hank found them to be as welcoming and friendly as Alanna, partly due to some good words spoken about him by Richard DeGaulle, but that didn't mean they approved of him. Mr. Moore was well aware of the over-turn of his conviction, and he asked several questions about it until Alanna begged him to change the subject, at which point he asked Hank about his business and how it was going. The easiest part of the conversation was when they ended up discussing the work the Moores had done when they first moved into their house, the only topic Hank felt at ease discussing. As he was leaving, Alanna's mother commented that it was good to see how he made Alanna smile again, a comment he wasn't sure how to take and which he considered asking Alanna about later. Once the evening ended, though, Hank was just glad it was over, hoping he had passed their test.

Due to her work and her parents' connections, Alanna was often invited to events around the city in addition to those she helped organize at Thalian Hall, so she began asking Hank to accompany her to those she didn't have to work. He didn't enjoy these gatherings as much as Alanna did, but he knew they were opportunities to generate business, so he would attend when he could. Alanna was more than happy to introduce him to new people, or to remind him of those he had already met and didn't remember, helping him in ways he appreciated greatly. He had gotten the job from Mr. Anderson, the largest renovation he had done yet, and he hoped when he completed the work that others would follow. He was still working out of his father's house, but in addition to having his father work with him, he had been able to start hiring a few fulltime employees. It was a slow process, but he kept reminding himself that as long as he did good work, it would eventually pay off.

Alanna recognized that Hank didn't feel like he fit in at times, and she did all she could to make him feel more a part of her world. One day she asked him to accompany her to pick up some clothes at a store in Lumina Station, a shopping village of locally owned upscale boutiques that Hank had driven past numerous times on the way to the beach. As they passed by a men's store, Alanna pointed to a jacket in the window and commented how handsome it would look on him, suggesting he try it on. Hank suspected this had been her intent all along. He would obviously need new clothes if he kept attending events, so he went along with the charade and let her help him pick out some items he could wear on their nights out. Later, when he brought Alanna over to Mike and Lila's house for dinner one night, Mike ribbed him for finally getting some style and told Alanna how she had quite the effect on him.

When it was just the two of them, Hank enjoyed his time with her, but it did not go as well when she tried to introduce him to her friends. She first brought him to a BBQ held at a beach house owned by one of her friend's parents. He could tell immediately that fitting in with this crowd would be difficult. Like Alanna, they were a few years younger than him, and after a few cursory questions on what he did, they switched the conversation to the latest car models or football season, all while drinking heavily. Hank felt more at ease once they moved on to these subjects since he didn't have to participate, just nod when appropriate. They had obviously all grown up together, given their inside jokes and how they treated each other, much of which he silently observed and didn't care for. While Alanna's girlfriends were friendly, the guys seemed much less enthusiastic about having him there, and as the drinking progressed, so did their disdain for him. Hank was grateful when the event was over, telling Alanna it had been fun, but knowing instinctively he was not welcome.

When they got back to Alanna's house, she asked if they could talk in the car for a moment. She had noticed some of the guys had not been welcoming and felt she should explain. She told him that before she had met him, she had been in a serious relationship with one of their friends, Jackson Causby. They had known each other in high school and started dating at Duke. They had talked of getting married after college, but when they graduated, Jackson took a job in Atlanta, despite her telling him she wanted to return to Wilmington. They had continued to date long distance for almost a year until she had broken it off when she realized he wasn't going to return home.

"So, now you know why they behaved as poorly as they did. It had everything to do with me and nothing with you," she said.

Hank's thoughts were on another matter. "Are you still in love with him?" he asked, not sure he wanted to know the answer.

Alanna reached over to touch his cheek. "No, that's over," she said, her eyes sparkling at him. "I am quite enchanted with someone else now."

Hank leaned over to kiss her and then looked at her, more relieved than he had expected to be. "That's good to know," he said.

"And what about you, Hank?" Alanna asked, looking at him coquettishly. "Was there a woman in your past that I should know about? Anyone break your heart, no matter how foolish she would be for doing so?"

Hank sat back in his seat, looking ahead and feeling uncomfortable. "That was a long time ago," he finally said, looking back at her and taking in her beauty and the way she looked at him. "I'm more interested in the present."

Chapter 45

Hank followed up with Alanna's suggestion to volunteer with the historical foundation. They were working on restoring a church from the 1800s, a job he was more than happy to assist with, and he spent a good part of his weekends helping out. It gave him a chance to display his workmanship and learn more about working on such a historic structure. There was also the added benefit that he could use his time volunteering as an excuse to pass on some of the weekend gatherings of Alanna's friends, letting her enjoy that time on her own.

The one other part of his life they did not share was the beach. Alanna repeatedly declined to join him there. She was not a fan of humidity or sand and preferred going to the gym to do spin classes or yoga in a more controlled environment. Hank didn't really mind since he liked to have that time to spend by himself or with Mike, when he could break free. Mike and Lila had just had their first baby, a little boy named Connor, and Mike was often tired between work and his new family life. Still, he made an effort to get out when he could, surfing with Hank when they could find a time to meet up. Hank enjoyed telling Mike how his business was going and hearing his opinion on current trends in the housing market.

"So how is it going with Alanna?" Mike finally asked at one of their outings.

Hank smiled, knowing Mike would eventually ask. "Great. We're having a good time together. It's not the fireworks I had with Jess, but I really like her. We have a lot of the same interests. And she is really helping me build my business. I don't know, maybe our relationship could become something more, but right now I am more focused on getting my business off the ground. Once I do that, I can think more about the future."

Mike listened quietly, hearing the words Hank wasn't saying. Hank clearly still missed Jess, though it was good to see him getting involved with a new woman. He patted his friend on the back in consolation, then said, "Yeah, I can certainly understand that."

As summer turned into fall, business was still trickling in, but Hank started to get more steady work. Most of his jobs were still smaller projects, and many of the properties he worked on were not historical, but he brought that expertise with him if he got the opportunity to work on an older home, and he preferred the challenges an older structure posed. His father was also quite happy to be back working construction jobs, and when Hank was lucky enough to have more than one job going on in a week, he was thankful for his father's help supervising the various sites since he had to spend more time at the office to coordinate supplies and other details.

Hank also decided it was time to move out of his father's house. He and his father had fixed up their house enough that he was proud to take Alanna there to show her their work, but he also wanted to have his own place. With Mike's help, he found a small rental down-town and within walking distance of Alanna's house, which would allow them to see each other more frequently. Alanna was delighted and helped him pick out furniture and find small items to taste-fully decorate the apartment. Hank was grateful for her help, having no idea how to put it together himself, and he especially liked the homey touches she added.

Between work and their social calendar, the rest of the year went by quickly. Soon it was the holidays, which were a blur of parties and celebrations. Hank was relieved when January finally came so he could get back to a more normal schedule. His business now needed more room than he had at his father's house, so he found some office space near his apartment, just off of Princess Street, and hired an office assistant to free him up to focus on the work itself. The business was slowly making a name for itself, and Hank was proud of what he had accomplished.

The added help also gave him some time to think about where his life was going. He noticed how happy Mike was with Lila and Connor, so his thoughts turned to his own future and whether he saw it with Alanna. At their last dinner, Lila had asked him when he was going to marry her already since they got along so well, a question that had been in the back of his own mind. He wanted to be able to support a wife and family before thinking about marriage, and with his income becoming steadier, maybe now was the right time.

If his business continued to go well, Hank felt confident he could provide for a family, though not the lifestyle Alanna was ac-customed to. That was still a strong concern. It was one thing for her to date him, but quite another to be married to him, and he wasn't sure she would be happy with what he could provide. He didn't enjoy the social events they attended as much as she did, seeing them only as a means to obtain business. He also did not yet feel fully relaxed around her parents or friends, hoping that would come with time. Hank recognized he loved Alanna, but it was a different kind of love than he had felt before. He felt comfortable with her, enjoying the time they spent together and hearing what she had to say. She was caring and thoughtful, and he knew she would make a good wife and a wonderful mother. She was the first woman he had been attracted to since Jess and he felt that must mean something. But he knew he couldn't keep comparing his feelings for Alanna to the love he had felt for Jess. That had been a summer romance, he told himself, that feeling of infatuation you only feel when you are young and attracted to a girl for the first time. It was not the mature type of love he believed he had now. He wanted a family, and Alanna was the best partner he had found to share that dream.

That Saturday was unusually warm for March. Hank and Alanna walked downtown to get a cup of coffee and then walked back to his apartment where there was a courtyard out back. The backyard was fenced in with a garden and a sitting area with two benches. He had spent a number of afternoons sitting out there with Alanna beneath the shade of an oak tree, talking and watching as an errant butterfly would swoop down to explore the colorful garden's array of wild-flowers and bushes. Today as they sat and talked, Hank looked at the way she sat with her legs crossed, so neat and contained, always looking so refreshed, even in the hot and humid weather. She would tilt her head back and laugh, making him want to laugh with her, and the way she looked at him was admiring and loving. While she talked, he thought about how well their interests in Wilmington aligned, between her work at historic organizations and his work restoring historic properties. And how despite the flack he suspected she got from her parents or friends, she made him feel a part of her world, a place he had never seen himself being included. He could see the wife she would be, someone kind and good to him. He could see them having a good life together.

Then nothing should be holding him back from taking the next step, he decided.

Chapter 46

Once Hank made his decision, he had to figure out how to do it. How could he ask Alanna to marry him so she would say yes?

It had to happen somewhere that meant something to them. He threw away the obvious ideas of doing it at Thalian Hall where they first met or the Riverwalk. He wanted a place he felt was theirs and that captured their relationship. He recalled all the places they had visited over the past year and then came upon the perfect place—the one place that had belonged to both of them from the beginning, where they would picnic and take long walks, where they had some of their better conversations uninterrupted, a place that captured the beauty and history of the Wilmington they found so captivating. He would do it at Airlie Gardens, particularly now that the azaleas and gardens would be in full bloom. He knew it was the right spot as soon as he thought of it, and he began planning his proposal.

Of course, he needed a ring, but he had no idea where to start looking. Luckily, Mike told him where he had bought Lila's ring and some other jewelry for their anniversary. Hank knew he could not afford an expensive ring, and he feared whatever he could afford might not be suitable to Alanna, but the salesman was very helpful.

He asked Hank several questions about what he was looking for and then showed him a collection of vintage-style rings. From these, Hank chose a marquise-shaped diamond framed on each side by smaller diamonds in the shape of leaves. Hank thought it would be perfect for Alanna, particularly in the setting he had chosen to propose. As he left with the ring in his pocket, he felt excited about giving it to her and starting their life together.

However, before proposing, he felt he should ask Alanna's parents for their blessing. He wasn't sure he needed to do it, but he was concerned they might expect it, so he decided to let her father know he intended to propose. Though he had been over for dinner several times in the past year, they had yet to develop a comfortable relationship. Mr. Moore seemed to enjoy being commanding over whoever was in his midst, a trait Hank had noticed even when he saw them out at events, and Sunday dinners at their house revolved around his direction. He had a sharp conversational style, which Hank attributed to his profession, and a large mustache he would sometimes stroke when thinking, giving him an authoritative air. Hank may have won over Alanna, but her father was a different story, having come from money and a long line of leaders in the community. The best he could do was state his intentions and how he planned to take care of Alanna, hoping her father had gotten to know him well enough that this would be sufficient for him. It would not be an easy conversation but one Hank felt he needed to have.

The next weekend when dinner was finished, Alanna and her mother stepped out for a moment to look at a dress her mother had picked up. Hank took the opportunity to ask Mr. Moore if he could have a few minutes of his time in private. As if already knowing what he was going to ask, Mr. Moore regarded him for a moment, then said, "Why don't we go into my study." Hank followed him down one of the long hallways to a room lined with cherry bookshelves filled with law books and a large desk piled with papers. Mr. Moore sat behind the desk, indicating Hank should take one of the adjoining chairs. He offered Hank a cigar, which he politely turned down, then lit one himself and settled down behind his desk, waiting for Hank to speak.

Hank was nervous, but he cleared his throat and started talking. "I have spent the last year getting to know your daughter, and I find her to be quite an amazing woman. While I know I must seem an unlikely choice for her affections, we actually have a lot in common in that we both love Wilmington and its history. It is what first bonded us together and has allowed us to create many happy memories that has led to a deeper affection for each other. Alanna has also been instrumental in helping me develop my business, which has grown to the point where I feel I am ready to take on a wife and family. I know I could be a good husband to Alanna and would do everything in my power to take care of her. What I am saying, sir, is that I would like to marry Alanna and would like your blessing when I propose to her."

Mr. Moore sat regarding him, thinking before he spoke.

"Do you enjoy these events Alanna takes you to?" he finally asked, looking at Hank quizzically, his drawl more pronounced.

Hank wasn't sure how to respond. "I have found them very helpful in meeting people and in obtaining business…" he started.

"Right, right," Mr. Moore said, waving his cigar as he cut him off. "But do you…*enjoy* them?"

Hank thought for a moment. "I enjoy being with Alanna. If it's what she likes to do, then I am happy to do it with her."

Mr. Moore nodded his head up and down as if in agreement, but Hank could tell he was planning his next words carefully.

"Do you know of my family's background?" he finally asked, seeming to take a different tactic.

"I know what Alanna has told me, sir."

"Then you know that I, like my daddy, was born into this life of big houses and fancy events. And that it is the life Alanna has always known, having been born into it herself. You see, it's one thing to be young and idealistic, thinking it doesn't really matter if you have such fine things, but it's quite another when you grow older and see all the things you used to have but can't have anymore because of your...idealistic choices."

"Sir, I am confident I can provide a good life for Alanna. Probably not to the extent she has grown up in, but one in which we could be very happy. Alanna has assured me that she doesn't need me to spend money on her to show her I love her."

Mr. Moore seemed to smile at that, taking a smoke from his cigar. "There's a big difference between doesn't need and can't have, son. You yourself have experienced that, I suppose."

Hank sat quietly, unsure what to say as Mr. Moore continued.

"You have been coming over here for dinners now for the better part of a year. You see the big house and the nice furniture. The staff that waits on us. The events we go to and organizations we are part of. You think it's all about just having money. But there's a lot more to it than how much I own. Even after the past year, I am not sure you understand just what it means to be a part of society."

"What are you saying, sir? Are you saying you do not approve of my proposing to Alanna?" Hank asked, getting frustrated with Mr. Moore's roundabout way of talking and wanting a definitive answer.

Mr. Moore regarded him for one more moment, almost impressed to see Hank stand up to him, then put out his cigar as he spoke. "I have raised my daughter to have her own mind. She knows what we think is best for her, but we have left it to her to decide her own future. She is my only child, so have no doubt that her welfare will always be my concern. But as for whom she chooses to marry, well, *that* is up to her."

And with these last words, he stood, indicating the meeting was over, and pointed to the door. "I believe the ladies will be looking for us at this point and we should return."

Hank thought about Mr. Moore's words over the next few days, but he wasn't sure what to make of them. Mr. Moore hadn't told him he wouldn't approve of Hank marrying Alanna, but he seemed to have his doubts about whether Hank fit into their social circles. That was the most Hank could take away from it. When Hank told Mike about the meeting, he agreed. But Hank was used to being challenged, and he had already decided he wanted to marry Alanna, so he did what he always did when put to a test. He vowed to do what he could to show he deserved Alanna. First, he had to see if she would marry him. If she turned him down, there was nothing more to do. But if she said yes, he was ready to do what he needed to show her she had made the right choice.

The following Saturday, Hank planned a picnic for them at Airlie. The first indication this was not a usual picnic was when he showed up in a jacket and tie, which Alanna found unusual. They drove over to the gardens and found a place by the azaleas to lay down a blanket and sit. It was a warm day for April, and he'd had to take his coat off as they walked. They talked for a bit, enjoying some of the food he had brought while idly talking about Alanna's work and her friends. Hank was visibly nervous and starting to question if he should wait to ask her. But then he looked into her eyes and saw her adoration for him; he listened to her laugh and her telling him how she had talked about him to her friends, building him up in slight but obvious ways. He would be a fool to walk away from this woman, he thought, and decided it was time. He stood up, put on his jacket, and straightened his tie. Alanna looked perplexed, asking if they were leaving, when he knelt down in front of her. Taking the ring from his pocket, he opened the box and held it out for her to see, saying the words he had prepared for this moment.

"Alanna, together we have shared a love of the history of our town, and now I would like to create our own history. I love you, Alanna. I want you by my side through all life has to offer. Alanna Moore, will you marry me?"

Alanna sat for a moment, stunned, looking at the ring and then at him, and then she threw her arms around his neck and kissed him.

"Yes," she said breathless and exhilarated. "Yes, I will be your wife, Henry."

Hank and Alanna spent a short while sitting there, enjoying the scenery and adjusting to their new status, until Alanna couldn't wait another moment to tell her parents. As soon as they got to her house, Alanna rushed in to tell her mother the good news. Mrs. Moore was delighted and hugged them both, saying how pretty the ring was that Hank had chosen. Her father came in a moment later after hearing all the commotion. When Alanna told him about the engagement, he didn't show any emotion, just said he was happy for them, giving Hank a look that reminded him he had a lot to prove. But today was about celebrating, so after they had shared their engagement with the Moores, Hank asked Alanna if they could tell his father next, anxious to get out from under the stare of Mr. Moore. Hank's father was, of course, delighted, giving Alanna a big hug and welcoming her to the family, and then Hank took her out to dinner so they could have some time alone.

They decided to go to the Bluewater Grill where they'd had their first date. Alanna was asking all sorts of questions about what kind of wedding Hank wanted and where and when, but he, who had not even thought about any of these details as of yet, felt it had already been quite a day, chose to sit back and listen to her talk excitedly about her ideas. *My wife*, he thought, looking at her fondly, *you are going to be my wife*.

After he dropped Alanna off, Hank called Mike, who congratulated him. Lila got on the phone to say it was about time, which made Hank laugh and feel pleased they were happy for him. He was relieved Alanna had said yes and that he had gone forward with asking her. It wasn't until he got home that another feeling came over him, a nagging uneasiness that he could not define. He stood in the kitchen drinking a glass of water and trying to put a name to it, but nothing came to mind. After a few moments, he pushed it away, attributing it to just being tired after the day's events, and started to get ready for bed, looking forward to his run in the morning.

Chapter 47

The next couple of weeks, Hank was met with congratulations from friends and other acquaintances on his engagement. Surprisingly, even Alanna's friends pretended to be a bit warmer to him when they found out the news, probably figuring that now that he was marrying Alanna, they should make the best of it. Hank felt good, happy with how his life was going and that his work continued to be steady. Everything seemed to have fallen into place for him after so much hardship, and he was now in a place he never would have guessed he would be. Alanna and her mother were already planning an engagement party and talked constantly about the wedding plans, coming up with several ideas. He would have preferred a small intimate wedding, but being socially prominent, the Moores saw this as an opportunity to put on quite the affair. Hank's job, as far as he could tell, was to sit back and let them handle it. As long as it made Alanna happy, that was good enough for him.

A few weeks later, Hank and Alanna were at a fundraising gala for the UNCW Center for Marine Science. Hank had never seen the facility, which was set back off of Masonboro Road, and although he didn't care much for modern architecture, he was impressed with the sleek silver-curved walls of the building's exterior and how the structure was incorporated into the surrounding marsh. The interior lobby was spacious, with a ceiling made of wooden planks that emulated waves with a school of metal fish hanging from it. Alanna had helped Hank purchase a new tuxedo a few weeks before, saying it was time he owned his own, and he was wearing it for the first time, knowing it fit him well. He felt like he belonged, something that didn't happen often at these affairs. He and Alanna went inside and found their table, then circulated around talking to various friends and acquaintances. He didn't feel he had to work so hard at driving up business now and appeared more relaxed, something even Alanna commented on. He was actually enjoying himself and was being congratulated by Richard on his engagement when a business call came in that he had to take. Hank headed out to a corner of the lobby where he could hear better without the noise of the crowd.

When Hank finished his call, he turned to head back to the main room but suddenly stopped short. Approaching him was the most beautiful woman he had ever seen. She had long brown hair cascading over her shoulders and the most striking eyes. Her long, royal-blue, silk dress was simple in design, with a suggestive but shapely cut that clung to her curves and remarkable figure. She was so stunning that Hank thought he was seeing things. She looked so much like Jess that it took his breath away. All he could do was stare as she walked directly toward him.

As soon as she said his name, he knew.

Jess had come back.

PART III

Jess

Chapter 48

Jess had never been so scared as when John had tried to pull her into that car. She saw the look in his eyes as he grabbed her, and worse, she saw a similar look in the eyes of his two friends inside, who were laughing and egging him on. She knew where this was headed. She'd heard about another waitress the year before who had not gotten away and left town shortly after. The rumor was she'd been paid a large sum to keep quiet and leave. Jess had seen enough of John's antics to believe it to be true, but she never thought she would be the one in this position.

And Hank. When he hadn't shown up as promised, Jess wasn't sure what to make of it and decided to walk home, not wanting to hang around the parking lot. He would know to head to her apartment to find her if he still wanted to talk. He must have been doing just that when he came across John attacking her. If he had not come when he did, she didn't want to think of what would have happened. When she broke free of John's grip, she ran away as fast as she could, turning back only once to see Hank repeatedly pummeling John, the sight making her turn back around and run faster.

What had been a relief at seeing Hank quickly became fear. That was the person Roxy had described, not the Hank she had known.

Between the darkness and her focus on getting away, Jess didn't see the large black sedan waiting at the end of the street until she reached the corner. She stopped just short of running into Mr. DeGaulle, who was standing outside the car watching as Hank beat up his son. She froze when she saw him, not sure what she should do, worried that somehow he would see this as her fault.

He looked at her with a strange sad look. "Get in. I'll drive you home," he said calmly, walking around the car to open the passenger door for her. Jess looked back at the scene and heard a strange laugh come from John, who was laying on the ground. She quickly turned around and got in.

"I'll be right back," said Mr. DeGaulle before he closed the door. He looked back at the scene and then walked over to John's car. Jess couldn't hear what he was saying, but the grip of fear returned. Hank was gone, though she hadn't seen him leave. Was Mr. DeGaulle going to blame her for what had just happened? Should she run? If she did, where would she go? She sat tensely, trying to decide what to do. After a moment, Mr. DeGaulle returned and got in the car. He started the engine and asked her where she lived so he could drive her home. At her direction, he made his way up the Island, turning onto her dead-end street and driving to the end to make the three-point turn to get out again. He stopped in front of her house, letting the car run as he thought for a moment. She wondered if she should just get out and leave, but before she could open the door, he turned to her.

"Are you all right?" he asked, seeing she was shaking.

His voice was soothing, which she really needed at this moment. She nodded, noticing the shaking for the first time. She wanted to calm down, but her nerves had caught up with her and she was having a hard time composing herself.

"Why don't you sit here for a moment and just breathe. You're all right now. It will help," he said, and she nodded again, unable to speak, trying to slow everything down. She took a few deep breaths, shaky at first, and then slowly they became more even. She could feel the adrenaline that had been coursing through her and urging her to flee slowly start to subside, and she was finally able to relax, albeit mildly. When she was ready to talk, she turned to look at Mr. DeGaulle, anxious to hear what he would say.

"Jess," he began, "you were very brave to come to me this afternoon to tell me of John's recent actions with the staff. It was why I followed him tonight—to see for myself what he would do. I can tell you I am ashamed of my son beyond words, and I promise you this will not go unpunished. I am going to make a big request of you. Let me handle this and don't go to the authorities. What John needs is help. Putting him in prison would not remedy what I saw him do tonight. Since I am the one who caused this problem, I would appreciate the opportunity to fix it. I am hoping you will give me the chance to do that."

Jess sat quietly, trying to take in what he was saying. She hadn't even thought of going to the police until he mentioned it, but she wasn't sure she wanted to make that promise.

Mr. DeGaulle continued, seeing her hesitation. "I do think you are owed something to compensate you for having gone through such a traumatizing event."

Mr. DeGaulle started to reach in front of her, causing her to jerk back a little toward the door. He pointed to the glove box to show her what he was doing, then slowly he opened it and took out a checkbook. He made out a check, tearing it out before returning the checkbook to the glove box.

"This is for you. With all the hard work you do, I assume you are working to pay for college. This will help with that. Do not ask me for more because I will not give it to you. If you were to report John, it would only be your word against mine since I doubt Hank will admit he was there tonight with all he has to lose if he did. I believe this covers any debt I may have with you, and I am very sorry this happened the way it did. But I think you have a bright future ahead of you, and I want to help you with that, Jess."

Jess took the check and mumbled "Thank you" without looking at it. She just reached for the door handle and opened the door, wanting to get out of the car and away from all this.

"One more thing, Jess," Mr. DeGaulle said just before she stepped out of the car. "You may want to think about finishing college elsewhere. This may not be the best place for you after this... incident."

Jess looked up, trying to determine if his words were meant as a threat, but Mr. DeGaulle was looking straight ahead with a strange, troubled look on his face. She could tell he was waiting for her to leave, so she opened the car door and stepped onto the sidewalk. As soon as she closed it, Mr. DeGaulle drove off while she just stood there, watching him go. After a moment, she remembered the check in her hand and looked down to see the amount for the first time.

What she saw surprised her more than anything she could have imagined.

Jess went into the apartment, thankful not to have to face Anne because she was in her room listening to music. She was doing all she could to hold it together and wanted to be alone. She went into her room and shut the door. She tucked the check into her top dresser drawer, not wanting to look at it, then curled up on the bed, trying to make sense of all the noise going through her head, and trying not to relive John's attack or how she had seen Hank hitting him over and over. She wondered if Mr. DeGaulle would turn Hank in and if he would go back to jail. She couldn't handle it if that happened. She should have asked Mr. DeGaulle if he planned to do just that, because if he did, she would have given him back the money to prevent it. No matter how confused she felt about Hank right now, she couldn't do that to him.

Jess lay there a long time hugging her pillow, trying to make sense of it all, but there was too much to process, and soon, the tears started spilling down her cheeks and she cried into her pillow, recognizing how scared she was and how she hated that she couldn't call Hank and have him comfort her. She could see on her phone that he had been calling, but she couldn't bring herself to talk to him right now. She didn't know what to say or how to think about him, so she turned off her notifications to avoid his calls and texts. Still, she really needed to talk to someone. It couldn't be Anne or Lynn because she didn't want anyone else to know what had happened tonight. She finally decided to call her mother, the one person she knew was always there for her and who would help her think through what she should do.

It would be a difficult call since she had never fully told her mother about Hank's past, only that he had been indecisive about what he wanted to do after high school, which was why he was working a delivery job. But tonight, Jess told her the whole story, explaining Hank's past and their summer together before telling her about the attack and the money. Then she moved on to what the event might mean to Hank, talking fast, as if she had to get it all out quickly before her mother responded. She apologized to her mother for withholding the information she had, explaining how she hadn't told her everything before because she didn't want her to judge Hank before she had even met him. Hank had been very good to her, but now she felt confused about who he was. And she was also worried about the money. Should she take it? Was it wrong to take it? What should she do? Once she had gotten it all out, Jess sat exhausted and waited for her mother's response.

Her mother had listened quietly, and after making sure Jess was physically all right, she walked her through the rest of it very matter-of-factly. She was relieved that Jess had gotten away from John, and she agreed that staying in Wilmington might put Jess in danger. She told Jess she should take the money and be thankful for it. What she had been through was horrible, and John's father appeared to have been through this before. At least he had the decency to try to atone for his son's wrongs. There would be no benefit in trying to prosecute John in a small town where his family was prominent. Hopefully, his father would do something about him, but her concern was Jess.

"The real question, Jess, is what do you want to do? You were devastated when you couldn't afford to go to UCF and now you have the money. I hate how you got it, but at least it gives you a choice. You've known Hank for three months. It was a wonderful summer, but you are only twenty years old. Forgetting everything else, it was unlikely to last merely because you are both so young and still figuring out who you are. Ever since you told me about your interest in sea turtles, I could see how passionate you are about them and how much you wanted to study them down in Florida. So if they would still accept you, do you still want to go to UCF?"

Jess thought for a moment. There wasn't any question that she still wanted to go. After all that had happened, the only thing that could keep her in Wilmington was Hank. She loved Hank, but so much had happened in the last week to make her question if he was the person she really thought he was. They had known each other such a short time. How could she ever believe again that he was the person she had spent all that time with this summer? If Hank was willing to fight John for her, to violate his probation just before it ended to save her, then she should realize he would do anything for her—that he truly loved her. But seeing him hit John had terrified her, confirming what Roxy had told her about Hank. She couldn't stay just to find out which version of him was the right one. Not when she could finally pursue her dream.

"I want to go to UCF," Jess said, feeling sure it was the right decision once she said it out loud. The call had calmed her as she had hoped, and now she knew what she wanted to do.

"Good," her mother said. "So, let's figure out how to get you there."

After packing late into the night, Jess left early the next morning before Anne woke. She left a note thanking her for everything and telling her she wouldn't be back. She didn't want to say anything about UCF because she knew Anne might tell Hank where she went, and she wasn't sure she wanted Anne to do that. Instead, she packed up her few belongings, then rode her bike over to campus to pick up her car and bring it back to the apartment. Once she packed everything inside, she started heading south to a new life, taking one long last look at Wilmington as it faded in her rearview mirror.

Chapter 49

Jess sat in a white van marked on the side with "UCF Biology Department." She was riding with three other volunteers, headed out to the Archie Carr National Wildlife Refuge on the coast. It was just over an hour drive from the university, and it was the first time Jess felt she had been able to stop and think in the whirlwind that had been the last seven weeks.

Jess barely remembered the eight-hour drive to Orlando. She had stopped only once to pick up food and do a rest stop before returning to the security of her car and what she felt was her mission. She found a hotel near UCF where she could shower and change, and she thought about what she would say when she went to the university the next day.

She showed up at the admissions office first thing in the morning and asked to speak to the director. Sitting down in the director's office, Jess explained that when she'd declined the university's acceptance offer, it had been due to her inability to pay for her tuition, but she'd recently come into some family money that would now cover those costs. The director talked to Jess for a while, and when she saw just how motivated Jess was and heard her reasons for wanting to get into the program, she felt Jess was the type of student they didn't want to lose. The director made some calls while Jess sat outside in the waiting area, anxious about what would happen and not wanting to think about what she would do if she didn't get in. But then the director came out and shook her hand, welcoming her to UCF. Jess could start classes next week.

Jess had a lot to do to get settled. After meeting with an advisor and signing up for classes, she immediately went online to look for a place to live. Most students had roommates already, but Jess knew with a school this size, there was a good chance someone's plans had fallen through. Sure enough, she found that was just the case with Kayla, an English major also in her third year. When Jess came over to see the apartment, Kayla explained that the friend she had planned to room with had suddenly decided to take the year off to "find herself."

"That's basically code for 'I don't know what to do with my life'," Kayla said, rolling her eyes. Kayla had a pixie haircut and the thin delicate features of a dancer. She was also friendly and seemed easygoing, exactly what Jess was looking for in a roommate. She showed Jess the living room, kitchen, and what would be Jess's bedroom, all of which looked comfortable. The apartment had lots of light and was bigger than Anne's beach place. Since the rent was in Jess's price range, she agreed to take it. The room came furnished with a bed, dresser, and desk, so having only a couple of bags and her bike, Jess was able to move in that afternoon and quickly get settled.

Once Jess had her school and living arrangements in order, she set out to do the one thing she had come for—to get on the Marine Turtle Research Group. She read everything she could find about the team on the internet, and even though she was not a fan of social media, she had set up accounts to follow them on Facebook,

Instagram, and Twitter. She knew the group was managed by Dr. Manning, one of the biology professors, and understood the process by which she selected interns from the university website. After a lengthy interview process, only twelve students out of more than a hundred would be offered a summer internship, a job that consisted of working several days a week from May through August to count new nests and watch for hatchlings along the beach on the Refuge. Jess was definitely interested in securing a position as a summer intern, but she had no intention of waiting until next summer to start working with the turtles. Making it to UCF had been a long and difficult path. Now that she was here, she wanted nothing more than to get involved with the Refuge in any capacity she could.

Jess knew the graduate students managed the day-to-day research at the Refuge. It was already September, which meant she still had a chance to see a green sea turtle nest hatch, since it was unlikely this far into the season that nests from the other turtle species would still be incubating. Jess didn't care which type she saw; she just wanted to be out there on the beach, like she had in North Carolina. After all the time she had spent monitoring that one nest on Wrightsville Beach, she was deeply disappointed that she would not see it finally erupt with hatchlings, a thought that led her to thinking of Hank. She put the thought of him out of her mind. She wanted another opportunity to see firsthand what it was like to see the hatchlings boil from their nest and head out to sea, and the only way to see that happen was to be out on the Refuge. She needed to find out which graduate students were running the internship program and who could use her help, so she went to the biology professors' offices to see what she could find out.

Once there, she wasn't sure what to do. There was a small waiting area outside a line of offices, each with a professor's name on the door. Should she knock on Dr. Manning's door, introduce herself, tell her how much she loved sea turtles, and ask to be part of the Turtle Team? Since it was such a competitive program, Jess was pretty sure that was not the right approach. As she stood thinking about her next move, she saw what she assumed was a graduate student leave Dr. Manning's office. He was tall and angular with thin, straight sun-bleached hair that was cut choppily around his round face. His forehead furrowed as he thought hard about something. He was wearing a light-green polo shirt and khakis and he looked very serious as he pulled on his dark green backpack. Without thinking, Jess approached him.

"Excuse me," she said. "Do you work on the Marine Turtle Research Group?"

He seemed to scowl in her direction before answering. "Yes. What do you want?"

Jess was a little intimidated by his terse tone, but ignored it. "I know you don't usually take on interns this time of year, but I was wondering...."

Before she could finish, he raised his hand and stopped her. "All the internship positions are filled. You will have to wait until January to apply for the next season." He began walking away.

"Wait," Jess said, jumping in front of him. "I realize this is not standard procedure, but I just transferred in from UNCW and I worked with an organization up there...."

"I'm sorry," he said and walked past her, leaving her deeply embarrassed. She turned around slowly, feeling defeated, wondering what to do next, when she heard a voice from the other side of the waiting area.

"Don't mind him," a young woman said, smiling as she walked in. "Nothing there that a good shark bite wouldn't cure." Jess took in the petite figure in a tank top and mini-skirt, her long dark hair braided down her back. Everything about her seemed tidy and well-placed, from the fit of her clothes to how perfectly her nails were painted. "And to think, this is one of his better days."

Jess knew the other student was joking, but she wasn't sure how to respond. "I'm Jess," she finally said, offering her hand.

"Leah," the woman replied, taking it. "So which organization did you work with up in North Carolina?"

Jess explained her work at the Turtle Rescue and with the Wrightsville Beach group. "I also did a lighting study for one of my classes at UNCW. I came here because, well, there are more turtles and nests here. But that doesn't help me if I can't see them."

"True. But unfortunately, what Chris just said is right. We aren't taking any new interns on this time of year. The season is slowing down, and we have all the help we can use. You need to wait until January to apply for the next nesting season."

Jess sighed. That seemed like a lifetime away. Certainly, there must be something she could do before then. "Are you one of the graduate students working on the research team?" she asked Leah.

"Yes, this is my second year."

"What are your graduate studies focused on?" she asked.

Leah explained she was researching how sea turtles knew how to navigate to their nesting beaches, a study that had to do with the Earth's magnetic field. Jess was fascinated and started asking questions. Leah asked her to wait a moment and then knocked on Dr. Manning's door before entering her office. She was gone about five minutes. When she returned, she asked Jess if she wanted to grab a bite at the Student Union while they talked.

Jess gladly followed along, sitting with Leah for an hour and asking detailed questions about how she was conducting the research and what information she had gathered. For a small woman, Leah must have had a fast metabolism because she ate a sandwich, chips, and an apple, finishing everything on her plate. When they were done eating, Leah looked at Jess and nodded her head.

"You would definitely be someone we would want on the team if you applied in January." While Jess was pleased by the compliment, she still felt disappointed that she couldn't start sooner.

Leah had a class, so Jess thanked her for her time. She gave her number to Leah, telling her to call her just in case anything changed.

"Really, I want to get involved in any way I can," Jess said, trying not to sound as desperate as she felt. Leah thanked her, saying she would keep her in mind. As she walked away, Jess had that sinking feeling again. *Patience*, she reminded herself as she walked slowly back to her apartment, thinking about their conversation. *Something will come up. It always does.*

Jess spent the next couple of weeks settling into her studies and getting into a routine. If she couldn't get out to the Refuge, she would do the next best thing by trying to get to know Dr. Manning. Dr. Manning's classes were very popular and filled by the time she signed up for her courses, but she found she could still audit a class, choosing one on animal behavior. Jess immediately liked the teacher and the class since sea turtle examples were often used in the discussions. She sat up front and would often participate, once mentioning the information she had learned from Leah about magnetic fields and nesting habits. After that class, Dr. Manning called on her by name, obviously impressed with what she had said. Jess hoped that showing how interested she was in the subject in class would help her when she applied for an internship.

Jess kept hoping Leah would call, but when weeks passed without hearing from her, she finally acknowledged she would probably not get to see the Refuge until next summer. Rather than lament about what she couldn't do, she focused on what she could do by working hard at her classes and getting acclimated to her new surroundings.

During her downtime, Jess went exploring on her bicycle. The Florida weather meant she could bike all year long, and even better, Florida was mostly flat, whereas North Carolina began to get hilly the farther west she went from the beach. She liked riding on campus, though she found she had to watch the guys on their longboards, who would often go fast and sometimes cut her off. She discovered a few trails she could ride, like around the Arboretum or the Little Big Econ Trail that took her through a forest. However, most rides tended to be on busy roads that wound through industrial parks or by shopping centers. She found she could even make it all the way to Downtown Orlando if she wanted to, but it just didn't feel the same as Wilmington. Here, the area was much more commercial and built up, and riding wasn't as relaxing as going through a quiet neighborhood.

On these rides, Jess would think about Hank and everything that had happened in Wilmington, trying to figure out what she had misread and whether she was doing the right thing by not responding to his efforts to contact her. But when Jess voiced these thoughts to her mother, she reminded Jess of how violent he had been in the end and would affirm that she had done the right thing by moving on because there was nothing she could do to fix a man like that. She would ask Jess if she could ever feel safe with Hank again, and Jess honestly did not know. She felt like she was putting together a puzzle that was missing pieces, but maybe she already had the most important one. If Hank really was capable of the actions Roxy had said he was, if breaking her mirror and hitting John were the first signs of what was to come, then Jess could not be with him. Maybe she had gotten out just as the honeymoon period was ending and the real Hank was emerging. There was no way to tell without going back, and Jess had no intention of doing that.

Chapter 50

It was mid-October when Hurricane Kara, a Category 2 storm, was reported headed toward the Gulf Coast and Louisiana. Florida had several hurricane warnings each year, with few actually panning out, so Jess, like everyone else, continued on with their day, believing such storms were unlikely to affect them except for some heavy rain. But as the storm made its way through the Caribbean, it developed into a Category 3, and worse, it unexpectedly turned, heading for Florida on its coastal side. At that trajectory, it would hit land about one hundred miles south of Orlando at Fort Pierce, and if it kept moving inland, UCF would be to the right of the eye, meaning there could be considerable damage. As the storm approached, the air grew increasingly humid and still, becoming muggier than usual. Friday classes were cancelled in anticipation of the storm, so Jess and Kayla picked up several days' worth of food and got ready to hunker down in their apartment and wait it out. But no sooner had they put away their groceries and gotten ready to watch a movie than Jess's phone rang. Looking down, she saw it was Leah.

When she answered, she heard Leah say the words she had been waiting to hear.

"Jess, we need your help. Can you meet me at the biology building in fifteen minutes?"

Not long after Leah's call, Jess was sitting in a van that was part of a caravan of trucks and cars filled with several other volunteers headed out to the bunkhouse on the Refuge where the team housed all its research gear. Time was tight, but they had to evacuate the boats, ATVs, and other equipment stored at the bunkhouse before the storm hit. Though it was not how she had hoped to get involved, Jess was excited to be there. She'd never been in a hurricane before. Now when she looked out the van window at the flat steel-gray sky and saw how hard the palm trees were being blown to one side, it gave her pause.

When they reached the bunkhouse, people scampered out quickly from the vehicles to get everything they could. Boat trailers were quickly attached to the trucks, and volunteers started loading up the ATVs while others ran behind the bunkhouse to the two storage containers, emptying their contents out into the vans. Everyone seemed to know exactly what to do except Jess, who stood there watching uncertainly before someone grabbed her arm.

"Hey, grab that strap so we can secure it," a male voice said. When Jess turned, she found herself face-to-face with Chris, who was equally startled to see her there, but didn't stop to ask questions. He told her what to do to help secure the ATV into the back of the truck. Jess stood there, holding the strap tightly while trying to avoid the sand being blown hard against her skin and into her eyes. She tried turning to her side and pulling up her T-shirt to cover her mouth and cheeks, but it kept falling down, leaving her having to endure the harsh conditions while continuing to help out. She helped secure the last two ATVs, then looked up at Chris to direct her where to go next.

"Go help them with the equipment," he barked, motioning to the sheds with his head as he went to work on moving some large containers into another truck. Jess ran over and grabbed whatever boxes she could, moving as many as quickly as possible into the vans until both sheds were emptied and locked. When everything had been packed up, they all quickly jumped back into the passenger vans, desperate to escape the stinging sand and harsh wind. Jess jumped into the first van she could to find Chris in the driver's seat. She hesitated, not sure whether she should find the van she came in.

"Just get in. We need to get off the island before they close the Causeway," he said, sensing her hesitation.

Jess moved toward the back to an empty seat and strapped herself in. A moment later, Leah jumped into the front passenger seat, quickly pulling the door shut. She was breathing heavily and had obviously been running.

"Did you get the pictures?" Chris asked her, as he started to pull out behind the others, the group leaving in a line just as they had come.

"I got what I could. Amanda came out yesterday and covered most of the Refuge. She felt pretty sure it was going to head our way before everyone else."

Jess turned to the female student sitting next to her. "What pictures is she talking about?" she asked.

"Oh, we take pictures of the marked nests on the beach so we can find them after the storm and assess the erosion damage."

Jess looked out the window at the waves coming in, one right after another, crashing hard against the beach, and she could see the gray sheet of rain in the distance stretching from the sky to the water, which signaled the downpour was making its way toward them. It was going to be a race to get across the bridge before it closed, and they weren't the only ones trying to make it in time. The call to evacuate the barrier islands had come late with the sudden turn of the storm, and the roads were filled with cars trying to get across to the mainland to find shelter. It was a relief when they finally made it across.

When they made it back to campus, there was more work to be done. Jess helped offload equipment into the turtle lab, while others secured the boats, trucks, and ATVs into the cement parking garages on campus. As soon as the work was done, the group disbursed quickly. They did not beat the rain, which was now coming down hard, with the wind strong enough to cause resistance when walking. When Jess finally made it back to the apartment, she was thoroughly soaked. Still, she was smiling. The whole experience had been exhilarating, and though it wasn't the experience she had hoped for, she still felt she had been a part of the team for a few hours and it felt good. At large universities like UCF, the advice given to students is to find the group they feel they belong to in order to find a sense of community in what is essentially a small city. Being out on the Refuge with the team, Jess felt like this was where she was supposed to be, and she hoped it wouldn't be too long before she was out there again.

That night and the next day, rain continued to pour down as the wind caused palm trees to bend and blow loose debris through the streets. Jess felt safe watching the storm from her apartment window. She was in an older building made from concrete blocks meant to withstand such storms, and being three floors up, she could survey the heavy rain without it affecting her apartment. She talked to her mother, assuring her she was safe from harm and telling her about her experience with evacuating the equipment. Afterward, she set out to get some studying done before hanging out with Kayla.

When she went to sleep that night, she could still hear the rain coming down as it struck the windowpane, the sound soothing as she drifted off to sleep.

When Jess woke the next morning, it took her a minute to figure out the rain had stopped, and rays of sunlight were coming through the sides of her curtains. Jess pulled them back to see a bright blue sky, making it seem as if the storm had never happened save for a few puddles and the scattering of palm fronds and other debris in the street.

Jess got up and was headed into the living room to see if Kayla was awake when her phone rang. The caller ID indicated it was Leah.

"We're headed back to the Refuge to return the equipment and check out the damage to the beach. Up for another field trip?" she asked, already knowing what Jess's answer would be.

Jess was dressed and downstairs in minutes, anxious to see what the storm had done to the beach and the turtle nests. She found out later that the team was often first on the beach after such a storm to assess the damage and replace lost markers on nests. After they reloaded the equipment that had been placed in the turtle lab, Jess piled into the van with the other students. They were all talking about how much rain they got and about a palm tree that had crashed into the front window of The Public House, a popular hangout with the graduate students.

The caravan returned to the bunkhouse around noon to find it had miraculously weathered the storm unharmed. Then everything they did before happened in reverse but with less urgency. Equipment was put back into the sheds, the ATVs were taken off the trucks, and the boats were once again parked in their trailers along the side for when they were next needed.

When that was done, Jess went up to Leah with the other volunteers to see what they needed to do next. Someone handed out sandwiches and water, which Jess gladly accepted. As they ate, Leah gave out clipboards to volunteers who were assigned different areas of the Refuge to check the status of their marked nests. She finished going through the list and then told them to head out. Not until most of them had left did she see Jess still standing there waiting for instructions.

"Jess, you go with…." She looked around and saw Chris gassing up an ATV and he didn't appear to have a partner. "…with Chris. He can show you the ropes."

Chris looked up at the mention of his name. He did not look pleased. In fact, Jess was beginning to believe being pissed off was his natural state. "I can't take her. I'm going to the south end of the island to check on my work."

"Great. She can check the nest markers down there while you do that."

"I don't have time to play teacher right now," he said. Jess didn't know why he disliked her so much, but she was beginning to get tired of it. She waited silently, hoping Leah would change her mind since going out with him was not her idea of fun either.

Instead, Leah walked up to Chris and talked calmly to him. "Look, she came out when we needed her. She has the pictures on her clipboard of what to look for. Once you show her what to do, you can check your samples while she checks markers. You know how it is this time of year. We are working with a smaller group, and need the help."

Chris glared at Leah, then jumped on the ATV angrily and started it up, the engine louder than Jess expected. "Well, are you coming?" he barked at Jess when she didn't move. Jess quickly threw on the backpack Leah was holding out to her and jumped on behind him, holding on tightly to the frame as he quickly took off.

Yeah, I didn't want to be with you either, Jess thought as Chris headed down the beach, the ride bumpier than she had expected. Right away, she could see the amount of erosion done to some of the dunes. As they drove down the beach, she saw where the waves had washed away so much sand that it had created a small cliff. In some places, sea turtle nests were exposed, showing large turtle eggs peeking out from the side of the cliff where the surrounding sand had been washed away to reveal the nest's contents. In other places, eggs just lay exposed on the ground. Jess was going to ask what would happen to those eggs, but she thought better of it, knowing Chris's demeanor. The less she asked him, the better, she decided.

They made their way to the south side of the island where Chris parked the ATV. Jess got off and looked around at the beauty of the reserve. Brush and vegetation were to her right, and to her left was a calm, beautiful ocean with green water gently lapping the shore. Any other day, it would have been considered a serene beach day, but Jess was not there to enjoy the view. It was late afternoon and already quite warm, so Jess was grateful to find another bottle of water in the side pocket of the backpack. She wasn't sure what else was inside, but she figured she would find out soon enough.

Chris got off of the ATV and walked over to her. "Give me the clipboard," he said. Jess opened the backpack, pulled out a clipboard with a pen attached by a string, and handed it to him. He flipped the pages to some pictures on the back. "Here," he said, pointing at the marker on the picture and then at the one on the beach about three yards in front of them. "Use this one as your starting point. It is still in place so you go here," he said, flipping to the first page in front of the clipboard, "and mark it as still standing. Then look for the next one in the pictures and do the same, marking down whether they survived the storm. Understand?"

Jess looked at the marker, then back at the clipboard, but before she could say anything, he shoved it back into her hands. "I have to check on my research site down the beach. If you keep walking, we will meet up at the end and I'll drive you back. Try not to take too long because the sun will start setting in a few hours, and I want to get back before dark."

All of this was said brusquely, and before Jess could say anything, Chris jumped back on the ATV and started it up, the loud noise once again startling her. He reached into his backpack strapped to the front of the ATV and pulled out a large black garbage bag. "And pick up any debris that washed ashore!" he yelled over the engine noise, holding it out for her to take.

"What if I have questions?" Jess yelled back as she took it, uncertain she had caught it all in his brief and curt description.

"Figure it out!" Chris shouted back, then gunned the ATV down the beach.

Jess stood there watching him drive away, confused about his attitude toward her and angry at how he was treating her. Sure, she wanted to come out to the Refuge and help any way she could, but she didn't know that meant taking some grumpy graduate student's abuse. She took a breath. *No, I am not going to let him ruin this for me*, she decided, and looked down at the clipboard. Certainly, she could figure it out. It wouldn't be the first time she had to do that.

According to the pictures, there should be two sets of stakes, one set in the area of the nest and a second set farther back in the dunes in case the first set of stakes got washed away. As Jess proceeded down the beach, there were some stakes in the dunes, but nothing on the beach, and sometimes, nothing at all. The storm had washed away many of the nests, and even though it was late in the season, she still felt saddened at losing them.

As Jess walked, she also picked up the debris she found on the beach, which included items she would expect, like fishing line and some dead sea life, but also several garbage items—like water bottles, plastic bags, and even deflated helium balloons—that made her shake her head. She stopped a couple of times to rest a moment, trying to ration out her water, but she still finished it before she had reached Chris. A slight breeze on the beach helped, but as the day grew later, she began to feel parched and hoped there was more water on the ATV.

By the time Jess reached the place where Chris was parked, she was beat and just wanted to head home. She threw the backpack and the full garbage bag next to the ATV and looked around. Chris was nearby, sitting on a dune looking out over the water, lost in thought. She walked over, hoping he would hear her approach, but when he didn't move, she finally spoke.

"Chris, are you ready to head back? I really need to get some water," she said, expecting him to give her one of his curt replies.

"We can't," he said dejectedly, with a big sigh. "The ATV has two flats from storm debris I ran into. I have to wait until the mechanic brings me spares."

"Well, how long will that take?"

"I don't know," he said. "I called the bunkhouse, but it could take a while until they can send someone to help me fix it."

Jess dropped onto the sand. She was hot, she was thirsty, and she was tired after walking all afternoon in the heat. The last thing she wanted to hear was that she had to sit and wait with Chris. It would be getting dark soon, and she was ready to go home. "So they expect us to just wait out here?" she asked, unable to contain her frustration.

"You don't know how things work around here. I am required to stay with the ATV until the mechanic comes. You'll just have to suck it up and wait. It's part of the job. If you really want to be out here, get used to it," he said as if that ended the conversation.

But Jess had had enough. She wasn't going to just sit here with someone she could barely stand and take his condescending remarks. She needed water and wasn't going to wait it out just because he said so.

"Fine, then *you* stay with the ATV and I'll walk back," she said, and before he could answer, she stood up and started walking away, glad to be away from him but not thinking about how she would have to walk several miles to get back to the bunkhouse. She could feel tears coming down her cheeks from the exhaustion and anger she was feeling, but she was not going to let him see he'd upset her.

"Wait, stop!" she heard him yell behind her, but that only made her go faster until she started running down the beach away from him and back to the north end of the island where she could catch a ride back to campus. What she didn't count on was his catching up and stopping her by standing in front of her and grabbing hold of both her upper arms. "You can't just walk all the way back. You have to stay with me. It's starting to get dark, and you are not allowed to be out here on your own, particularly since you haven't been through the training."

"Let go of me!" Jess yelled, yanking herself out of his grip. "All you have done is try to get rid of me. Well, here's your chance." She started to walk past him again, determined to walk back if it killed her, but Chris got in front of her again, this time not touching her, just walking backward while facing her so he could talk to her.

"All right, all right, you're right. I've been a jerk. I admit it. I have been nothing but rude to you since I first met you. Probably because of when I first met you, but please, *please*," he said, suddenly pleading with her, "do not walk back by yourself. It will only get you and me into trouble, and it would hurt your chances of being a turtle intern next summer."

At that, Jess stopped, some sense starting to infiltrate her determined spirit. Even in her angered and weary state, she knew she didn't want to give up her chances of working with the team, so she stopped and almost crumpled onto the sand, defeated.

"Wait here," Chris said, hesitating for a moment to see if she would get up again. When it looked like she would stay put, he quickly ran back to the ATV, taking something out of a cooler strapped to the front, and then ran back and handed it to her. It was a cold water bottle, which Jess immediately took and downed in one long swallow. When she was done, he took the empty bottle and handed her another one, which she took another large sip from before stopping to catch her breath.

"Does that help?" Chris asked, talking to her in an unfamiliar way. She realized this was the first time he was actually being kind to her. She nodded, taking another sip and then just sat, looking out over the water, trying to calm herself down.

Chris sat down a few yards away, giving her some space and waiting a few moments before talking. "Look, I owe you an apology. I've been going through a rough time and have been taking it out on you and everyone else, which I shouldn't have done. So, I'm sorry. It's hard to explain...."

"Why did you say it was because of when you first met me?" she asked, recounting his words from earlier.

Chris took a moment before he answered. "The day you approached me by the biology offices, I had just been told if I didn't get my act together, I would be asked to take a leave of absence from the program. You see, I was engaged up until a couple of months ago. Basically, my fiancée broke up with me to be with my best friend, and after that happened, I…stopped functioning. I couldn't eat or sleep. I stopped doing my work. I was finally pulled in and told that if I didn't get my head back into my studies, I would need to take time off, which could really affect my ability to finish my degree. So you see," he said, turning to look at her, "it was not the ideal moment for a starry-eyed undergrad to come asking me how to get into the program."

Jess sat taking in his words. She could feel her own pain at losing Hank rising inside her as it did at unexpected moments. She spent a lot of time pushing it down, but right now, her defenses were down and the sharp pain of loss suddenly seemed to creep its way up and hit her fully.

"That must have been hard, losing your fiancée," she finally said. "I had someone, too, that I left…." Being out here on the beach where so many of her memories with Hank were formed was adding to her sadness, and she needed to find a way to stop thinking about him. She took another sip of water and closed her eyes, trying just to breathe and let the feelings pass. She looked away from Chris while she gathered herself, trying not to let the flood of emotion show on her face. "What was she like, your fiancée?" Jess finally asked, wanting to focus on something other than her own memories.

Chris gave a short laugh. "Honestly? A lot like you. It's probably why I was so hard on you. We met in the program our first year, though she went on to do her graduate studies in Texas. I thought when Cameron, my best friend, also went, it was just a coincidence. We joked he would look after her. He certainly did," he said, the last part with some bitterness.

"It must have been really hard to lose them both. You didn't deserve that," Jess said, with true empathy. "Even if you are rather unpleasant to be around…." The last was said in jest since she was starting to feel like herself again. Chris looked at her, taken aback, but when he saw she was joking, he nodded his head.

"Yeah, I deserved that," he said, a slight smile on his face as he looked back out at the water.

Chris told her how he'd gotten into the program and about the nest incubation experiment he was working on that he was concerned the hurricane had disrupted. Jess spoke a little about her life in Wilmington and how she got to UCF, making her breakup with Hank seem more practical, due to distance than for the real reasons she had left. When they ran out of things to say, they sat quietly, listening to the sound of the waves hitting the shore as night fell around them, waiting for help to come. Jess was deep in thought when suddenly she felt the sand begin to shift a few feet to her right. She jumped back slightly, tensing as she tried to figure out what it could be, only to see something dark start to emerge from the sand.

But it wasn't just one creature. It was dozens of little creatures crawling up and over each other, having broken free from their eggs buried deep in the sand and now making their way to the surface. Here they were, all these baby turtles bubbling out of the nest right before her eyes with a sudden and urgent motion, crawling up and over each other. Jess and Chris sat silently watching their tiny flippers push them toward the water, guided only by the light of the moon reflecting on the ocean.

"What do we do?" Jess finally whispered, not daring to move in case it scared them, but Chris spoke in a normal tone.

"Nothing," he said, shrugging his shoulders. "It was an unmarked nest. All we do is watch."

The hatchlings came scrambling out, leaving tiny tracks upon the sand as they made their way to the waves. Jess thought of her nest on Wrightsville Beach that she had never gotten a chance to see hatch after all the time she spent watching over it. Again, she felt that pang of sadness that Hank was not here to share the excitement of finally seeing it with her. Her thoughts went back to all the nights he had come out to be with her while she monitored the nest. How even in the darkness she could see him watching her and smiling, never looking like he was bored and wanting to leave. Even then, she had known not many boyfriends would have done that for her, and she remembered how special it had made her feel.

Remembering those nights always brought back her feelings of uncertainty at leaving. She'd thought of calling Anne to find out what had happened to Hank after that night, but she wasn't sure what kind of response she would get after leaving so abruptly. She thought of calling Lynn, but she didn't want to explain the details of why she chose to leave. For as long as Jess could remember, she had always forged on by herself, creating her own path and not worrying about what anyone thought or said, but the loss of Hank made her feel a loneliness she'd never known before. She missed the closeness they had shared and the ease of their relationship—how the two of them had just seemed to fit together. But now it was over and she didn't know if she would ever find that type of love again or if it had been real in the first place. Every time she thought about it, she wanted to cry.

But she couldn't let herself succumb to those feelings right now, she told herself. She had finally made it to the Refuge and was doing the one thing she had set out to do, which was watch a turtle nest hatch. Even if it was not with Hank, as she had thought it would be, she was not going to let such a special moment pass. And so despite all she had been through that day, she sat there quietly, watching the turtles as they scurried to the water's edge, in awe that these tiny creatures were born already knowing what they needed to do.

Chapter 51

After their day together on the beach, Chris and Jess became friends. For the rest of the season, which went into November, she would walk the beach with him twice a week in the mornings, recording hatched nests for the team while he documented the findings of his experiment. During these outings, he asked what her goals were and what she ultimately wanted to accomplish. Jess was excited to do field research, and she knew she would need a graduate degree to do it, but she hadn't thought further than that. His questions made her think more specifically about what she wanted to do, explaining how getting a doctorate would give her the autonomy to do her own research.

When she wasn't out on the beach counting turtle nests, she was working hard at school. Being at a larger school meant some of her classes were bigger than she could imagine, with up to several hundred students. She was grateful that most of her biology classes were a manageable size where she could interact with her professors and lecturers, which she would often do after class and during office hours. Though Dr. Manning was quite popular with the students, Jess still managed to talk to her both after class and sometimes at the bunkhouse when she was out there with Chris. She hoped her professor would see the effort she was putting in out on the beach and take note of her interest by the questions she would ask during class.

While Kayla was quite studious herself, she wasn't about to let Jess miss out on some of the traditions that were integral to UCF. She convinced Jess to come with her to Spirit Splash, an event designed to get the students excited about UCF's football team and promote school spirit. It started with a rally that ended with thousands of students rushing into the large fountain in the center of campus. The really adventurous ones would scramble to catch plastic baby ducks thrown by the team mascot, who looked like a cartoon version of a knight. Kayla warned her to be careful because some of the students did not hold back when going after those ducks and would push anyone out of their way to catch one. Jess was happy to stay in the back rather than be part of the crowd that went rushing in, but she loved feeling the excitement of the other students and being part of the event.

Kayla also informed Jess of the school superstition that if you walked over the Pegasus seal in the Student Union, you wouldn't graduate. Not that Jess could have walked over it, since it was roped off. Still, though not superstitious herself, she was not willing to test this belief, and instead just noticed it as she passed by, wondering how many students held such a tale to be true.

By the second semester, Jess felt she was a part of the school, having a small group of friends and a schedule that kept her more than busy. When the graduate students came around in January to talk to the undergraduate biology classes about becoming a turtle intern, Jess sat listening and smiling to herself. She already felt she was part of the team, but she knew she would have to go through the process to get into the summer program. That evening, she sent an email stating her interest in being an intern and asking for an interview. The meeting was scheduled a couple of weeks later with Leah and another graduate student. Jess hoped to impress them with the knowledge she'd gained in working with Chris on the Refuge during the short time she'd been there. If she had any concerns with how the interview went, they were quickly allayed by Leah's smile and wink as she gathered her things and thanked them for their time.

The next step was an invitation to join a netting day. Potential interns were invited out on a boat trip to help capture juvenile turtles and take various samples from them before releasing them back into the Indian River Lagoon. The potential interns were evaluated on their participation and enthusiasm, as well as if they were team players. Chris told Jess that when they worked in the summer program, the quarters were close and everyone got pretty tired after weeks of working nights and trying to sleep days, so you wanted to find students who would pull their weight and fit in well with the rest of the group.

Jess was on one of the two boats set up to capture the turtles. They motored out into the muddy green water with Jess taking in the sea breeze and salty smell of the water. She loved being out on the lagoon with the sun shining down on them through the cloudless sky. She helped set the large mesh net in the water that would allow fish to go through but would trap anything bigger. When the buoys holding up the net started to "dance," they grabbed their dip nets and tried to pull up whatever the net had captured. A few times, they pulled out some stingrays and even a four-foot shark, which they immediately threw back, but soon they were pulling up turtles, reaching down to carefully lift each one onto the boat. Jess was glad she was strong since it took some arm strength to pull them in. She quickly learned that while the green turtles were mostly amiable to the whole process, the loggerheads wanted nothing to do with it and put up a bit of a fight. Jess had to be careful where she put her hands so she didn't get bit while trying to haul one in.

They would pass the turtles onto a third boat called the "work up" boat, where other students would take measurements and samples of blood, tissue from a rear flipper, and a piece of scute from the shell before giving them flipper tags. If the turtle had a tumor, they would take a biopsy of that as well. Jess quickly realized several, if not half, of the turtles they caught had cauliflower-like tumors on their necks or skin. When she asked one of the graduate students about what caused them, he said a lot of research was being done on why they were forming, but they suspected it had to do with the stress of turtles transitioning from living offshore to closer to land and experiencing more coastal contaminants in their food from pesticides and other pollutants that found their way into the water.

They pulled up a green turtle with a particularly large tumor that was limiting its ability to use its eyes. It was determined the tumor hampered his ability to find food, so they decided to take it to one of the nearby sea turtle hospitals to be looked at by a vet. It reminded Jess of when they had found Waffle when she was back in North Carolina and how she had gone to visit him at the Turtle Rescue.

At one point during the day, Leah had pulled Jess aside to ask if she was dating Chris with all the time they spent together, but Jess explained they were just friends. One reason Jess was available to volunteer at the Refuge as much as she did was her disinterest in dating. Leaving Hank had left her uninterested in finding another boyfriend. As far as Jess was concerned, she'd worked hard to get to UCF, and she wanted to prove they had made the right choice in accepting her, especially considering her last-minute arrival. There were guys who approached her on campus, but they were no different than the guys she had known at UNCW, looking for a good time and nothing else. She didn't have to worry about any of that with Chris. They seemed to have an understanding from the beginning that their relationship was platonic, focused purely on researching sea turtles. He was more like the big brother she'd never had the way he made her think about what direction she was going and imparting knowledge through his own experiences.

Later that day, Jess was on the work up boat with Chris, learning how to tag a turtle, which required her to crimp a tag on the flipper using pliers.

"Does it hurt them?" she asked, holding the tag pliers in her hand. They were restraining a juvenile loggerhead on the deck of the boat, and she was a little hesitant about how to approach it. Chris was pointing to where she was supposed to tag it. The turtle did not appreciate being restrained and was struggling to get away. Jess didn't know why she was hesitating. She was told it didn't hurt the turtle, but when she watched Chris do the last one, she noticed the turtle flinch slightly, so now she wasn't so sure.

"Go ahead, do it," Chris said, holding the turtle, which was now trying to bite him. "Quickly, Jess...."

Jess started to reach for the flipper when the turtle turned its head and tried to bite her, causing her to jump back.

"Here, let me do it," Chris said, getting impatient and reaching for the pliers.

But Jess wouldn't back down. "No," she said, backing away so he couldn't take them from her. She stepped up again, trying to get a hold on the flipper, but the loggerhead was fighting hard, and when he turned toward her, she stepped back again. This time, the turtle reversed his head quickly and managed to slap Chris with a flipper. Chris yelled and instinctively pulled back in pain. When Chris let go, the turtle stopped fighting and Jess saw her moment, quickly grabbing the flipper and attaching the tag, hearing a muffled crunch as she did so.

"There," she said, proud of herself. "All done."

She smiled up at Chris, who was holding his slapped arm, scowling at her. "Why didn't you just give it to me when I asked?"

"Because you were teaching me how to do it," she replied, used to his moods by this point and knowing she could joke him out of them.

"But you weren't doing it. You waited too long," he said.

"Hmm. I think that had something to do with the teaching I was getting," she said, smiling innocently.

She could see Chris was starting to calm down, the slap on his arm not as severe as he had indicated at first. She'd heard about another graduate student who had lost part of his finger because he had put his hand in the wrong place at the wrong time and been bit. Chris was certainly not in that category, though it would be like him to play up an injury just to prove a point.

"The teaching you were getting was top rate," he replied, trying to sound superior and regain the upper hand. "It's the student that had the problem."

"Well, the student got the job done and the teacher got slapped. You do the math," she said, laughing.

At that, Chris had to smile. Jess had a way of getting him to relax his defenses, despite his reluctance to do so.

"It's a good thing you are as stubborn as you are," he finally said. "You will need to be to do this kind of work."

"My mother calls it being strong-willed," Jess replied.

"Your mother was being kind," Chris said, giving her an elbow to show he was kidding.

"Probably," Jess nodded with a smile.

Chapter 52

Before Jess knew it, her second semester was over and her first summer as a turtle intern had arrived. Even with the half week on, half week off work schedule, which she heard would be tough, she didn't care. Her goal had always been to be out on the Refuge, and now she was finally an official member of the team.

It took Jess a few weeks to get the routine down and learn the various things she was supposed to do, but once she understood her role, she felt right at home. One particular night, she was out with MacKenzie, another turtle intern she was paired with, to mark and flag new turtle nests and gather samples from turtles that came ashore to lay their eggs. Jess was lying down on her back on a sand dune, trying not to swat at the mosquitos that were descending on her despite the long-sleeved shirt, long pants, and gallon of bug spray she was wearing. She focused instead on how bright the moon appeared this evening. It was a hot July night with little breeze, but the clothes were a necessity on the Refuge at this time of year.

Jess was waiting for MacKenzie to come back and report what the green turtle was doing. They had seen it come up the beach, and they now needed to wait until it finished digging its nest and started laying its eggs before they could tag it and get their samples. With a green turtle, that could mean a few hours since it would dig a deeper nest than a loggerhead. If they made too much noise, the turtle might abandon its digging and head back into the ocean before it was done, leaving them to search for another nesting turtle, so they lay there quietly until the time was right.

MacKenzie came crawling backward down the dune on her elbows, trying to stay low and not startle the turtle.

"Not yet," she whispered as she joined Jess, turning on her back as well. Like Jess, MacKenzie was also studying biology and had just finished her junior year. She was from the area, and during their walks on the beach, she would tell Jess stories about how the theme parks had changed over the years. When she found out Jess had yet to go to any of them, she was shocked. "You can't live in Orlando and not see at least of one of them," she had said. "What have you been doing with yourself?"

What Jess had been doing was studying. Some of her classes were more challenging than she had expected, and if she had any down time, she spent it with Chris or helping out the team. Kayla had invited Jess to go with her to the theme parks a couple of times, but she just hadn't been interested. She thought they were more geared toward kids, and even if she went, what would she do? She hated roller coasters and most amusement park rides, and if she had free time, she would rather head to the beach or ride her bike.

They'd already witnessed two false crawls from turtles that came to shore and then left before nesting, and they wanted to tag this one so they could get in before 1 a.m. As they waited, Jess could hear the recurring sound of the ocean waves in the distance. She was trying not to let it lull her to sleep, as this was her third night of her rotation for this week—three nights on, four nights off—and she was feeling the repercussions from having been up late each night and out early in the morning to count nests before trying to sleep the rest of the day. It was a hard schedule, but she had known what to expect when she signed up, and the benefits of being out here far outweighed the inconvenience of an upside-down sleep schedule. Still, the third night was always the hardest. She just needed to make it through tonight, she reminded herself. She could rest when she returned to her apartment for the second half of the week.

Jess reached down absentmindedly to scratch at a mosquito bite, then stopped herself. The more she scratched, the more it would itch, and with the dozens of bites she and MacKenzie had counted on her last night, she knew she didn't want to start down that path. So she did what she could to bury her legs and arms in the sand for protection and take her mind off it. The bugs were the only part of fieldwork she didn't like. Instead, she made herself focus on how much she loved being out here surrounded by nature. She would look up at the sky and never cease to be amazed by the number of stars that would come out at night. She remembered looking at the stars on the beach in North Carolina, but light coming from the homes around the beach made them harder to see. Here on the Refuge there were far fewer artificial lights, and without them, the sky just lit up in a way she had never seen it do before, with shooting stars that would streak across the sky on a nightly basis.

Jess was doing well at building a new life for herself here, but the return of summer and being back at the beach at night made her start thinking of Hank again. He was always in the back of her mind, even after she had tried so hard to convince herself she just needed to forget about him and move on. She could feel herself start to revisit their nights together when she felt a nudge from MacKenzie.

"Your turn," she said quietly.

Jess nodded and rolled over, then crawled on her elbows to the top of the mound. The large green turtle had finished digging its nest and was now sitting over it, dropping her eggs. Even though the turtle could lay up to two hundred eggs, it was possible she could also have a smaller clutch of only about seventy-five, so they had to move quickly. She scooted back down to MacKenzie and signaled to her that it was time to move.

Working in unison, Jess and MacKenzie grabbed their backpacks and quietly came up behind the turtle, each getting ready to do their specific tasks. They had been warned early on not to get in front of the turtle because they could get bit or cause her to abandon the nest before she finished laying her eggs. Jess acted first, taking a biopsy from the trailing edge of her rear flipper. Unlike the docile juveniles they captured when they were netting, full grown green turtles were known to be sassy, so Jess proceeded cautiously, keeping an eye on the turtle as she did so.

Next, MacKenzie took a blood sample from a sinus in the back of the turtle's neck. Greens had comically small heads compared to their large lumbering bodies, whereas the loggerheads had such huge heads that Jess and MacKenzie sometimes took pictures with their hands held over them to show how enormous they were. When she was done, Jess quickly pulled out the measuring tape and read off the size of the carapace to MacKenzie, who wrote it down. She then took out the calipers to measure the turtle's skull. The turtle had finished laying eggs and was now covering the nest, which meant Jess and MacKenzie's remaining time with her was limited, causing them to work quickly. The turtle was kicking sand everywhere in trying to cover its nest, which made it hard for Jess to see as she reached into her backpack to get the tagging pliers. She went home most nights to find sand in her ears, hair, backpack, and underneath her clothing, and tonight would be no different, but she tried hard to stay focused on her task.

"She's on the move!" MacKenzie cried out, trying to get the chip reader out. Jess's job was to tag both front flippers, which meant running after the turtle as it hurried back down the beach toward the ocean. She managed to secure one tag and was trying to get behind the turtle to the other side when she tripped and fell face down in the sand. MacKenzie ran up behind her and managed to wave the chip reader over the turtle before it reached the water's edge, and then, just as it had suddenly appeared from the ocean, it was quickly swallowed up by the waves. MacKenzie looked back at Jess and laughed, seeing her wipe away the sand from her fall.

"Oh, sure, it's funny when it happens to me and not you," Jess said, knowing full well MacKenzie had experienced her fair share of face plants. "Did she have a chip?"

"Thankfully, yes. She was a recap," she said, meaning a "recaptured" turtle who had nested there before. MacKenzie reached down to help Jess up.

"Good because I only got one flipper tag on her," Jess said, a bit disappointed.

"That's one more than she had when she came in," MacKenzie replied. Jess nodded in agreement. *Next time, I'll get it right*, she told herself. Then she followed MacKenzie to mark the nest with stakes.

While it was hard to wake up after only a few hours of sleep, the sunrises made getting out of bed worth it for Jess. Mornings were easier in lots of ways. For one, she could ditch the protective clothing and only needed some shorts and a tank top when doing the morning rounds, though a hat and lots of water would also be necessities once the sun came up. Florida was known for its scorching and humid summer weather, making even Jess avoid the beach during midday. But in the mornings, the sky was something out of a movie. It was larger than anywhere else she'd ever seen it, with its incredible pinks and yellows and lumbering, heavy clouds that reflected these colors as did the substantial ocean beneath them. She never ceased being amazed by this sight, nor at the multitude of turtle sightings and nests she routinely saw in the short time she'd been interning. If she wanted to see turtles, this was the place. Every time she walked down the beach, Jess was reminded of this fact from all the tracks in the sand that the turtles had left from the night before.

Jess and MacKenzie went back out on the ATV to mark some of the new nests in their designated section of the Refuge. Because such a large number of nests were laid on a nightly basis, their job was to only mark every seventh or eighth nest. Once they reached their area, they jumped out of the ATV and got busy marking, driving over the turtle's tracks once they were done to show the nest had been recorded. They could tell what type of turtle it was just by looking at its tracks. A loggerhead would have an alternating gait, but today, they saw tracks that looked like the turtle had pulled herself up with both front flippers at the same time, indicating these nests were made by greens.

"You're right; it's going to be a high green turtle year," Jess said to herself as she marked another nest on the clipboard.

"What's that?" MacKenzie asked, coming up next to her.

Jess didn't realize she had said it aloud. "Oh. It means that we can expect more green turtle nests this year." She'd gotten this information from Chris on their last day on the Refuge when he'd come to finish his research project. He had completed his master's degree during the spring semester and had left shortly after to work on a research project in Nicaragua. It was strange being out here without him, but she was really enjoying the team that was put together this year.

"That explains why we've been so busy," MacKenzie said, looking down the beach. "Let's mark a few more nests over there." She started walking in the direction she had pointed.

The two of them headed over a short distance to where some tracks had been laid, but when they found the nest, it was covered in fire ants.

"Raccoons," Jess said, shaking her head. Sometimes, raccoons dug up the nests and ate some of the eggs, leaving a mess of broken shells with the insides spilled on the sand. When they left, fire ants would take over. Jess hated to see a nest destroyed like that, but she understood such things were part of nature; she had to develop a thick skin in order to become the scientist she wanted to be. They marked three more nests, then got back on the ATV, finishing up just before 10 a.m.

When they got back to the bunkhouse, Jess was too tired to drive back to Orlando, so she thought she would take a nap. MacKenzie, on the other hand, quickly changed and freshened up.

"See you later," she said to Jess with a smile before heading out, closing the door of their bedroom behind her. The other two interns had not yet returned, so Jess had the room to herself. She knew MacKenzie was romantically involved with another intern, which was not uncommon. It made sense the students would gravitate toward each other while living in this secluded area and unable to talk to friends because they were up nights and sleeping days. But it made her think again of her own situation. That place inside of her since she had left Hank still felt empty, and she lay quietly wondering if that feeling would ever go away.

If July was terribly hot and humid, Jess was told August would come with a whole new level of discomfort. Still, her love of being on the beach and working with the turtles overcame having to endure the heat and mugginess. The summer was going by so fast, and she was enjoying it so much, learning something new every day. As it got later into the season, Jess witnessed multiple nests hatching. She also got several opportunities to educate well-meaning passersby who happened upon a nest at the right time, informing them of the plight of the baby turtles yet to come. It reminded her of her time with the Wrightsville Beach group and how much she enjoyed talking to the beachcombers there.

Three days after a nest hatched, the team would inventory the eggs, seeing if there were any unhatched eggs that had proven not to be viable and to count the remaining shells to get an idea of the overall clutch size. This was done to determine why some eggs didn't hatch and to estimate how many hatchlings made it to the ocean. It was fascinating field work, but it came with one major downside: the insides of the unhatched eggs smelled quite rancid, and if you got any of the egg on your clothes, it was impossible to get out the smell.

Jess learned this early on when she and MacKenzie had been instructed to inventory their first nest. Together, they had dug up shells, opening the few eggs that had not hatched to see what stage the embryos had been in when they had stopped developing. When they returned to the bunkhouse, they tried everything they could to wash the smell out of their clothing, from dishwashing liquid to toothpaste, but nothing worked. In addition, even though they wore gloves, they could still smell it on their hands after multiple washings. They finally conceded that on inventory days, it was best to wear clothes they could later throw out and to avoid eating with their hands until the smell dissipated.

But that didn't deter them from wanting to explore why some eggs were not viable. To Jess, opening up unhatched eggs was like opening up presents. She was so curious to see what was in there. Just by holding an egg in her hand, she could feel if there was something inside, and what they would find was often unexpected. Just in their research alone, they found everything from partially developed turtles to ones that were not developed at all. It was fascinating to see the different embryonic stages the turtles went through. Today, as they opened the unhatched eggs, they found one hatchling with two heads. It was an unusual find and Jess was excited to have discovered it, taking a picture to show to the others later. When they were done digging up and cataloguing the nest, they put all the opened shells and dead hatchlings back in the ground and covered it up, returning it to the earth.

As they headed back to the ATV, Jess was still feeling excited over her find when MacKenzie looked down at her phone and stopped short. "Jess, there's a leatherback on the beach…" she said, looking up excitedly.

A leatherback sighting was rare, especially this late in the season, and if someone happened to catch one coming up on the beach, they immediately put out a call to the others. It was possible to go the whole season without seeing one, though Jess had secretly hoped she would get lucky, and now here was her chance. They ran for the ATV and started it up, rushing over like many of the others to capture a glimpse of this large lumbering creature.

When Jess saw the huge turtle digging its nest, she was awe-struck. It was much bigger than she imagined it would be, looking like some sort of prehistoric creature. Its shell was very much like she had read, more leather-like than the hard shell common on other sea turtles. The leatherback was distinctive because it had a layer of soft skin that covered the bony plates composing its shell, which were supposed to have a leathery feel. She had read they could weigh any-where from 600-1500 pounds, yet were known to be gentle giants. The graduate students around her were guessing this one was about 900 pounds, and to see it in action was mesmerizing. The group stayed to watch it lay its eggs and cover its nest before heading back out into the ocean, excited to have caught such a sight. It would be the topic of conversation for weeks to come, and the next shift of interns would be jealous they had missed it.

That night, lying in bed thinking, Jess admitted to herself she had made the right decision coming to UCF. She loved being out on the Refuge doing field work and had never felt so certain about what she wanted to do as when working with the turtles here. This was where she belonged, even though the road that led her here had not been one she would have chosen. She'd loved Hank, that she didn't doubt, but she still didn't know how to process the person she had known with the events that had happened at the end. Even if she wanted to find out, so much time had passed that he might not even talk to her at this point. After not replying to his texts last fall, they had stopped coming, meaning he had probably moved on. Which was what she needed to do as well. She needed just to leave all that behind her. She had to stop questioning herself over whether she had done the right thing in leaving and not looking back. As best as she could tell, she had.

Chapter 53

Senior year came quicker than Jess could have imagined. She had taken a couple of courses over the summer during the second half of the week when she wasn't busy being a turtle intern to make up the credits she had lost with her transfer. Even after doing that, she still had to carry a full course load in the fall. Not that Kayla was going to let her spend all her time studying sea turtles. She seemed to make it her mission to find Jess a boyfriend, despite Jess's attempts to convince her she didn't want one. First, Kayla talked Jess into joining her on a double date with her boyfriend and his roommate, a guy named Rich who was a business major. Rich was pleasant enough, but after a dinner of listening to him talk about day trading and the stock market, Jess had to wonder why Kayla thought they would be a match. Next, Kayla set her up with a guy from her humanities class who met Jess for coffee. He was from New York, a transplant from the Northeast like Jess, who loved the beach, but all commonality ended there. He didn't have any interest in her science studies, only wanting to talk about his thoughts on classic literature and various books Jess had never heard of, much less ever wanted to read. It didn't take long before their conversation fell flat. Not that this stopped him from inviting her up to his place afterwards, which she curtly declined.

After that meeting, she firmly informed Kayla that she would not be going on any other dates, saying she could get her own if she wanted to. Jess had no shortage of opportunities to date, as a number of guys had tried to ask her out, but she just wasn't interested. She knew what it was like to be truly attracted to someone, and until she felt that connection again, she was content to focus only on her work.

Jess felt good about how her life was going. She'd made lots of friends, she knew what she wanted to do, and she knew she wanted to be the best at doing it. That took concentration and dedication, two traits she had in abundance. While she enjoyed occasionally going out to dinner or catching a movie with friends, she never felt she was missing anything by passing on parties or hanging out in bars.

What energized her was being outside, exploring the habitats that were native to Florida but so exotic to her, having grown up in New Jersey. In North Carolina, she had come across certain birds and animals that were not native to the cooler climate of the Northeast, but Florida offered a whole new array of wildlife to explore. While biking around different lakes, Jess would often see different types of cranes wading around in the marsh, or spot large alligators sunning themselves, some up to twelve-feet long. More than once, she came across a flamboyance of flamingos that would suddenly lift off and fly over her head, their unusual pink feathers brightly contrasting against the blue sky. Occasionally while walking around at night, she would even spot an armadillo scampering away. It was an unusual sighting to her, but she soon discovered they were an unwelcome pest that they dug burrows that damaged peoples' gardens and lawns.

One particular encounter was both unexpected and exhilarating. A graduate student on the team the previous summer had left behind a paddleboard. Jess had avoided surfing since coming to Florida, but quietly paddling her way through some of the waterways surrounding the Refuge struck her as a peaceful way to explore the more out-of-reach areas. She particularly liked gliding around Mosquito Lagoon to see the wildlife there. On days when she visited the Refuge and had a few hours to spare, she would borrow the board to enjoy some time on the water.

She knew there were manatees in Florida, grayish-brown creatures described as giant sea cows, but seeing one in real life was much different than seeing one in a short video online. During one of these paddleboard outings, two manatees came up beside her, a mother and her calf, their large plump bodies playfully doing barrel rolls in the water as they swam gracefully alongside her. The mother was at least ten-feet long and Jess, knowing such mammals averaged about 1,000 pounds, would have been frightened if she didn't know from her animal behavior class how gentle manatees actually were. She remained still on her board as she watched them bob alongside her. Barely daring to breathe, she was amazed to see them up close like this, and she only resumed her paddling after they decided to swim away and were well out of sight.

The thrill of the encounter stayed with Jess for days. She felt invigorated to see such marvelous creatures and was anxious to see what else would reveal itself to her during one of her paddling excursions. It was yet another reminder of how lucky she was to have transferred to UCF.

When Jess's senior year was over, she was extremely proud of what she had accomplished. She'd earned her Bachelor of Science degree and had been accepted into the UCF Biology Doctoral Program, guaranteeing she would spend more summers on the Refuge. Her hard work was paying off, and it felt like everything was falling into place.

Jess's second summer on the team was even more eventful than the first. Now that she was in the PhD program, she was involved with training the interns, plus collecting data while she determined what the focus of her research would be. She found she acclimated to the schedule a little easier this time since she didn't have to switch back to a daytime routine for classes. By keeping to a consistent schedule of working nights and sleeping days, even when she was back in Orlando, she felt more rested than she remembered being the previous summer. While it did mean that any extracurricular activities like biking or paddleboarding would have to be done in the late afternoon, she didn't feel like she was giving up anything. She liked the person she was becoming, and her enthusiasm was contagious. The interns sought her out when they had questions, and the other graduate students were equally drawn to her. There was no question she played a key role in solidifying the group.

What Jess loved most, though, was being on the Refuge. She loved seeing the turtles dig their nests and lay their eggs, their resolve not deterred by the interaction of the interns. She loved seeing the hatchlings erupt from their nests and how they would find their way down the sandy beach with nothing but the light of the moon and the pull of the ocean waves calling to them. She loved the smell of the salt water and the sound of the sea grass rustling with the wind. She loved the sunrises in the morning and how at night the sky would be so full of stars that it looked like the universe could barely contain them all.

But at odd moments when she would look up to see a shooting star, the loneliness would sometimes come. She missed having someone who made her feel special. Any hopes that she would someday meet someone who made her feel the way Hank had were quickly pushed down. Better to concentrate on the things she did have than to think about those she didn't. What was important right now was that she was in the exact place she wanted to be. She told herself that was enough, or for now that it had to be.

Chapter 54

That fall, Jess began her doctoral studies working with Dr. Manning, assisting with her current research project, which focused on the "lost years" of baby sea turtles. This was the period from when the hatchlings first broke free of their eggs and swam offshore until they returned years later as juveniles to forage closer to coastlines. Very little was known about this time, and since so many turtle hatchlings never made it to adulthood, understanding where they went during their early years would help scientists understand what threats these young turtles encountered and why so few of them survived. The work involved attaching small solar-powered satellite tags to loggerhead juvenile turtles that were less than a year old to track their movements, but the biggest problem Dr. Manning's team was having was getting the tags to stay on the shells of the turtles. Using methods like harnesses and hard epoxy had proven faulty, so Jess and another graduate student were experimenting with using different mounts and glues. However, as Jess started her third summer working at the Refuge, it was clear nothing they were using was working, and her frustration grew as she recognized they needed a solution.

Jess was an active participant in putting together the Turtle Team this year. She had helped pick the new interns and was assisting in running the program. While she was still an asset in training the interns and keeping the group running smoothly, she started to become increasingly engrossed in her research project, paring down her other duties where she could. She spent night after night on her computer, often staying at the bunkhouse for days while she researched a solution for keeping the transmitters on the turtles long enough to gather information on their early behavior and habitat choices. The other graduate students were also deeply invested in their own studies, but even they started to grow concerned about Jess's unrelenting focus on her work. It became a game among them to see who could lure her from her computer, by asking her out on dates or inviting her to hang out with them. But while she would join the others for meals or group meetings, the rest of the time she waved them off and kept to herself, absorbed in her quest to solve her research problem. When Dr. Manning pulled her aside, telling her she would think clearer if she took a break and to focus on a better work-life balance, Jess listened and nodded in agreement, but then went right back to work. Nothing could deter her from her task, and after a while, the group left her alone, not knowing how to break the spell she was under.

Everyone, that is, but Thomas. Thomas was a graduate student from Australia, and like Leah, he had a strong interest in the migration patterns of sea turtles and how they were able to return to the beach where they were born to lay their own nests. This was his first year at the Refuge while he was working on his master's degree. Jess welcomed him on his first day, showing him around the Refuge and introducing him to the rest of the team before excusing herself to let him get settled. He immediately took to the group and was instantly popular due to his unusual Aussie accent and gregarious manner. But he found it odd that after such a warm welcome, Jess barely acknowledged him whenever he encountered her around the bunkhouse, making him think he had done something to put her off.

Thomas began watching how Jess interacted with the others, and after a few days, he realized she treated him no differently than anyone else. When she wasn't guiding the interns, she spent the majority of her time working, rarely socializing with anyone. In the rare moments when he managed to talk to her in the lounge area, he could feel the intensity she gave off and how passionate she was about her work. Though he admired her dedication, he sensed something else about her. He could tell she was missing something. He wasn't sure what that something was, but at some point, he decided he wasn't going to let her work away the summer without enjoying some of the marvels that surrounded them. Here they were in a place filled with natural wonders that never failed to leave him captivated, and he wanted to share some of those discoveries with someone he felt would enjoy them as much as he did. From what he heard about Jess from the others, the Jess they knew before she became so focused on her work was that person. He just needed to figure out how to bring out that side of her again.

So one night while Jess was busy at her computer typing away, Thomas came in and handed her a windbreaker. "I need you to come with me," he said, as if this were a common occurrence and not the first time he had approached her in such a manner.

Jess looked up, unsurprised to see him. She was aware it was a game to the others to see who could get her to leave her computer, and she figured it must be Thomas's turn to play.

"Thanks, but I am in the middle of...." she started, trying to dismiss him, but he put up his hand and spoke quietly but authoritatively.

"I have something to show you that I guarantee you will want to see, but if you are going to see it, you have to come now." He then turned and left the room, not waiting to see if she would follow.

Jess sensed something different about this request. Thomas was exactly what you would expect a field biologist to look like with his shoulder-length brown hair tied back in a ponytail, his Birkenstocks, and his tall and lanky frame. But there was also an energy to Thomas that made you believe when he was around that something exciting was about to happen, which drew people to him. When he looked into Jess's eyes, she felt that energy and a promise of something else. She thought for a moment, recognizing her research was not going anywhere tonight, then decided to shut down her computer and put on the coat. Maybe a walk outside would clear her mind, she thought.

Thomas was waiting by the front door, and when he saw her emerge from her room, he turned and walked out of the bunkhouse. Jess silently followed, uncertain where they were going. They started walking down the beach with Jess just a bit behind him, trying to keep up with his long strides. At first, she felt a little bit hesitant—where in the world was she going with this guy she barely knew down a deserted beach in the middle of the night? But then she saw some of the undergraduates out marking a nest and could hear one of the ATVs further down the beach, reminding her that they really weren't alone after all.

Not that she'd ever gotten the impression she should worry about Thomas. She'd seen him work with some of the undergraduates, and she was impressed with his patience in teaching them, even the female students who would ask questions just to hear his accent. She could see how they would find him attractive, though it was not something she thought about. But right now, she didn't know what to make of him. They continued to walk down the dark beach in silence until their only guide became the light of the moon and the soft sound of the waves in the distance. He made no effort to talk to her or even look in her direction to see if she was still there, and didn't seem to notice that his long strides required her to work to keep up. After they'd been walking for what seemed like forever, she started to wonder if this was just a waste of her time. Maybe he was just playing the game like the others. Maybe she had misread him and he was just seeing how far she would go.

With this thought, she stopped, ready to tell him she was done playing and was going to head back, when Thomas also suddenly stopped and looked up at the dunes.

"There," he said, his hand motioning to a loggerhead turtle in the process of finishing up a nest. Loggerheads were known to acquire a good amount of algae on their shells, and this one's shell was especially covered. Thomas walked slowly up behind the turtle, trying to find a spot so as not to get hit with the sand being flung by her flippers. When he was close enough, he slowly reached out his hand and rubbed the algae on the turtle's shell while she continued to bury her eggs.

What happened was something Jess had never seen before. The shell actually lit up where Thomas rubbed it, emitting a pale green glow that quickly faded, making Jess wonder if she had actually seen it. She had read about bioluminescence in jellyfish, but she had never seen it on a sea turtle. She came up next to Thomas and also rubbed the turtle's shell, watching the greenish color flare bright again before disappearing. She smiled at him, astonished and not knowing what to say.

"I thought you should see this," Thomas said, smiling back, proud that he was able to impress her. They turned back to the turtle rubbing her back to make the shell glow until, without warning, the turtle finished covering her eggs and headed back to the ocean, remnants of light still flickering off her back like a scattering of fireflies as she made her way down to the shoreline and into the water.

The two of them stood there watching the turtle disappear into the waves, speechless at the beauty of what they had seen. It wasn't until many moments after the turtle had disappeared that Thomas turned to Jess.

"Will you go to dinner with me?" he asked as if he already knew her answer.

"Yes," she said, knowing there was no other reply.

Chapter 55

What to wear? That was always the dilemma. Jess hadn't spent as much time the past year or so hitting the consignment stores, so coming up with a dress for dinner was proving difficult. *This is one of the reasons I don't date*, she thought. All this effort for what was usually a disappointing event. Though the excitement over having seen the turtle glow was still with her, the tension of going on a date was starting to outweigh the delight it had given her.

"You can borrow one of mine," Kayla said from the living room where she was watching TV. Even though Kayla had graduated the previous year, she'd stayed on in Orlando for a job, allowing their roommate situation to continue. Kayla was especially pleased with the way the arrangement worked. When Jess stayed at the Refuge, Kayla had the whole apartment to herself for days. And when Jess was there, she got to hang out with her. But when Jess told her she was going on a date for dinner, Kayla became downright giddy, making several suggestions about what she should wear and how to do her hair before Jess kicked her out of her room.

"No thanks. I think I found something," Jess replied. While she appreciated Kayla's advice when she needed some tips on makeup or the best shampoo to use, she had learned long ago that Kayla would happily take over Jess's social life if given half a chance. What made them compatible roommates was Jess appreciated her advice when she needed it and she was able to tune her out when she didn't. Jess found a black halter dress with white polka dots, something attractive without seeming like she was trying too hard—a choice she felt was just right for tonight, along with a pair of silver earrings. She had enough of a tan to forego having to wear makeup, so with a quick brush of her hair and a dab of lipstick, she was ready to go.

"Do I get to meet the mystery man?" Kayla asked with a gleam in her eye as Jess slipped on a pair of sandals and gathered her purse and keys. Kayla was in the middle of gluing on some fake nails with intricate floral designs on them, a habit she had recently picked up, saying it was easier than painting them. Jess stopped for a moment and watched with curiosity. She'd never been interested in spending the time other girls did to learn makeup techniques or play with different hair styles. It was easier to rely on Kayla's knowledge of such things the rare times she had needed to know them. She was lucky to find the time to dab a clear coat on her nails when she could, knowing she not only lacked the patience to wear long nails but would never be able to keep them on with all the field work she did.

"I am meeting him there," Jess said, looking at her watch. "And I better be going if I don't want to be late."

As Jess headed out of the apartment, she could hear Kayla's cheerful send-off. "Don't do anything I wouldn't do," she said with a laugh. "Or better yet, do!"

Jess smiled as she closed the door behind her.

Jess met Thomas at a restaurant in Winter Park, a city just out-side of Orlando that was a favorite with the locals due to its old-world charm. They were seated on the patio at a table that over-looked a large lake with a clear view of the setting sun. Thomas was more dressed up than usual, if you could call chinos and a short-sleeved, button-down shirt dressy, but it was certainly a step above the usual field clothing they normally wore. Jess could tell he was freshly showered, having combed his wet hair back into his signature ponytail, and she liked the way he smelled. Thomas was obviously thinking the same thing, letting her know how pretty she looked as he pulled her chair out for her. He started out more reserved than usual, which Jess found interesting, considering how gregarious he normally was at the Refuge. However, once they started talking, he relaxed and the confidence he normally exhibited with the team resurfaced as he talked about how he chose UCF and what he hoped to accomplish by getting his master's degree.

Jess asked Thomas questions about what it was like to grow up in Australia and how he had developed his love of sea turtles. She enjoyed how he described his family back home, including the pranks he would play on his brothers, which made Jess laugh out loud. She watched him as he told his stories, realizing how much she liked hearing him talk. She noticed how animated he could be when he was excited about a subject and how his exuberance would draw her in. At the Refuge, she found his outgoing manner almost too much sometimes, as if he were actively seeking attention. But being here alone with him, she found him engaging and sincere. While he talked, she looked at him, finding him very physically appeal-ing. For the first time in a long time, she found herself attracted to him, and though the idea took her by surprise, it seemed so natural just to be sitting here with him. While he may have been slim, she could see by his arms that he was quite strong and wondered what it would be like to have him hold her. And while she typically didn't like beards, she found his close-shaven look worked well on him, and she wondered how it would feel for him to kiss her. More importantly, she understood the passion he felt about his work, feeling she had found a kindred spirit.

They stayed until after the sun had long set, lingering as long as they could until the restaurant informed them it was closing. Neither of them was ready for the night to end, so they decided to go for a walk along Park Avenue, past the high-end shops and various restaurants with tables overflowing onto the sidewalk. Here the conversation switched to Jess, who talked about growing up in New Jersey before giving her rehearsed version of how she had ended up at UCF, which led to what she was doing with her own research. As they were crossing a street, Thomas took her hand and she found herself gravitating closer to him, liking the warm feel of his arm against hers. They ended up strolling through Greeneda Court, with its narrow brick walkways and decorative shrubs, stopping to view the fountain in the courtyard that was lit up at night.

"It would go so much better if we could solve the problem of getting the transmitters to stay on the turtles' shells," Jess said with sigh. "It seems like instead of doing research, that's where all my focus has been. I have been working on it for months, and if I don't find an answer, I won't be able to get the data I need to write my dissertation."

"It sounds like quite a perplexing problem," Thomas replied.

"It really is," Jess said, suddenly getting worked up. She had promised herself not to talk about her work, but once she got started, she found she couldn't stop. She threw her hands up in frustration. "I have researched every type of gluing compound I can think of, and nothing has worked. If I could just...."

But before she finished her sentence, Jess suddenly stopped, holding her hands frozen in mid-air. She could feel her mind racing, working through something, and she stood still, waiting for it to finish. She was looking at her nails. It made her think of Kayla and how she was gluing fake nails onto her real nails. Turtle shells were made of the same material as fingernails, her brain was telling her. Could what Kayla used to glue on her fake nails work on a turtle shell?

"That's the answer I've been looking for," Jess said out loud without even realizing it, almost certain it would work as soon as it came to her.

Jess suddenly turned to Thomas, threw her arms around him, and kissed him on the lips, stunning him in the process. Before he could react, she stepped back. "I've got it, Thomas! I think I know what will work! Of course, why didn't I think of it before?"

Thomas answered by pulling her back to him and kissing her again, the kiss lasting much longer, leaving Jess feeling flustered when she pulled back. She was amazed by how good it felt to be kissed again, and once more, she felt an attraction to Thomas that was making her heart race.

But even that special moment could not subdue her delight over possibly finding the solution to her long-standing problem. She took his hand and started explaining to him the connection she had made as she led him back to her car. Jess didn't want to waste any time in researching this new idea and wanted to get started right away.

At her car, she gave Thomas one more quick kiss, hesitating a moment to look into his eyes, then told him she would see him at the Refuge, before she got in and sped away. Thomas just stood there watching her leave, reeling from the depth of her passion and completely enchanted with everything else about her.

Jess spent the rest of the weekend researching her idea. When she presented it to Dr. Manning on Monday, the professor was extremely impressed with Jess's solution and gave her the go-ahead to see if it would work. Jess experimented first with some turtles in the lab. What she found was it didn't work on the green turtles because their shells were too waxy, but it did work on the loggerheads because the acrylic would seal the shell that would normally peel away as a natural part of their growth, allowing her to attach a tag with an aquarium silicone that would stay put. Finally, she had a way to start collecting data to put toward her dissertation, so she set out to start attaching transmitters to juvenile turtles in the field.

Jess practically lived at the Refuge now that she had had a breakthrough. She was anxious to start collecting data, but she no longer isolated herself from the others. She started to join them for social events or to hang out in the lounge after her work was done, reverting back to her old self. For the first time in a long time, she felt happier and wanted to connect with the team again like she had when she first became a turtle intern.

It wasn't difficult to figure out what had inspired the change in her. After their first date, Thomas and Jess became inseparable, only apart when doing their individual fieldwork. At the end of the day, they would meet up at the bunkhouse to eat dinner with the rest of the team and help prepare the undergraduates for their evening shifts before going off to spend time together. Once alone, they would discuss any findings they came across that day and relay any happenings that would make the other laugh. Thomas was especially good at turning his sometimes less-than-successful attempts to work with the turtles into outlandish stories of courage and adventure, a trait that drew Jess to him just like it did the others.

Jess enjoyed how easy it was to be with Thomas and how comfortable she felt with him. He filled the emptiness left by Hank, making her believe again that she could find someone who could make her feel special. Being with Thomas made her realize how much she'd shut down in order not to think about how much she had missed being close to someone. Having him reawaken those feelings was both exciting and scary. She worried about getting so close to Thomas so quickly, but one look from him made all those thoughts disappear. In him, she had found someone she could talk to at length about her work and who shared her passion to discover the answers to all the questions their research raised. She felt he understood her. He made it so easy to let her guard down and let him in.

Chapter 56

One afternoon, Jess took Thomas paddleboarding. They rented a couple of boards and headed out into Mosquito Lagoon with Jess leading. She first determined which way the current was flowing, then headed upstream.

Thomas had never been on a paddleboard before, which surprised Jess.

"I thought you knew how to surf," she said when she saw how wobbly he was. He fell off when he stood for the first time and again shortly after they started out.

"Why would you think that?" he asked, trying to maintain his balance and not fall in again.

"Because you're from Australia." Thomas had no problem pointing out some of the stranger habits of Americans, so Jess would often tease him about his Aussie roots whenever the chance arose.

"Not everyone from Australia surfs. Some of us don't live by the beach."

"Ah. So you're from the Outback. That would make you more used to wrestling alligators."

Thomas chuckled. "No one in Australia tussles with alligators because we only have crocs."

"All right, crocs. Then you can save me if one of those makes his way out to us." She motioned to a couple of alligators sunning themselves on the shore of the barrier island they were gliding by.

Thomas eyed them warily. "You're dreaming. If they so much as look like they are headed our way, I'm going to do the Harry," he said, referring to an Australian phrase for beating it out of there.

"That's going to be tough if you can't stay on your board," Jess replied.

"I'm thinking that if I can make a fair go of it, mate, and just outrun you, I'm better than a ham sandwich."

"I'm not sure what to make of that," Jess said, chuckling. Sometimes the language barrier was more than she would expect from two people who spoke English. "Let's hope they're chockers so we don't have to find out." Thomas had told her he felt "chockers" one night after a particularly big dinner and explained it meant full. He laughed heartily at her using his own vernacular back at him.

They continued paddling, the water a crystalline blue and almost glasslike. It was a beautiful day to be out on the water, and Jess would sometimes stop paddling and just close her eyes as she glided along, feeling the sun warm her face and arms, a slight breeze against her skin. Staying close to the shoreline, they managed to remain clear of the fishing boats, though when one would pass, the waves it would cause would sometimes make Thomas fall in again. Jess pulled up next to him and showed him how to turn the board into the waves so that he hit them directly rather than have them hit his board from the side, rendering it unsteady.

"It's easier to keep your balance this way," she said.

"Yes, but not when this happens," he said, playfully pulling her off the board and into the water with him. He pulled her close to him, each holding onto their board with one hand so it would not float away. "I guess now we're both off-balance."

"Don't think I'm going to let you get away with doing that," Jess said, shaking the wet hair out of her face.

"I'll take my chances," he said, leaning in to kiss her.

Jess's relationship with Thomas continued into the school year with both of them spending time together daily. Kayla immediately took to Thomas, partly due to his Aussie accent, like most girls, but mostly because she liked his outgoing manner and the effect it had on Jess. Sometimes he would conspire with Kayla to come up with different ways to break Jess out of her comfort zone. Kayla was particularly fond of having game nights or throwing themed parties, which Jess had begged off of in the past but now was participating in thanks to Thomas. When Jess started worrying that she was taking too much time away from her work, Thomas would reassure her that her work was proceeding fine and that it was good for her to enjoy some time off once in a while.

Between Thomas and working on her research, the first year of dating went quickly. The only time they were apart was during the holidays when Thomas flew back home for a couple of weeks while Jess returned to New Jersey for a visit with her mother. Even when they were on different continents, they stayed in touch by FaceTiming each other daily, working around the time difference. The next summer, they were back out at the Refuge, working on their experiments. With the transmitters staying on the turtles, Jess was starting to collect data, and as always, she enjoyed working with the new interns. Her and Thomas's enthusiasm brought a certain energy to the group that motivated the others through the long nights and strenuous fieldwork. Jess could not have asked for a better way to spend her summer, studying turtles and having Thomas to share it all with.

After their second summer together, Jess started to wonder where their relationship was headed. It wasn't something they talked about since neither of them knew where their work would take them, making such a conversation premature. And when she listened to Thomas talk about the future, it was clear he planned eventually to return to Australia. While Jess thought it might be interesting to spend some time conducting research in another country, she'd never considered living somewhere else, and she wasn't sure she wanted to settle down in a place so vastly different from what she had always known. Rather than think about what might happen, Jess put it out of her mind, telling herself it was not something she needed to think about yet with so many variables still uncertain.

Once in a while, her thoughts returned to Hank. Now when she thought of him, she only thought about how he'd always been there when she needed him. She would never forget that it was because of him that she had gotten away from John that night. For a long time, the memory of John's attack had stayed with her, making her relive the fear she had felt. It had taken a couple of years before she had recognized that what had happened was not her fault. It was just a matter of being in the wrong place at the wrong time, and she was lucky that Hank had showed up when he did. Over the years, her fear had turned to anger, and now if she saw John again, she would have no problem letting him know just what she thought of him.

Now at times she wished she had talked to Hank to hear his side of the story. The more she thought about the things Roxy had told her, the more unlikely they seemed. Maybe breaking her lamp could be explained as an accident, distorted by Roxy's words going through her head. Or was she just making excuses, wanting to believe Hank was someone he was not? Maybe she would never know the truth about who he really was, but she could remember the way he made her feel and how much she'd loved him. It was the only way she could put it to rest in her head.

Not until well into their second year together did Jess start noticing little things about Thomas that bothered her. For instance, Thomas often sought to be the center of attention at group gatherings, which grew tiring. At times, Thomas was so wrapped up in whatever he was working on that he forgot about plans he had made with Jess, often showing up late and one time not at all. She understood about being so engrossed in your work that you lost track of time, but when he completely forgot they had plans, her first thought was Hank would never do that. Having been in only one serious relationship, it was hard not to compare them. But then maybe she wasn't being fair to Thomas. She'd only dated Hank a handful of months during a summer when they'd had few obligations. And when Thomas did show up, he would be apologetic and completely focused on her, making her feel as if she were the most special woman in the world, then would charm her into some group activity he wanted to do. More and more often, she found herself accommodating his desire to always be interacting with the world over her own preference to enjoy quiet nights at home.

In their third year together, Thomas completed his master's degree and made plans to stay on in Orlando to work with a research group studying the effects of plastic waste on sea turtles. It was part of a collaborative effort that meant working with researchers in several other countries, including Australia. Thomas seemed excited about the project, but once he started working on it, he started to change. At times, he would grow sullen, avoiding Jess and not going out. If they did go out, he would get easily aggravated over things that never seemed to bother him before, like getting irritated at the slow service at a restaurant or frustrated when they unexpectedly hit traffic, incidents he used to shrug off. When he started talking more frequently about his family and what his life was like back home, Jess realized how much he missed being there and knew it was only a matter of time before he would be going back.

Sure enough, when Thomas's year with the research group came to an end, it was no surprise to Jess that he had secured a position back home, not informing her about it until he'd already accepted it. He knew Jess had another year before she would complete her doctorate, so he made the one offer they both knew was merely to delay the inevitable: they could continue to date long distance and see how things went. Jess saw it for what it was. She knew she did not want to move to Australia, and that Thomas did not want to stay in America. So that was it. It was time to let Thomas go. And while she was sorry to say goodbye and to end what had been a special time together, Jess also felt a strange sense of relief come over her when it was said and done, knowing it was the right thing to do.

Chapter 57

After Thomas left, Jess didn't really miss him. She felt his absence only because he'd been her sole companion for the past year, particularly after Kayla had left for another job in Tampa and many of her friends from college had gotten married or moved away. What Jess did miss was having someone to talk to at the end of the day and to maybe watch a movie with or go out to eat. Being alone gave her more time to think, and after some time apart, she admitted to herself she had never pictured herself marrying Thomas. Her hesitancy to bring up the subject earlier in their relationship was a sign that she knew their differences were too great, and now she was glad she had never broached the idea with him.

Not that having that understanding eliminated the loneliness she felt after he left, which was only compounded by the sudden influx of wedding invitations she was receiving from college friends, reminding her of her newly single status. The heavy cream-colored note cards embossed with swirly gold lettering announcing such upcoming events made her think about how she, too, would like to get married someday and start a family. She had always pictured herself sharing her life with someone. But here she was, almost twenty-seven, with only two serious relationships in her past. It didn't seem like a lot when she thought about how many relationships some of her other friends had gone through. That worried her and made her wonder if she would ever find someone with whom she wanted to settle down.

To take her mind off of her worries, Jess decided to do a deep clean of her apartment. She went through her closet and her desk, pitching old clothes and notes she didn't need anymore. The act of cleaning out her living space gave her a feeling of renewal. After all, her life was about to change in new ways once again, so why not start it without the clutter she'd accumulated during her time in Florida? And the cleaning project had an added benefit. As she got rid of the items she no longer needed, she also came across others that brought back fond memories. She was warmed by some heartfelt graduation cards she found in a drawer and was happy to find a sweater she thought was lost, but had only fallen down into a corner in her closet.

But Jess's biggest find was in the back of a drawer behind some T-shirts she no longer wore. It was a small black velvet bag, and in it was a silver turtle with swirls on its shell hanging from a chain. It was the necklace Hank had given her all those years ago, the night she first told him she loved him. She looked at it thoughtfully, thinking what a beautiful piece it was, then opened the clasp and put it on. She had put it away when it made her think of Hank, but now she was happy to have found it again. To her, it represented the beginning of her journey to become a sea turtle biologist and for that reason alone, she should wear it proudly.

Without Thomas around filling her social calendar, Jess had time to start biking again, using the regular physical motion and fresh air to clear her mind. She liked how riding helped her thoughts flow and gave her perspective as she thought about her life. During one ride, she remembered a conversation with her mother in high school that she'd not thought about in a long time. She recalled complaining one evening about how no one ever asked her out, yet her friends seemed to be constantly dating and moving from one guy to the next. She remembered how her mother just smiled and looked at her, holding her chin in her hand. "You are not going to have those types of casual relationships," she had told her. "Just give it time."

Jess didn't understand what her mother had meant at the time. It was easier to believe she was deficient in some way and that was why the boys didn't like her. But now she understood what her mother was trying to convey. She was not the type of girl who was with a guy for the sake of saying she had a boyfriend. Although she'd only been in two relationships, they were heartfelt and meaningful, enriching her life in ways she had never imagined they could. That she had found two men who had touched her deeply gave her hope that one day she would find someone she could spend her life with. After all, what was it her father had told her? *Love will find its way to you when the time is right.* She just needed to believe that.

Feeling more hopeful about her future, Jess turned her thoughts to focusing on what she wanted to do now she had almost completed her degree. She had applied for a postdoctoral fellowship grant with the National Science Foundation to study sea turtle interactions with gillnets. Jess knew firsthand how badly being entangled in such a net could harm a sea turtle, drowning it if held under water too long or causing deep cuts that could lead to infections or the loss of a limb. She wanted to explore ways to deter the turtles from getting too close to the nets to avoid such injuries. If she received the grant, she could set up her office anywhere she chose that allowed her to conduct the research she proposed.

So now she needed to figure out where she wanted to go if everything fell into place. There were aspects of being in Orlando that she really loved. Like how she could see so many different creatures just by taking a paddleboard ride. Or how she liked to breathe in the tropical air and watch how the wind would make the palm trees sway. She'd loved that she was able to work with an abundance of turtles and with people who enjoyed them as much as she did. No doubt, coming to UCF was one of the best decisions she had ever made. But when she thought about the modern buildings that made up Orlando and the number of tourist attractions it had, as well as the city's size, she did not picture herself staying. She'd never gotten used to how little change there was from season to season, finding herself missing the colors of fall and the emergence of spring blooms she had grown up with. And she really disliked the number of hurricane warnings each year, knowing there was always the chance one would hit. She felt she'd gotten what she came for and now it was time to move on.

She felt her next move should be to a place where she could think about building a home. When she closed her eyes and thought about where that would be, she saw herself back in Wilmington. Memories of her time there had been popping up in her thoughts, and she felt a longing to return. Her mind would reminisce about all the bike rides she had taken through its quiet rambling neighborhoods, walking through the downtown area with its historic homes, and all the good times she had enjoyed out on the beach. The quaintness of the town gave it charm and a homey atmosphere she'd never forgotten, and she had felt a sense of belonging when she was there. It was where she'd discovered so much about herself, and deep down, she'd always felt a sadness at having to leave it behind. As her time at UCF was coming to a close, she felt herself being drawn back to it.

She would be lying to herself if she didn't admit that she wondered what it would be like to see Hank again. She was curious to know what had happened to him after all these years and whether she would ever know if she had made the right decision to leave him. After all, he was her first love, the one against whom she had measured every guy since, at least in the way she chose to remember him. But there was no telling what he would be like now. Best to leave it in the past and focus on her own life, she told herself. Who knew what the future held?

When the grant came through, providing her with funding for her research for the next three years, Jess was elated. She finally had the job she'd spent years working toward and now the freedom to do it in the one place she hoped to return. There was nothing left to do but start packing.

Jess was going back to Wilmington.

PART IV

The Return

Chapter 58

As Jess drove into Wilmington, she could smell the start of spring in the air. She opened her windows and breathed it in, letting it flow over her. She felt welcomed home as the scent of magnolias wrapped itself around her, calling her attention to how the trees and other plant life were starting to blossom with the start of April. Driving through town, she passed by several familiar landmarks and saw her old haunts as well as new stores and developments that had popped up since she had left. And as she drove closer to the beach and inhaled the ocean breeze, it reminded her that she'd returned to a warm and familiar place.

Settling back in Wilmington was surprisingly easy. She reached out to her former advisor, Professor Williams, who was pleased she was returning. She helped Jess secure space at UNCW's Marine Center for Marine Science, which had offices available for visiting scientists. Jess was very excited about working at the Marine Center. While she'd done class work there as a student, she felt proud to be returning to it as a PhD. It drove home the extent of her accomplishments since she'd left and made her even more determined to do her best to succeed.

Jess also found another roommate online, a woman named Jenna who was a graduate student at UNCW, examining how North Carolina could increase resilience against flooding from storms. Jenna was slightly overweight with medium-length brown hair that she often wore in two short braids and granny glasses that made her look older than her twenty-five years. She had been born and raised in North Carolina, having completed her undergraduate work in biology at UNC Chapel Hill before coming to UNCW to do her graduate work in geoscience studies. When she was not in class, she spent a lot of time reading and was a virtual encyclopedia on the hurricanes that had traversed the North Carolina coast. She could cite from memory each one that had wreaked havoc through the state, citing dates, names, and the amount of damage each storm caused.

"Did you know that six of the seven largest rainfall events of the last 120 years occurred in the last twenty years...?" Jenna would start, looking at her textbook, making Jess uncertain if she was talking to her or just reciting the information she was reading to herself. Jess didn't mind because she admired Jenna's passion for her subject, much like Jess was drawn to her sea turtles. Occasionally, they would make some tacos and watch a couple of episodes of *The Bachelorette*, laughing as they discussed the antics of the men on the show, but that was the extent of their camaraderie. Jenna had a boyfriend, Mark, who was getting his graduate degree studying coral reefs in Hawaii, which meant she spent a lot of time FaceTiming with him when she wasn't studying. Jess felt right away that she and Jenna were a good fit as roommates since they had enough in common to spend the occasional evening together while not getting in each other's way.

As soon as Jess was settled in, she went to the beach. She made her way down the sandy path between the dunes, letting the long strands of sea grass gently brush against her until they parted to reveal the ocean. So many times, Jess had sat on this beach, looking out across the greenish-blue water, letting the steady flow of the waves soothe her while she figured out how to solve her problems. She had so many happy memories of days spent here with friends. No matter where she might go, this would always be her beach, with its long piers, its lifeguard stands, and its groups of pelicans flying overhead. Standing there taking it all in and smelling the salt spray from the ocean, she realized how much she'd missed being here.

The first chance she got, Jess also went biking down her old familiar trails. She rode through the UNCW campus, the trail that took her downtown, and every other path she could remember, noting the extent of new construction in some areas and how other areas looked exactly the same. One of her first rides was to reacquaint herself with the streets of large oaks that she loved to ride beneath, still humbled at how their gnarly trunks were so thick and sturdy, and how their large, jagged limbs could reach out so far and wide, as if embracing her return.

Revisiting each of her familiar places, Jess felt more certain she had made the right decision in returning to Wilmington. What she didn't count on, however, was how strong Hank's presence was everywhere she went. Even though she hadn't run into him, the memory of him was everywhere. She thought about their time surfing together, their walks on the beach, and how he would sit with her when she monitored the turtle's nest. She recounted their lunches at the Trolly Stop and their bike ride downtown. When she drove by Oceanside, she remembered how he would pick her up from work, waiting by his Jeep until she was ready to leave. She started to remember just how much he'd meant to her, and the heartache that was long forgotten started to rise within her.

But Jess couldn't go down that path again. It had been too many years, and Hank had most likely changed in ways she could not even fathom. Reliving her time with him brought back happy memories, but it also reminded her how confused she'd felt when she left. She reminded herself that the reason she had come back was not for him. Rather, she came back because she felt like this was her home. If she was going to live here, she needed to put all that behind her and look toward what new memories lay ahead.

Chapter 59

A few weeks after she returned, Jess ran into Lynn at the supermarket. Lynn was now married and had a two-year-old with her, sitting in the cart. She was also quite obviously pregnant with a second child, looking every bit the harried mother.

"Yes, it's hard, and I rarely get any sleep, but I wouldn't have it any other way. We're having another one soon," she said, pointing to her protruding belly. "How about you? How do you like being back?"

"I love it. I didn't realize how much I missed being here."

"It seems like it was just yesterday that we were working together! Do you remember John who used to harass us at Oceanside?"

Jess flinched a little at hearing his name, but then realized Lynn didn't know about how he had tried to attack her. "Who can forget?" she replied, remembering their mutual disdain. "What a jerk."

"Well, he got his. Did you hear what happened to him?" When Jess shook her head *no*, Lynn said, "His family said they sent him to North Carolina State to finish college, but the rumor was he was in and out of rehab. He ended up dying in a car accident. Everyone was sure he was drunk when it happened. Not that anyone would miss him. How's Hank? Did you two stay in touch?" Lynn was talking quickly because her two-year-old was getting antsy and starting to fuss. She was trying to appease him with a pacifier, but he was pushing it away.

"No, we didn't," Jess said, surprised Lynn would even remember she had dated Hank.

"What that poor guy went through back then. Everyone thinking he'd started that bar fight because of the story some girl told the police. I'm so glad he got that conviction overturned. Now he has his own business building houses, I think." Lynn's son was now trying to climb out of the cart, so she picked him up and put him on her hip, bouncing him to quiet him down.

Jess tried to understand what she had just heard. "I'm sorry, what? What did you say about his conviction?"

"Oh, I thought you knew. It turned out he was set up. Some girl told the police he had hit a guy with a beer bottle when it was the bartender who did it. It was quite the story for a while. I think she even ended up in jail for making it all up." Lynn's two-year-old started to wail. "Jess, it was so good seeing you, but I have to go. I'm on baby time now," she said, rolling her eyes. She gave Jess a quick hug. "Let's catch up soon!" she said as she quickly headed down the aisle, trying to hush her little one as she hurried away.

Jess immediately pulled out her phone and typed in Hank's name and Wilmington. A number of articles popped up. "Local Man Wrongfully Charged," said one headline. "D.A. Overturns Wrongful Conviction," was another. Apparently, Roxy had given false testimony, which was affirmed by two other bar customers hoping to reduce their own criminal charges by turning her in. She ended up getting jail time and Hank's name was cleared. As Jess scanned the articles, it was clear everything Roxy had told Jess about

Hank being violent was a lie. He hadn't done it. He hadn't done any of it. He'd been innocent all along.

Jess stood for a long time staring at the phone as two distinct feelings coursed through her. The first was a feeling of relief that she'd been right about him all along. The second was harder to admit to herself and it brought a strong sense of guilt.

She should never have left the way she did.

After running into Lynn, Jess started thinking more about Hank. She didn't know what to do with this feeling that she'd acted badly by running away from him without giving him a chance to explain. She wished she could apologize now that she knew the truth, but how would he react to her after all this time? Certainly he had moved on long ago, she told herself, but with this new information, she felt a yearning to know what became of him. Now whenever she went out, her eyes would search for him, imagining what it would be like to run into him again.

That is, when Jess had time. There was a lot of work involved in setting up her office and getting everything in place to conduct her studies, so Jess did what she always did when faced with a challenge—she worked hard. She was exhilarated and anxious to be running her own research experiment, never sure what she would come up against on any given day. When she wasn't working, she was out riding her bike, sometimes pedaling hard as if to physically push away her worries about whether she was on the right track. There were times she felt she had no idea what she was doing and just had to learn as she went along. Her first part of the project required she acquire data to prepare her for the field work that would come next.

While she preferred being out in the field, even the desk work was bearable because it was her project.

Jess was friendly enough with colleagues she met at the Marine Center, but like she did at the Refuge, she mostly focused on her work. She joined some of them for drinks or dinner a couple of times, but more often begged off such invitations, preferring the comfort of riding for a couple of hours or walking along the ocean. She hadn't quite felt like herself since her conversation with Lynn, and she was trying hard to get her bearings back. The one event she could not avoid, though, was the big May fundraiser the university hosted at the Marine Center to inform the community of the work it was doing while raising funds for its future endeavors. Jess didn't want to go, but it was considered a mandatory gathering for everyone working there, leaving her no choice.

David, a fellow researcher with an office near hers, offered to drive Jess to the event. He was paying her too much attention lately and was obviously angling to ask her out. She had already politely turned him down a couple of times, but that didn't seem to dissuade him. When she arrived at the gala, he was waiting for her and ushered her to a place at the table next to him. He kept complimenting her, clearly taken with her choice of dress, but Jess wasn't interested. She did her best to ignore him, though it was proving more difficult tonight since he was drinking, something Jess knew not to do at a work gathering.

When David started to get a bit tipsy and leaned in too close to talk to her, touching her arm, she got up and excused herself from the table, thinking she would go outside for a moment to get some air. She went into the lobby, making her way through the groups of people talking, when the crowd parted, giving her a view of a handsome man in a tuxedo talking on a cell phone in the corner. It took her only a second to realize it was not just any man. It was Hank. He finished his call and put the phone in his pocket, and as he turned to leave, he stopped and looked right at her.

Hank stood there motionless, staring, no expression on his face. Jess felt like she had suddenly gone back seven years in time to when she had first looked into his eyes and felt that electric charge. It shot right through her, and her first reaction was she wanted to run, but the force between them was so strong that it was pulling her toward him, causing her to slowly walk forward until she was right in front of him.

"Hello, Hank," she said, her voice a little breathless, unsure how he would react.

"Hello, Jess," he said. God, she wished she could interpret his expression, but he wasn't giving her anything. Where his looks had been average at twenty, he had grown into his features with his hair cut in a more professional style and his face taking on more definition. Her first thought was what an extremely handsome man he had become. Even in his tuxedo, she could tell he was still in great shape and that he exuded an air of confidence she'd never seen before. He looked so grown-up from when she had last seen him, yet so familiar.

"You look amazing," she said, looking him over. "How are you?" She was unsure what else to say.

"I'm good. I'm very good."

"I hear you have your own company," she said, looking for any clue that he was glad to see her.

"Um, yeah, I started a business restoring some of the older homes downtown and around the Island."

"That seems like something you would be very good at," she said, smiling. "You always liked those houses."

"Did he?" a woman's voice said. A tall, beautiful blond walked up next to Hank and linked her left arm into his, indicating they were together. "Hello, we haven't met. I'm Alanna Moore," she said, holding her right hand out to Jess. "So how do you know Henry?"

Jess glanced quickly at Hank, who still appeared stoic, then back at this stunning woman in front of her, and gave her a quick handshake. "We were in college together for a short time," she said, ending the contact and not wanting to divulge more. She gave a wary smile to Alanna. "I'm Jess. Jess Wade," she said when Hank didn't introduce them.

"How wonderful to run into an old friend," Alanna said, looking at Hank while making sure her engagement ring was prominently displayed on his arm.

"Wow, your ring. It's beautiful," Jess said, now feeling incredibly stupid for having talked to Hank at all. Of course he was engaged. It was amazing he was not married yet. "When is the wedding?" she asked, trying to be polite.

"Well, it's all so new we haven't really set the date yet," Alanna said, happy to share the good news. "Maybe in the spring around Azalea Festival? That is, if I can wait that long," she said, smiling at Hank and giving his arm a squeeze.

Hank was visibly uncomfortable and sought to end the conversation. "Well, it was good seeing you, Jess," he said, unwinding his arm from Alanna's grasp and reaching out to shake her hand. She took it and gave a short shake while looking at him. *Oh God*, she thought, *I can't believe that is Hank*. And when he touched her, she felt that charge again—that old connection to him.

"You too," she said, her voice breaking as she quickly withdrew her hand. "It was very nice meeting you, Alanna." She tried to maintain a normal voice, but was barely able to look at her.

Jess quickly turned away, heading out the doors that led to the parking lot, desperate to get away from them and to escape from the gala. She found her car and got in, quickly heading out and back to her apartment where no one could see just how distraught seeing Hank had made her.

Chapter 60

Back at the apartment, Jess had quickly undressed and gone straight to bed. She found lying in bed to be comforting, a place where nothing could happen to her and she could be alone with her thoughts. Now she lay here thinking of her meeting with Hank and how he was nothing she had imagined he would be. Part of her wanted to see him again, to have a chance to talk just a little longer and find out what he had been doing since she had last seen him, but the rational part of her mind told her that time had passed. He was engaged, and from what she saw at the gala, had a much different life from when they had been together. She knew she shouldn't be thinking about him, but couldn't stop thinking about their brief meeting. No matter how many times she went over it in her mind, the heartbreaking end result was always the same. He had moved on and she should do the same.

You knew him for one summer, she reminded herself. *And you left because you felt you didn't know who he really was. Either way, he's got a new life now and you need to let it go.* But seeing him again only reminded her of just how much she had missed him. Why had she believed a few words from that waitress over what she had known from being with him? How could she have seen his hitting John as anything more than saving her? Over and over she questioned herself, wondering why she had made the decisions she did.

Jess finally told herself to stop. *It's over now.* She had made the best decision she could with the information available at the time. There was nothing she could do to change it. It was better to keep her mind off of Hank and focus on the work she was here to do. That's what she would tell herself as she fought to push the thoughts of Hank from her mind, wondering if she would ever forgive herself for making the decision she did. She lay there waiting for sleep to overtake her and drown out her thoughts, but it felt like it would never come.

The Saturday morning after the gala, Jess was sitting in her apartment trying to find something to do. She had no desire to go back to the Marine Center today, but she had woken early out of habit and eaten breakfast, and she was now just sitting around being idle. She needed a distraction. It was unusually muggy outside, making it a bad time to go for a long bike ride, so her thoughts turned to going to the beach. Her eyes drifted around the room to a surfboard that sat idly against the wall behind the couch. She'd noticed it numerous times before, but now she kept eyeing it, and she finally asked Jenna, who was reading at the kitchen table, why she never used it. Jenna looked up, surprised to know there was a surfboard in the apartment.

"Oh, that. That's Mark's board," she said, when she realized what Jess was talking about.

"He's a surfer?"

"Well, he never got the hang of it even when he was here and gave up after a few tries," Jenna said, going back to her reading. "You're welcome to use it if you want."

Jess was instantly interested. She always thought of surfing as something she did with Hank and not something she would do on her own. But if she were going to live here, she knew she couldn't let his memory keep her from doing a sport she had really enjoyed. She'd not done any surfing since she had left for that very reason, but that board was calling to her, and she finally gave in. She wanted to remember what it felt like to ride on top of the water and to see if she still remembered how to do it.

Jenna told her there was a bike with a surfboard carrier on it in the shed out back that she could use. It seemed Mark had inherited both from an old roommate who didn't want to take it with him when he took a job in Asheville. Jess went out back and found the beach cruiser. It had wide, heavyset tires that she supposed helped balance the bike with the added weight of the board. The tires needed to be pumped up, but other than that, it was in decent enough shape to ride. Jess loaded up the board and pedaled east to the beach, figuring any ride in this heat would soon be alleviated by being in the ocean.

She expected the beach cruiser to be harder to ride than her much lighter road bike, but Jess was pleasantly surprised to find it easy to handle. The board put a lot of weight to one side of the bike, which took a bit of getting used to, but she soon got the hang of it. As she crossed the bridge over the Intracoastal, she caught a glimpse of the Café to her right, bustling even this early on a Saturday morning. She saw a number of early risers were on the Loop, a roughly two-and-a-half-mile path that started on the Island, crossed the bridge, and circled the park and surrounding marsh, only to cross the adjacent bridge and bring you back on the Island and through the town. It was a favorite of locals and visitors alike who used it to run or bike in the morning, and the familiarity of seeing it all reminded Jess of what her life had been like when she lived here.

When Jess crossed the bridge over the Channel that brought her onto Wrightsville Beach, she felt herself getting anxious. What if she ran into Hank out there? She pushed the thought of him out of her mind. The Island was big enough that the chances of them running into each other were slim, and she couldn't let such thoughts stop her from doing the things she enjoyed.

Jess rode down the side street near where she had once lived with Anne, locked up her bike on the bike rack by the path, and picked up the board. She eyed the walkway for a moment and then took a big breath and marched forward, determined to give it a try. *After all,* she told herself, *the worst that could happen is I wipe out a few times, give up, and go home.*

Stepping onto the beach, Jess was once again reminded of the solace it gave her. She stood for a moment taking in the deep blue of the water which today had lightened into an emerald green along the shoreline. The light blue of the sky was dotted with white clouds, and she felt the inviting sea breeze. Jess let the calming effect of seeing the ocean flow through her, once more feeling the connection to this place she'd always loved, telling herself she never should have stayed away so long.

Jess started walking toward the water. Halfway down, she dropped her towel, shorts, and shoes on the beach and then made her way to where the water reached the sand. A few surfers were already out there, their boards bobbing in the water, but it wasn't too crowded yet, which she was grateful for. She knew it was better to surf with other people around for safety reasons, but she also didn't want to have a bunch of teenage guys who could surf circles around her watch her fumbling attempts to get back on a board. It was May, and surfing season was starting up again. She was glad she had come out early since it was hard enough to give it a try without an audience. She eyed the surf as Hank had taught her and saw that the tide was coming in and the waves were well spaced. She stepped into the surf, gingerly testing the water temperature, which was a bit cool, but she was wearing a rash guard and knew that once she started swimming, she would warm up. She dove in to acclimate herself, then got on her board and started paddling out.

Jess was amazed how much of it came back to her so quickly. At first, she missed a few waves by being too far behind them, but when she paddled harder, she managed to catch them at the right time. Once she remembered how to catch a wave, it took her a few attempts to relearn how to leap to standing and where to situate herself on the board. She was wobbly at first, but after a few wipe-outs, she started to get the hang of it again. At one point, her body remembered how to turn the board into the wave just enough to keep riding it down the shoreline, giving her a run that lasted an impressive length. After that last ride, she came in, exhilarated at her success and loving it so much she wondered why she'd avoided doing it for so long.

Jess returned to her towel, sitting down on her board while she sipped some water and looked out at the scene before her. She missed being out by water every day like she had been able to do at the Refuge. When she looked at it, she thought of how beautiful and mysterious it was, and how an entire world lay underneath. She loved her work with the turtles, remembering how it had all started with finding Waffle in her freshman class. She thought about how her job challenged and excited her and how despite the memories that sometimes arose, she was glad to be back. And now she was re-discovering surfing, which she realized she had sorely missed. She sat there just taking it all in, enjoying the moment while letting the sun dry her off. She took a deep breath in, and then with a long exhale, let all her worries flow out of her, feeling a sense of calm.

Everything is going to be all right, she told herself. *Just focus on what you came here to do.*

Chapter 61

Once Jess started surfing again, she became addicted. Mornings were spent checking the surf report to see if it was a good day to be out, and if it was, she would drive down for an hour of surfing before work. Though she liked the beach cruiser, she had limited time before work on weekdays, so she bought a roof rack to carry the board for shorter visits. She would get out early just as the sunrise was turning from shades of red and purple to an orange glow that would part as a glowing yellow sun arose. The water would be a silvery translucent hue that would turn a blue metal color and finally a deep turquoise as the sky above it went from muted to bright and became a sunny blue. Sitting on her board and watching the world wake up was her favorite part of the day.

Jess still thought about what she would do if she ran into Hank. When she arrived, she would scan the beach to see if he was there, but as time went by and she never encountered him, she eventually stopped worrying she would run into him. Maybe he had stopped surfing like she did, due to no time or work, or maybe he was doing it at another part of the beach. There was no way to know. All that mattered was she was back on a board. Surfing made her feel energetic and connected to the ocean she loved and studied, and she wanted to keep doing it.

Jess loved the calmness she experienced on her board, bobbing on the water and feeling the ocean breeze while waiting for the right wave. She always felt so present when she surfed, concentrating on nothing but the coolness of the water on her legs and waiting for her next ride. When her mind drifted to her times with Hank, they felt less painful now. She would turn her thoughts to how grateful she was to be back and even feel thankful to Hank for introducing her to surfing. She wanted to remember the good times and not just the ones that had made her feel sad or the guilt she still felt for having left so suddenly.

And it was good to feel something other than sadness when Jess thought of Hank. He had been on her mind since their meeting at the gala, but now that she had settled in to a routine, she felt herself making peace with why she had been so scared to face him all those years ago, and sometimes she even thought she might explain to him one day why she had left so abruptly and apologize. While on the water, her mind would imagine chance encounters with him where she would have the opportunity to tell him all these things she'd been thinking about. In her mind, these fantasized conversations helped to resolve any tension between them and usually ended in their being friends again. Jess knew that was unlikely, but it made her feel better to think that one day she could put it all behind her and not feel the ache she did now when she thought of how hard it had been when their relationship had ended.

What Jess was less certain about was whether Hank needed to hear the things she wanted to say. She knew she had hurt him back then, but his stoic reaction when she ran into him at the gala could just mean she was a distant memory to him—a summer romance that had ended suddenly and was long over. He was engaged to be married to Alanna now. Jess didn't need more than their one meeting to see that Alanna was beautiful, smart, and someone who came from Wilmington money. She belonged at events like the gala with her poise and easy manner. She, more than anything, showed Jess how much Hank had changed. When her mind went in this direction, she thought she should forget about the past and leave well enough alone. How humiliating it would be for her to bring it up just to have him say what happened all those years ago didn't really matter to him anymore. That would cut her deeply because she had truly loved Hank back then, and she wanted to believe that she had meant the same to him as he had to her.

Since Jess was at the beach most mornings, she started to get to know some of the regulars. There was Jack, who grew up on the Island and brought his ten-year-old son out to ride waves before he went to school, and Clark, who was in his sixties, who'd retired in the area and wanted to keep in shape, as well as others. They would greet each other and talk about the wave conditions and where the best surf spots were. Jess started venturing to some of the other beach areas they mentioned and found she liked being on the south end of the island best. It was less crowded and the sandbars seemed to create the best waves. This became her go-to spot, enjoying some time in the water before stopping in for a quick bite at SUNdays, a coffee shop over the surf supply store that was popular with the locals. After, she would head home to get ready to work. It was becoming less the place where she had dated Hank and more the town she had come to because she wanted to live near the beach. Even though she went to the beach early, Jess found she had to search a little harder for a good spot that wasn't too crowded. One day, she was enjoying a particularly beautiful morning with a sunny sky and water so translucent that she could see to the bottom even this far out from the shore. Some pelicans flew overhead, and she wondered if she would see some dolphins today like the week before, a pod of them darting nearby in joyful leaps. Other surfers would come and go nearby, but she rarely focused on them anymore, other than to make sure they didn't crowd her. Her only concentration was on finding a wave she liked and then riding it in. She caught a few good waves and was bobbing along watching the horizon for her next ride when she suddenly heard him next to her.

"You're leading with your right foot. You always did better leading with your left and using your right to steer from the back of the board."

Jess was shaken out of her reverie and looked over, instantly recognizing the voice. There was Hank, sitting on his board next to her, looking right at her. With just his swim trunks on and a tight-fitting rash guard, she immediately saw how he had maintained his physique in the seven years since she had last seen him. If it were possible, he looked even better than when she had seen him at the gala. The suddenness of his approach and the directness of his stare made her speechless and she looked away. This was not how she had pictured them meeting up again, and she was unprepared to meet him here, but she didn't want him to know it.

"Maybe I've learned some tricks since you last saw me surf," she said, trying to regain her composure. "I haven't seen you out here. How are your skills these days?"

Hank smiled at the challenge. "Let me show you," he said, and he started paddling as a wave came up from behind. She saw him jump up on the board and down into the crest of the wave, maintaining perfect balance as he rode it down the beach, jumping off his board when the wave started to flatten. He got back on the board and paddled his way back to her. Jess felt like she had been transported back to their summer together, feeling all her emotions swell up again. *Keep it together,* she told herself. But it was all she could do to stay calm. She was just so glad to see him and have him talk to her again. She had missed him so much.

"And that's how it's done," he said as he came up next to her, bringing his board alongside her and sitting up. He had a big smile on his face that she reciprocated, remembering how much she liked it.

"Yeah, that was all right. For someone who is out of practice."

"Out of practice?" Hank said with mock surprise. "That was a perfectly executed ride. I would have gotten a ten from the judges if it were being scored."

Jess laughed. "Sure, if the judges were three elderly women with bad eyesight who liked surfers," she replied.

"Are you saying it's only my good looks that would have earned me that score?" he asked, playing along.

"I said they had bad eyesight," she said, giving him a look that said she had gotten him. He shook his head in disbelief, then smiled at her, feeling their old connection instantly come back.

"I always liked your laugh," he said. Jess suddenly felt uncomfortable, not knowing how to handle the compliment, so she looked behind her and saw a wave coming up.

"Bet I can catch this wave before you," she said and started paddling fast. He quickly came up behind her, but she was up on her board first and surfing down the crest, riding it into shore. He watched her on the board, remembering the first time he had seen her ride a wave, and he was struck by how graceful she was, like it required no effort at all.

Hank was able to catch another wave a few minutes later and rode it in. Jess had gotten out of the water and was toweling off. He picked up his board and walked over to her.

"Great ride. I told you leading with your left works better for you." Jess hadn't even realized she had changed her position until he had said something. All he'd had to do was mention it and she had done it without even thinking. She could already feel his influence over her, and she didn't trust herself to talk to him right now. After all the times she had pictured running into him, she wasn't prepared for it to happen here where they had spent so much time together.

"You really do look good, Jess," he said, standing with his board next to him. "It's really great to see you."

Jess gave him a wary smile, not trusting herself to speak. She picked up her things and then looked at him. "It's great to see you, too," she finally said, wanting to say something but not knowing what. Then she turned and started heading back to her car. She walked a few steps and then turned around again.

"I'm here most mornings if you ever need a lesson," she said with a smile, then turned around and walked off, not wanting to see his reaction. What if it had been the wrong thing to say? The man was engaged to another woman. She didn't want to look like she was coming on to him, but she would welcome a chance to see him again, to get that chance to talk to him like she had hoped. She was just caught off guard seeing him here. So many feelings had risen unexpectedly, and she needed to compose herself before having the conversation she had pictured.

Yet as Jess walked back to her car, she felt a slight spring in her step at having seen him again. It had gone well. She had not said anything she would think back on later and regret. And yes, he looked good. Too good. But she knew she could not let herself think about that. It would just break her heart all over again to know he was back and yet gone forever.

Chapter 62

Hank had known about Jess's surfing schedule for a while, after coming across it by accident. He came to the beach one morning to surf, and while sitting on his board getting ready to head out, he watched the other surfers as he tried to wake up. The night before, Alanna had taken him to a fundraiser for coastal wildlife, making it the second late night in a row. He did not care to go to so many social engagements, particularly during the work week, but Alanna reminded him how much it helped his business when he networked. He did get some inquiries from the people they met, so she was right about that. He just didn't like having to sell himself so much.

So there he was, trying to get his energy up before he went out into the water, when he saw her. He hadn't known it was Jess at first. He saw her catch a wave and watched as she came in, admiring her form and how clean it looked, though it was obvious she was a little unsteady. It wasn't until she came all the way in and hopped off the board that he recognized her. He felt his heart drop at seeing her again, the feeling even more crushing than when he first saw her at the gala.

When Jess had walked up to him that night, Hank could not believe it was her. She had matured into a truly gorgeous woman, and his heart ached just looking at her. It was all he could do not to reach out and take her into his arms, but he knew there were so many reasons he couldn't. He had convinced himself he would never see her again. And yet, here she was, the scent of her reminding him all too well of his longing for her. And then Alanna had appeared. It had been all he could do not to show his feelings for Jess with her there. So he had stood there, conflicted and unable to speak, not knowing what to do.

Jess had left as quickly as she had appeared, heading out the front entrance. Hank had let Alanna lead him back into the festivities, but as soon as she was occupied talking to a group of friends, he had excused himself, claiming another business call. Once he was in the lobby, he headed straight out to the parking lot hoping to find Jess and see if he could talk to her. But just like before, she was gone, leaving no trace that she had ever been there, once more reminding him of all the pain and heartbreak he'd felt all those years ago.

Now, seeing Jess at the beach, Hank pulled his baseball cap low on his forehead and looked down, hoping she wouldn't notice him. He knew they would run into each other at some point, but he wasn't ready to face her just yet. He wanted a chance to talk to her, to find out why she had left so quickly and what had happened to her since he had last seen her. But this was not the time to find out. Not when he was off his game.

He waited as she finished her ride and then swam back out to catch another wave, oblivious to his presence. While she was swimming, he grabbed his board and towel and headed back to his car, slipping away as fast as he could.

Hank thought about Jess all that day, wondering if he went back to the beach whether he would see her there again, and if so, if he could bring himself to talk to her. He tried to talk himself out of it, but the pressing need he felt to look into her eyes one more time and feel the connection they had shared was unrelenting and he finally gave in. The next morning, he got up and dressed for a run, then went back to the same stretch of beach where he had seen her, doing warm-ups by the access point while watching the surfers. When he didn't see her there, he started running north up the beach. She wasn't there either, so he looped around and headed back to the south end of the Island. Just when he was about to give up, he found her. Still uncertain whether he should approach her, he stayed back where she was less likely to see him so he could watch her for a while.

Jess was out there, talking with two other locals he sometimes ran into. The amount of jealousy he felt at seeing her talk to them surprised him, even though he knew them both. He watched for a while as she surfed, the memories flooding back to him. Eventually, he knew she would be heading in, so he headed back to his car, getting away before she saw him. While driving home, he came up with his plan to bring his surfboard and meet her on the water like he was casually running into her. It was the best way he could think of to try to talk to her before she slipped away again.

Since it was Friday, Hank knew it would be a few days before he could put his plan into action. Alanna had made a number of plans for them, including boating with her friends on Saturday and a BBQ get-together with her family on Sunday. Monday he had early meetings. So it wouldn't be until Tuesday that Hank would be able to grab his board and head out to the beach.

He felt a twinge of guilt that he hadn't told Alanna that Jess was his college girlfriend. He thought of saying something now before he talked to Jess, but he quickly put it out of his mind. There was no need to concern Alanna unnecessarily as his intent was only to find out why Jess had left all those years before. Jess had been his first love. He had pictured a future with her, even in the short time they were together. It had taken him years to get over her, and he wanted to understand why it had fallen apart, if only to put it behind him. He rationalized that it was his business to rectify those feelings before fully committing to Alanna in marriage.

And so on Tuesday morning, after days of having all these thoughts run through his head, Hank swam out to talk to Jess, uncertain what feelings seeing her again would bring.

Chapter 63

The second time Hank came out, Jess was ready to talk to him. After their first meeting, she had continued to surf in the same spot, keeping an eye out for him. Just when she wondered if she'd been a little too cavalier, making him think she wasn't interested in talking to him, he showed up. She breathed a sigh of relief when she saw him put his things down on the beach and swim out toward her. She didn't want to admit how much she had been hoping he would return.

"I thought I scared you away with my surfing skills," she said when he reached her.

"No, I was just giving you time to get a little more practice in so you didn't embarrass yourself," he replied with a smile, obviously happy to see her.

After about an hour of trying to outdo each other, Jess called it a day and asked if he wanted to join her for a quick breakfast before work. Hank readily agreed and together they headed in, picking up their gear and agreeing to meet at Port City Java, a local coffee shop just off the Island but tucked away from the usual tourist spots. They found a table outdoors and sat drinking coffee and talking about how Wilmington had changed over the years. The time was over faster than either would have liked, but both had work obligations. Hank asked if she would be out again soon, and when she said she came out most days, he said he would look for her again. Then they said their goodbyes, smiling at how easy it was to be together again and not wanting to touch on any subject that might take that good feeling away.

It quickly became a regular thing. Any morning he could, Hank would grab his board and head out to do some surfing with Jess. They would meet at the beach north of the pier, and after spending some time surfing, they would go to Port City Java for coffee and something to eat while talking. Hank told Jess about how he had gotten into UNCW and then how he decided to start his own business and about all the headaches and successes that came with it. Jess told him about Florida, the Refuge, and the research she did there, plus the work she returned to do at the Marine Center. As she talked, he remembered her excitement when she first told him about her interest in sea turtles; it was obvious that excitement had only increased. She loved what she was doing, and her whole face lit up as she talked about her work. It made him realize her leaving was probably the best thing for her. It gave her opportunities she never would have had if she had stayed in Wilmington.

The one subject they did not talk about was Jess's sudden departure. Neither of them seemed to want to explore that particularly emotional moment. It was easier to talk as if none of it had ever happened and just be friends. At least that was what Hank told himself. They were building a friendship where a relationship had once been. Jess was a connection to his past and an important one. She was the reason he was where he was today. He didn't want to give that up, particularly since he enjoyed talking to her and spending time surfing with her. She reminded him just how far he'd come, and he was glad to finally be able to share that with her.

Which was why he held back from telling Alanna about Jess. It was one thing to be out with other surfers since the surfing community was a friendly and inclusive one. But he could see how the coffees he shared with Jess could be misconstrued. One reason he kept the conversation with Jess focused on catching up was subconsciously to build an alibi that it was all innocent and he was just reconnecting with an old friend. After all, they were always out in public, so it wasn't like he was hiding anything. But the idea that he was keeping something from Alanna bothered him, and he knew eventually he would have to tell her if the meetings continued. Just not yet.

Jess also enjoyed their time together. While Hank had matured in some ways, he was still the Hank she remembered—like when he teased her about her surfing abilities or how he always insisted on carrying her board to her car even while carrying his own. It was as if they'd never been apart, though she was very much conscious of keeping herself physically distant from him. The few times they had accidentally touched while in the water or when he handed her the board had sent shock waves through her that she fought to keep down. *He is engaged*, she told herself. *He is off-limits as a romantic interest*. And though that saddened her to some extent, it made it easier to know where she stood and that they could spend time together without worrying if it meant something more.

A couple of times Jess thought about explaining why she had left, but after a while, there seemed no reason to bring up the past. Their relationship was moving in a new direction, and though she would have dated him again if she had the chance, she respected that he was not available. *It's just surfing and coffee*, she told herself.

Don't read any more into it, and let it be what it is. At least she got to share this with him.

Week after week throughout the summer, they met, talking and laughing together, enjoying the time they spent getting to know each other again. Hank found that very little had changed about her. She still had the same determined and unyielding spirit she'd had when they had met all those years ago. He could see how dedicated she was to her work and enjoyed hearing humorous stories about her colleagues and what it was like to be on the Refuge in Florida. She talked about similar studies being done in Costa Rica and how she would love to see such exotic places one day.

Hank liked to listen to Jess talk, watching how she seemed to glow with delight when her work progressed. He remembered how she used to look at him with the same sense of excitement and how he missed that. He thought of how she had made him feel alive again all those years ago when he had thought his life would never be better. He would carry the good feeling that he got from these meetings with him throughout the day, sometimes smiling to himself when remembering something she had said, and always remembering how she would shine when saying it.

When Hank and Alanna weren't attending a social event, many evenings were spent at her house while she and her mother worked on the wedding. Hank had had no idea there was so much planning to do—the guest list, the invitations, the flowers, the cake, the menu, and the reception setting, followed by bridesmaids dresses, suits for the groomsmen, gifts and hotel arrangements, plus so much more. He would sit, nodding his head, as they showed him their choices for each item. He didn't offer any opinion but went with whatever Alanna wanted mainly because he didn't care about any of these details. His preference would be to do something where it was just family and a few friends, where the ceremony focused on them, not the reception. But it became clear early on that Alanna and her mother had been looking forward to this day for a long time and already had developed ideas about what this day should be like. Overwhelmed by the grandeur of the event they were putting together, Hank found some relief in remembering his conversations from earlier that day with Jess, sometimes sitting with a smile on his face for no apparent reason.

"Henry. Henry! Are you listening to me? We need to pick which invitation we want to use," Alanna would say, waking him from his reverie.

"I had no idea that invitation fonts were so humorous," Alanna's mother would say, not pleased with her future son-in-law's disinterest in such matters.

Hank would let these comments, which were coming more often, slide and turn to Alanna. "It really doesn't matter to me, Alanna. I am happy with whatever you pick," he would respond, hoping that would be enough for them to go on without him.

Alanna would give him a quick kiss and start talking again with her mother at an excited pace, finally making a choice they felt sufficiently represented the event.

Not that Alanna would let Hank get away that easily. More than once after such evenings when they were alone, she would look at him quizzically. "What on earth are you grinning so much about lately?" she would ask, pretending to be suspicious.

He knew what she wanted. She wanted him to say he was thinking about her, but he couldn't bring himself to say that. "Just some jokes the guys at work were making earlier," he would answer, or "I was remembering something Mike said the other day." He knew it was no use to explain how little he enjoyed planning the wedding, an event he felt less and less involved in. To him, the wedding was something to get through so they could start their life together—a life he was thinking about a lot lately as he tried to picture what it would be like and how much it would include Alanna's family. Rather than think about it, he retreated to his thoughts of being on the beach and out on the water. It was the one place where he always found peace, not admitting to himself that the comfort he found there had more to do with a woman than the ocean itself.

Chapter 64

With the approach of fall, the summer crowds dwindled and the students returned to school, making the beach less crowded. Hank and Jess were sitting on their boards in the water, idly watching for waves, but far more interested in their conversation than surfing. Jess was recalling a funny event that had happened to her over the weekend. Hank teased her about being a Northern girl who just didn't understand the Southern ways and Jess had splashed him, saying that with all the time she had spent below the Mason-Dixon line these past years, she had become an honorary Southerner and deserved some respect. The conversation was interrupted by a sudden voice behind them.

"So this is where you have been hiding out."

They both turned to see Mike joining them on his board. Hank had told Mike about Jess's return but failed to mention they were spending time surfing together. He suddenly felt self-conscious, like he'd been caught doing something wrong.

"Hey, man, good to see you out," Hank said, trying to act casual while working hard to avoid the look Mike was giving him.

Mike turned to Jess. "Hey, Jess, good to see you again. I heard you were back in town."

"Hey, Mike," Jess said, a little surprised by Hank's reaction but happy to see Mike. "Yeah, I came back to work at the Marine Center at UNCW. It's been a long time. How have you been?"

"Mike's a married man now," said Hank, smiling at his friend. "And has a son."

Jess showed surprise. "Really. Who's the lucky woman?" she asked.

"No one you know. Her name's Lila," he said, smiling and looking proud. "And we have a second one on the way."

"That's great, Mike," Jess said, amazed by how much older he looked and that he was settled down.

"Yeah, but it really cuts into his surfing time," Hank added, ribbing his friend. "It's been a while since he's been able to get out here."

"That doesn't seem to have stopped you," Mike said, alluding to his being out with Jess. "Just give me a couple of years and I'll have Connor out here on a board. Then you better watch out."

"You think your son is going to out-surf me?" Hank replied, laughing.

"Oh, I know any son of mine is going to dust you, Atwater," Mike said.

Jess laughed. "Are you still working with your dad?" she asked Mike.

"Sure am," he said. "We've opened a second office that I run. It's going very well."

"Mike helped me find a couple of cheaper houses to renovate and resell when I first started," said Hank, "but now he only deals with higher-end properties."

"Hey, I go where the money is. I have a family to support now," Mike replied.

Jess loved the camaraderie between the two of them and realized how much she missed the days when they all hung out at the beach with Anne. The three of them spent some time talking and rode in on some waves but then decided to call it quits. When they were toweling off, Jess asked Mike if he wanted to join them for coffee. Mike looked at Hank, who again avoided his eyes, then thanked her and declined, saying he needed to get ready to go to work. Hank said he was actually running late and had to get to his office himself, quickly saying his goodbyes and exiting first. As Jess gathered her things, Mike watched Hank walk away, reading his quick departure for exactly what it was—avoiding having to talk to him about what he was doing here with Jess.

Mike thought for a moment and then offered to walk Jess to her car. "You should come over and meet Lila," he said nonchalantly. "Why don't you come for dinner on Saturday night? I'm sure she'd like to meet you." Jess appreciated the invitation and accepted, giving him her number so he could text his address to her.

"Great. See you then," he said, giving her his charming Mike smile and heading off to his own car.

Mike wasn't worried that Hank had been busy lately. The summer months were always a busy season for Mike, and he hadn't been able to get out at all this summer due to either work or life with a toddler. The few times he had reached out to Hank to get together, Hank was either too tired from one of his social engagements or his work made it difficult. Mike didn't think anything of it because he knew that eventually they'd find the time to reconnect. But now Mike suspected Hank was avoiding him because of Jess.

Mike hadn't known that Hank was out surfing that morning. He had woken and made a last-minute decision to grab some waves to relieve some of the stress he was feeling. He didn't plan to surf in that area, but their usual spot was taken over by a summer surfing class, so he headed north and pulled into one of the side streets where he saw Hank's Jeep. Elated to run into his friend, he parked and headed out to find him.

Looking out across the surf, he could tell Hank was already out there with another surfer, which didn't surprise him because they both knew most of the locals who came out here. It wasn't until he swam out to meet Hank that he saw he was with Jess. Hank had told him he'd run into her at one of his events, but he hadn't mentioned her again, so it had seemed like a passing thing. Watching them kid around in the water as he swam up immediately told Mike just how comfortable they were with each other, and that concerned him. That Hank had not told him about her was not a good sign, nor was the way he avoided Mike's look and left so quickly when they returned to the beach. Something didn't feel right, which was why Mike extended the invitation to Jess for dinner. He wanted to get a better idea of what was going on and what her plans were now that she was back in Wilmington.

Mike didn't believe Hank would do anything that would hurt Alanna. He had seen them together and knew how important she was to him. But he wanted to hear directly from Hank what was going on. So Mike called Hank later that day and then again the following day, leaving messages for Hank to call him back. When he got no response, he left a third message which got right to the point.

"Either meet me tomorrow at our surfing spot or I'm storming your office," was all he said.

Mike wasn't going to let this one go.

When Hank got Mike's third message, he knew he couldn't keep putting him off. Having Mike show up that day while he was surfing with Jess had caught him off-guard. He knew Mike would ask him questions he wasn't ready to answer yet, so he was avoiding him. But he knew that not answering Mike's calls was even worse than saying he was too busy. He wanted to talk to him about seeing Jess again, but at the same time, he didn't want to really think about what their getting together meant to him. He saw their time together as separate from his life with Alanna. With Mike now knowing they were meeting at the beach, it changed things, and Hank didn't know where those changes might lead him.

The next morning, Mike was sitting on his board when Hank made his way out to him through the waves. Hank felt tired and uneasy, but he greeted his friend and waited for him to start the conversation.

"So, are you going to tell me what's going on?" Mike asked right away.

Hank shook his head and looked out at the water. "I don't know, man. We ran into each other at the gala, and then one day I came out to surf and she was here and we just started talking again like old times. We've surfed a few times and have gone for coffee, but that's it," he said. Hank recognized he was downplaying it, but he wasn't sure how much he wanted to admit to Mike, or even to himself. He really enjoyed spending time with Jess and didn't want that to end just yet.

"How has it been seeing her again?" Mike asked.

"Great. I mean, I think seeing her again is making what happened when she left easier to deal with. Maybe this is what I need to put it behind me, you know? To move on," Hank replied, trying to put it into words, but Mike could hear the uncertainty in his voice and wasn't buying Hank's story.

"Did she ever tell you why she left?" Mike asked.

"No, it hasn't come up."

Mike thought about that for a moment. "Just be careful, man," he finally said.

"I always am," Hank said with a wan smile, glad the discussion was over and they could just focus on surfing.

But Mike was even more certain that inviting Jess to dinner had been a good idea.

Chapter 65

When Hank texted that he would not be able to go surfing that morning, Jess went in to work early. She was almost finished gathering the data she needed and was preparing to move into starting the field work she was excited to do. She had chosen Wilmington because she knew she could work with the Turtle Rescue to gather information on the injuries they were seeing in their rescues as well as work with certain fisheries open to her ideas to lessen the bycatch of sea turtles in their nets. She was also in touch with another scientist stationed at the Virginia Marine Science Museum who was conducting a similar study. Jess went to meet with her in July to discuss coordinating research data and they got along very well. She was even told there was a place for her there if she wanted to work more closely together, but Jess declined since her permits were to do her research in North Carolina, and she wasn't sure how long it would take to get Virginia permits.

But Jess's real reason for staying was she didn't want to leave Wilmington. She enjoyed being back and getting to know the city all over again. She had made new friends at the Marine Center and was discovering new parts of the area. And yes, she didn't want to give up her mornings surfing with Hank. It felt so good to be reconnected to him, and it made her feel more a part of Wilmington than ever.

Jess didn't think about what their time together meant to his relationship. She knew he was still planning a wedding with Alanna and the time he spent at the beach with her hadn't changed that. If anything, she didn't want it to. Jess had no intention of breaking up his relationship. She recognized they were acting on borrowed time, and eventually, that time would come to an end. She just didn't want to think about how she would feel when that time came. Rather, she pushed the thought from her mind, telling herself they were just friends.

It would only pain her to think about him living a life that didn't include her.

Airlie Gardens held concerts on Fridays that were a very popular summer event. Jess had never visited the famed garden reserve when she was a college student, but a number of her coworkers were going together as a group, and Margie, another colleague, convinced her to join them, offering to pick her up with some other folks, including David. Jess had become friendly with David now that he'd stopped trying to ask her out, so she agreed to go with them. She figured with a group this size, she wasn't sending the wrong message, and besides, she really wanted to see the place she had heard so much about. She'd passed it several times over the years on the way to Wrightsville Beach, preferring the quiet and less traveled Airlie Road when biking her way down to the ocean, and now she would finally see what she'd been missing.

Jess followed her coworkers and a large crowd through the elaborate black, iron-wrought, scrolled gates that opened up to the driveway and onto a path that led them through a sprawling garden. At the end of the path was a large open area known as the Oak Lawn. It was an appropriate name. The Airlie Oak, a massive, nearly 500-year-old oak tree draped in Spanish moss, stood at one end while a bandstand was erected at the other. A band was preparing to play while the group looked for a spot to set up. It was not an easy task since almost all the space on the lawn had been taken up by chairs and blankets of the other concert-goers, but they finally found an open space. The group unfolded their chairs, then laid out their food and drinks and sat down to chat and eat before the concert began. David handed Jess a glass of wine, something she rarely drank, but it was a warm evening and everyone was in a festive mood, so she indulged herself, letting the setting of the lush gardens and overgrown trees wash over her.

The music started and people danced up front with their children while others stood in groups talking. It was a very social event, and Jess liked watching the crowd when she wasn't talking to her own group. Even though she only drank one glass of wine, she was feeling a bit tipsy, probably because she had not eaten much that day. She decided to go for a walk to clear her head and get a closer look at the oak tree Jenna had told her so much about.

When Jess had told Jenna she was going to Airlie, Jenna had rolled off some impressive facts about the Airlie Oak. It was said to be the largest and perhaps oldest oak in North Carolina. The trunk had a circumference of twenty-one feet and a crown spread of its branches of 104 feet. Seeing the tree up close was even more spectacular than the facts suggested. The magnificent tree looked as if it were made up of several trunks woven together at the base, only to separate and sprawl out on top into its various lumbering branches. Jess stood marveling at the beauty of it, wondering how it had managed to survive all these years.

As her eyes traveled down the trunk, she looked past the tree and across the lawn filled with people. Not far away, one particular group caught her eye. Six attractive and preppily dressed men and women stood in the shade of the oak with drinks in their hands. They were all focusing on an attractive blond woman talking animatedly. Jess immediately recognized the hair formed in a loose blond bun and the tall, elegant shape of Alanna, whom she had not seen since the gala. Alanna looked just as regal as she had at the formal event, this time wearing a floral sundress. Jess stared at her for a moment, watching as she transfixed the group, when a handsome man in a blue polo shirt and khaki shorts came up next to her and handed her a glass of wine, then put his arm around her shoulders. It was Hank standing next to her, raptly listening to her as the others did, with a loving look in his eyes.

Seeing them so cozy together startled Jess, and she quickly retreated to her own group, sitting down with her back to where she had seen Hank and Alanna. Someone offered her another glass of wine, which she took without thinking, drinking it down quickly. She sat there quietly while the others joked and laughed, not really paying attention to what was said as numerous thoughts rolled through her head. While she knew Alanna was Hank's fiancée, somehow not seeing her had made her less real in her mind. But seeing Hank and her together made Alanna's presence suddenly all too real, and the pain Jess felt at how Hank looked at Alanna was distressing.

While Jess's thoughts were elsewhere, David had sat down next to her and was trying to draw her into the conversation, but it was obvious she found it difficult to talk. When the concert ended, she immediately started gathering her things as the others did, grateful that she could now go home, but she seemed unable to do the simple task of folding her chair and putting it back in its carrying bag, making her frustrated. She was so flustered by seeing Hank and Alanna together that she had forgotten to eat when she had returned to her group, and now the wine had gone to her head, making her drunk.

David could see she was visibly distraught and offered to help her. He folded her chair and took it with her bag in one arm while gently placing his other arm around her, leading her out through the crowd. She allowed him to do this, and put her arm around his waist to steady herself since the wine and the lack of food made her feel weak and unsteady. He talked quietly to her as they walked out, helping her back to Margie's car, where she explained she must have been more tired than she realized and appreciated his help. Margie drove her home first, by which time she felt a little better, having gotten away from the scene on the lawn. She gave a quick thank you to Margie and her other coworkers in the car, anxious to get inside because the image of Hank and Alanna was replaying itself inside her head like a broken record.

Once inside, Jess quickly ate some crackers and drank some water to offset the alcohol. Then she joined Jenna on the couch to watch a movie. When Jenna asked about her evening, she told her she felt queasy and didn't really want to talk about it right now, leaving them both to watch in silence. She tried to focus on the movie, to drown out the thoughts that kept swirling around her head, but no matter how hard she tried, her thoughts kept going back to that moment at Airlie when she saw them together.

All she could think about was how Hank used to look at her in the same way.

Chapter 66

Attending concerts at Airlie with Alanna was one of the few social engagements Hank truly enjoyed. He could dress casually, they were outdoors in a beautiful garden setting, and somehow the usual chitchat wasn't as boring as he normally found it, possibly because everyone was more relaxed than at the formal events they so often attended. They would meet up with a particular group of young professionals, some of whom worked on committees with Alanna. Hank saw it as the up-and-coming crowd of Wilmington's elite, and though he was honored to be part of it, he knew his inclusion was based solely on his being with Alanna. He often wondered why Alanna chose him when so many other men in her crowd were obviously interested in her, but he always put it out of his mind before he tried to answer. Better not analyze it and just accept it, he thought, though it continued to remain a question in his mind.

It was a comfortable night for this time of year, warm but with less humidity, and the conversation was jovial. Hank didn't talk much at these gatherings, preferring to listen to the music and watch the crowds, but he would participate if there was something he wanted to add to the discussion. Alanna asked him to get her a glass of wine, which he did willingly, taking a moment to take in the view before him as he did so. He thought about his talk earlier that day with Mike and looked over at Alanna. He saw how lovely she looked, her manner inviting and entertaining, and wondered what it was he was really doing by meeting up with Jess. *You have this beautiful woman who has chosen you over all these other men*, he told himself, *who cares about you and who said yes when you asked her to marry you, who has helped you build your company in ways you could not have done on your own. You chose to be with her. Why would you do anything that would jeopardize your own happiness?*

Hank felt the familiar pang of guilt he got when he thought of Jess and shook it off, deciding this was not the time to be thinking about her. To refocus his attention, he walked over to Alanna to hand her the glass of wine, then put his arm around her, pulling her close to him. He watched her talk, not really listening to what she was saying, but thinking about how lucky he was to have her. She rested her arm around his waist for a moment, then giving him a squeeze, disconnected herself from him. Hank was a little disappointed to have her pull back like she did, but Alanna did not like to be too familiar in public, so he took it for what it was. Still, he watched her admiringly as she interacted with her friends.

When it was time to go, Hank packed up their items, slinging their chairs over his shoulder while carrying the cooler in his other hand. He walked alongside Alanna, who was recounting a story he had missed when he went to get her a glass of wine. Alanna was excitedly talking when she stopped, her gaze focused on someone in the crowd.

"Henry, isn't that your cute college friend I met at the gala?" she asked, pointing up ahead to their right. There up ahead was Jess with her arm around some guy Hank had never seen before. He only caught a quick glimpse of her face before she and her companion turned down the path and were swallowed up by the crowd.

Hank stopped and looked in Jess's direction in disbelief. He had purposely been avoiding thinking about her, but to have her appear so suddenly, and with another man who had his arm around her, completely threw Hank off balance. The surge of jealousy he felt was overpowering, and for the moment, he was unable to conceal his look of surprise.

"Henry, hon, is something the matter?" Alanna asked, touching his arm, unsure what to make of his reaction.

Hank shook off the feeling, knowing this was not the time to deal with his emotions about Jess. He turned to Alanna and forced himself to smile. "No, nothing's the matter. It's not her," he said, continuing to walk toward the parking lot.

He maneuvered them through the crowd, trying not to appear like he was actively searching to see if he could find her again. He needed to know if what he just saw was really true. Jess had never mentioned a boyfriend, but then why would she? They never talked about the other people in their lives since their time was spent solely focused on each other. But certainly an attractive woman like Jess would have lots of men seeking her out. Why should he be surprised if she were out on a date? Intellectually, he knew this was true, but seeing her in the arms of someone else unnerved him in ways he didn't expect.

They walked back to the car in silence without Hank seeing Jess again. He put their items in the trunk and then opened the door for Alanna, who was waiting beside the passenger door.

"Are you sure everything's all right?" she asked again softly before getting in, her woman's intuition telling her something was off.

"Of course," said Hank, giving her a small smile and a quick kiss. "I think I'm just tired. It's been such a busy week."

Alanna gave him a long look, trying to read his mind, then smiled as if she accepted his explanation and got into the car. However, as Hank got in the driver's side and started to drive them home, she had one thought that resonated through her and seemed to sink into her bones, one she had never worried about before.

Hank had lied to her.

Chapter 67

Jess woke up Saturday and immediately cringed, remembering the night before. Seeing Hank with Alanna had been enough to deflate her in a way she did not think possible. It surprised her how much it had affected her just to see them together. She put it out of her mind, focusing instead on the beautiful sunny day she could see out the kitchen window. It was the perfect day to go for a long bike ride and then head out to the beach to take a long swim. She did both activities with vigor, pushing herself until she felt the tiredness in her muscles and her body relaxed. Only then did she let the thoughts running through her head come to the surface.

Jess admitted to herself that she acted as if Alanna didn't exist and she had let herself get caught up in being with Hank. But now that she had seen Hank and Alanna together, it was obvious he loved her. As hard as that was to face, it was the reality of the situation. Any fantasy that their meetings together would lead to something more was dashed in that moment. *You're just friends*, she told herself. *He's moved on.* She said it to herself like a mantra, over and over, hoping it would subdue the hurt she felt at having him so close and yet unattainable.

She was relieved to be going to Mike's that night; it would take her mind off the previous night's events, even if she was slightly anxious about why Mike had invited her. She could sense him watching her and Hank closely while they were all surfing, and she wondered if there was more to the invitation than catching up with an old friend. Whatever the reason, she welcomed the chance to meet Mike's wife and son and see how much he'd changed from the fraternity boy he was in college.

Jess pulled off of Masonboro Loop into one of the newer housing communities she noticed were popping up all over Wilmington. She wound her way around the various one- and two-story traditional homes with well-kept lawns, porches with rocking chairs, and children's bicycles strewn on driveways until she found his address. At the door, she was greeted by Mike's wife, a pregnant Lila, and their two-year-old son, Connor, a shy but curious boy who hid behind his mother's skirt.

"You must be Jess. Come in! I am so happy to meet you," said Lila, her motherly warmth exuding from her as she invited Jess in, instantly making her feel at home. Lila was very attractive and had on a yellow sundress that looked comfortable but stylish, making Jess wonder if she should have worn something nicer than the skirt and sleeveless top she had thrown on, thinking it was a casual dinner. When Connor stepped out from behind his mother and Jess got a better look at him, she instantly saw traces of Mike in his young features.

Lila scooped him up and held him, asking him if he would like to meet one of Daddy's friends from college.

"He's adorable," Jess said, shaking the little hand he offered. "I can see both you and Mike in him."

"He's got his father in him all right, let me tell you," Lila said with a cheerful wink.

"Meaning he is just as charming and handsome as I am," Mike said, appearing behind Lila, giving her a squeeze and a kiss. "Come on in, Jess. Glad you could make it." He took the bottle of wine she had brought and waved her into the family room, a large open room with a two-story ceiling painted in beige. A fireplace was centered on the wall at the far end with windows on either side. There was an overstuffed leather couch with chairs on each end and a wooden coffee table made from what looked like long planks of driftwood. Scattered about the room were pictures of the three of them as well as what looked like Mike and Lila's parents in various settings. A box of Connor's toys was in the corner, its contents spilling over onto the wooden floor just outside the area rug. The room had a decorated but homey feel, and Jess was once more amazed by how domestic Mike had become.

"I was so glad to hear Mike invited one of his old college friends over. I enjoy hearing about his wild college days," Lila said, looking teasingly at Mike.

"Not me, honey. I was in the library studying the whole time. There's nothing to tell," Mike said with mock seriousness while giving Jess a playful look.

"That's my recollection," said Jess, innocently looking at Lila and playing along.

"Oh, I know that's not true," Lila said, laughing it off, "but I can wait until dinner to hear about it. Now, who can I get a drink for?" she asked, picking up Connor again and sitting him on her hip.

"Beer for me," said Mike.

"A glass of water would be fine," said Jess. After the night before, she had no desire to drink again.

"Coming right up," said Lila, cooing at Connor as she headed into the kitchen to get their drinks.

Jess offered to help her with dinner, but Lila would hear nothing of it and told them to sit and relax and think of some good stories to tell her. Once Lila had them settled with drinks and a platter of cheese and crackers, she retreated into the kitchen to feed Connor and finish making dinner, giving Mike and Jess a chance to talk.

"Mike, this is not how I would have imagined you living when we were in college," Jess joked when Lila left the room.

"Yeah, I didn't quite seem the family man type back then, did I?" he replied, taking a sip of his beer and smiling at the thought.

"No, but it obviously suits you now. Lila is wonderful. How did you two meet?"

"Well, not in the way you would expect," he said, putting his beer down and thinking of the story. "Lila's parents had come down from Charlotte wanting to buy a beach house. I spent a lot of time with them showing them places and helping them to get to know the area. They ended up buying a place on the north end of the Island, and after we finished the sale, they asked me if I would like to meet their daughter who was coming down to see the house. I didn't want to say no, being as I had just made a large commission on the sale, so thinking they were nice enough folks and it was all in the name of business, I agreed to meet her for dinner the next time she came down."

"You were set up?" Jess teased, remembering how popular he was with girls when she knew him and how he'd never had a problem getting dates. He was the last person she imagined going on a blind date.

Mike laughed. "Yeah, I was. I mean, I wasn't dating anyone at the moment, and I figured it was one night; I could say I went and then be done with it. Keep my clients happy, and hopefully, they would keep referring me to their friends and everyone's happy."

"Yeah, but that's not the way it worked out, is it?" Jess said. "So what happened?"

"Well, it didn't go well at all at first," Mike admitted. "I was working with another client on a contract that needed to be done at the last minute, making me late to the restaurant. When I finally arrived, the hostess informed me we had missed our reservation and would have to wait for another table. As it was a hopping Friday night in downtown Wilmington during the height of tourist season, I knew that could mean a good amount of time. We sat down at the bar to wait, but it was so loud we could barely hear each other talk, so conversation wasn't possible. I just sat there not knowing what to do and worried it would get back to her parents that I didn't show her a very good time. That was when she leaned over to me and said, 'Let's get out of here.' Relieved, I followed her out the door to a place she said she knew a couple of blocks over. It turned out to be an oyster bar that I had gone to a number of times and really liked. We were able to get a table right away and started talking."

"Were you attracted to her right away?" Jess asked, wondering if his experience was like hers with Hank.

"Let's just say that yes, I found her attractive at first, which made me think the night would be a little easier to get through. She was definitely a Southern girl with the blond hair and not too much makeup, and a nice white dress that was fitting but not too provocative, you know, with the right shoes, the right purse. Since she was the daughter of a client, I certainly wasn't going to put any moves on her, which defined the evening from the outset. Just drinks, dinner, and then I walk her back to her car and say goodnight. How hard could it be? Who knows, maybe it was because I had no intention of seducing her that I was able to just relax and be myself. She told me about herself, and I talked about myself in a way I never had before. We ended up closing down the restaurant, and when it was time to say goodnight, I knew I wanted to see her again. So we started dating, and after a year of getting to know each other, I proposed."

"What was it that drew you to her?" Jess asked.

Mike thought for a moment. "I know it sounds cliché," he said, "but the best way I can put it is she made me feel like less of the rowdy college student I still had in me and more like the man I wanted to become. I respected her and felt the need to treat her in a way I had not always treated other women. I felt...protective of her, in a sense."

Jess sat thinking of how that was the same feeling she got from Hank when they were dating, and she had liked how it felt.

"And she liked oysters," Mike said, breaking the serious tone the conversation had taken, emphasizing his point by holding up his beer and taking a long swig.

Jess laughed. "As all good women do," she remarked.

"Amen," said Mike, clinking his bottle to her glass of water.

It turned out Lila was also quite the cook. Dinner was a delicious combination of pan-fried flounder, garlic mashed potatoes, and green beans, and Jess was duly impressed, complimenting Lila several times on how tasty it all was. When they were done, Mike insisted on clearing the table while Lila said she was going to put Connor to bed. Jess helped him bring the dishes into the kitchen and offered to help clean them, but Mike said he would do them later and brought her back into the family room.

"You know, when you first invited me over, I thought it was to talk about Hank," Jess said as they sat down, believing her concerns had been wrong.

"Actually, Jess, there is something I wanted to talk to you about," said Mike, looking a little more serious and sitting forward, leaning on his knees as he thought about what he was going to say.

"Hank has been my best friend practically my whole life, and I love him like a brother. I am breaking the best friend code by telling you this, but when you left that summer back when we were all in college, well, you devastated him. I was there when his mother died, and I saw how badly he handled it when Rob was killed, but with you, it was different. I knew you had broken something in him. After you left, it was like a part of him left with you. He focused on studying and working, and though he wouldn't admit it to me, I knew he did those things for you. It was as if he was hoping someday he could show you that your belief in him had been right all along so he could win you back. It took a long time before he gave up that idea and started living his life again. He tried dating a couple of girls, but it was never serious. Once he found his calling with restoring houses, he put all his time and energy into it, spending every waking hour making it work. I began to think he would never get over you until he met Alanna. She urged him to open up and got him to start enjoying life again. Not to mention, she helped him grow his business when it was just starting out. Maybe he never fell for her the way he did for you, but maybe she is what he needs now. She's good for him, Jess. He loves her and they work, you know? They have a lot in common being from here and all, and that's a good thing for Hank."

Mike hesitated and took a breath, looking for the words. "Look, I saw how he looked at you when we were all out surfing together last week, and it's obvious he still cares about you. The question is how much do you care about him? Is it enough to walk away and let him have this bit of happiness he finally found with Alanna? Or do you see something happening between you two?"

Jess was taken aback by the directness of his question. She was still processing everything he had just told her and was unprepared to explain her motives when she was just starting to examine them herself. "Mike," she said, trying to sound reassuring, "We're just friends. Whatever you think Hank is feeling, he hasn't conveyed it to me. I know he's marrying Alanna, and I'm happy for him."

"Are you?" Mike asked, looking questioningly at her. "Because hanging out with him like you are, that may not be how he sees it. At one time, Hank wanted you more than anything else. It was never a summer romance to him, Jess. He loved you more than I have ever seen someone love another person. But you left and never contacted him again. That hurt him more than you understand. It took a lot of time, but he finally got over it. And now you're back, which is obviously causing him a lot of confusion. You, more than anyone, have the ability to hurt him deeper than anyone else. If you really care about him, you need to do what is best for him," he said, leaning back, having finished what he wanted to say.

Jess was surprised to learn all this. "Mike, you know I would never do anything to hurt Hank. I feel terrible about what happened...."

Mike raised his hand to stop her. "I believe you, Jess. Really, I do. I always liked you. I just want you to think about what you are doing to Hank by coming back into his life like this. Because I can already tell that to him, it's not as harmless as you think."

The conversation dwindled after that. Jess was grateful when Lila came back down a few minutes later. She was ready to leave after her talk with Mike, thanking them for dinner and saying her goodbyes as soon as she could. Mike's parting words to her were to think about what he had told her, confirming her belief that this evening had been more than a friendly get-together. He had given her a clear picture of what her leaving did to Hank, and it had been hard to hear.

Jess thought back to when she had returned and hoped to run into Hank to explain why she had left. But after they struck up such an easy friendship, she could never bring herself to raise the subject, thinking the past was behind them. To do so would only seem to open old wounds that were better left in the past.

But from what Mike was saying, those wounds had never closed.

Chapter 68

Jess lay awake that night for a long time going over Mike's words. When she woke on Sunday, her first thought was to take a long ride to sort out her thoughts. But looking out the apartment window, she saw a light rain was starting, killing any chance of riding. Jenna was already at work at the kitchen table, which meant Jess would need to go elsewhere if she wanted time alone to think. She grabbed her raincoat and decided to go for a walk in the chilly gray morning, weather that seemed aligned to her mood.

Jess knew it must have hurt Hank when she left, but she had never really thought about what he went through until Mike explained it to her. After she made it to Florida, it was too painful to think about him. Since she had returned, she had figured that whatever hurt she may have caused him in the past was long forgotten. Not once did he bring up her leaving, and Jess told herself that was because he had moved on with Alanna. But to hear Mike confirm how devastated Hank was and how much her presence now affected him forced her to admit she had been lying to herself. Obviously, Hank still cared about her. And if that was the case, she really needed to understand her own motives in spending time with him because she never wanted to hurt him like that again.

Jess knew very well why she wanted to spend time with Hank. She was still in love with him. So many good things had happened to her while she was in Wilmington. She had discovered her love for the sea turtles, a passion that helped her create her purpose in life. And she had discovered love through him. No one else had made her feel so special since her father. She hadn't even known how much she missed that feeling of security until Hank came along. Even after all these years, she had never met another man who had made her feel the same way. Their time together surfing and talking over coffee gave her the chance to get to know him all over again, and if she was captivated by him in college, he had now matured into a man who was everything she wanted. She loved the passion he had for his work and hometown, as well as his loyalty to his father and Mike. He was strong in so many ways he didn't even recognize, yet so gentle and kind with her. She could see him being such a good husband, a good father, and the kind of person she wanted to spend her life with. When she thought of Wilmington, she thought of being with him. It was clear the two were entwined and inseparable.

But the fact was Hank was marrying Alanna. Jess started imagining what might happen if she had stayed. She had been avoiding the reality that in just a few months, Alanna would be his wife. Jess hadn't wanted to think about it, but there it was. Seeing them together at Airlie was hard enough, but seeing them together as husband and wife, and later as a family, was something Jess did not think she could bear. There was no question that she needed to end their time surfing together, for her sake as well as his. After what she had learned from Mike, she knew she needed to find a way to end these outings without putting them both through the anguish she had caused the first time.

It was chillier than usual, particularly with the rain, so Jess jammed her hands deep in her pockets and pulled her hood on tight. She looked down as she walked, letting her feet take her wherever they wanted to go, and she wasn't surprised when she found she was headed toward the beach. She walked past the Café where they met, over the Channel where they watched the sunset together, and past all their familiar places until she came to the street where she had once lived with Anne. She stood for a long time staring up at the house they had lived in, the rain streaking down her face, thinking about the night when she and Hank had made love and how he had made it so memorable.

When Jess couldn't bear to look at it anymore, she headed up to the beach. The sky was covered with dark clouds that hung low over the rough water. The rain soaked her, making her feel even more chilled as the wind cut through her. Nothing about being there felt peaceful the way it always had in the past. If this was the place where she felt most connected to the world, it now seemed cold and uninviting.

She thought of the offer she received to do her field research in Virginia and how she could make it work there if she could get the permits and work out a few other details. It wasn't Wilmington, but it would give her a fresh start. Mike had made it clear she was only causing Hank conflict if she stayed, and if she still loved Hank, she owed it to him not to interfere with the life he had created for himself. It was too late to resurrect their relationship. She was better off going to a new place that held no history for her.

There was no reason to stay anymore.

Chapter 69

Hank was withdrawn and silent the whole weekend, deliberating over the thought of Jess with someone else. Try as he might, he couldn't let it go, the image of her creeping into his thoughts even during his Sunday run. He thought about mentioning to her that he had seen her at Airlie and asking who she was with, but he didn't know how she would react to the question. She didn't owe him an explanation, but Hank couldn't let it go. He needed to know how serious it was. He went back and forth on whether to bring it up or to pretend he hadn't seen them together. When Monday morning came, he still couldn't decide whether he should ask her.

In the end, it didn't matter, as Hank never got a chance to ask. Shortly after they were out on the water, Jess told him she was moving her research project to Virginia to collaborate with another research team. She mentioned it nonchalantly as they were bobbing on their boards, talking about what a great opportunity it was for her to work with another group that would provide even more information for her study. He told her it sounded promising, but it was clear he was taken aback by this change of events. He asked her a few rudimentary questions about logistics, then grew quiet, a pained look on his face. They fell into an uneasy silence that was lasting too long when the sound of thunder rumbled in the distance. A storm was blowing in behind them, and it started to rain. Once thunder started, it was unsafe to be in the water, so with a quick look at each other showing they both recognized the sound, they paddled in.

As soon as they made it to the beach, the rain started coming down in sheets. Storms often came in hastily at the beach, dropping heavy rain, then just as quickly stopping and allowing the sun to break through the clouds, but right now it was pelting their skin hard, so they needed to find shelter. They motioned to each other to take cover under the pier, scooping up their items on the beach as they ran for its protection. Once they were safely underneath, they propped their boards up against the support beams and stopped to catch their breath.

Hank was surprised by his reaction to Jess's news that her research would take her away from Wilmington. His first thought was to convince her to stay. They had just gotten to know each other again, and he didn't want her to leave.

"How important is it that you go to Virginia?" Hank asked, trying not to let the despair in his voice show as rain poured down around them. He had been telling himself they were just friends, that that was enough, but now he felt her slipping away again, and the thought was unbearable. They were alone under the pier, disconnected from the world, and Hank was remembering the first time they had walked in the rain together all those years ago and the first kiss that he had savored for so long after. There were so many good memories with her. If she left, there would never be the chance to create new ones.

"I need to be there as soon as possible so we can coordinate protocols and share data," Jess said, not really focused on what she was saying. She, too, was recalling the memory of their first kiss and was trying desperately not to let herself fall back in time. Once she let those memories resurface, she knew she wouldn't be able to stop herself from where this was going. She didn't trust herself to look at him, choosing to look out over the beach and the rain as it fell.

Hank looked at her with all the desire he felt for her, taking in the wet dark hair slicked back and seeing the beauty of her features as they glistened with rainwater. He reached out and touched her cheek, and without even thinking, she leaned into his hand, closing her eyes and allowing herself to be drawn into the soft, warm feel of his touch. Her body reacted by turning toward him and leaning her head against his chest as his other arm wrapped itself around her protectively. He pulled her in close, resting his head on top of hers. They stood there quietly with the sound of rain falling around them, and then Jess looked up at him, her eyes filled with all the love she had for him, all the love she'd kept hidden, wanting to stay like this with him forever. He couldn't hold himself back any longer. He leaned forward and kissed her, all his desire coming to the surface, wanting to feel her in his arms and never let her go. He had denied his feelings for so long, but now he had to show her how he felt and to keep her from leaving him again.

Jess kissed him back with just as much passion and desire, pressing herself against him and wanting to be consumed by him. Everything she loved about him, from the sensuous feel of his kiss to the way she felt when his arms were wrapped around her, was even more intense than she had remembered, and her body ached at reclaiming it. She let herself get lost in the moment, allowing it to overtake her, thinking how badly she had missed being with

Hank like this and how right it was, when a small voice in her head shouted for her to stop. She broke out of her trance, and realizing what she was doing, jerked herself away from him.

"Hank…we can't…" she said, stepping back and looking at him standing there, her hand touching her mouth, the longing to be with him stronger than it had ever been and wanting nothing more than just to lose herself in him, seeing the yearning in his eyes. But she couldn't. This was wrong. It was all wrong, and she knew she needed to get out of there, had to get away before she did something she would regret forever. She grabbed her surfboard and started running up the beach to her car, needing to get away from him and from the beach. It suddenly became starkly clear that the life she so desperately wanted to have here could never happen the way she had hoped.

"Jess, wait…." she could hear Hank yelling behind her. But Jess didn't wait. She ran all the way to her car and quickly latched her board on top before getting in and driving away as fast as she could, angry for allowing herself to be drawn in by him and a dream that could never happen.

Chapter 70

Hank knew not to follow Jess. They had gone too far, they both knew that. He had been wrong to kiss her for so many reasons, but while he felt guilt for doing it, he didn't regret it. The kiss had been more than he imagined it would be, showing him that their connection was just as deep as it had always been. Seven years apart hadn't changed how he felt about her and never would. The feel of her against him lingered, his body physically remembering all too well all her curves and softness, how perfectly she fit in his arms. His mind played the moment over and over, wanting to stay there and not think about how it had ended or that it could not happen again.

He also knew that kiss was a betrayal to Alanna. He was not proud of himself for doing something that would hurt her, but he recognized it was just the culmination of all the things he had been doing with Jess that were wrong. He'd been living in denial, telling himself that what he was doing was innocent. But now he had to face the truth. He cared deeply for Alanna, but he had never stopped loving Jess, and try as he might to figure out what to do, he had just endangered his relationship with both women. He needed to choose one, yet there was no clear answer. He was planning a wedding with Alanna. He would never have proposed if he did not see them building a life together. But Jess seemed able to reach deep inside him and get to places no one else could. She made him feel things no one else ever had. Yet here she was getting ready to leave him again by moving to Virginia. How would he survive it this time if he were to tell her he wanted her to stay and she left again?

He tried to put it out of his mind while working, trying to put together some applications for permits that were needed and reviewing some invoices that had come in. But his mind could not focus. After a few minutes, his thoughts would go back to the feel of Jess in his arms, her lips so warm and soft, and how he never wanted to let her go, and then he would be off into his own thoughts again.

Hank wrestled with his feelings off and on until finally he decided enough was enough. He needed time to think. Shortly before lunch, he announced he would be out for the rest of the day, leaving the work in his father's hands.

"Everything all right, son?" his father asked when Hank called him into his office. "You seem a bit distracted today."

Hank thought about telling his father what had happened, but then he thought better about it. Right now, no one else knew about the kiss he had shared with Jess, and maybe it was better to keep it that way. He could only imagine what his father would think of his actions, particularly since he liked Alanna.

"Just tired, Pop. Too many late nights with Alanna," he said, trying to downplay his need to escape.

"Yep, you've got yourself a good woman there. Don't ever forget it," his father said, smiling, not realizing that he had played right into Hank's guilt. Hank nodded, feeling the pain of that comment and what he had done, leaving as quickly as he could.

Hank went home and changed into some running clothes. He didn't usually run in the afternoon, but his thoughts were racing and he felt anxious. He needed to do something physical to calm himself down and allow himself to think. He didn't want to return to the beach, so he figured he would just head out his front door and run through the downtown area to clear his head.

He started running at a relaxed pace. He could feel his body was tense and his legs needed some time to warm up before he could pick up the pace, but even knowing this, it was hard to hold himself back when his mind wanted to go hard. When he reached the point where he could feel his breath start to even out and his body to relax, he picked up the pace. He went faster and faster until he was sprinting under the shade of tree-lined streets past the historic homes he so loved but which were a blur as he ran past them. Right now, it was all about pushing himself until he felt the rush of endorphins surge through his body, easing the pain he felt in his heart, trying to get to the point of feeling anything but the emotions that had paralyzed him since this morning.

Hank ran until he was out of breath, and then he slowed down, thankful for the calming effect running was starting to have on him, for being able to concentrate on the aches in his legs rather than the jumbled thoughts that ran through his head. When he had thoroughly worn himself out, he made his way back to his apartment, walking the last few blocks before heading inside, wiping his sweaty brow with a kitchen towel and taking a long drink of water.

He sat in a chair at the kitchen table looking out the window, giving him a view to the back of the building where the patio and garden were located. He thought of the afternoons sitting out there in the garden with Alanna, talking together. He remembered the way she sat with her legs crossed, so neat and contained, always looking so refined even in the hot and humid weather. How she would tilt her head back and laugh, her smile flirtatious, and the way she looked at him, admiring and loving. It was during one of these afternoons together that he had really felt her love for him. He could see how well their interests in Wilmington aligned, between her work at historic foundations and his work restoring historic properties. And how she made him feel a part of her world in society, a place he had never seen himself included, yet by being with her, he felt accepted. He could see the wife she would be, someone kind and good to him who would care for their children and home. It was what drew him to her.

Hank thought how far he had come from his early days when his life was nothing short of a mess. To Alanna, that time was just a story in the paper she had once read, not knowing what he was like back then or what he had gone through. She only saw him as the person he was now, a hardworking man who was running his own successful business, of which a lot of that success was due to her influence. He liked the version of himself that he saw in her eyes.

Jess, on the other hand, knew him better than almost anyone other than Mike or his father. She had lived through that time with him, and when most people chose to condemn him merely due to what they had heard, Jess had taken the time to get to know who he really was. Jess had been the one to believe in him when no one else had and help him break free of the image he had of himself as someone with limited capabilities and choices in life. It was through Jess that he had opened up his heart, and if she hadn't come along, he didn't know where he might have ended up. She'd been such an integral part of his life and the changes that brought him to where he was today. And he had been so grateful to have her back, feeling their old connection as if no time had passed, and discovering that not only was she just as dedicated, smart, and beautiful as she was then, but that he'd never stopped loving her.

But none of this mattered if he couldn't be a part of the life she wanted. The one thing he worried about with Jess was how easily she found it to leave. She had a career she loved and worked hard to develop, but that career demanded she go to other places. From what Hank could see, Jess needed to go wherever her work would take her, and taking her work to Virginia was just the next step in what he imagined would be more moves. Making a life with her would be impossible because his livelihood was here. He had built his life in Wilmington and had no desire to leave, particularly after he'd worked so hard to make a name for himself. He was doing work that enriched him and made him feel like he was making a difference. The more he thought about it, the more he believed he would only be holding her back if he were to ask her to stay in Wilmington with him. Maybe she would for a while, but how long would it take before she started resenting him for it? The only thing that would give him more pain than seeing Jess with another man was if she were to stay with him, then blame him for holding her back. If he really loved her, he needed to do what was best for her. He needed to let her go to fulfill her dreams, no matter how much it broke his heart to do so.

As the sun sank in the distance, Hank thought long and hard about his relationship with both women, recognizing the roles they had played in his life and what each of them had meant to him. And after sitting there for an extensive time thinking it through, he came to a decision. He had to let Jess go. The thought of doing so was excruciatingly difficult, but he could see no other way it would work. He wanted Jess in his life, but more than that, he wanted her to have the life she wanted and had worked so hard to build. He saw the way she talked about sea turtles and the work she was doing, her enthusiasm still apparent after all these years. He knew she would not be doing the work she was if she hadn't left the first time. He couldn't be the reason she gave up the aspect of her life she was most passionate about. And if she was already considering working elsewhere, it was obvious her passion wouldn't be satisfied by staying in Wilmington.

And then Hank did something he had not done since Jess had left all those years ago, remembering the night he had sat by the turtle nest and watched the hatchlings dig their way free and head out to the ocean. Sitting alone in his kitchen, now darkened by nightfall, Hank put his head down on the kitchen table and cried harder than he ever had, allowing the sorrow of letting Jess go overtake him.

Chapter 71

Jess spent the next couple of days working out the details for moving to Virginia. She worked as fast as she could to tie up loose ends so she could get there as soon as possible, knowing she did not want to linger in Wilmington any longer than she needed to.

If she had thought about leaving before, the kiss with Hank had only reaffirmed her decision. She briefly wondered what their relationship would have been like if she hadn't left all those years ago. What would have happened if she'd contacted him from Florida and let him know she missed him and given him a chance to explain his side of the story. But she couldn't linger on those thoughts anymore. If she let her mind wonder about what might have been, she would be forever stuck in the past. If Jess was anything, she was practical. It didn't matter that she had wanted to make Wilmington her home. Now that she felt connected to Hank again, she could not imagine a life there without him. And that was not going to happen. She had no choice but to leave.

But she couldn't leave without talking to him one more time, knowing that would be too much like the last time. She had never told him all those things she had wanted to when she first came back, and if she didn't do it now, she would never get the chance to again. He deserved to know the truth about what had happened and to know she wasn't leaving because of what had happened between them at the pier.

Jess texted Hank and asked if they could they meet for coffee in the morning at their usual place. He replied within minutes, saying he would be there. There was no turning back now. She just hoped she had the courage to tell him everything she needed to before she left for good.

The next morning, when Hank arrived at Port City Java, Jess was already there, sitting at one of the outdoor tables and looking nervous. He wasn't sure if he would hear from her again after the way things had ended at the pier. While he was glad she had offered to meet, he knew it wasn't going to be an easy conversation. He sat for a minute in the car, not knowing what to expect of their meeting, finally opening the door and stepping out into the warm and hazy day. The sky was a bit overcast, indicating rain would be coming soon, and the katydids were humming around him, but all he could focus on was the beautiful woman he already believed he would probably never see again.

"Hello, Jess," he said, disrupting her thoughts. She looked up, a bit startled, and then gave a small but nervous smile.

"Hi, Hank. Thanks for meeting with me," she said, sitting very still. The tension between them was palpable, and he wondered if there was a way to diffuse it. "Please, sit," she said, motioning to the chair opposite her when he remained standing.

"Did you want me to grab us some coffee?" he asked, noticing she had nothing on the table and anxious to do something to make it more normal.

"No, thank you. I can't stay long. I just wanted to talk to you one more time before I left. To clear the air after…all our time together," she said, glossing over their last encounter.

Hank hesitated, then slowly took out the chair across from her and sat down, crossing his legs and leaning back as if wanting to create as much distance from what she was going to say as he could. Jess hesitated, then took a deep breath and plunged in, hoping she would be able to get through it all.

"First, I never thanked you for what you did for me all those years ago. When John tried to pull me into that car with his friends, I knew what was going to happen. I'd heard all the rumors and knew I was in trouble. I fought so hard, harder than I ever had before, but I couldn't get away. Even drunk, John was so much stronger than me. It was terrifying. And then you showed up and saved me. You were always showing up at the right time in my life back then, and that moment could have changed everything for me. I was so grateful that you had come and yet…I felt so scared of you as well. After talking to Roxy, she had me convinced how violent you were. Then when you broke my lamp and I saw the look on your face when you hit John…" she paused, trying to slow down and not get too emotional. "I thought maybe Roxy was right. I was wrong, Hank. I was young and scared and didn't know what to think or what to do.

"I didn't learn the whole story of what Roxy did to you until after I returned. All those years, everything I had believed to be true about you had been based on a lie." Jess shook her head, still angry that she had believed it for so long. "I owe you an apology for that. For ever thinking that you could be the type of man who couldn't control his anger. For not trusting myself enough to believe I knew who you really were. I was so wrong in so many ways, and I'm truly sorry for all of it."

Hank listened quietly as Jess took a breath, knowing this next part put her in a bad light, and she didn't know how he would take it.

"You should also know there was another reason why I left. When I got into UCF that spring, I wanted to go more than anything. I had worked so hard to get into their program, only to discover I couldn't afford it. They didn't offer me any money like UNCW had, and covering it with loans was just not an option. I felt I'd finally discovered what I wanted to do with my life, and then was told I couldn't go because I didn't have the money. That night, when I ran away from John's car, I ran into John's father about a block away. He had been watching the whole thing. He told me to get in his car and he drove me home. When we got there, he gave me money for not telling anyone about what John had tried to do to me. A lot of money. Enough to cover both college and graduate school. There was one condition. He recommended that I finish school elsewhere. I was worried about what would happen to me if I stayed or how I would feel seeing John again. And when I calmed down, I recognized it was my chance to go to UCF. That is why I left so quickly the next morning.

"Once there, I told myself I needed to protect myself from you, that what I saw those last few days were just the beginning. I tried so hard to believe that, to convince myself I had been wrong about you. Everyone I talked to said I was doing the right thing by moving on—that I needed to forget about you. But no matter where I went or what I did, I just couldn't. Deep down, I never believed you were capable of doing the things Roxy said you had, and the more time that went by, the more I questioned if I had been right. I missed you so much, and I thought about you so many times, but I didn't know if I could trust that I knew the real you. When the opportunity arose to return here, I wanted to come back not just because of how much I had loved Wilmington, but because I wanted to find out if I had done the right thing by leaving all those years ago. Even though I wouldn't admit it to myself, deep down I had hoped to see you again, to see for myself if I had been right to leave and never look back."

Hank had been fingering his keys to focus on something without having to look directly at her as she spoke. But now he stopped and looked right at her. He uncrossed his legs and leaned forward. Anger about having to live down his past yet again rose within him. "And what did you decide, Jess? Were you right not to contact me, even just to let me know you were all right?" His voice was unable to hide the hurt that still lingered from that time.

Jess didn't blame him for getting upset. She felt her eyes tearing up and her mouth start to tighten. She knew she had to hold back the tears and explain it all to him. "No, I was wrong," she said softly, looking at him with the love she felt for him. "You were a great guy, Hank. You were always…a really great guy. I loved every minute we spent together that summer. And what I have learned since I have returned is that you've grown into an amazing man. You have accomplished so much by getting your degree and starting your own business—"

"Which I never would have done without you, Jess," Hank interrupted, leaning forward on the table and looking at her earnestly. "Certainly, you know it was you who got me here?"

Jess shook her head. This was heading down a path they could not go down, and she had to stop it. She took a deep breath and made herself calm again, then reached over and took his hand.

"No, Hank, it was you who got you to where you are today. I may have helped you start thinking about it, but it was you who got into UNCW and did the work that made all this possible. I was not here for any of it, so I can't take the credit. Though, I understand Alanna did play a part in it. You deserve someone like her by your side helping you do all the things you dreamed of doing. I cannot be that person. I need to do what's right, not just for me, but if I really care about you like I say I do, for you as well. And what's right is that I take my work elsewhere and let you live the life you have built for yourself. I love you, Hank. I always have and probably always will. But there's no way for us to be together. Too much has happened since that summer, and while this time we've spent together over the past summer has meant so much to me, I think we both realize it's better if I leave."

Hank sat frozen, knowing she was right, knowing what he had already decided, and yet, he still didn't want to let her go. But before he could say anything, Jess let go of his hand, reached down to get her purse, and stood, indicating the meeting was over. Hank stood up as well, knowing this might be the last chance he had to explain to her how he felt, but unable to form the words. "Jess…I care about you…so much. I just want you to be happy…." he started, but didn't get the chance to finish.

Jess stepped forward and gave him a hug, holding him tight for just a short moment, then letting him go, trying to maintain her composure and not break down. "I know you do. I want the same for you. I wish it could be different, but we know this is the right thing to do. Goodbye, Hank."

She turned and walked away, wiping away a tear from her eye as she headed to her car, telling herself not to turn around because she knew if she saw the pained look in his eyes, she would go running back to him and throw herself in his arms. Instead, it took every fiber of her being just to get into her car and drive away as fast as she could, not wanting him to see the tears streaming down her face at having done the hardest thing she'd ever done.

Chapter 72

Hank was not surprised by how his last meeting with Jess had gone. He had not known about the money she received from Richard, but he didn't fault her for taking it. Everything else she had explained was exactly as he had deduced. She had believed the lies Roxy had told her about him, and though it hurt him to think she would believe Roxy over their time together, he couldn't blame her for doubting him. Maybe he should have just driven down to see her in Florida to talk to her. But would she have listened to him? Would he have been able to change her mind? What held him back from doing it? Was it pride at having to prove himself yet again to the one person he thought loved him? He had so many unanswered questions of his own. But it was over now, and thinking about it wasn't going to change anything. It was better just to get on with life, focusing on work rather than the dull pain in his heart.

The next day, Hank started a new renovation on one of the older homes on Market Street that had suffered extensive water damage. Working with his father, Hank found where the water had started to infiltrate the inside of the house, due to a faulty fix on the roof by the former residents, and explained to the owners what repairs were needed. In addition to the repairs, they wanted to put on an addition to the house, a suite to house an aging parent or their soon-to-be graduated college student. Hank drew up the plans and obtained all the necessary city permits to proceed. It felt good to have something to occupy his mind, and this job promised to keep him busy, particularly since the damage was more extensive than they had initially thought.

Work was also a way for Hank to turn down one of Alanna's events that week, plus a get-together Friday night with some of her friends, claiming how tired he was from his current job. It was just too difficult to see her while the pain of losing Jess was still fresh and hard to hide. Saturday they had plans to work on the wedding, but Hank said he needed to finish some demolition, so could they push it to the next weekend? Alanna was disappointed but understanding. He knew he couldn't get out of seeing her Sunday without raising suspicion, so he came by to take her out for coffee, then told her he had promised to help his father out with a project at his house. She seemed a little taken aback at the shortened visit, but she hugged him and told him not to push himself so hard and that she would miss him.

Hank didn't want to hurt Alanna, but his heart was not into being around her right now. After he left her, he went for a run and then headed over to his father's house. There was no project, but he hoped that being in familiar surroundings would make him feel better. His father sensed something was bothering him, but in his typical fashion, he didn't push. They ate dinner together, and then Hank headed back to his own place. When he arrived, he just wasn't ready to go in, so he took a long walk through the town, watching the people hanging out at the bars and the tourists walking along the river. He knew he had made the right decision in letting Jess go, he reminded himself. He just had to keep repeating the thought over and over again until he actually believed it.

The next week went a little easier with Hank again burying himself in work. Though he talked to Alanna every day, he didn't see her until the following weekend. Alanna had chosen the Bellamy Mansion for their wedding site and reception, an 1861 mansion that had been preserved and seemed the ideal place for them, considering it embodied so much of Wilmington's history. Hank and Alanna were to do a walk-through with the event coordinator, a friend of Alanna's mother. Hank needed to be there so they could plan out how they would stage the ceremony. He really didn't feel up to it, but maybe this was the thing he needed to get his head back into being with Alanna and start looking forward to their upcoming wedding.

"I feel like I haven't see you in ages," Alanna said ecstatically, giving him a big kiss when he arrived at her door to pick her up. Hank smiled and kissed her, but it was obvious he seemed off. "Is anything wrong?" she asked, immediately sensing something was different.

"I'm just tired," he said, holding her close for a moment, making it seem like he just missed her, but really trying to avoid any more discussion. When Alanna pulled back, she couldn't hide her excitement.

"Mother and I have been working on this for a month. She has some wonderful ideas about the centerpieces and placement of the tables. You don't mind if she meets us there, do you?" she asked.

"Not at all," he replied, grateful to have someone to share Alanna's excitement so he could just blend into the background.

He had taken a long run that morning to clear his head, and although he was happy to see Alanna, he would rather not be doing this today if he had his choice. As they walked through the mansion, Mrs. Moore and Alanna happily discussed the details of the nuptials while Hank followed along, responding when needed, but relieved not to have to be overly involved.

The walk-through took most of the afternoon, and when they were finished, they said goodbye to Mrs. Moore and then Hank took Alanna out to dinner. He wanted to feel connected to her again, so he took her to a small Italian restaurant they had been to before with candles on the tables and a romantic setting. Hank looked across at Alanna and told himself he was a lucky man to have her. He asked about her work and what she did that week, but Alanna kept turning the conversation back to the wedding planning, excited about what they had accomplished that day. Hank knew he should be more excited about it, but what he really needed was to feel close to her and talking about the wedding was not helping. After several attempts to change the subject, he finally stopped trying and let her go on about the setup at the mansion and how beautiful it was all going to be. When dinner was over, he took her home, claiming he was exhausted from his new job, gave her a quick kiss, and told her he would call her in the morning.

The next day, Hank worked out even harder, doing one of his workouts at the beach before changing at home and calling Alanna. The October weather meant that the beach was less crowded and it was getting a bit cooler, which he preferred since the heat made it harder to push himself. The ocean water still maintained some of its summer warmth as he swam laps between circuits of exercises, the coolness a relief to his sore muscles. When it was done, he felt more relaxed and ready to be with Alanna again.

They spent the afternoon walking around Airlie, noting how the leaves were starting to change. Alanna talked about what had happened at her job at Thalian Hall that week, sensing he needed a break from talking about the wedding plans, as they wandered about like they had in the past. At the end of the day, Hank was holding her hand and just enjoying being with her again, remembering what had drawn him to her in the first place.

Over the next few weeks, Hank's work picked up substantially, which meant cancelling on more events with Alanna. She was always understanding, encouraging him not to work too hard, and telling him she would be waiting for him, but he knew she was disappointed not to see him. He felt some guilt since he didn't always cancel due to work. Sometimes he just needed a night to himself to sit, unwind, and read some books the way he used to. The one thing he didn't do was allow himself to think about Jess. He was doing everything he could to get back to feeling like himself, forcing himself through the motions and telling himself that at some point it would get easier, if he just waited long enough.

He just wished he knew how long that would be.

Chapter 73

Alanna wished Hank was as excited about planning the wedding as she was, but he often seemed undecided or just deferred to whatever she wanted. Her mother told her most men were uninterested in such details, so it didn't surprise her, and she thought it sweet that he wanted her to have it "the way that is most special to you," as he put it, but she couldn't shake the feeling that there was more to it. He was tense a lot lately, and he was even short with her a few times, something he attributed to his increased workload. Right now, all she could do was wait it out and do what she could to help him through it, hoping it was just a phase he was going through.

But finally, after Hank cancelled on her for another event, Alanna knew she needed to find out just what was going on with him. That weekend, they went out for coffee and then sat in the garden behind his apartment. The leaves were falling from the trees, and it was a bit cool out that day, but it was quiet and a place where they could talk.

Alanna snuggled close to Hank and linked her arm in his. She looked at him lovingly, and talked gently, hoping to get to the heart of the matter. "I know you've been so busy these past few months.

I am so proud of how hard you have been working. I just hope you aren't working yourself so hard because you think I expect certain things from you," she started off.

Hank looked at her, a little surprised. He thought he'd been doing a good job of keeping his feelings to himself, but obviously he had not. "No, not at all. I mean, I want to be able to provide for us. To be able to buy us a place to live and all, but it's just that…the work has come in faster than I expected. I am just figuring out how to keep up."

"Well, that's good," she said, squeezing his arm. "But I would rather have a happy husband than a tired and worn-out one." When he didn't smile or react to her kidding, she went on a bit more seriously. "But there is obviously something on your mind. Maybe you can share it with me and we can work it out together…."

Working out his feelings was not something Hank wanted to burden Alanna with. He knew it was something he would have to work out on his own, and he needed to do so without her knowing about it. He removed his linked arm and turned to her, taking her face in his hands and looking into her eyes. "I am sorry I have not been as attentive as I should be lately. Starting my own business has been much harder than I thought it would be, and I can see that I am letting that affect our time together. I will work on not letting that happen anymore, particularly as our time lately has been so limited." Then he leaned in and kissed her in a way he'd not done in some time—a long, soft kiss, followed by resting his forehead on hers with his eyes closed and inhaling her scent. He wanted so much to get back to the place they were before the summer had happened. But deep down, he wondered if he could ever get back there again.

During November, Hank remained pleasant enough, paying attention to Alanna when they went out together and treating her sweetly, but something had changed. He stopped accompanying her to events, claiming it was because of work, and even when they did get together, he seemed distant. His interest in the wedding had dropped to the point where he joked that she could handle the details and just let him know when to show up. Alanna couldn't blame him. Even she felt like her mother had taken over the wedding planning and it had become more of their party, since her parents were paying for it and they were used to putting together such elaborate events. Even though she had helped organize such events for work, Alanna also felt a bit overwhelmed by it and found herself deferring to her mother's choices more and more. She could only imagine how Hank must feel at how large the wedding had become.

This was their first holiday season together as an engaged couple, and it was obvious where they would spend the holidays. Alanna invited Hank and his father to Thanksgiving dinner, which consisted of about a dozen other members of the Moore family who came in from other parts of the state. Hank stayed close to his father for most of the night, which Alanna assumed was to make him feel more included since the Moore clan could be quite boisterous. Alanna did everything she could to make them feel included by sitting with them and explaining family jokes, but she could tell they were having a hard time fitting in. When she later mentioned to her mother that she felt bad they had not had a good time, her mother said to just give it time. First holidays as a couple were always hard, but they would find their place.

A week later, Hank and Alanna walked hand-in-hand through the historic district to look at the Christmas decorations, enjoying the displays and the festive spirit in the air. Alanna tried to talk a few times, but Hank would just nod in agreement, not having much to say. They made their way downtown where they walked along the river, and at one point, they stopped to look out at the stars reflecting off the water, sparkling with the holiday lights of the restaurants along the walkway. Hank put his arms around Alanna and looked deeply in her eyes before pulling her close to him, holding her for a long time.

Alanna hugged him back tightly, trying to convey all the love she felt for him. But in that moment, she'd seen the sadness in his eyes, and she finally admitted to herself it was not just work stress. Something hurt in his heart, something deep she could not reach. And worse, it was a pain she suspected she would never be able to assuage, no matter how he tried to fill that void with her.

Chapter 74

On Sunday, Hank went over to Alanna's for brunch with her and her parents. It had become a weekly event where they could discuss wedding plans and enjoy some family time. Hank recognized early on that these brunches would continue through their marriage. However, today he was unusually quiet, polite but preferring not to engage in the lively conversation between Alanna's parents. Alanna was also unusually quiet, not eating and looking at Hank several times throughout the meal. When her mother asked her what was wrong, she just said she was tired, but it was obvious there was more to it. Hank knew she was worried about him, but he didn't have the strength to play the part he was supposed to today, so he excused himself from the table as soon as he felt it acceptable to do so.

Though the weather was chilly, Hank sat outside on the porch to think. Alanna came out and sat down next to him on the porch swing. He tried to muster a smile, but it was hard.

"Something on your mind?" she asked, trying to be gentle. She started to stroke his hair, but he took her hand in his and asked that she just sit with him for a while as he looked out over the green lawn that led down to the street. He was always amazed by how the house being set back like it was gave it so much privacy from the cars and passersby below. Alanna realized he was shutting her out again and she couldn't pretend it wasn't happening any longer.

"You know, I always thought it was being male that prevented you from expressing your feelings. Most men don't use a lot of words, so I told myself the things you did for me showed me you cared. That I shouldn't expect you to express your feelings like I would."

She stopped for a moment as Hank sat there, unsure where this was going.

"But that really isn't the case, is it?" she continued. "I know you just don't have the same kinds of feelings for me that I have for you."

The words hung in the air between them, her hoping beyond hope they weren't true now that she had finally said them out loud. Hank looked at her and wanted to say something, but he didn't know what. She was right. He had never felt as strongly for her as he had for Jess. He might never feel that way about anyone ever again. But he couldn't live his life comparing every woman to the one who had broken his heart and he now knew he would never be with.

"I do love you, Alanna…" Hank started, but she held up her hand to stop him, not wanting to hear the rest.

"I believe you do, Hank," she said, her voice steady but sad. "I believe you are an honorable and upstanding man and that you would have gone through with this wedding and tried to be the best husband you could be. But I would never be enough. I saw how you looked at that woman at the gala and then again when you saw her at Airlie. The first meeting I was able to dismiss as running into an old college sweetheart. But that second meeting? You were transfixed, and what's worse, you lied to me about seeing her. Whatever you felt for her is still there." She let that statement hang for a moment, hoping he would deny it, but when he didn't, she went on, her words becoming more emotional. "I don't want to be the second choice in my marriage. I want someone who loves me and looks at me the way you looked at her. And you can't give me that."

She slowly took her hand out of his, then took off the engagement ring he had given her and put it on the table in front of them, looking at it sitting there for a moment with tears in her eyes.

"I would have been a good wife to you," she finally said, staring at the ring.

Hank put his arm around her and held her. "I know you would have. That's why I would have married you," he said softly.

She got up, straightened her skirt, and wiped a tear from her cheek, then stood proudly, looking at him one last time. "Goodbye, Henry. I hope it all works out for you the way you want it to," she said, and then she turned and went back into the house.

Hank watched her go and then sat there a long time, staring at the spot she had been, not sure if he should go in to say his goodbyes or if he should just go, knowing she was telling her parents that the wedding was off. After a while, he decided it was best just to leave. He got up and put the ring in his pocket, feeling sad that his relationship had just ended, but also feeling unexpected relief.

Hank walked back to his apartment where he called Mike and told him what had happened.

"Man, that's pretty tough. I'm really sorry. Do you want to come over here and hang for a while?"

Hank didn't know what he wanted. He knew something bad had just happened, but he didn't feel anything. He wondered if he was just in shock and that the realization of their relationship ending would hit him later.

"No, I think I'm going to go for a run," he finally said, wondering if that would help deter the pain when it came. "I need some time."

Chapter 75

The pain Hank was waiting for never came, only a numbness that seemed to dull his feelings. He went about his days working and going for runs, which was more than enough to keep him busy. He spent Christmas with his father, having a quiet dinner and watching a movie, a welcomed difference from their Thanksgiving celebration. New Year's he spent with Mike and Lila and a small gathering of friends. As winter came, his work was going well with new projects coming in and the business growing. It filled his days and kept him occupied both mentally and physically, creating a rhythm in his life that was comfortable and familiar.

Though he missed being with Alanna, he never felt the sadness he thought would come with the ending of their relationship. When he thought about it, he questioned if they'd gotten engaged too quickly. He felt relieved that he didn't have to attend the functions they'd gone to on such a regular basis, and he was thankful he no longer needed to hang out with her friends or have brunch with her parents. He admitted to himself he'd gotten caught up in being a part of Wilmington society because it had never been open to him before. He'd felt love for Alanna, but he could see it had never been the kind of love that would sustain a marriage. In the long run, their differences would have only widened, no matter how much he thought they had in common. He was only sorry he'd hurt her and that there was no way to make it up to her.

Trying to help out, Lila mentioned several times that she knew a few women who would love to meet him, to which he would politely decline, saying he wouldn't be good for anybody right now. In all honesty, he just didn't have the energy to try meeting someone new. He'd been lucky enough to meet two women who'd touched his heart, but for different reasons, he couldn't be with. The idea of opening up again was just too difficult. In those moments when he felt a pang of loneliness, Hank told himself his heart had been through enough. He was lucky to have people he cared about and success from his work. Maybe one day he would meet someone else, but right now, he wanted to keep his life simple.

Like always, Mike worried about Hank the most. He invited Hank over for dinner one night, and while Lila put Connor to bed, they sat in his family room with Mike drinking a beer while Hank had his usual club soda.

"So, how's it going?" Mike asked, taking a sip of his beer.

"Good, actually. I landed the Spencer project this week, and while it means I have to do more hiring, the project promises to be one of the bigger ones that I—"

"I meant with you," Mike interrupted. "Since you and Alanna broke up."

Hank sat silently for a moment at the change of subject, then shrugged. "Fine, man. I mean, I'm disappointed it didn't work out, but I think it was for the best."

"What about Jess? Do you ever think about her?" Mike asked, getting to the heart of the subject.

Jess was always in the back of Hank's thoughts, but he wasn't going to admit that to anyone. He hadn't told Mike about how their friendship had ended last fall, just that her work required her to move to Virginia. "It would never work, Mike. She goes where the work is. My life is here."

"Are you sure? I got the impression she was pretty happy to stay if there was a good reason to," said Mike.

Hank gave a short laugh. "How would you know? You only saw her the one time surfing."

"Because she came over for dinner before she left."

Hank was stunned. "How come you never told me that?"

Mike picked at the label on his beer bottle, choosing his words carefully. "When I saw you two surfing together, I could tell you both still had feelings for each other. I was worried about you, Hank. You were so destroyed the first time she left. And you were finally happy again with Alanna. I just wanted to ask Jess if she realized the effect she'd had on you in returning to Wilmington."

"And what did she say?" Hank asked, trying to be stoic but feeling the pain starting again.

Mike sighed and shrugged. "She said you were just friends. But it was obvious she was lying."

Neither of them said anything for a minute. Hank could feel the wound Jess had left reopening, and he couldn't have that. It was over between them. He had let her go. No matter what he wanted, she would never be happy living in Wilmington.

"Mike, I appreciate you looking out for me, but Jess and I are done," he said. "She knows what she wants, and it wasn't me. Really, you need to drop it."

Mike nodded, knowing that tone in Hank's voice. "Whatever you say, man," he replied, standing up. "I'm getting another beer. Want anything?"

Mike and Lila had their second child in the spring, a little girl they named Charlotte after Lila's mother. While he couldn't be happier for them, Hank felt a pang of sadness when he looked at Mike's family, wondering if he would ever have one of his own. He liked hanging out with Mike and Lila on the weekends when he wasn't working, often spending time with Connor to give them time to take care of the new baby or catch up on some much-needed sleep. Hank bought Connor a construction playset, and they would go around the house pretending to fix things.

"Look, you can fix things better than your daddy," Hank would say when Mike was around, ribbing him.

"Oh, very funny," Mike would say, scooping up Connor in his arms and swinging him around. "Tell Uncle Hank that Daddy just doesn't want to embarrass him with his own handyman skills."

"Daddy no want to embrass you," Connor said in his toddler language.

Hank laughed at the interpretation. "Tell Daddy not to worry about that," he replied. "You can show him how to fix things when you grow up."

After these visits, Hank thought about what it would be like one day with his own son and all the things he would teach him if he had one. As the days grew warmer, Mike brought Connor down to the beach and started teaching him how to boogie board, which consisted of Mike putting him on the board close to shore to catch the smaller waves. It wouldn't be long before he had him on a surfboard, Hank thought when he saw them.

When Hank wasn't with Mike and his family, he still spent some weekends doing work for the historical foundation. It was the one place where it was possible he might cross paths with Alanna, until one day he heard she had left her job there. No one would tell him why, but it wasn't long before he found out. The announcement in the paper was large and hard to miss, much larger than theirs had been. Alanna Moore to marry Jackson Causby. The story talked about how they had parted ways when Jackson had moved to Atlanta, but then he discovered he just couldn't stay away from his one true love, so he returned to Wilmington to be with her. Hank was glad Alanna had moved on, and he hoped she was happy. Jackson seemed a better fit with her life than he would have been, so it seemed appropriate. He was happy for her.

He just hoped he would find that kind of happiness himself one day.

Chapter 76

Moving to Virginia had not gone well for Jess. For one, finding a place to live was difficult. She left the first apartment she had settled into because her roommate forgot to mention her boyfriend lived there, too, sending her scurrying to find another one. The collaboration with the other team was going well, but Jess was having difficulty getting the Virginia permits she needed to conduct her field studies. When she hadn't acquired them by spring and found out they might take as long as another fifteen months to be issued, she knew this move would not work out. Her grant was only for three years, and waiting that long for the permits would not leave her enough time to do the actual field work. She finally acknowledged that she needed to return to North Carolina to finish her study and to figure out where she would go next. While Wilmington was no longer an option, there were some aquariums she thought might work. She needed to get some advice, so she made plans to go back to Wilmington for the weekend to meet with Professor Williams and visit with her friends at the Turtle Rescue, to get some ideas.

Jess drove in early, meeting Professor Williams for lunch. While Professor Williams tried to talk Jess into returning to UNCW, Jess made it clear she would love to continue her work there, but for personal reasons she could not explain, she needed to conduct her work elsewhere. Professor Williams said she understood and told her there might be a place she could go in the Outer Banks. She promised to make some calls and let Jess know.

Jess thanked her when they were done, but she felt despondent that their talk had not led to a more concrete solution. Next, she drove out to the Turtle Rescue to visit with friends there and see how their work was progressing. She talked with Kathy, the director, about an injured turtle that had come in the week before that fit right in with her study, and she took several notes. Jess also asked Kathy if she had any ideas where Jess might find another office to conduct her field work. Kathy couldn't think of anything offhand, but promised to let her know if she did. When she was done there, Jess headed back to have dinner with Jenna and catch up with her. She was happy to hear Jenna's boyfriend would be returning soon, and she could see how excited Jenna was about being together with him again.

When she woke early on Saturday, Jess thought about doing some surfing, then thought better of it. She didn't want to risk running into Hank, so it was better just to avoid the beach altogether. Instead, she took a bike ride through UNCW and down the familiar streets that took her to the downtown area. Later, she met some of her former friends from the Marine Center for dinner and then turned in early, thinking it would be best if she got an early start back the next day.

Jess sensed this trip was her final goodbye to Wilmington. She felt a certain sadness in leaving behind what still felt like her home. It felt good to see everyone one last time, knowing what they meant to her. She wished it didn't have to be this way, but she knew she was making the right decision.

Jess left early on Sunday, keeping the windows open as long as she could to take in the smell of the sea air and the feeling of the heat already beaming down from the sun. As she drove down College Road one last time, she felt certain this was the last time she would see it since there was no reason left for her to return. As she merged onto the highway, she rolled up the windows and turned on some music, hoping to make the drive back go quickly.

She was on the road less than fifteen minutes when her phone rang. It was Kathy.

"Jess, I'm so sorry to bother you, and I know you are probably headed out of town. I wouldn't call if it wasn't urgent."

"What is it?" Jess asked, pulling over to the side of the road so she could talk.

"It's Scutes. He washed ashore on Wrightsville Beach, and from what I understand, he's badly hurt. I drove up to Virginia last night to visit family or I would get down there myself, but we're talking hours. Is there any chance you can go? The two other staff members I would normally call are unavailable, and the new volunteers will not know what to do...."

"Of course. I just left so I'm still close. Text me where to find him and I'll go there now," Jess said. Jess had been at the Turtle Rescue the year before when Scutes was brought in with bacteria on his shell and she had helped treat him. He was a green turtle, which was rare in this area, making his rescue and release a significant event. That he was back and hurt did not bode well, and Jess was immediately concerned.

Jess turned her car around and headed back to the one thing that could still draw her back to Wrightsville Beach.

Chapter 77

Hank woke up with the voice already in his head.

Go to the beach.

It was Saturday, and since it was May, the summer season had started. Still, it was early enough that he could catch some waves before the beach crowds arrived. Hank assumed it was just his mind telling him to go to the one place he found peaceful. It had been a busy work week, and getting out into the sun and waves would relax him and make him forget his worries for a while. He grabbed his board and was out the door within minutes, feeling the warm breeze rush by him as his Jeep headed toward the Island.

Hank was able to find a place to park, and then he grabbed his board, noting there were a lot of people, but it was not too crowded yet. He dropped his clothes, towel, and keys on the sand, then dove into the refreshing cool water, immediately feeling more calm as he paddled out. He started catching waves fairly quickly, working his legs, torso, and arms to relieve his stress. After an hour, he felt relaxed and sufficiently hungry to call it quits. He rode in one last wave and walked up to where he had dropped his personal items.

As he reached down to pick up his things, Hank noticed a small crowd gathered slightly farther down the beach and he wondered if someone had been hurt. It wasn't uncommon for a swimmer to get pulled into an undertow or for a child to swim out too far and need rescuing, but this seemed different. He watched a few minutes as he drank some water, then decided to check it out himself, picking up his board and walking to where the crowd was gathered.

He heard Jess's voice before he saw her. She was talking to another volunteer about the turtle laying on the beach, looking still. Its shell was cracked, most likely from a boat strike. She was trying to figure out how to get him back to the Turtle Rescue since he was not doing well and she wasn't sure they had time to wait for someone to drive the van down from the facility.

"I can take him," Hank said without thinking. Jess looked up, startled to see him there, wet and holding his surfboard. "We can use my surfboard to take him up to my Jeep. He'll fit in the back and I can drive him there."

Though Jess was surprised to see Hank, she didn't have time to figure out how he had suddenly appeared. She quickly agreed and he laid the board down next to the turtle, covering it with his towel. She and Hank and two other men who had been watching the incident gently lifted the 250-pound turtle onto the surfboard, and then working together, carried it to Hank's Jeep. It took all four of them to lift the turtle up by using the towel to get him into the back. Then Hank put his board aside and got in.

"What about your board?" Jess asked, getting in beside him.

"I'll pick it up later," he said, not thinking twice about it.

"No worries! I'll put it by Jess's car," said the volunteer who had been working with Jess. "Good luck, Jess. Let me know what happens."

They sped off for the Turtle Rescue, with Jess navigating while Hank focused on driving as fast as he felt he could without going too far over the speed limit. When Jess noticed the turtle was worsening and voiced her concern that they might not make it in time, Hank decided it was more important to help the turtle, so he drove as fast as he could. Neither of them mentioned how odd it was that they'd both made their way to that particular stretch of beach at the same time, instead focusing on getting the turtle to the Turtle Rescue.

When they reached it, several volunteers were in the parking lot waiting for them. Together, they gently lifted the turtle out of the car and put him on a gurney so they could quickly transport him inside. Jess started to follow them, but then she turned back to Hank, who was standing by the car, uncertain what to do. "Thank you," she said, looking at him with a look of tenderness, unable to think of what else to say. Then she turned and hurried into the building with the others.

Hank parked and then sat in his car, waiting while Jess worked inside. He sat quietly, reflecting on their moments together and all that had happened between them. He closed his eyes and sat back, once in a while feeling a cool breeze come over him, briefly brushing away the mugginess already so prevalent this time of year. The Turtle Rescue was not open to visitors this time of day, so Hank was alone in the hot parking lot with the cicadas as the only nearby sound on this back road.

"You always did know when to show up at the right moment," he heard Jess say. He opened his eyes, startled out of his thoughts to see her standing by the passenger door. "I would have thought you would be long gone by now."

"I thought you would need a ride back," he said, sitting up. "How's the turtle?"

Jess shook her head. "We don't know yet. He was hurt pretty badly. I did all I could. A vet is coming in from Raleigh to look at him." She looked tenderly at Hank again. "He wouldn't have made it at all if you hadn't shown up when you did and helped me get him here. Really, thank you. It means a lot."

"Well, anything for a sea turtle…" he said lamely, trying to make a joke, but neither of them felt very lighthearted. "Do you need to stay? I was going to grab something to eat."

Jess hesitated for a moment, then smiled. "No. I'm done here, and I am hungry. Plus, I could use the ride back."

She got in the car and Hank drove a short ways until they found a CookOut, a local drive-thru burger place that specialized in shakes. After getting their food, they parked in a nearby parking lot to eat.

Jess asked about Hank's father and Hank told her about how he was such a great help at his business, managing a number of the projects. Then she asked about Mike, whom Hank said had just had a baby girl and was doing well. They went as far as they could with polite conversation, then sat silently eating.

"So how's married life?" Jess finally asked, figuring she had avoided it long enough.

Hank swallowed hard. "I didn't get married. Alanna and I broke up a few months ago."

Jess stopped eating and looked at him in surprise. "Hank, I'm so sorry," she said sincerely. "What happened?"

Hank chose his words carefully, not looking at Jess as he spoke. "She knew I didn't love her the way she loved me. And she was right. She decided she wanted more, so we ended it. Last I heard, she is marrying her college boyfriend."

Jess sat thoughtfully, taking in this unexpected information, not knowing how to respond. He didn't marry Alanna. So why hadn't he called her? She watched Hank closely. While he was there helping her out by getting Scutes to the hospital and driving her back to her car, she also was starting to notice how reserved he was. In the past, their conversation had been playful and easy, but now it felt constrained. She observed how closed off his body language was and how he kept to surface conversation. A feeling of dread started to wash over her as she began to wonder if he was over her. She thought back to their last conversation and how it must have changed everything. And why shouldn't it have? She'd told him they couldn't be together. Even though she had explained it had to do with his marrying Alanna, it didn't change the fact that once again she'd left. As Mike said, it was devastating to Hank the first time she went away. How could he possibly still love her after she left him behind a second time?

"So how's life in Virginia?" Hank asked, changing the subject.

"Not as good as I had hoped," Jess replied, trying not to show how devastated she felt if she was right that everything had changed. She explained that she couldn't conduct the fieldwork she needed from the location she had moved to, choosing her words carefully and not giving him half the details of how disappointing it had been. She couldn't let him know what a terrible mistake she had made in leaving, not if this was how things were going to be. "So, I am basically looking for my next move."

Jess explained she had come down for the weekend to talk to some of her colleagues at the Marine Center and the Turtle Rescue for leads, which was why she had been available to go to the beach when they received the call about Scutes. What she wanted to tell Hank was she would return to Wilmington for good if he still wanted her to. She was trying to think of what she could say to let him know she still had feelings for him, when he told her he needed to get back and started driving Jess back to her car.

As they drove, Hank talked about a house he was working on and some of the issues he was having, but Jess was only half-listening. She used the opportunity to look at Hank and remember their kiss on the beach, recalling the feeling of having him touching her and how lost in him she had been in that moment. She was still in love with him and perhaps always would be, but something always got in the way of them being together. Jess felt that all too familiar ache in her heart at being so close to him yet knowing he was out of reach. She closed her eyes, feeling the wind swirl by her face through the Jeep's open windows, remembering that same feeling from when she had rode around with him during the summer they were together. *If only I never left*, she thought. *If only I did so many things differently.*

In too short a time, Hank pulled up to the side of her car and stopped. He got out to retrieve his board, putting it in the back of the Jeep, then walked over to the passenger side where Jess had already gotten out, keeping his distance. She stood facing him, taking him in one last time, hoping to see something in his face that showed he still cared, but there was nothing there.

"Thank you, for everything..." she started, looking deep into his eyes one last time, trying hard to convey her feelings for him. But Hank just looked down awkwardly, making it obvious he was ready to go.

"Glad I could help," he finally said, giving her a small sad smile.

Jess didn't want him to leave, but she knew she didn't have a choice. She offered her hand in farewell, which he reached over to give a quick shake before turning around and getting back into his

Jeep. The feel of his brief touch lingered on her fingers, reigniting her feelings as she watched him drive away.

Hank drove to the end of the dead-end lane and did a three-point turn to get back out to the main road. As he started to head out, he suddenly came to a stop. Jess was standing in the middle of the road, blocking his exit. As soon as he had driven off, she knew she couldn't let him leave without telling him how she felt. There had been too much between them for her just to walk away. Jess walked up to his window with a determined look, placing her hands on his door to keep him from leaving. She didn't know what she was going to say, but once she started, it all came out in a rush.

"When I first came back to Wilmington, I didn't know how I would feel about returning. For those seven years I was away, I always questioned if I had made the right decision in leaving like I did. When I came back and found out your conviction was overturned, I knew how terribly wrong I was not to have returned your calls. When I saw you at that gala, it was like time had stopped. I knew instantly I had never stopped loving you. Even if I didn't want to admit it to myself, I knew I came back hoping to find you again, to see if what we had that one summer was real. All that time we spent together surfing and hanging out, I was pretending we were just friends, but deep down, I was trying to figure out if there was still a chance for us to be together. When you kissed me under that pier, I fell in love with you all over again in a way that was even deeper than before. But you were engaged to Alanna and had built a new life. I saw you with her, Hank. I could see you were happy together. I went over and over it in my head, and every time I came up with the same answer. I had returned too late. If I really loved you, the best thing I could do was leave so you could have your life with Alanna. All I wanted was to do what was best for you. Even if it meant I had to give you up.

"But now you tell me she's gone and you didn't even try to contact me. Why didn't you call me, Hank? I need to know. I need to know if you felt everything I did when you kissed me under the pier? And most of all, I need to know if those feelings are now gone forever?"

Her voice cracked at the last sentence, knowing she was laying herself bare, but she couldn't stop herself. She had to know if it was truly over. She wouldn't believe it until she heard him tell her it was so.

Hank listened as she said her piece. Then he turned off the engine and stepped out of the car, standing in front of her.

"Jess," he said, putting his hands on his hips and looking around nervously, trying to find the words. "You would never have been happy here. When you told me you were going to Virginia, I knew your work would always require you to go somewhere else, and I could never keep you from doing what you love most. I've seen how important your work is to you, Jess. Even today, I saw how much you cared about that turtle. But that passion takes you away from Wilmington, and I can't follow you. My life is here. You would never be happy being in a relationship that prevents you from going where you need to be to do the work you so love to do. I'm sorry. I wish it were different, but that's the way it is. I have made my peace with it. You should, too."

Hank said these last words gently but mournfully, then turned and was reaching for the door handle to get back into the car when Jess put her hands on his arm to stop him.

"I don't have to leave, not you or Wilmington," Jess said, starting to understand what was holding him back.

Hank shook his head and turned to her. "What are you saying, Jess?"

Jess took a deep, shaky breath. "When I came back here, I felt like I'd come home. I loved my time in Florida, but I never felt I was meant to stay there. I kept trying to find the feeling that I have when I am here because this is where I feel like I'm supposed to be. I didn't want to go to Virginia. I left because I couldn't bear to stay here and see you marry Alanna. It hurt too much to know I had lost you again. But if you are not marrying her, I don't want to leave. My work can be done here. This is where I want to build my life. And the only thing that would make it all perfect, the only thing that would truly make me happy..." Her eyes filled with tears and her words started to choke up, "is if there is any chance I could make that life with you."

Jess stood there, her heart totally exposed, tears streaming down her face as she looked up at Hank, waiting for his reaction. This was not the way she had wanted to tell him she loved him, but the fear of losing him forever was too great. If he drove away now, she would never get another chance. She couldn't let him go without telling him everything she felt for him and to find out if there was any way he could still love her.

Hank stood silently for a moment, taking in everything she had said. He'd convinced himself that she was gone forever and there was nothing he could do to make it work. For months, he had distracted himself with work to make himself forget all his feelings for her, reminding himself over and over that it would never work out. Even today, his offer to help had been an impulsive one upon seeing her there so unexpectedly. Being so near to her in the car had been painful, reminding him how much he had missed her after all the work he had done to push those thoughts away and he had fought to remind himself why they couldn't be together. But now she was telling him that everything he'd told himself so he could let her go had never been true, that she could do the work she loved here and that she wanted to do it while being with him. And if that was the case, then he wanted her, he wanted her more than anything.

"Do you mean that, Jess? I mean, really mean it," he asked, wanting so much to believe it was true, but not wanting to open his heart all over again if there was any way it wasn't. He could feel the emotions rise up within him, wanting to believe her, to let his love for her rise to the surface again, but he had to be sure. If she left him again, he would never be able to survive it.

Jess nodded hard, the tears coming quickly now, making it difficult for her to talk. "More than anything. I love you, Hank. I have never stopped loving you and I never want to let you go again. You are the one I was always meant to be with. I left because I could see the conflict I was causing you by returning. I never wanted to do anything that would hurt you. But if all the reasons I left are now gone, I want to come home and be with you."

As she stood there, Hank caught a sudden reflection of light that made him look down, catching a glimpse of the turtle necklace around her neck. His mind went to the night on the beach when he had given it to her and the first time she had told him that she loved him. Here they were eight years later, and his love had only grown deeper after all that time.

He reached out to wipe the tears from her face, the very act of just touching her making him remember all the feelings he'd held back. He could feel them surge through him, awakening from the place where he had pushed them down, racing to be freed again. He reached out his other hand to hold her face in his hands and looked deep in her eyes, wanting to convey everything he was feeling, trying to find the words to explain them.

"I love you, Jess. I have always loved you," he said as he leaned down and kissed her, gently at first and then harder as she wrapped her arms around him, kissing him back while laughing and crying at the same time. They stayed that way for a long time, neither of them wanting to let go now that they had found each other again.

Epilogue

"Wait, one minute," Lila said, adjusting the veil on Jess's head. "There. Now it's perfect."

Jess looked at herself in the floor-length mirror and couldn't believe she was getting married. She had chosen a simple sleeveless dress made of white silk that flowed over her body. Her veil softly framed her face and hung down her back to her waist, fluttering lightly on the backs of her arms. Behind her stood Lila, her maid of honor, dressed in a tailored, light blue sheath dress that made her eyes sparkle.

"My, but you do make a beautiful bride!" Lila said to Jess, staring at her admiringly in the mirror.

The last six months has been a whirlwind of activity. After she and Hank had gotten back together, Jess had wasted no time moving back to Wilmington, and once she returned, every free moment she had was spent with Hank. Mornings they would surf and grab breakfast. After work, they would eat dinner and go for long walks or stay in and read. Weekends were spent exploring old familiar places and discovering new ones. Jess could not have been happier, and she could tell Hank felt as lucky as she did that they were back together again.

The first time they went over to visit Mike and Lila, Mike gave her a big hug. "Good to have you back," he said, his eyes showing he really meant it. Lila fixed them another delicious meal and the four of them talked and laughed through the evening. Jess held Charlotte in her lap while Mike and Lila cleaned up and Hank ran around with Connor. More such evenings followed and as Jess got to know Lila, she found that beneath Lila's warm and motherly exterior was a very smart woman with whom she could talk for hours. Hanging out on the weekends became a regular event for the two couples, making them become quite close.

Jess was able to get her office back at the Marine Center and resume her field research, which was progressing well. At night, she would share some of her findings with Hank, who would prod her for more. She didn't think he would be as interested in her work, but he asked questions and showed a genuine interest in what she was doing. Likewise, she would ask about his day at work and get him to talk about the houses he was working on. Even if she didn't understand many of the technical terms he used, she liked to listen to him talk, amazed by how knowledgeable he was about construction and how much he cared about the work he was doing.

The engagement came quickly, only a few months after Jess returned, and though it surprised her, she knew they had waited longer than most for it to happen. Hank took her on a moonlit walk on the beach one night, suddenly stopping at the same place where he had first kissed her and dropping down on one knee. He took both of her hands in his, gazing at her with an earnest and heartfelt look.

"I never told you this before," he said, "but the first time I met you at the Café, I heard a voice inside me say I would marry you. I didn't believe it at the time, but when I kissed you here that first time in the rain, I knew at that moment my heart would always belong to you. Even during all those years apart, when I thought I would never see you again, you were always with me. You are everything to me, Jess, and I want to be with you for the rest of our lives. I want to wake up next to you each morning thinking about how I can make you happy that you chose me as your husband. Jess, I love you with all my heart. Will you marry me and be my wife?"

And now here they were at the Blockade Runner Resort on Wrightsville Beach, about to be wed just a month after Hank's proposal. Neither of them had wanted to wait any longer to make it official, and they both wanted a small intimate wedding, which could be quickly planned. Jess thought for a moment about all they had been through to get to this point. Not too long ago, she had wondered if she would ever find someone to spend her life with, and now, here she was in a wedding dress about to walk down the aisle to commit herself to the man she loved.

"So, are you ready to get married?" Jess's mother asked as she entered the room. When Jess turned to face her, there were tears in her mother's eyes. "You look so beautiful," her mother said, gazing adoringly at her. "Your father...would have loved to be here."

Jess walked over to her mother and gave her a hug. "I am just glad I can share it with you."

Together with Lila, they took the elevator downstairs and made their way to the back of the resort, which faced the ocean. Jess stepped outside and looked across the lush green lawn, which ended with thick brush separating it from the beach. At the end of the lawn in front of the brush was a white trellis covered with white roses, light blue hydrangeas and delphinium, much like the bridal bouquet Lila was handing to Jess. Underneath the trellis stood the officiant, and to the right stood Hank and Mike. Mike was holding a very sleepy Charlotte in a lacey pink dress in one arm and Connor's hand with his other. Connor looked adorable dressed in a miniature navy suit like his dad and also looked like he was ready to run around, held there only by Mike's firm grasp. On the other side of Connor was Hank's dad. All of the men looked handsomely dressed in their suits with the backdrop of the beach behind them.

"Whenever you're ready," Lila whispered to her. Jess nodded and Lila signaled to a quartet on the side. The quartet started playing as Lila began walking in rhythm to the music toward the trellis. Jess took her mother's arm and followed, taking in the light ocean breeze and the bright blue of the sky, thinking this was exactly how she wanted this day to be with everyone she loved around her. When her eyes met Hank's, she held his adoring gaze as she made her way forward, once again feeling the familiar charge when she looked at him. She couldn't believe he was going to be her husband, that she was going to be his wife and that they would finally get to build their home here together.

When they reached the trellis, Jess's mother kissed her cheek and told her how much she loved her, then stepped back. Hank took Jess's hands and looked deeply into her eyes as the ceremony began. They took their vows, promising to love each other through sickness and in health, through good times and bad, each conveying to the other the love in their heart. When the officiant declared them man and wife, they shared a long kiss while everyone let out a great cheer and applauded.

The journey to finding each other had been filled with pain and sadness but also moments of elation and self-discovery. Now that they each knew what loss felt like, they promised to always hold the other dear in their hearts so as never to experience it again. Neither of them knew what ups and downs the future would hold, but there was no question that it would be better because they would be going through it together.

The End

Why I Love Sea Turtles and Put Them In My Book

Sea turtles are among the oldest creatures on earth, having remained essentially unchanged for 110 million years, and yet somehow, I never paid them much attention. That changed in August 2016, when I went to Wrightsville Beach with two of my best girlfriends. We stayed at a condominium overlooking the beach near Mercers Pier, and right in front of our condo on the beach was a sea turtle's nest. Volunteers from the Wrightsville Beach Sea Turtle Project had marked it by putting stakes in the sand and then tying rope around them to keep people on the beach from interfering with the nest area. I didn't recall seeing turtle nests on the beach before, but then maybe I just wasn't paying attention. My friend, Erin, however, is a lover of all things animal, and she was fascinated. We ended up talking to the volunteers monitoring this particular nest and were told it was very close to hatching. When they described how the hatchlings would come out in a way that made it appear like the sand was boiling, we decided that was something we wanted to see. And that is how we ended up sitting on the beach each night during our visit hoping to catch sight of this amazing event.

Fortunately, the hatchlings decided to come out on one of those nights we were there. Unfortunately, they came out about an hour after our 11 p.m. bedtime and we missed it. When we talked to the volunteer the next night, we were told there was still the chance that "stragglers" might come out after the nest had hatched. These were the hatchlings that, for whatever reason, decided to wait a day or two before they left the nest. So the following night, we went ahead and set up our blanket on the sand, hoping to get lucky along with a handful of other people who were hoping for the same thing. To pass the time, Erin decided to pull up some YouTube videos of turtle nests hatching on her phone and we sat watching them, figuring since we missed the real event, at least we could see what it looked like.

We suddenly noticed a small group of people watching something by the nest. We went over to find out that sure enough, a straggler had emerged and was making his way down the beach toward the water. We all followed him at a safe distance as his little flippers worked their way toward the water, excited to catch it happening. But suddenly, he became sidetracked and started heading toward the pier, drawn in by its lights. The group started talking about what to do since the volunteer had left and we knew we weren't allowed to touch the turtle. It was Erin who came to the rescue, taking off her black flip-flops and blocking the turtle's path with them when it tried to turn left toward the pier, directing it back to the ocean. The turtle finally made it to the water and was quickly washed out to sea, hopefully to live a long and healthy life. A few days later, I came and saw the excavation of the turtle eggs, learning even more about sea turtles and their breeding habits.

I attribute the start of my interest in sea turtles to the informative and friendly volunteers of the Wrightsville Beach Sea Turtle

Project. I saw these volunteers repeatedly answer such questions as: How long do the eggs incubate until hatching? How many eggs does a turtle lay? What kinds of turtles nested there? And how long do they live? They also explained, each time with patience, why people shouldn't flash their phone camera lights on the nest. Their passion in monitoring the nests and educating the public made learning about the sea turtles fascinating, and I have been a big fan ever since because of my interactions with them.

Once I became interested in sea turtles, I made a visit to the Karen Beasley Sea Turtle Rescue and Rehabilitation Center, about a thirty-minute drive from Wrightsville Beach in Surf City, North Carolina. This is where sick or injured sea turtles are sent from all along the eastern seaboard for medical treatment. As a visitor, you can see the sea turtles as they recover in big blue tubs and talk to volunteers about the work they are doing in hopes of releasing the turtles back into the ocean. They see all sorts of injuries, such as turtles getting tangled in fishing lines, being harmed by boat strikes, or getting cold-stunned. The work they do is extensive and admirable, and to see the beautiful shells on the turtles up close was captivating.

When I had to choose a college degree and career path for Jess, there was no question she would be a sea turtle biologist. I researched what educational path she would take, which led me to the University of Central Florida and the Marine Turtle Research Group, who conduct studies on sea turtles at the Archie Carr National Wildlife Refuge (NWR). The Archie Carr NWR hosts the largest nesting population of loggerhead and green sea turtles in the U.S. It is responsible for a quarter of all loggerhead sea turtle nests (between 9,000 to 17,000 nests) and a third of all green sea turtle nests (between 2,000 to 16,000 nests) that are laid each year. Leatherback sea turtles are rarer, but still annually produce between

20 to 50 nests. It is a great place to experience turtles in their natural habitat.

As of the writing of this book, six out of the seven sea turtle species are classified as threatened or endangered. Some of the biggest threats include sea turtles being entangled in fishing gear; coastal development affecting their breeding grounds; the consumption of their eggs and meat as an aphrodisiac or delicacy; and the amount of plastic in the ocean that they ingest or get caught in. I am making contributions to the organizations I discuss in the book because I want to make sure sea turtles survive and hopefully thrive. I was amazed to find out during my research just how little is known about these ancient creatures, and I applaud those people who have made it their life's work to help them.

If you enjoyed reading about the sea turtles, then I encourage you to reach out to one of the organizations below, or to one that is local to your own area, since there are dozens in the United States alone. Follow them on social media to see current information about what the turtles are doing, and if you get the chance, I highly encourage you to attend a Turtle Talk, which many organizations offer for free, or tour a visitor's center. Some centers have very cool gift shops that allow you to order items online. Just about everything looks better with a turtle on it (including my turtle hat from the Karen Beasley Center!) The Karen Beasley Center even has a way for you to "adopt" a turtle, which turned out to be a great gift for my friend Erin. And of course, donations are also always welcomed and appreciated because they allow these organizations to keep doing the work they do.

Wrightsville Beach Sea Turtle Project
Wilmington, NC
https://wbstp.org

Karen Beasley Sea Turtle Rescue and Rehabilitation Center
302 Tortuga Lane
Surf City, NC 28445
https://www.seaturtlehospital.org

Archie Carr National Wildlife Refuge
For Visits:
Archie Carr NWR – Barrier Island Visitor Center
8385 South US Highway A1A
Melbourne Beach, Florida 32951
https://www.fws.gov/refuge/Archie_Carr/visit/plan_your_visit/
https://www.brevardfl.gov/EELProgram/Sanctuaries/
BarrierIslandSanctuary

For Donations:
Friends of the Carr Refuge
https://www.carrrefuge.org

You can also follow the **Marine Turtle Research Group** in its
research of the turtles on the Archie Carr NWR and other study
areas on the following sites. The pictures alone are worth it!

Web:https://sciences.ucf.edu/biology/marineturtleresearchgroup/
Twitter/Instagram: @UCFTurtleLab
Facebook: https://www.facebook.com/watch/ucfmtrg/

Acknowledgments

This book has taken a few years to write and has allowed me to meet some of the most interesting people. It amazed me how many people contributed to what I hope you found to be an enjoyable and heartfelt read.

During my research, I found Dr. Kate Mansfield and the Marine Turtle Research Group. There have been times when I have been lucky enough to find people who are excited about their work and are generously willing to share their knowledge. That was Kate Mansfield. I cannot thank her enough for the time she spent providing me the information I needed for Jess to sound like a sea turtle biologist and the work she put in editing my manuscript, particularly when it was in its early stages. Her enthusiasm pushed me along when I really needed it.

Though the book was started a couple of years before COVID-19 hit, the section where Jess goes to UCF was written during the height of the pandemic. That meant no traveling to experience for myself what it was like to be at the University of Central Florida or the Archie Carr National Wildlife Refuge. Once again, Kate proved helpful by introducing me to three of her former interns: Leah

Rittenburg, MacKenzie Tackett, and Kayla Burandt. Using their stories and experiences, I was able to create Jess's experience of being a fictional turtle intern, and I hope I did it justice. I found all three of these former students to be such intelligent and directed women, and I wish them all the best in their future scientific endeavors.

I also thank Kate for getting me in touch with Dr. Amanda Southwood Williard, another scientist and professor at UNCW. Amanda runs the intern program for UNCW students to volunteer at the Karen Beasley Sea Turtle Rescue and Rehabilitation Center. She was very helpful in helping me figure out how Jess would conduct her studies at the Center for Marine Science when she returns from Orlando. I appreciated her time and insights into a world with which I am unfamiliar.

At the Wrightsville Beach Farmer's Market, I met Mary Flinn, another author who writes about Wilmington and who planted the idea for me to self-publish this book, something I had not considered before. Mary was a true mentor in sharing her knowledge and experience in how to publish and market my book, and I cannot thank her enough for all the time, resources, and advice she provided. If you enjoy reading about North Carolina, including Wilmington, I encourage you to go to her website and pick up some of her novels at: https://theonenovel.com

Mary was kind enough to introduce me to her editor, Tyler Tichelaar, who I am now proud to call my own. I cannot thank him enough for making sure I was grammatically correct and for his help in taking this book from a rough draft to a finished novel. I truly enjoyed his commentary and felt a sense of accomplishment whenever he pointed out I had successfully conveyed a scene. His changes and direction helped me make this a better book, and his guidance in this new and challenging process was extremely helpful.

Mary also introduced me to her graphic designer, Shiloh Schroeder, who created such a wonderful cover to represent the book and who was instrumental in guiding me through the process of preparing the book for printing.

I want to give a great big thank you to Deborah McGuire, my friend and early reader of the manuscript. I truly appreciate her plowing through the first draft of the novel, which at the time I thought was complete. Such are the misguided beliefs of a new author. She gave me important feedback and was a great cheerleader who kept me going! She also put me in touch with her husband, Mike McGuire, who provided me with in-depth knowledge of what it was like to start a construction business. I appreciate him providing Hank with the correct terminology to sound like a builder and for lending me a few of his own experiences to make Hank and Tim appear more authentic.

In October 2020, I made a visit to the Karen Beasley Sea Turtle Rescue and Rehabilitation Center, where Kathy Zagzebski, the Director, was kind enough to give me a tour of the center's inner workings. I thank her for sharing the information and resources she did and for all she does for the turtles!

Thanks to Cameron Paradiso for giving me pointers on how to make two twenty-year-old male college students sound like two twenty-year-old male college students. Hopefully, I got it right.

I was able to visit Wilmington many times while writing this book and would often step out with my computer to find a location to hang out and spark my imagination. I spent many days sitting at coffee shops like SUNdays, with its great view and friendly staff; Port City Java at Lumina Station with its great lattes and peaceful setting; and Café del Mar, which had the best toffee coffee freezes. I always enjoyed hanging out at the tables outside of the Trolly Stop, which is a Wrightsville Beach institution and where I met Michelle, one of my favorite baristas. I even spent an afternoon sitting on the porch at UNCW's Fisher Student Center, where I wrote about Hank's early days at college. I really enjoyed walking around the campus and believe I would have enjoyed going to college there myself.

Having visited Wrightsville Beach since the late 1980s, I have so many memories there. My husband and I spent years with our kids eating at Tower 7 and going to Wings to get kites and look at the hermit crabs. Even now, after they are grown, we keep going back. When I walk the Loop, I am amazed at the work of the Harbor Island Garden Club, who has created an oasis to walk through. Walking through town, I meet people like Jazz, who runs a local art shop and is always happy to give our dog a treat. Good people doing everyday things that they do not realize add so much to those of us who are lucky enough to come in contact with them. I am grateful to you all.

To my two best friends, Armella Schroder and Erin Schultz, thank you for letting me share Wilmington with you and for sharing experiences with me worth writing about. You are always there when I need you and I could not ask for two better friends.

I want to thank my family for their support and patience. This book was written for my daughter, Taylor, when she first started dating. I wanted her to see what a loving relationship would look like and to know that whoever she dated should treat her well. I am lucky that she has made good choices in that regard, particularly as her dating life developed faster than this book. I also thank my other daughter, Carly, who provides in-depth and honest critiques and won't let me get away with bad writing. I love our conversations on characters and story lines and can't wait until she starts finishing her own books. And to my handsome husband, Tyler. You support me in so many ways, constantly reminding me that I chose well.

Lastly, thank you, reader, for choosing this book. I hope it was a story you enjoyed.

About the Author

I discovered Wilmington in the late 1980s when my mother relocated there. At the time, the last leg of I-40 had just finished construction, a feat that would drastically change Wilmington in the following years, since it made getting to that section of the Carolina coast a much easier trip. My mother moved down there because she fell in love with the historic charm of the city and had always wanted to live by the ocean. I was equally captivated by it, and over the years as my family and I made frequent trips to visit, it became my home away from home.

I developed an early love of reading and by the age of ten, had started writing as well. By age thirteen, I was sending out queries to publishers and magazines alike. I managed to get published in *Teen* and *Seventeen* magazines in high school and while I was at Tulane University, where I worked to further my writing skills while obtaining my Bachelor of Arts in English. The summer after graduating, I attended Bennington Writing Workshops in hopes of pursuing a writing career, but I still felt like I had not found my voice. Shortly after, I visited a fortune teller named Emily who told me I would be a writer one day but that I had "a lot of other things to do first."

Whether due to Emily's influence or the need to earn a living, writing was put aside while I went to New York City to pursue work in television and film production, and then working for a couple of years at HBO. Still looking for my path, I went on to earn my degree from New York Law School and worked in two law firms in Washington, DC before opening my own law practice. All through this time the idea of writing was always very much with me, but there was little time and I was waiting for when, as Emily put it, I finished a few other things first.

Two of those other things included getting married and having children. It was while raising my two daughters that I finally found my writing voice. Late at night or whenever I had a few spare moments, I would jot down thoughts about being a new mother, relationships with family, and all the trials and tribulations that a parent goes through raising two headstrong and extremely bright girls. Add in that one of the girls had extensive medical problems, and writing became my way of expressing all the emotions that comes with managing such difficulties. As teenagers, when they didn't want to listen to what mom had to say, I would write stories to convey my advice to them hoping I could reach them that way. That is exactly how Wrightsville Beach came about. It was written to show my daughters what a loving relationship should be like in hopes that they would find someone who would treat them well in their own dating lives.

So much of my life has happened in Wilmington. My wedding dress, which had been my mother's, was altered there. We spent our first Christmas down there after my first daughter was born. Every summer, I would bring the girls down for marine science camp at UNCW and surf lessons, after which we would get lunch at the Trolly Stop or soft serve ice cream at Dairy Queen. We got hermit crabs, our first pets at Wings, where we would also buy kites to fly on the beach. As my kids got older, we would rent kayaks and paddleboards to take out on the Channel and go shopping downtown. It was where I first developed an interest in sea turtles upon seeing their nests on the beach. It was where I did a half iron triathlon, running through the cheering crowds on Front Street and around Greenfield Lake. It was in Wilmington where I helped my mother during her last two years when she discovered she had pancreatic cancer, taking her to doctors' appointments and spending weeks in Hanover Hospital and finally, at the Lower Cape Fear hospice center. Even after her passing, we continue to return year after year, building new memories and finding new friends while watching how Wilmington continues to grow.

My first novel tries to capture so many of the feelings and experiences I have had throughout the years in Wilmington, while telling the story of two people finding their own paths. It has been a tremendous experience to put all these thoughts down on paper and to imagine a life there if I had it all to do again.